'Dark humour, a fast pace and gritty plot'
LoveReading

'Highland history and dark humour . . . drips with tension'
Press and Journal

'Skelton's talent is casting his descriptive eyes on the familiar
and rendering truthful characters with a believable backstory'
The Scotsman

'If you don't know Skelton, now's the time'
Ian Rankin

'Immersive, compelling and shot through
with Skelton's pitch-black humour'
Neil Broadfoot

'Pitch-black depiction of the competition between the
police, the press and the powers-that-be . . . Skelton's first-
hand experience of real-life crime enriches his writing'
Dundee Courier

'The plot is compelling . . . savour some of the gorgeously
lyrical prose that's sitting in there amongst all the drama'
Crime Fiction Lover

'A layered, intelligent plot that captures both the
heart and the mind. Absolutely unmissable'
Live and Deadly

'A master of his craft'
Scots Whay Hae

'A stand-out thriller'
Scots Magazine

A note on the author

Douglas Skelton was born in Glasgow. He has been a bank clerk, tax officer, taxi driver (for two days), wine waiter (for two hours), journalist and investigator. He has written several true crime and Scottish criminal history books but now concentrates on fiction. *Thunder Bay* (longlisted for the McIlvanney Prize), *The Blood Is Still*, *A Rattle of Bones* (longlisted for the McIlvanney Prize), *Where Demons Hide*, *Children of the Mist*, *The Hollow Mountain* (also longlisted for the McIlvanney Prize) and *The Other Side of Fear* are the first seven novels in the bestselling Rebecca Connolly thriller series.

Also by Douglas Skelton

The Davie McCall series
Blood City
Crow Bait
Devil's Knock
Open Wounds

The Dominic Queste series
The Dead Don't Boogie
Tag – You're Dead
Springtime for a Dead Man (novella)

The Janus Run

The Rebecca Connolly series
Thunder Bay
The Blood Is Still
A Rattle of Bones
Where Demons Hide
Children of the Mist
The Hollow Mountain
Death Insurance (novella with Morgan Cry)

The Jonas Flynt series
An Honourable Thief
A Thief's Justice
A Grave for a Thief
A Thief's Blood

THE OTHER SIDE
OF FEAR

A REBECCA CONNOLLY THRILLER

Douglas Skelton

Polygon

First published in Great Britain in 2025 by
Polygon, an imprint of Birlinn Ltd

Birlinn Ltd
West Newington House
10 Newington Road
Edinburgh
EH9 1QS

www.polygonbooks.co.uk

1

ISBN 978 1 84697 714 5
eBook ISBN 978 1 78885 784 0

British Library Cataloguing-in-Publication Data
A catalogue record for this book is available
on request from the British Library.

MIX
Paper | Supporting
responsible forestry
FSC® C018072

Typeset by Biblichor Ltd, Scotland
Printed and bound in Great Britain by Clays Ltd, Elcograf S.p.A

In memory of Denzil Meyrick,
author, raconteur and my friend

The End . . .

The sound of the surf is punctuated by the boom of the waves in the sea caves. It is dark. It is a warm night, would be a lovely night, but the wind still surges in from the Atlantic as if this is the only place it ever wished to be.

Legend has it that this remote bay is where spirits come to sail into the west. It's where the wind comes to die, Rebecca had been told once too, but she knows that isn't true. It may come here to rest but it doesn't die. The wind never dies. It exists, it continues, it grows and diminishes and blows and blows, in from the sea, up from the beach, across the island to the mainland and around the world, until it comes back here again. Back to Stoirm. The wind is everlasting. The wind is forever.

Unlike life.

She knows that. She has learned the hard way that life is loss.

And now it looks as if she may be joining those who've passed, right here on this wind-raked beach on an island that she doesn't particularly like but to which she has found herself drawn back time and time again. Like the wind.

Her eyes are locked on the man in front of her. He is tall and keeps himself in good shape. He is handsome, if you like your features perfect, though Rebecca has never fully trusted

1

perfection. It's usually hiding something. And this man has plenty to conceal. She knows she is about to experience that ugliness at first hand.

It's fitting that things end here, she supposes. After all, much of what her life has become began here, with the death of a young woman.

She closes her eyes, listens to the birds, to the sea, to the boom, to the wind.

And she waits . . .

1

The Beginning . . .

It was Emily Thorne's black Labrador that alerted her to the intruders.

Katy had slept at the foot of Emily's bed since she was a pup, thirteen years before. Her husband, Tariq, had voiced reservations from the start because he had not been raised with dogs in the house, but Katy soon wormed her way into his heart, and he'd loved her unconditionally. Even though she was Emily's dog, the lab gravitated towards him, but Emily never felt any bitterness over that – though when Tariq died, she had worried that Katy might pine away. The dog did grieve for a time; they both did. Katy would enter a room expecting to see him sitting in his chair, or she'd wait in the hallway, head between her paws, watching for him to come through the front door. That passed, as grief does, even though it never fully goes away, and Katy settled into the new reality, curling against Emily's legs every night in bed.

Over those eight years Emily had become attuned to the dog's movements, so she awoke as soon as Katy sat up straight, her ears cocked, her eyes fixed on the curtained window, a low growl scraping her throat.

The sound of a fist banging the windowpane made them both jump.

Then she heard noises that were alien to the island at night. Laughter, guttural cries, howls swirling around the cottage. Another rap at the window.

Katy lowered herself to the floor with a little less care than what had become usual in her senior years and barked. Then her muzzle lifted, and her black nose swivelled slightly as she detected an odour. Emily smelled it too: something on fire. But not in the cottage – no, it was coming from outside.

The wailing and shrieking continued and there was a third thud against the window, which made her jump again.

Her heart palpitating, Emily eased from the bed and crept to the window. She was a Londoner by birth, so even though she had been on Stoirm for eight years and lived two miles outside of Portnaseil, and there was nobody close to her converted croft to look in, she still closed her curtains at night. Old habits die hard. She reasoned that it was always possible someone would be wandering the moors in the dark, and she didn't relish the thought of a stranger peeping at her while she slept. Now she hesitated because she didn't want whoever was outside to see her, even though they would know she was at home. She thanked God that another old habit was to lock the front door.

She waved a hand towards the dog, who was still barking, and Katy quietened, but her old eyes remained fixed on the window. The burning smell grew stronger. Oh my God, what if they had put something up against the front door?

She shuffled through to the living room, where the curtains were also drawn, but she could see a glow outside and was able now to hear the crackle of flames. Not at the door, thankfully. Katy followed her, still growling, still giving the occasional bark, her gait more of a lurch thanks to her arthritis. The howling issued from all around the house, but she was unable to identify how many voices there were, or who

4

they belonged to. There was at least one female among them, which disappointed her.

She retrieved a key from within a fake leather volume on the bookshelf and carefully turned the lock of the metal cabinet in the small porch area beside the front door. Her fear told her that she should simply let them do what they want, then they would move on, but her rational mind countered that if she did, they might feel emboldened to take their intimidation further, perhaps actually set fire to her door. And her pride told her that she didn't know who these idiots were, but she wouldn't cower away inside while they rampaged.

The cabinet open, she hesitated, looking first at the Browning Maxus 12 gauge, then at the box of cartridges. She'd bought the shotgun second hand because she'd always fancied doing some shooting – clay pigeons only because she'd never shoot at anything living, not even these morons. She wouldn't load it. They won't know the weapon was empty. She merely wanted to scare them off.

She motioned to Katy to stay where she was, then rested her hand on the key in the door. She paused, swallowing hard, her breathing growing a little frenzied. She shouldn't do this. *What the hell are you doing, Emily?* She shouldn't do this.

But she had to do this. Tariq had told her that you have to tackle situations like this head-on. These people were cowards at heart, he'd say. They can talk a good game, they might even try bluster, but in the end they will back down. It's the quiet ones you have to watch out for, the ones who stand and watch and wait. They're the dangerous ones.

She took a few deep breaths, willed her heart and the nerves jumping in her stomach to calm the hell down, then unlocked the door.

Flames licked into the night sky from the small outhouse in which she kept her wheelie bins, the smoke from the wooden frame and burning plastic obscuring the array of stars and drifting in a thick noxious veil across the grass and driveway. Although shocked, she was confident that the blaze was too far away from the cottage itself to cause any damage. Even if a spark managed to fly across to her roof, the tiles were still wet from that day's rain.

A figure ran by her, screaming something in her direction. A male, slim, probably young, his face concealed under a hood made of canvas, with eye holes and an opening for the mouth slashed in the material. Another sprinted in the opposite direction, wearing an identical hood, but stopped a few feet from her and did star jumps as he threw back his head and howled. She raised the shotgun, and he bolted beyond the limits of her security light. She heard others laughing as they ran through the darkness.

She considered fetching the extinguisher from under the kitchen sink, but the flames had too firm a grip of the structure, so instead she cradled the shotgun in the crook of her arm and reached for the phone just beyond the entranceway in the living room.

'I'm calling the police now,' she called out, her voice, to her shame, trembling. That only provoked more howls.

She was about to thumb 999 when Katy darted out, barking. Emily followed her, calling her back, fearful she would get too close to the blaze, but the dog was astute enough to keep her distance.

At that moment, all the howling and laughing and whistling stopped, as if someone had simply flicked a switch. The only sound was the crackle and snarl of the flames and the slight breeze rattling the mesh of her perimeter fence.

Katy had come to a halt in the middle of the small garden, barking not at the blaze but at something beyond the thick smoke swirling across the driveway, her hackles razoring the fur of her neck and shoulders. They were still there. They had fallen silent, but they were there.

Emily raised the cordless phone still in her hand. 'I'm calling now,' she shouted, thumbing 999, even though she knew she was too far away from the cottage to pick up a signal. She made a show of putting it to her ear. 'Hello, police, please,' she said to dead air.

And then four figures stepped forward from the darkness in a line, one female by her shape. They were all hooded.

She gripped the shotgun in both hands, the phone still in her right, and pointed it at them, regretting now that she hadn't loaded it. A warning shot into the ground would have been ideal at that moment. 'Who are you?' she said. 'What do you want?'

And then a further movement, at first only a disturbance in the swirl of smoke, then every nerve jangled as a new figure appeared. There was something different about this one, even though his hood was the same as the others, the flickering shadows caused by the flames making its blank expression more disturbing. There was something about the way he moved, the way he carried himself. He wasn't tall but he was burly, his worn denim jacket straining at his chest and gut. He wore jeans and work boots and a pair of thick gloves.

This was the quiet one.

This was the one who watches.

She raised the shotgun higher, her arms, hands, legs all trembling. 'Who are you?'

'Take this as a warning, hen,' he shouted. 'We don't want incomers here any more. It's your shed the night, but next time . . . who knows?'

Katy took a few bouncing steps towards him, still barking.

'Katy, no!' Emily rushed to squat beside her, wrapping one arm around her chest, pulling her back, the other straining to keep the shotgun level.

The figure stepped back, reaching behind him to produce a long, broad knife from his waistband. He pointed the tip at Katy.

The knife still raised, he stepped back into the smoke, into the darkness, and became one with it, his four companions following. She heard the sound of car doors closing, then engines gunning and rocketing off down the road. She tried to identify the cars – to note the make, the colour if she could, a registration number – but no lights flicked on until they were too far away. Her heart hammering, she hauled Katy back into the house – despite the dog's old legs, it wasn't easy – and locked the door. With the phone signal restored, she dialled the emergency number while peering through the curtains, worried that the hooded man would return and make good on his promise to torch the house.

Donnie Kerr enjoyed being near the water after the sun had gone down. The island wasn't exactly a bustling metropolis in daylight, but there was still noise. Cars moving along the Spine, tractors in fields, hammering, voices, the throaty roar of the ferry as it slowed on arrival or pulled away from the jetty. He liked to hear the water lapping against the stonework of the harbour and the occasional soft splash as a seal surfaced or submerged. He enjoyed the stars spreading above him like millions of fairy lights laid on black velvet. When he could see them, that is, because cloud cover was more common on the island. Not this night, though; tonight it was clear and warm. Even the breeze coming off the water carried heat, and it eased itself through the grassland on the other side of the harbour as if caressing a lover, causing the blades to moan.

He lingered on the quayside, enjoying the moment. He breathed in the air, thought he could detect a floral scent he couldn't identify. Looking back towards Portnaseil, the buildings were only shadows within the darkness. Although the largest settlement on Stoirm, there was no street lighting, and Donnie liked that. There was too much light in the world, as if all darkness must be banished. Its absence allowed him to

8

see the stars, and anyway, there was little need for it here. The island was peaceful.

He amended that thought immediately. The island had been peaceful, but not so much now. Yes, there were fights, disagreements, feuds, because that was human nature. There had been murder, too, but he didn't like to think of that too much. That had been a bad time in his life: drug addiction, larceny, lies told to those he loved. To those he ultimately let down.

He cut the introspection off. He was a different person now, he hoped. He would always be an addict but he hadn't touched drugs, had even stopped smoking, and if he drank, which wasn't often, it was non-alcoholic beer. He had to let the past lie where it belonged, and that place wasn't in the here and now.

He took one last deep breath, savoured it, then stepped closer to his boat, the *Kelpie*. He had come to pick up his phone, which he'd left in the wheelhouse after the day's sailings. He did that too often, but he hated the damn thing. There were times when he simply wanted to be on his own, without the threat of someone phoning him, or messaging him. He had a landline and an answering machine at home and if anyone wanted to contact him, they could use that. He couldn't remember the last time someone had left a message on his machine, though, let alone called his landline number. It was all mobile phones and social media, the latter being something he didn't do on a personal level, but he did use it to promote his whale and dolphin tours, and that was onerous enough. The last thing he wanted was to spend hours scrolling through endless shots of people's dinners, their dogs, cats and budgies, eternally discussing and dissecting the most recent episode of whatever TV show was currently in vogue or spouting bile-filled political views that were often both partisan and ill-informed. His daughter, Sonya, teased him about his Luddite tendencies towards modern means of communication, pointing out that they were necessary if she needed to contact him urgently. She had a point, but he still continued to forget to pick up his mobile. He'd leave it at home or on the boat, as was the case this time. He'd already been in bed when he remembered and he'd lain awake for some time wondering whether he should fetch it, Sonya's words about contacting him in an emergency echoing. Yes, if she couldn't get him on the mobile, she could call the landline, but she was a child of the twenty-first century and probably wouldn't consider such an outlandish notion. Finally he'd got up, dressed and, as it turned out, enjoyed the walk down from Portnaseil.

He sensed something wrong as soon as he descended the ladder set into the harbour wall and stepped over the *Kelpie*'s gunnel onto the deck. No, not wrong. Something different. Something not right.

He stood perfectly still and surveyed the shadows of the deck. He saw nothing unusual but his skin tingled. There was something amiss. It was the first time he had ever thought of that word, amiss, let alone said it out loud.

You're jumping at shadows, Donnie, letting all the shit on the island get to you. You were never of the *fey*, those islanders who could foresee the future and commune with the spirits they said hovered in the machair, and on the moors, and on Beinn na Sìthichean, Ben Sheen, where all sorts of supernatural beings were reputed to live. The breeze in the grass was their song, the *fey* would insist, and anyone who listened too long or too intently could be stolen away. Donnie thought that anyone who believed that – fewer certainly than ever before – were themselves away with the fairies.

But now, standing on the deck of the vessel he had cleaned, repaired, sanded, painted and sweated over for so long he knew every square inch intimately, he felt something alien.

Something amiss.

He shook his head, feeling a smile come on. He told himself to behave and fished out his key to unlock the wheelhouse door.

That flutter of concern took flight when he found the door already unlocked. He could forget many things. His phone, people's birthdays, his own birthday. But he never left the wheelhouse door unlocked. There wasn't a great deal of crime on Stoirm but there was some, especially during the summer when there was an increase in visitors lured by the promise of clean waters, sandy beaches and breathtaking scenery, if not the guarantee of decent weather. The Portnaseil Hotel was closed but there had been an explosion of Airbnb properties as well as traditional boarding houses in the larger properties.

And then there was all the crap that had plagued Stoirm of late.

He was certain he had locked the door when he finished for the day; he'd checked before he headed home, which was his habit, sometimes more than once. His phone was unimportant to him but the *Kelpie* was a big part of his life, second only to Sonya.

He eased the boat hook from where it hung beside the wheelhouse door and, holding it at the ready, pulled the door open with his left hand.

The wheelhouse was empty, but nevertheless he peered round the door to ensure that nobody was hiding in some confined place that he had never himself discovered. Lowering the boat hook, he laughed softly. Jesus, Donnie, you're getting jumpy.

It was as he reached for his phone, tucked away in a little cavity beside the wheel, that he saw the photograph stuck to the window. It was a picture of Sonya, smiling as she spoke to someone in a Glasgow street. He had no way of knowing exactly when it was taken but he knew it was recent. She'd had her hair cut only two days before and had sent him a selfie. He'd thought it was too short but it wasn't his business, so said it was lovely. In this pic, printed on ordinary copy

11

paper, her hair was short and she was even wearing the same clothes as the selfie.

He looked at the time, after midnight, but he had to gamble that she was awake. If she wasn't, that was tough, because he had to know she was safe and well. The irony that he was proving her correct about mobile phones wasn't lost on him. In Glasgow, the phone rang and rang. With each ring he grew more fearful.

Pick up, he willed. For God's sake, pick up.

It rang.

It rang.

It rang.

His heart hammered, his mouth dried. Oh my God, Oh my God . . .

And then there she was, her voice sleepy. 'Dad?' There was an edge to the word, though, as if she realised that something might be wrong.

Amiss.

'Sonya, are you okay?'

'Of course, I'm okay. Are you? What—' She stopped, no doubt looking at the clock. 'It's after midnight.'

'Everything's fine,' he said, feeling shame at his fear. But he had to know. 'Just thought I'd give you a call.'

'After midnight?'

'I've had a busy day.'

She knew him well enough, and was sufficiently wise, to know he was hiding something. 'What's wrong, Dad? You don't phone anybody at this time of night.'

He decided to tell the truth, at least partly. 'I just had this urge to hear your voice, that's all. Sorry for it being so late. I didn't think you young students went to bed before two.'

'This young student has an exam tomorrow, so she needs her beauty sleep.'

'You need sleep, but not for beauty.'

'Oh, shut up,' she said, laughing.

It was true, though. She was the image of her mother. He hesitated before asking the next question, fearful of what the answer might be.

'Are you alone?'

If she was, that was a worry. If she wasn't, if someone was sharing her bed, that was something the father in him didn't want to know. But the father in him needed to know. He wasn't terribly impressed by her boyfriend, Albie. He'd met him a couple of times and he struck Donnie as being something of a narcissist. That said, he would have relaxed a little if he was there. Or perhaps not. Shit, being a dad wasn't easy.

'Angelique is in her room. She's asleep, too.'

He was relieved. He was dismayed. He was driving himself mad. Angelique was her flatmate, a stunningly beautiful young woman from somewhere in Africa. She was slender and small and unlikely to prove an impediment to anyone meaning Sonya harm.

'Anyway,' he said, 'I was wondering if you'd like to come back home early.'

'How early?'

'Tomorrow?'

She paused for a moment. 'What's up, Dad?'

'Nothing. I just want to see you and you're coming back at the end of the week anyway . . .'

'I can't come back tomorrow. I've got an exam, remember?'

She'd just told him that, but his mind didn't seem to be working at the moment. 'Of course,' he said. 'It was just a thought.'

'Okay,' she said, but he could still hear doubt cloud her voice. She knew something was up. 'I'll get back as soon as I can, I promise.'

'That's good,' he said. But it wasn't good. It was far from good. She was down there alone, Angelique notwithstanding.

13

He wanted to tell her to make sure she was never alone, but he couldn't find a way to say it that wouldn't increase her concerns. He recognised that the photograph in the wheelhouse was a scare tactic, but it had worked. He didn't think they would actually do anything. Would they? He wasn't even sure who *they* were.

The call ended with him wishing her goodnight and her suspecting there was something hanging between them. He pocketed the photograph along with his phone and locked the door. At the top of the ladder he paused and surveyed the few lights of Portnaseil and then the quayside. The breeze still blew, and whatever lived in the machair still sang, but he saw nobody.

Now, what had been a beautiful night had become dangerous.

2

The River Ness was blue. The sky was blue with hazy, puffy little clouds hanging around as if they were enjoying the view, the kind of blue seen on early summer days that are glorious, not too warm, certainly not cold, and dry, which in Scotland is a win. On the walkway beyond the restaurant window a jogger passed, her blonde hair tied back in a ponytail and topped by a baseball cap, a dog on a lead attached to her belt – a big dog which perhaps couldn't run terribly fast but would certainly make any man think twice about making a pest of himself. Across the water, the twin square spires of Inverness Cathedral stood out solidly against the sky, the sun somewhere beyond it thinking about heading further west but having such a good time giving people pleasure after a long, wet winter that it was reluctant to leave. It was close to idyllic out there – warm and peaceful and lovely, everything Rebecca Connolly wanted her life to be. And she was getting there, she really was.

She felt the touch of Stephen Jordan's hand on hers and she saw him smiling at her. 'You're away somewhere,' he said.

She returned his smile. 'Just enjoying the moment.'

Stephen was about to say something further but the arrival of the waiter with their drinks caused her to slide her fingers from under his. She had been going out with him for two years now but she was still uncomfortable with public displays of affection. The waiter laid the sparkling water in front of

Stephen and the gin and bottle of tonic before her, then departed without a word.

Stephen didn't show any sign of being hurt by her pulling away. He was, after all, used to it. He sipped his water and said, 'So, how was your day?'

'The usual,' she said, pouring half the bottle of tonic into the gin and giving the glass a swirl. She didn't know if that improved the taste, but it was something she did, almost a ritual. 'Apart from one guy who came in claiming his neighbours were trying to kill him.'

'Really? Why?'

'It seems they had a dispute over the noise he made when he was walking across his floor – it's one of those four-in-a-block flats and he's above them.'

'Cottage flats.'

'Yes. If that's what they're called . . .'

He sipped his water. 'That's what they're called.'

'Well,' she said, 'life is all about learning. Anyway, he lives in this block of cottage flats, thank you very much Mr Estate Agent-speak, on the upper floor and he has wooden floors, no rugs, and they claimed he was stomping around at all hours of the night . . .'

'Which he denies, of course.'

'Of course. Anyway, the argument became bitter and now they don't talk.'

'But he says they're trying to kill him?'

'Yes.'

'And how are they doing that? Have they hired a hit man? Or those two you told me about?'

Rebecca's mind returned briefly to one night in an Inverness cemetery when she encountered two people who killed for a living. That it had not ended with her lying dead over another's man grave was entirely down to Bill Sawyer, a former police officer who had for some reason cast himself as her occasional protector. They had a curious relationship, she and Bill, but then he was a curious man.

'No, nothing as simple as that,' she said, feeling a smile coming. 'You won't believe it when I tell you.'

'I'm all ears.'

'Always knew there was something different about you.'

He grimaced. 'So, what then? Poison? Force-feeding him episodes of *Made in Chelsea*? What?'

'None of the above.'

'You going to tell me, or do I have to tickle you until you do?'

'While that might be fun, you wouldn't do it here.'

With eyebrow raised, Stephen's broad face attempted a Roger Moore impression, though his misshapen nose, the result of a break from playing rugby in his younger years, did not make it in any way accurate. 'You want to put me to the test?'

She decided against stretching this out further, as Stephen was not as averse to public physicality as she. 'Okay, I'll tell you,' she said. 'He believes they have drilled holes in his floor and are using powerful air pumps to suck the air out of his flat.'

His mouth hung open slightly. 'You're right, I don't believe it.'

'I kid you not. He thinks one night he'll suffocate.'

'Not if he opens a window.'

'I didn't say it was foolproof and I'm not sure he's thought of that.'

'You didn't point it out to him?'

'I just wanted him out of the office smartish, to be honest.'

'So, what does he want you to do? Write a story?'

'I think so. He saw me on the telly.'

Her old boss, Elspeth McTaggart, had written books based on some of the stories Rebecca had worked on. One had been made into a Netflix documentary and another was in the offing. It was while they had been in Glasgow filming interviews that Elspeth was murdered. Rebecca missed her guidance, her acerbic tongue, her bitching about not being allowed to smoke anywhere she pleased. She missed *her*.

She pushed the latent grief back down, where it joined other sad memories. 'He wanted me to investigate this couple and expose them as would-be murderers.'

'Which you can't do.'

She cocked her head. 'Well . . .'

The way she stretched the word made him frown. 'You can't be seriously considering following it up.'

'It's a slow news week.'

'Becks, the guy is clearly troubled. You can't feed that kind of madness.'

'It won't do any harm to go see him, check out his floors, maybe speak to the neighbours.'

'Are you kidding? The guy needs help with his issues, what-ever they are, not a journalist looking for a scoop.'

She hid a smile. There was a time when that comment would have sent her spiralling into rage, but not now. She felt she had grown as a person. And anyway, she knew he was right. That didn't stop her having some fun. 'But what if there's something in it?'

'Something in it?' He stopped short, sat back and gave her a sideways squint. 'You're winding me up, aren't you?'

'Just a little.'

'Does this guy even exist?'

'Oh, he most certainly does. I felt sorry for him. He was so convinced by this fantasy that he'd created. I don't know what has gone on in his life to cause it, but he needed help, so I phoned Val Roach to see if there was anything she could do.'

'You could have dialled 999 or 111.'

'Didn't want to tie up their lines but I thought Val would be able to circumvent any red tape. She said she'd get a couple of uniforms round to check up on the guy and take it from there.'

He blew out his cheeks. 'I really thought for a minute you were going to go see him.'

'You think I'm stupid? That would be unbelievably irresponsible.'

He laughed. 'And you've never been unbelievably irresponsible in the past, of course.'

Again her mind flashed.

Her breath catching in the cold, dark waters of a loch . . .

A gun in the hand of a young man high on drugs and rage . . .

A group of men in the shadow of a Highland castle with violence in mind . . .

'Never,' she said, giving him as sweet a smile as she could. Those images of the past were just that: the past. She reached out and placed her hand on his. She didn't even look around to see if anyone was watching. She really was growing as a person. 'You don't need to worry, Stephen. I've learned my lesson. I'm never going to put myself in danger again.'

He didn't look convinced but he squeezed her hand while reaching into the inside pocket of his jacket with his other. 'Okay, I suppose this is as good a time as any . . .'

She felt a flicker of apprehension as she guessed what was coming. It had been inevitable, she supposed, that it would come to this. They had been seeing each other for two years. They had a relationship that could be extremely physical when they were both in the mood, or had the energy.

She had even said the L word to him, and he had said it back. They had been through all sorts of shit, or rather, he had put up with all sorts of shit from her, although he was no saint. He could be distant when he was caught up in a case, but then so could she. His mistrust of reporters and the media had caused something of a strain, but they had come through it. The fact that he had nearly been shot by an angry rich boy with a shotgun had gone a long way towards repairing that. She loved him, of that there was no doubt.

But that said, when he pushed the small ring box towards her, she eased her hand away from his and stared at it as if it was about to explode.

'Aren't you going to open it?' he asked.

She blinked at him, wondering where this sudden urge to cry came from. She opened the box.

It was empty.

She looked back at him, a quizzical frown puckering her forehead.

'I thought we could go buy one together,' he said.

Rebecca stared again at the box, at the little mound of lining, at the slot where the ring would sit, her mouth suddenly dry, her heart pumping like the bilges on the *Titanic*. She heard Elspeth's voice, the same one she'd heard in the wind as her ashes were spread on Loch Ness.

Be happy . . .

She wanted to say yes.

Be happy . . .

She wanted to say let's go find a jeweller's now, and if it's not open we'll find a brick and open it.

Be happy . . .

She wanted to say that it was time to settle down . . .

To be happy . . .

... and he was the one she wanted to settle down with. They went well together. They clicked. They worked.

She looked back at Stephen – at his eyes filled with expectation, with questions, maybe even with dread – and gave her answer.

3

PC Rory Gibson stared at the blackened wooden hut, his face grim. The blaze had long been extinguished by the island's retained firefighters, but the lingering odour hung in the sunlight like a bad memory.

'And you didn't recognise the man's voice, Ms Thorne?'

Emily, standing nearby, Katy at her feet, shook her head. 'No. I don't think his accent was local, though.'

'But it was Scottish?'

'Oh yes, I'd say Central Belt somewhere. But I'm English and sometimes I find it difficult to tell the accents apart.'

'It could have been someone adopting a Glasgow accent, say?'

'Of course.'

'And the others?'

'Youngsters.'

'How could you tell?'

She conjured them up in her mind. 'They way they moved, their look. Just a feeling, I suppose.'

'Recognise any voices?'

'They didn't say anything, just noises. But you know who it was.'

He looked back at her. 'Do I?'

'Darren Yates and his cronies.'

Darren Yates was a troublemaker and, supposedly, a drug dealer. His family was notorious, and there were families like them everywhere, even in islands like Stoirm. His older brother was in prison for attempted murder, his mother was easily the most unpleasant woman Emily had ever met, his father not much better. Emily tended to avoid them all as much as possible, but if there was trouble, it was believed that he was behind it. On occasion, he was even innocent.

Rory didn't respond as he nudged a charred plank to the side with his foot. 'What did you keep in here?'

'Firewood. Garden tools. A wheelie bin. The lawnmower.'

'Petrol driven?'

'Yes.'

'Was there petrol in it?'

'If there was, it wasn't much.'

'Any petrol containers?'

'Yes, one, but it was empty. I'd intended to get it filled today.'

Rory looked towards her battered old Land Rover. 'You were lucky that didn't go up, too.'

'It was parked round the back last night. When I was told you wouldn't attend immediately, I drove into Portnaseil this morning for some groceries.'

The police officer ignored the slight rebuke in her tone as he walked around the ruins of the hut, sniffing the air. 'Some sort of accelerant was used, the firefighters said. I can still smell it. Probably petrol.' He looked at the ground. 'No footprints, ground's pretty hard. Apart from that rain yesterday we've had a decent May. And you were asleep, right?'

She nodded. 'The yelling and howling woke me.'

'Nobody spoke but the man in the hood?'

'They were all wearing hoods but, yes, only the man who threatened me.'

'And you couldn't identify the vehicles used?'

'It was too dark.'

'How many vehicles?'

'Two.'

Rory studied the land beyond her garden gate. The moor stretched to a line of trees, the heather not yet purple. Beyond the trees Ben Shee rose into the blue sky. 'Witch Mountain', some folk called it, the home of three witches. Sometimes, the islanders said, you could hear them cackling, but Emily believed it was just the cry of gulls carried on the winds – winds that were sometimes strong enough to uproot trees that didn't have the foresight to lodge themselves deep in the ground. Stoirm was a place where a person's roots have to be deep in order to hang on, and she thought she had managed to achieve that, but the previous night's events had made her question her belief.

'And they headed to the Spine, right?'

The Spine was Stoirm's central main road, running the length of the island with other, minor roads threading away from it to reach farms, crofts and small settlements.

'There's nowhere else to go, as you know.' She pointed to the right beyond her garden gate. 'The road peters out that way.'

He followed her finger as if he might see something that would contradict what she'd said. He didn't, though. The young officer was merely taking in all the details he could.

'Tell me again what he said, Ms Thorne.'

She repeated the man's words from the previous night, was glad to see the policeman's eyes hardening and his jaw tightening.

'I know prejudice, PC Gibson. I was married to an Asian man, so I've experienced it first-hand. It's ugly and it's frightening, and we got it from both sides. But I've been here for eight years. When I first came, I know there was some muttering about me and people like me being white settlers, even those who were Scottish but not island-born, but that was all there was: mutterings. Not a great deal, just from the

24

likes of Darren Yates and his family. I've been largely welcomed. I know there can be friction over incomers buying up property for second homes and Airbnbs, but there really wasn't much of that on the island, to be honest. Not until recently, anyway.'

He didn't follow up on her last words. He knew what she meant. 'You've had no threats before this?'

'No.'

'Not seen anyone hanging about?'

'Only the occasional tourist walking in the summer.'

She watched the police officer studying the blackened ruins.

'You know what's behind this, PC Gibson. You know who those young folk were.'

He was about to say something but thought better of it. 'No, I don't, Ms Thorne. I have no evidence. They could be yobs up from Glasgow deciding to make trouble, have some laughs. You said the man wasn't local . . .'

'There's a pattern.'

He paused, knowing exactly what she meant. 'Not officially.'

'Unofficially, then.'

Rory Gibson pursed his lips, took off his hat and ran his fingers through his short, fair hair. He pulled at the collar of his shirt and squinted up at the morning sun. 'It's going to be a hot one today, you can just feel it. They say we're heading for a heatwave and I think they're right.' He replaced his hat. Sighed. 'Ms Thorne – Emily – there's a world of difference between what I know – or what I think I know – and what I can prove. There could be any number of motivations behind this.'

'Like what?'

'Simple vandalism.'

'Oh, come on . . .'

'The anti-incomer sentiment could be indicative.'

Her laugh was short and bitter as she caught his meaning. 'You're going to try to blame Callum McMaster but not Darren Yates and his friends?'

'I'm not trying to blame anybody,' the police officer said. 'I'm only mentioning a possibility.'

'I've met Cal, spoken to him many times. He has his views and we disagree, but he wouldn't do anything like this.'

'He's done a lot worse.'

'And he paid the price. And if there's no evidence against Darren and his gang, then there's none against Cal.'

He looked away again, knowing she was right, knowing he had spoken out of turn.

'You know what this is all about, Rory,' she said, using his Christian name purposely. 'They want to stop us.'

'I know, but there's nothing I can do without proof.'

'The people behind this are not playing by the Marquess of Queensberry Rules, you know that. They see us gaining ground and they don't like it and they're stepping up the pressure. You know what's been happening.'

'I don't know anything,' he insisted, although reluctantly. 'I've had reports of incidents – nothing like this, certainly – and they've been investigated.'

'And nobody has been arrested.'

'There was no—'

'No evidence. Yes, we all know that,' she said, her irritation noticeable. 'So, what will have to happen before this is all taken seriously?'

'It is being taken seriously.'

'Not seriously enough. You're undermanned on the island – there's you and, what, another four PCs? And a sergeant, of course, but let's be frank, he's as much use as a chocolate teapot.'

'Sergeant Nisbett is—'

'Sergeant Nisbett is a lazy so-and-so serving out his time till retirement. I mean no offence, but with that kind of manpower there's a limit to what you can do. When will they send a detective from the mainland to investigate this properly?'

He stared again at the smouldering ruin. 'There's been nothing serious enough to merit that.'

She indicated the smoking wood. 'Even this?'

'Even this.'

'So, what then?' she snapped. 'Does somebody have to be assaulted? Or worse?'

The police officer couldn't reply. Emily felt her sudden anger give way to guilt over attacking him in such a way. His hands were tied and he was only doing his job. He also couldn't agree with her view that events would have to take a more dangerous turn before the mainland would pay any attention, but it was to his credit that he didn't try to defend the police's lack of action in any forceful way. And he was correct. They needed evidence and that was the one thing they didn't have. The youths and the man the night before had been careful not to reveal their identities, although him speaking to her was at least something to work on.

Emily and others had already discussed what should be done about the worsening situation on Stoirm. If the mainland wouldn't send an investigator, they had decided to call in their own.

Molly Sinclair had fought it, but the committee had voted overwhelmingly against her. She didn't know what they were doing. Donnie did, though, but she had expected nothing less of him. He had never believed that Rebecca was bad news for the island, had always defended her.

But Molly knew. The reporter was nothing but a self-seeking muck-raker who cared nothing for the lives she might ruin. All she cared about was the story she was following, and if they brought her back to the island then nothing but heartache would follow.

She looked at Hector in his usual chair, watching the morning news. She saw him every day and saw no difference in him, but her sister had visited more recently and had commented on how much he had aged.

Molly had laughed a little, but she knew it to be forced. 'We all have, Myra. You and I are no spring chickens, are we?'

Myra didn't even smile. 'No, it's more than just the years, Molly,' she'd said. 'It's as if there's a weight around his neck, dragging him down.'

'Aye, well,' Molly had said, knowing full well what her sister meant. 'Losing a boy to the drugs and having your only daughter murdered, then seeing the man accused of it walk free from court will do that.'

Hector hadn't been the same, not since Mhairi died and then the year Roddie Drummond had returned to the island. How that man had the barefaced cheek to show his face on Stoirm after what had happened, she never understood. Even though the courts had cleared him of their daughter's murder, he was still guilty in most people's eyes. Including her and Hector's. Of course, Drummond never left the island again. Maybe he deserved what he got, maybe he didn't – true judgement would be in the hands of the Almighty – but whatever the case, even his death hadn't given Hector real peace; if anything, he had become more withdrawn than before. Molly had found acceptance. You have to accept what is given to you, otherwise you turn bitter and hollow. Her husband had never accepted it, that was his trouble.

And now she had to tell him that Rebecca Connolly might be returning to the island. She couldn't bear the thought, knowing how he would react. Time was, he would have flown into a rage, but now he just let the knowledge soak in, his face blank, but his eyes dark and . . . haunted. It was the only way she could put it.

4

'So, what did you say?'

Alan Shields leaned forward in his chair, his thin face brimming with its customary eagerness, his eyes alive behind his glasses. He had long used spectacles when reading, but now he wore them all the time. His love of books was evidence of the fact that he was one of the most curious people she knew, rivalling even her own insatiable need to know. He loved to gossip, loved to probe, to research, and he had been useful to her more than once. But this particular enquiry didn't relate to any story she was working on; this was about her personal life. There was a time when that would have rankled, but not now. Alan and his husband, Chaz Wymark, who also waited for her response, were her closest friends and they had been through a great deal together.

They had popped into the office for a quick cup of coffee, Alan being on a day off, Chaz heading out on a job. He was a photographer with another agency and was off to cover the visit to Inverness by a government minister who had come north to show how much they cared about the Highlands. Rebecca had told them about Stephen's proposal the previous night, and even though they expressed surprise, she had a feeling that they had known in advance and that this quick coffee break was not born out of any spur-of-the-moment decision.

They knew everything about her. Almost everything. There was one thing she had never shared with them and never would. Not even her mother knew. She wasn't ashamed, for the miscarriage hadn't been her fault – they'd told her it was merely an issue with chromosomes, in that there weren't enough of them, but the baby still died before it had lived. The father – who, like Stephen, was a solicitor she had met during the course of work – had wanted to marry her when he heard about the pregnancy, but she declined. He wasn't the one for her, and she knew it. He was a decent man, and she felt bad about the way it all ended. Stephen was also a decent man and part of her told her that he was the one for her. But there was that other part of her that pulled back . . .

Be happy, Elspeth had told her . . .

'I said I'd have to think about it.'

Alan's eyebrows shot up so quickly he almost had a nosebleed, but Chaz didn't even blink. His head was slightly cocked, eyes narrowed, lips slightly pursed, as if he knew all along what her response had been. Of the two, he was the one who knew her best. They had met on her first visit to the island of Stoirm. He had been the local contact for the *Highland Chronicle*, the weekly newspaper for which she worked at the time, and she had defied the editor's instruction not to visit the island for a story. Newspapers had reached the point of actively avoiding sending reporters out of the office – a story wasn't a story unless it could be done on the phone, she had been told. That approach to reporting didn't sit well with her. She had a personal connection to Stoirm in any case, which she had been keen to explore.

'And how did he take that incredibly romantic response?' Chaz asked.

'He understood,' she said.

Stephen hadn't, really. He'd said he would have preferred a flat-out no to vacillation. He hadn't stormed off, which was something, though the rest of the dinner was cool enough to make their breath frost. He drove her back to her flat but didn't come in, a fleeting peck on the lips the only sign of warmth. He was hurt and angry and confused, and he had every reason to be. They both knew that their relationship was headed this way, and yet still she held back.

The increased puckering of Chaz's lips told her that he believed her as much as he thought pigs would rival the Red Arrows, but he didn't say anything. It was left to Alan to fill the void.

'Becks, I say this with love, but what the hell is wrong with you?'

She didn't reply. It was a question she had been asking herself all night.

'You love Stephen, right?'

She looked away from him, uncomfortable with confessing the concept. It had taken her a long time to even say it to Stephen, let alone admit it to her friends. Rebecca had spent most of her adult life masking her feelings. Alan wasn't to be ignored, however.

'You. Love. Stephen. Right?' he repeated, his voice harder than she had ever heard it before.

'That's not the point.'

'That *is* the point. You have a man there who is absolutely nuts about you, though God knows why, the way you have treated him. And you, Rebecca Connolly, are nuts about him, whether you admit it or not. So, why hesitate?'

Yes, Rebecca – why hesitate? What are you afraid of? These were also questions she had asked herself and had come up with only one answer.

'I don't know,' she said.

'You don't know?' Alan's exasperation was clearly evident. 'How can you not know?'

Chaz rested a hand on Alan's arm. 'Leave it, Alan.'

'No, I won't leave it. Rebecca's our friend, we love her, and if we can't tell her when she's making a mistake – and we both know she's prone to poor decisions – then who can?'

Chaz shook his head and then leaned over the desk towards Rebecca, his voice soft. 'How did you leave it with Stephen?'

She thought of that fleeting kiss, the way he didn't look at her as he drove away, no wave, his lights vanishing as he turned out of the small car park. And, importantly, her standing at the open door feeling that she had blown it.

Yeah, Becks, what the hell is wrong with you?

She was saved from having to explain herself further – or, really, in any way – by her phone ringing; her personal mobile, not the agency one. She saw a name she recognised on the read-out and snatched it up from the desk all too eagerly.

'Fiona, how are you?' She could hear the tension in her own voice and hoped the woman on the other end wouldn't catch it and ask her the same. Fiona McRae was a Church of Scotland minister on Stoirm, and even though Rebecca wasn't a believer, she didn't fancy lying to a woman of the cloth.

'I'm here with Donnie Kerr, Rebecca,' Fiona said, getting right to the point, telling Rebecca that this was no social call.

'Chaz and Alan are here,' Rebecca countered. 'I'll put you on speaker.'

She laid the phone on the desk, avoiding Alan's accusatory gaze. And Chaz's disapproving one. 'What's up?'

Another voice chimed in, a man's voice, and one she recognised, though she hadn't heard it for years. 'We have a story for you, Rebecca, if you're interested.'

She had met Donnie Kerr on Stoirm during the same trip in which she met Chaz for the first time, though she had spoken to him only once or twice since. He owned a fishing boat but didn't fish. Instead, he took tourists out into the stretch of water separating the island from the mainland, called the Sound by locals, to see whales and dolphins. The Roddie Drummond story she had been following had concerned a murder fifteen years earlier which had involved Donnie and old friends of his. The return of the man accused but acquitted of the killing on a Not Proven verdict had opened up all kinds of wounds on the island. There had been further death, and Donnie himself was badly beaten. Chaz hadn't emerged unscathed from that period, either. He had been targeted by a bunch of local youths and almost died when the vehicle in which he and Alan had been travelling was forced from the road.

'Hi, Donnie, good to hear from you – what's the story?'

'What do you know of what's been happening over here?'

'I know Lord Henry's estate is up for sale.'

Lord Henry Stuart's family had been lords of the manor on Stoirm for centuries. While following up on the murder story, Rebecca had discovered that Henry Stuart was none too fussy about how he made money to support the estate. Although he himself was wealthy, he wasn't keen to sink his own capital into it. That lack of scruples had led to some questionable alliances. Following his accidental death, his wife had put the estate up for sale. Rebecca wondered if those questionable alliances had a hand in said accident.

'It is, and the community is trying to raise the cash to buy it,' Donnie said. 'We believe it's best in our hands. We've registered our interest, and that gives us first shout if we can raise the money, but there's someone else interested.'

'Who?'

'A consortium of rich bastards . . . Sorry, Fiona.'

'That's okay, Donnie,' said Fiona. 'They probably are rich bastards.'

Chaz leaned forward again, now more interested in this than in Rebecca's love life. 'My mum and dad told me there was big money involved in the consortium but they were being held back by the community bid.'

'That you, Chaz?'

'Yes, hi, Fiona. Hi, Donnie.'

Chaz's father was one of the doctors on the island. He wasn't island-born but had decided long ago that his family – his wife and baby son – would be better off there than in London. When he was of a sufficient age, Chaz, like many young people raised on Stoirm, decided that there were few prospects there for him as a photographer and so had decamped to Inverness. He managed to make a living but, like Rebecca, was in no danger of going into tax exile.

'Which rich bastards are we talking about?'

'We don't know, that's the annoying thing,' Donnie said. 'It'll be hedge funds, insurance companies, finance firms, that sort of thing. The only name we know for certain is a solicitor in Edinburgh called Terence Williams, but as to who he acts for, it's kind of a mystery. But I'm telling you, they don't have the island's interests at heart. It's time the land returned to the people, Rebecca. It's time to stop this parcelling off of the country to people with money who don't really care.'

'And is Lady Stuart minded to flog it to them?'

'Lady Stuart will sell to anyone as long as the price is right. She never much cared for the wellbeing of the island, and I really can't blame her, given her husband was shagging the local MP. Sorry, Fiona.'

'That's also okay, Donnie. He was, indeed, shagging the Right Dishonourable Viola Ramage, even after she fell from grace. I suppose that shows some kind of loyalty in the man, God rest his soul.'

Viola Ramage had been caught in a newspaper sting accepting cash to lobby ministers on behalf of a foreign group looking to muscle in on the country's energy industry. Unusually for her party, she resigned her seat, which was later won in a by-election by the candidate from the opposition party, and she was now presenting a political show on the UKB satellite channel. Rebecca never watched the channel, which put her in the majority, but she supposed Ramage no longer holding a seat in Parliament made a change from constituency MPs appearing on it and pretending to be impartial.

'So, do you want me to do a story on the community buyout, Donnie? Are you and others willing to speak about it?'

Rebecca's mind was already turning to the human-interest aspect of the story, wondering who she could flog it to. It was an issue, true, so that might hook a broadsheet, but the 'David and Goliath' aspect could be of interest to the tabloids, the magazines, maybe even TV. She thought perhaps Leo Cross, who owned the TV production company that had made the documentary, might see some mileage in it. Scenery, drama, history . . .

'The thing is,' Donnie continued, 'there have been . . . incidents.'

His words pulled her from her forward planning. 'What sort of incidents?'

'Windows broken. Cars vandalised. Homes broken into but nothing taken, though the owners know someone's been in. We don't get a lot of that on Stoirm, as you know, but there's been a rash of them. The police put it down to local yobs.'

Alan sat forward, really taking an interest now. He had lived on the island for a time; in fact, it was where he and Chaz had met. They both had experience of those undesirable elements.

'Don't tell me: I sense the hand of the Yates family in this.'

Donnie laughed. 'Yes, if we're right, then they will be up to their necks in it. There's one thing that connects all the victims.'

'What's that?' Alan asked.

'Guess,' said Donnie.

'They're all part of the community buy-out?' Rebecca asked.

'More fish for the redheaded lass.'

'That's okay, I'll settle for chocolates.'

'The most serious incident took place last night. Emily Thorne moved here just after you left, Chaz. Nice woman, loves the island, lives on her own in the old Ramsay croft on the Ben Shee road. You remember it?'

'Yes, the place was a bit rundown,' Chaz recalled.

'Emily has completely renovated it. It was targeted last night. Gang of neds woke her up shouting and screaming and banging on windows.'

'Is she okay?' Rebecca asked.

'She got a hell of a scare but she's unharmed. Anyway, one of them set fire to her wood store. Only this time someone spoke to her. He wore a hood, like the others, told her to leave the island, that she wasn't wanted.'

'He wore a hood?' Rebecca asked.

'Yeah, very Ku Klux Klan.'

'If the other attacks—'

'Incidents, according to the law,' Donnie corrected, his voice heavy with irony.

'Sorry, if the other incidents were clandestine, then the fact that she saw him and he concealed his identity means that he intended to be seen. They could be ramping up the pressure.'

'That's our thinking, too,' said Fiona.

Rebecca fell silent as she considered this. 'What do the police say?'

'What can they say?' Donnie replied. 'There's only a hand-ful of them and there's no evidence to lead them to anyone in particular, not even Darren Yates, who as we know is the boy most likely to be behind any shit. Sorry, Fiona.'

'Will you stop apologising, Donnie. I've heard the word before. I've even used it myself.'

'Aye, sorry.' He laughed. 'Anyway, it has to be people working for the consortium.'

'If they are responsible,' Fiona added, ever the fair-minded part of any conversation.

'It is them, you know it, Fiona.'

'I know nothing of the sort, Donnie. I know it's a possibility, but that's all.'

'Aye, right,' said Donnie, disbelief heavy on the two words.

'Donnie, we have to be fair about this. It could be just as the police say – local kids up to no good. And if it is, they'll get them.'

Donnie mumbled something that Rebecca didn't quite catch, then spoke up. 'So, what do you think, Rebecca? You think there's something in this?'

Rebecca made a mental list of the work on hand. She had a couple of court reports to write up for the nationals, but that wouldn't take her long. The cases were complete. She had an interview to complete for a magazine, which she could write anywhere, and some bits of research for Leo Cross, but they could wait a few days. And there was the Stephen situation, of course.

'There is something in this, Donnie,' she said, avoiding the accusatory stares from both Chaz and Alan, instead looking at the clock on the wall behind them beside the office's small kitchen area. 'I can be over there this evening if I can get to Oban to catch the last ferry. Failing that, the first one in the morning. Can you arrange for me to speak to a few people while I'm there?'

'Yes, everybody is keen to get all this in the open,' he replied.

'Well, perhaps not everybody,' Fiona said. 'You know there are always those who don't want outsiders placing their lives here under scrutiny.'

'It's an island thing,' Rebecca said, parroting the phrase she had heard so many times on her first visit, when she had placed lives under scrutiny. It hadn't turned out too well for some of them.

'There are a few who are sympathetic to the idea of a community purchase but really don't want outsiders to start meddling.'

'That's why they support the buy-out rather than a consortium taking ownership,' Donnie jumped in, making Rebecca wonder what he didn't want Fiona to say. 'At least we're local, even if some of those involved are incomers. This consortium would bring more people from across the water to the island but only to use it as a playground. Stoirm islanders would take their money, certainly, but you know the old Stoirm adage – come here by all means, but we'd rather you simply came over on the ferry, left your money and caught the next one back.'

'The point is,' Fiona said, 'those on the committee who are not island-born will speak to you, but you might meet resistance from a few of the others.'

Rebecca knew all about that resistance, although she had managed to break through before.

'I'm used to people not wanting to talk to me,' Rebecca said, prompting a snort from Alan.

'I know how they feel, right now,' he muttered.

'You can stay with me,' Fiona said.

'No, that's okay. I'll book a room in the hotel,' Rebecca said, not being keen on staying in someone's home, especially while they were there. She liked her own space. Was that one of the reasons she had hesitated in accepting Stephen's proposal?

'The hotel's closed, Rebecca,' Fiona said. 'It's being renovated. You're welcome to stay here, I have plenty of room.'

Rebecca would have preferred finding a boarding house or an Airbnb, but she knew she couldn't snub Fiona's offer. She thanked her, told them she'd let them know if she was able to catch the evening ferry and the conversation ended.

As she hung up she caught Alan's reproving look.

'You know what the truly sad thing about this is?' His earlier exasperated tone had been replaced by something softer. Mournful, even. He didn't wait for either of them to reply. 'That you really think you're hopping on a ferry in pursuit of a story.'

She knew what he meant but feigned ignorance. 'Is that not what I'm doing?'

'No, you're running away, Becks, and as usual using a story as a barrier against life.'

'I'll speak to Stephen before I go.'

'Of course you will, and then off you'll pop off like the eager little newshound that you are, and you'll speak to people on the island and you'll sympathise and you'll get to the bottom of it all, of that I have no doubt. But the real story, that of you and your life, will be abandoned again, although you'll convince yourself that this was something you *had* to do, right now, right away.'

'My work is important, Stephen understands that.'

'Yes, he does, because his work is important to him. But you know what's more important? Life. Living. Chaz's work is important to him, but he makes time for living. I, on the other hand, think life is important so I make time for work. It's just something I do to make some money, whereas you three have a calling, I suppose, but both Chaz and Stephen know how to manage it. Even Elspeth knew the importance of enjoying life.'

Be happy . . .

'The sadness is that you believe this calling is more important than anything else, but it's really not. And if you don't wake up and smell the percolator bubbling, you'll find that calling is all you have. Then one day you'll realise that you're nothing but a bitter old woman, looking back on her life and wondering where it all went wrong.'

5

Ryan Duffy had known since he was a boy that he could frighten people.

It wasn't just because of his size, which was considerable. It was something in his broad face, in the way he held himself, that seemed to intimidate others without him having to do or say anything. It was a skill, if you want to call it that, but not one of which he was particularly proud.

The thing of it was, all Ryan Duffy had wanted as a boy was to be a carpenter. At school, his favourite class had been woodwork and he had shown very early expertise in wielding a plane and a hammer. He had grown up in the Edinburgh streets with the unusual collective name of Bingham, Magdalene and The Christians, where carpentry was an unusual ambition, and his love of working the wood was not something that ran in the family. His grandad had been a safeblower – what they once called a peterman – before, during and just after the Second World War. Ryan's own father, Jimmy Duffy, was not so skilled, as he was too big and clumsy for the careful work of applying gelignite, lighting the blue touch paper and retiring quickly. He was a hulk of a man, with more muscles in his fingers than most had in their entire body, so went to work for a city gangster by the name of Artie Rose, earning the nickname 'Jimmy the Snap', thanks to his facility for breaking bones. He had also shown some flair with weapons, but Jimmy was a foot soldier and always would be, and that grated on him and turned him into a bitter and vicious man.

His son also grated on him.

Ryan wasn't interested in blowing things up, shooting things down or lacerating flesh. Though he shared his dad's muscle gene, he wasn't inclined to hurt people unless they intended to hurt him. Such scruples didn't lend themselves to future employment with Artie Rose, and that annoyed the hell out of Jimmy because he had visions of him and his boy becoming a team and, if the lad had his mother's brains (which he did), perhaps finally rising to something more than muscle to be ordered hither and thither. Ryan inherited the family's larcenous gene and, being somewhat more dexterous than his brute of a father, developed an enviable skill in opening lockfast places in order to steal everything from here to the horizon.

His aversion to inflicting pain didn't mean he kept out of trouble, though. Being Jimmy Duffy's boy meant that there would be no end of that, and Jimmy himself wasn't sparing with his fists after a day of boozing in order to drown out the disappointments of his life. Ryan drifted into a life of gangs and violence, finding himself doing a ten stretch for mobbing and rioting before he was twenty – just a bunch of pals drunk on cheap bevvy getting out of hand – then later another stint for serious assault. A bloke thought he would show off by pushing Ryan around, thinking that because this big guy tried to avoid trouble that he was somehow open to the experience. Push came to shove, shove came to punch and, when the bloke was down, punch came to kick. As a young man, Ryan's temper was not something of which he was proud and he really, *really*, had to force it down sometimes, but on that occasion it boiled over and before he knew it the guy was unconscious and bloody at his feet, and the law had been called. That he had been provoked, that he had acted in self-defence and the boy himself was no angel only went so far in the eyes of justice; he ended up in Saughton, with a stinging reminder from the judge that might is not always right and sometimes it's best to walk away. While Ryan recognised the wisdom in those words, he also knew that he wasn't built like that. If someone pushed his buttons, he reacted, simple as. He didn't much like that part of himself but there it was.

He was granted parole, thanks to keeping his nose clean and expressing sorrow at his wicked ways, and while at liberty he met a red-haired Irish girl called Maureen, who liked to be called Rina. He also managed to get her up the duff the first time their winching got beyond kissing and groping, but he did the decent thing and married her. They had a son – against Ryan's wishes they named him Patrick after her dad – and Ryan found work with a joiner working out of Niddrie, a decent man. But the siren call of larceny was too strong and he was nabbed red-handed in a Morningside villa, having taken care to gain access without noise or damage, but failing to take into account an alarm that neither he nor his accomplice, who had selected the house as ripe for plucking, knew existed.

He was duly sent back to the hallowed halls of Saughton to complete his previous sentence and another few years on top for the housebreaking. Once there he kept his joinery skills sharp by being assigned to the workshop, where he could work the wood. That ended when one of the other blokes took a chisel and went to town on a prison officer – someone said that Ryan had handed it to him, but he hadn't, he'd actually been trying to stop the bloke from going spare, but that's not the way the prison service, or the courts, saw it. Another few years were added to his sentence, during which young Pat died of an overdose. He was only fifteen. Ryan wasn't even allowed out to go to the funeral because he was seen as a risk to the public. And all because he tried to take a chisel away from a bloke who had gone mental and went for a screw.

When he got out, he did odd jobs here and there, none of them in any way legal, always trying to avoid anything that involved violence. He didn't want to go back inside. He owed the memory of his boy that much. His dad had died a couple of years before, dropped dead in the boozer in the middle of downing a pint, probably lying to someone about how he used to be a somebody when he worked with Artie Rose, when the reality was that he was just another thug. Artie Rose himself was dead by that time, shot in his car on some country road. Jimmy had actually wept at the funeral, Ryan had heard, which further pissed him off because he never shed a tear when his own wife had died after being bullied and beaten into an early grave. Maybe she had once loved him; Ryan could never tell.

In his memory his mum always had a worn look, as if life had squeezed her dry, only coming alive when she was reading. She loved books and perhaps used them as a means of getting away from her own life, which had not turned out to be the answer to a maiden's prayer. She was affectionate to her son, certainly, but only when his father wasn't around. Jimmy Duffy didn't do affection. Sudden blows to the head, vile insults and vicious putdowns of both his son and wife he could manage, but not anything remotely resembling fondness.

It was an acute massive pulmonary embolism that took him, the doctor said. He had been coughing blood that morning, his then current girlfriend told Ryan when he met her later, and had been complaining of a pain in the leg prior to that. Deep vein thrombosis, Ryan was told, and a blood clot had broken away and travelled to his lung. Just like that. One minute he was draining a pint and smoking and laughing with his mates, and the next minute he was lying on the floor, gone for a Burton. Even though he hadn't seen him for years, his passing was like a weight being lifted from Ryan's shoulders. He had known he was there, in the city, and that was enough. Frankly, the world was a much better place without Jimmy in it. There were still some blokes who took liberties with Ryan because of things his dad had done, but he handled them easily enough, mostly without delivering a slap but sometimes it was unavoidable. When he did, he ensured his temper didn't get the better of him. He didn't want to end up back in jail. He was done with all that.

Then the opportunity came up to do some joinery on a contract basis on some island off the west coast, way past Mull and the last stop before you hit Canada and the USA. It was Rina's dad, Patrick Murphy, Big Pat to his friends, who gave him the steer, saying some guys he knew had a job to refurbish the local hotel. The boss was a good man, Pat said, who wanted men he could rely on.

Ryan should have known there was more to it right then, Big Pat himself being someone who needed satnav to lead him to the straight and narrow, but he saw the chance to maybe get back to what he wanted to do, and he took it. So, he travelled to Stoirm with a bunch of blokes he'd never met, some who had a trade, but one who Ryan soon found out wasn't handy at all. Not in that way, anyway. The boss was a Glasgow guy by the name of Matt Coyle, who explained that they had all been hired by the new owners of the hotel in a wee place called Portnaseil. He added there were a few other jobs to do as well, and at first Ryan thought that meant more refurbishment somewhere else on Stoirm.

But it didn't. And he found out why the other bloke who didn't have a trade was there.

The night before, Matt had handed him the keys to a motor and told him to drive one of them – Elton was his name – somewhere. Ryan asked what it was all about, but

Matt told him not to worry. It was sorted. Ryan didn't know what the fuck was sorted, and he didn't like the idea, but he went along with it. He'd sat in a car near to a wee cottage on some godforsaken road leading to nowhere, where they were joined by a bunch of locals who arrived in an old pick-up truck that looked as if it had been in some war. He supposed that it was a veteran of these island roads, some of which were little more than dirt tracks. A tall blond fellow piled out and Elton pulled on a sort of hood, then went out to meet him. Ryan couldn't hear what was said, but at one point the blond boy looked towards the car.

Okay, Ryan thought, what's that about?

The confab over, Elton came back to him while the blond lad motioned to his pals in the pick-up, two boys and a lassie, to follow him. They all pulled hoods over their heads and trooped past the car, the tall one peering in at Ryan through the driver's window. Ryan gave him the stare as he passed.

Seriously, what was going on?

'What's the deal?' he asked Elton. 'What's with the masks?'

Elton just waved him off, took a can of petrol from the boot and followed them, leaving Ryan wondering just what the holy fuck he was involved in.

All he knew was that he hadn't a Scooby about what was going on, but it was far from kosher. That was proved when he saw flames in the cottage's wee garden. He jumped out and ran to the fence. The kids were running around the cottage like Comanche surrounding a wagon train, whooping and screaming. They all had hoods on, and Ryan knew that he should just get back to the car, put the pedal to the metal and get the hell out of Dodge.

Then a woman came out, with a bloody shotgun, in the name of Christ, and Elton told her to get off the island, calling her an incomer, whatever the fuck that was about. Ryan had then beetled back to the motor before anyone saw him. Later, Elton came running back, throwing the empty canister into the back seat.

'Floor this fucker, for God's sake,' he said. 'No lights till we're well away.'

The kids were piling into their truck and taking off. Ryan did as he was told, mindful of the woman's shooter and not fancying the idea of her taking out the back window. Or taking him out. He floored the fucker, as instructed.

'I don't like it, Rina,' he said on the blower to his wife the next day. He was in his room in the hotel – they all had their own, which was a good thing, but as they were all being done up he dossed on a fold-out camp bed, wrapped in a sleeping bag.

'We need the money,' she said, her sigh all the way from Edinburgh sounding harsh. 'You know that.'

Between them, Rina was always the more pragmatic. Her dad was as hard a bastard as you could ever meet, and she had inherited much of his grit. Big Pat hadn't been too keen on his daughter marrying him, but not because he was Roman Catholic and Ryan was Protestant – to be fair old Pat didn't give a monkeys about that stuff, and neither did Ryan. Jimmy Duffy had a few things to say, though, him being a member of the Orange Lodge even though he only graced the doors of a church for weddings or funerals, but by that time Ryan wasn't interested in anything his dad had to say.

No, Pat wasn't happy with the match because he thought Ryan was a useless loser. Pat had known Jimmy and respected him. He liked men who could drink hard, smoke hard and fight hard, and not be too choosy about their level of devotion to any marriage vows. Ryan gave up the bevvy after going down for the assault, had never seen the sense in sticking tubes of burning tobacco between his lips, and didn't screw around. Rina wasn't the first lassie he'd shagged but she was

48

certainly the last. You'd think old Pat would've appreciated that, if not for his own sake but for that of his only daughter, but he didn't get it and never would.

The problem was, Ryan believed that Rina had come around to her dad's way of thinking. Not about the shagging – because if she caught him with another woman, she'd cut his tackle off with a rusty spoon – but in thinking that the man she had married was a loser. Judging by the tone of her voice down the phone line, he suspected he was right.

'Just get it done, Ryan, for fuck's sake,' she said. 'Pocket the cash.'

'Someone's going to get hurt,' he said.

'So what? They teuchters are nothing to us.'

'I think some of them are English.'

'Even better. They bastards have exploited us for far too long.'

Ryan wasn't a political animal, but Rina spent too much time on social media. 'Come on, Rina, they're just people, you know? Good and bad, like—'

'Ach, Ryan, when you gonnae grow up, man? The only people that matter are those who share your blood, you should know that by now.'

He thought of Jimmy. His father had been his blood relative and there had been bugger all about him that mattered to Ryan, not for a long time. Rina had four brothers and, if rumours were true, a couple of half siblings in Belfast, Pat being one who practised what he preached, shagging wise, if not family loyalty.

'So, suck it up, do what has to be done and stop greetin' about it,' she said. 'I spoke to my da – he knows this Matt Coyle bloke and says he's well connected, so you keep in with him and do whatever the fuck he wants you to do. Don't question it, just do it.'

'But someone could get hurt here.'

'Jesus! For once in your life show some balls! Can you no just do what needs to be done and don't question?'

He pictured her face, her teeth gritted in anger, her once coal black hair, now threaded with grey, swept back from her face, a cigarette no doubt burning between her fingers. He loved her but he didn't think she loved him, not now, not since young Patrick died. She blamed him for not being there to help her when their son was losing himself to drugs. She didn't blame him for getting lifted in that house, but she did blame him for being daft enough to try to stop the rammy in the prison woodshop and getting his sentence extended. The fact that both their fathers had, in the past, been part of the machinery that took those drugs onto the street seemed to have escaped her. In the eyes of his daughter, Pat Murphy the elder could do no wrong.

The conversation ended abruptly, because Rina hung up, saying she was tired of hearing him whine. He didn't think he'd been whining. He thought he had been sharing his concerns with his partner, but if he had said that she would have sneered and made a fool of him.

His was a small single room at the very top of the hotel with a window looking down the hill towards the stretch of water that locals called the Sound. If he stood on a chair, he could also see the Square, with its shops, its grocery store and post office, and the modern civic building that he'd been told housed a sort of town hall. It also contained the island's police station, so he'd made a point of never going near it. He didn't take in the view, though. He sat on the bed, his phone still in his hand, and thought about Rina's words. Maybe she was right, maybe these people didn't mean anything to him. He was being well paid to fix skirting boards, fit doors and replace dry wall – paid well over the odds, if he was honest. She was definitely right that they needed the scratch, and he was smart enough to know that the wee side jobs he'd been doing, last night's being the most recent, were the reason for the extra. What all this was really about was none of his business.

But he couldn't shake off the feeling that this could all turn nasty. And in his experience of life, when things turned nasty, he generally ended up worse off.

6

Stephen was fond of claiming that the lane that curved up from the pedestrian precinct opposite Inverness's Eastgate Shopping Centre was named after him. Rebecca had no clue as to why the pathway that took people to the Crown area was called Stephen's Brae but she was fairly certain it had nothing to do with him. It was much more likely that his parents, who had begun the practice and sited their office on the brae, named him after it.

She'd often thought it would be pleasant to live up in the Crown, close to the city centre, in a Victorian or Edwardian villa with some history. Her own flat was of more modern construction and, although functional, it had no character whatsoever. Having grown up in a pre-war semi-detached villa in Milngavie, outside Glasgow, she felt herself drawn to older properties. She wanted plaster mouldings. She wanted old wood. My God, she wanted a dado rail. She had said all these things to Stephen once, and he'd pointed out, rightly, that there was nothing stopping her from at least having the mouldings and the rail, but she dismissed the suggestion. It wasn't the same. She wanted the knowledge that these things had been part of the property since it was constructed, not bought from B&Q and stuck up there with super glue. Stephen had countered that older properties come with all sorts of issues, but she responded that she had heard of new-builds that are riddled with damp, so you pays your money and you takes your chances.

The conversation had been good-natured, with each of them poking a little fun at the other. It wasn't serious, it wasn't drama. It wasn't a deal-breaker.

The conversation they were about to have might prove to be all of the above. And she wasn't looking forward to it.

She was greeted by the customary glare through the protective screen from Elaine, Stephen's red-haired receptionist. Rebecca had never found out her age, but she had to be in her mid to late forties, and she had never taken to her, right from day one when she showed up at the office, as she had on this occasion, to speak to him about a story on which she was working. Even though Stephen had been expecting her, she still had trouble getting past her that day, and this one was shaping up to be the same.

'I'm afraid Mr Jordan is busy,' Elaine said. 'He has court.'

Rebecca knew that wasn't true. Stephen didn't talk much about his work but he did tell her when he was in court, and he was scheduled to be in the office all day. Elaine knew they were seeing each other, so Rebecca found it curious that she might think that they didn't share such information. Of course, it was possible Stephen was so pissed off with her that he had instructed his receptionist to lie, should she call or visit. The woman's expression told her nothing, because she always bore a look of faint disdain. And sometimes not so faint.

She decided not to query the lie. She didn't have time. 'I won't take long, Elaine.'

Her lips compressed like a vice. 'Was he expecting you, Ms Connolly?'

Always Ms Connolly, never Rebecca, even after all this time. Rebecca suspected there was a little bit of jealousy there, but Elaine sported an engagement ring that looked like the Koh-i-Noor's little sister and a gold wedding ring that probably cost some miner in South Africa quite a bit of sweat to hew out of the ground. As for Stephen expecting her, the answer was – very probably – yes. He knew her too well. Knew her strengths and weaknesses and generally accepted them both, knowing that he himself wasn't Mr Perfect. Until now, perhaps. Now she might have gone too far.

'No, but I do need to speak to him.'

For a moment there was a look behind Elaine's glasses that she was going to continue to stonewall her, but she pressed a button on the phone, lifted the receiver and told Stephen that Ms Connolly was here. Stephen obviously told her to let her through because the security door clicked open. Okay, so maybe he hadn't told her to guard the gate. Elaine was capable of assuming that responsibility all by herself.

'Thank you, Elaine,' she said, giving her the sweetest smile she could muster, even though she was dreading her encounter with Stephen. Elaine, she could handle. Stephen would be more difficult.

He was still angry from the previous evening. She could tell by the way he barely raised his eyes from the paperwork on his desk. She had hurt him, she knew it. She hadn't wanted to, but she had.

'I'm sorry,' she said. As a start it was hackneyed but heartfelt. She really was sorry.

He didn't reply. Didn't look up. His pen glided over the paper. His handwriting was always impeccable. *He* was always impeccable. Today he wore a grey suit, white shirt, blue tie. She couldn't see them but she knew his brown brogues would gleam. His hair was neat – it was always neat, even after they'd made love, when hers was tousled and tangled. Of course, his was a lot shorter. Even though she wasn't close enough to smell it, she knew he would exude a glorious scent, a mix of aftershave and, well, Stephen Jordan.

'I reacted badly,' she continued.

Still no eye contact. The pen moved on. What was he writing? His life story?

'So, I'm sorry.'

'You said that.'

He didn't look up. His writing didn't even pause. His voice was cold. Okay, she deserved that.

'Because I mean it.'

'Sure.' More ink flowed but no rise of the head. 'Fine, apology accepted.'

His tone of voice made a lie of his words. He really was angry, angrier than she had ever seen him before. When she had almost died making that swim for shore after being left stranded on an island in the middle of a loch, he had been relieved that she hadn't, in fact, drowned, and that tempered the anger he had over her going off on her own and getting into trouble. She wished he would snarl at her, even shout at her; this calm, polite, cold demeanour was unsettling.

She took a seat. He still didn't look up. The pen left its ink trail on the paper. The moving finger writes, and having writ, moves on. Jeez, Rebecca, what brought that line from some school lesson into her mind? She couldn't even remember who the hell wrote it.

'Look,' she said, 'can't we talk?'

The pen stopped, then was dropped and, finally, he looked at her. His eyes weren't exactly dead, but they did seem in need of some life support. 'Is there anything else to say?'

That was a good question, and she wished to God she had a good answer. She had to try, though. 'You can let me explain.'

He propped his elbows on the desk and threaded his fingers together. 'What is there to explain, Becks? I asked you to marry me, you said you'd have to think about it. I'm letting you think about it.'

'I think I need to tell you why I want to think about it.'

'No, you don't.'

'I think I do.'

'No,' he said, with added emphasis, 'you don't. Because I know.'

That caught her by surprise because she wasn't even sure herself. 'You know?'

'You want me to tell you?'

His calm tone was beginning to grate on her, so, when she replied, there was more tension in her words than she would have wished. 'Yeah, I'd really like to hear it.'

A slight narrowing of his eyes told he had caught the edge in her voice, but he didn't comment. 'You're afraid of being happy, Becks.'

'That is utter—'

'You said you wanted to hear it, so do me a favour and listen.'

She decided to do him a favour and listen, even though he was talking utter bollocks.

'Okay,' he said, 'this is what I believe. You won't accept it but I'm going to say it, anyway. You really are afraid of being happy because you fear that something will come along and take it away. And I think it all goes back to your dad, and it's been further compounded by what's occurred since.'

He was right about one thing: she didn't accept it. But she played along, even though she had never heard so much non-sense in her life. 'Like what?'

He took a deep breath. 'Elspeth's death, most recently. She was happy with her life with Julie, her books were selling, the TV thing had finally come together. Her happiness had even transferred to you, because things were going well, especially with us. We'd reached a point where we were comfortable with each other, with the boundaries our different professions imposed on our relationship, with the disappointments of past relationships. We worked, Becks, for the first time we actually worked. You understood that I couldn't tell you certain things about my clients, and through you the mistrust I had of the media lessened.'

'It never went away completely.'

'No, but the main thing is that I trust you. In return, I came to understand that you will go off and do your thing without consulting me—'

'I didn't know I had to clear my every movement.'

He sighed. 'We're doing what you wanted, Becks, we're talking about it. Don't get annoyed. I really don't think that's your right, is it?'

She was about to retort but realised that, this time, she really didn't have any right to be annoyed.

'The death of your dad affected you deeply, you have to admit that.'

'Of course it did!'

She was growing defensive, she knew it, but couldn't help herself.

'You saw how happy he and your mum were, how happy you all were, and then it was taken away from you both.'

She had loved John Connolly, her father. Even when she discovered he wasn't as perfect as she believed, she still loved him. It was cancer that had destroyed that happiness, but her mother had now found new contentment with another man – a relationship Rebecca had resisted at first. She had since come to realise that she was being petty and, yes, spoiled. She had been a daddy's girl, she recognised that, and though James Wilton would never replace her father, he at least made her mother happy.

'Your mum is moving on now,' he said.

'She deserves every moment of joy she can get,' she mumbled.

'And so do you.' When she didn't reply further, Stephen waited a beat. 'Then there was Nolan Burke . . .'

That she couldn't accept. 'Come on, Stephen, he meant nothing to me!'

'Maybe you didn't know that he did. Or that he might.'

'He was a crook, for God's sake. Do you think I'm one of those women who's impressed by a bad boy?'

'No, I don't. But I knew Nolan Burke slightly. I acted for one of his friends and he was a witness for his defence. There was something different about him. He was better than the sum of his parents' parts, if you get what I mean. His dad was and is little more than a thug; his mother . . . well, Mo Burke was something else. Clever but vicious. But Nolan was certainly nothing like either of them, and most certainly better than his brother. And he was interested in you.'

She remembered the rain falling on the canal towpath. The wind on the water. The gunshot.

'I wasn't interested in him.'

The bullet had been meant for her but had hit Nolan.

'Maybe not, but it was around this time that you finished it with Simon.'

'It was before all that,' she said, her voice coming from a long way away because her mind was off to the west of Inverness, at Clachnaharry, where the Caledonian Canal met the Beauly Firth.

'Because of the baby,' Stephen said, snapping her back to the here and now.

'How do you . . .?' She stopped. Only one person knew she had lost the baby, and that was the father. 'Simon told you, didn't he?'

Stephen at least had the decency to look uncomfortable over knowing something he shouldn't.

'Of course he did,' she said, bitterness coating her words. 'Men always talk.'

'And women don't? Come on, Becks, don't make this a gender thing. There's enough of that nonsense in the world. He was drunk one night, a legal do, and he told me, nobody else. He blamed himself for what happened.'

It wasn't anybody's fault, the doctor had said. A mix-up of chromosomes. Nobody's fault. Nobody to blame.

'He had no right telling you,' she said.

'Probably not, but the question remains: why didn't you tell me?'

'It's not . . .' she began.

'It's not what?'

Your business, she was going to say, but thought better of it. 'Never mind.'

His look told her that he had surmised what she was about to say, but thankfully he didn't pursue it. 'Fine, but that's another reason why you're afraid of happiness.'

'Don't go there, Stephen,' she warned. 'Please . . .'

It was still raw. She hadn't planned on getting pregnant, had never properly thought about motherhood, concentrating more on her work than anything else, but it happened, and when it did she had looked forward to being a mother. She didn't know whether it was the chemicals raging through her body changing her views or whether she had actually decided she wanted to have the child. In the end it didn't matter because the baby died. Inside her. She killed the child she had wanted. It didn't matter what the doctor said, it didn't matter what medical science said, or biology, whatever. The child was inside her body and had died, ergo, she was responsible.

Stephen took pity on her, his eyes softening. 'Okay. But listen to what I'm saying, Becks. Life is made up of a series of opportunities. Some we take, some we miss, some we allow to pass us by because we're too afraid of where they may lead. Don't let the past dictate the future. It can be a guide, an influence even, but in the end you have to make the most of what time there is, because we, none of us, know how much we actually have.'

She forced a lightness into her voice that she really didn't feel. Some things he said had hit home. 'Have you been reading those inspirational memes again?'

59

For the first time he smiled. It wasn't much of a smile, there was more sadness than levity in it, but it was an improvement. 'Think about what I'm saying, Becks. I know you're prone to introspection, so do it now. Go away for a few days, if you can, find somewhere quiet to think. And when you come back, tell me what you decide. I still want to marry you, make a decent woman of you . . .' It was his turn now to force some levity into his voice. 'But if you decide that's not what you want, then fine. I can't force you. I won't try to convince you, talk you round, I promise.'

Go away for a few days. She'd come here to tell him that that was exactly what she intended to do. It's funny how things work out sometimes.

7

She spotted the woman very quickly because her gaze was a little too direct for it to be fleeting.

Rebecca had entered the Eastgate Shopping Centre in search of a quiet table where she could have a coffee and a pastry and spend time digesting what Stephen had said. They had parted amicably enough, but the sadness in his eyes remained and she felt responsible for putting it there – which, of course, she had. It had cost him a great deal to make his proposal: he'd been burned once before by a fiancée who put work before life, and there he was in the same position – at least that's what he believed. Rebecca, though, wasn't putting work before life. She was merely concerned that she would, somehow, hurt him even more deeply. Listening to him talk, she realised just how well that man knew her. She was scared of happiness because she had learned that it was transient, fickle even. Just when you thought everything was going along nicely, something came along to pull the rug from under you. She was also sufficiently self-aware to recognise the possibility that she was being too cautious, that life isn't like that, really – that, as the philosopher once said, shit happens and it's nothing personal.

And yet . . .

She carried her coffee and the pastry to a table. At this time of the morning the ground-floor food court was relatively quiet, so she was able to keep herself apart from other customers, which made it easier for her eye to fall on the young woman scrutinising her from the Falcon Square entrance. She was in her early twenties, maybe five years younger than Rebecca, her hair auburn like hers, but a much darker shade and falling to her shoulders, much as Rebecca's did when she didn't have it tied back in a ponytail. Her face was thin, not sharp exactly – elfin-like was the way Rebecca would have described it. She was put in mind of Val Roach. My God, she could be her daughter. She was about Rebecca's own height and slender and her clothes were expensive, though Rebecca, who favoured utility and comfort over style, was no real judge. She carried over one shoulder a large brown leather bag – Prada, no less, and the branding looked genuine – while the other hand held an iPhone.

At first Rebecca thought the woman might have recognised her from the TV documentary. That had happened a few times and although it hadn't yet affected her work either positively or negatively, there was always that danger.

She held her gaze long enough to let her know that she had seen her, then set to pouring some sachets of sugar into her coffee and stirring it with one of those long, thin slivers of wood they issued instead of a spoon. The problem was that she had to swirl the coffee so much that she practically created a whirlpool that would pose a danger to any trawlers making their way through the Eastgate. She took a bite of her pastry – she'd wanted a fruit scone, but they were all out – and let the sweetness run riot round her mouth, raising her dopamine levels, because after the session with Stephen she really needed those suckers to have a wee party in her brain.

When she looked up again, the woman was about two feet away from her, uncertainty clear in her features. 'Sorry . . .' she began, then stopped, her fingers working at the strap of her bag.

'Can I help you?'

The woman opened her mouth, then closed it, then said, 'Sorry . . .'

Rebecca smiled. 'You said that.'

The smile in return was tremulous, a little embarrassed. 'I know . . . Sorry . . .' A little laugh, then. 'There I go again.' She paused, took a breath. 'Look, I don't mean to disturb you, but my name is Dot Blair. And you're Rebecca Connolly, right?'

Her accent was upper-class Scots. Not quite English – there were still traces of old Caledonia present – but putting the voice, the clothes and the Prada together, Rebecca came up with enough money in the bank that this woman needn't worry about paying the gas bill.

'Right, what can I do for you?'

Her shoulders relaxed with relief. 'Thank God, I was worried I'd made a terrible mistake. You look slightly different in real life, you know? I mean, from the way you look on the TV.'

Rebecca had heard that before. 'The lighting here isn't as flattering as it is in a studio.'

And she looked fatter on the screen. They said the camera can add ten pounds, and there were three of them on her during recording. That was the way she looked at it, anyway. Stephen said she had looked gorgeous and indeed was so swept away by it on first viewing he had taken her by the hand and led her into the bedroom where there was all sorts of X-rated activity.

Stephen . . .

She had let him down.

No time for that now.

'What can I do for you?' she asked again.

Dot Blair hesitated, her fingers brushing the back of the empty chair in front of her. Rebecca motioned that she should sit.

'Okay,' Dot said once she had settled, placing her bag on the floor at her feet, the iPhone on the table in front of her. 'Okay,' she repeated. 'Again, I'm sorry for disturbing you.' There was a more businesslike sound to her voice now, as if the invitation to sit had given her confidence. Maybe she learned that from Mummy or Daddy, who were no doubt something big in the city. Pick a city, any city, and there are people who are big and who have kids called Peppa or Tarquin – or Dot – who grow up never knowing what it's really like to have to live within a budget and can afford actual Prada. Rebecca once had a bag like that, but it was spelled Pradda and fell apart after two months.

Stop it, Rebecca, you're profiling this girl and she doesn't deserve it. She reminded herself that her father had been a senior police officer and her mother a head teacher in English, and though they weren't exactly rolling in it, growing up there were never any real money worries. A former prime minister once seemed to suggest on TV that his childhood had been tough because his family couldn't afford Sky TV. The Connolly family could afford satellite. Yes, she had to struggle a little now that she was making her own way in the world, but she wasn't on benefits and she didn't have to use food banks, so she told herself to stop being a snarky little bitch.

'That's okay,' Rebecca said. She had wanted time to consider Stephen's words and her own shortcomings but found herself intrigued by why this person had sought her out.

'I called in at your office first,' Dot said, 'but you weren't there.'

'That's because I was here,' Rebecca said, flashing her a quick smile.

'Yeah, right. Okay. So, I was coming here to kill some time, grab a coffee, and then I saw you. It's a small world, right?'

'But I wouldn't like to paint it,' Rebecca said, quoting some comedian or other.

Dot frowned slightly, then understanding dawned. 'Yeah, of course. That's funny.'

'I'm here all week.' Rebecca sipped her coffee before she repeated, 'So, what can I do for you?'

'I want to talk to you.'

'I gathered that. And you *are* talking to me.'

'No, you don't understand. I have a podcast, true crime. It's called Dot Com. You can find it on all the usual platforms. I've not got a sponsor yet but I'm hopeful.'

Oh God, Rebecca thought, I've been suckered by an amateur podcaster. They were just one step up from an influencer, in her opinion. Her earlier prejudices were now superseded by a new one.

'I see,' Rebecca said, hoping that she conveyed her waning interest sufficiently to perhaps scare her off.

However, Dot leaned forward, her enthusiasm building. 'I'd like to talk to you about your work. About the cases you've worked on. I've read all of Elspeth McTaggart's books and watched the Netflix documentary on the Culloden murders so often I know it off by heart.'

The mention of Elspeth brought the unwelcome image of her lying on a cobbled roadway in Glasgow, blood pooling around her, her limbs at awkward angles . . .

Stop it, Becks. Stephen is right, you wallow too much in these things.

'But it would be a real honour to me if you would agree. I'm a big fan, Rebecca, I really am. I can call you Rebecca, right? I mean, it's okay to call you Rebecca?'

'It's my name.'

The young woman beamed as though Rebecca was royalty and she had granted her some sort of honour. 'And you must call me Dot, short for Dorothea.' She rolled her eyes. 'I know, I know, the Victorians want my name back, right? But it was my grandmother's name, and my mother wanted me to have it, too, and she hates me shortening it to Dot. But, seriously, who is called Dorothea in the twenty-first century, right?'

If this was the way she presented it, Rebecca wondered what the podcast sounded like.

As if she had sensed her thoughts, Dot said, 'Sorry, I'm babbling here. I don't usually babble but, honestly, I'm nervous. I mean, it's not every day you meet your role model . . .'

Role model. Jeez. Rebecca was nobody's role model. And if she was, then the person who thought so was in serious trouble.

Dot was still talking. '. . . initially, I wouldn't take up too much of your time, I promise, an hour maybe, in your office or somewhere else, if you'd rather. I have my recorder here' – she motioned towards the bag under the table – 'and we could go anywhere you like, somewhere quieter than here, obviously, because there's too much ambient noise.'

'Initially?'

'Yeah. Right.' Dot paused as if she was berating herself for using the word. 'Look, here's what I thought. I do an interview, okay? That's fine, but why not do something different? What if I, you know, shadowed you for a while, be with you for whatever you're working on? I wouldn't get in the way, and I'd promise – sign anything you like – not to put anything online until you had given the go-ahead, published whatever it was first, okay?'

She stopped speaking suddenly, and there was a brief lull as Rebecca realised she was finally expected to make some sort of response.

'Dot, I'm afraid—'

Her face crumpled a little. 'Don't say no, please don't say no. I've come all the way up from Edinburgh to see you.'

'You really should have phoned first.'

'I know, but as Elspeth said in the book about the James Stewart case, sometimes it's best to simply turn up. And you said it in the documentary, too.' She closed her eyes. '"Some people you have to forewarn by necessity, but others you are better to approach unannounced. They might still send you on your way, but it's not so easy."' Dot's eyes opened again and she leaned forward eagerly. 'I got that right, right? That's what you said, word for word?'

Rebecca shrugged. She had no idea what she had said in the interview and was probably talking nonsense anyway. 'If you say so.'

'As I said, I'm a big fan and I've learned everything I know from reading her books and your work. And my university course, of course. I'm studying media at the University of East Scotland.'

A media studies student who does a true crime podcast. Fabulous.

'Sorry, but I've really not got the time right now to do an interview.'

Dot's glance at the half-eaten pastry and container of coffee was telling. 'It wouldn't take long.'

'Even so, I'm leaving Inverness soon on a story.'

Her eyes widened eagerly. 'Is it another book?'

'No.'

Rebecca didn't write books. That had been Elspeth. And she was gone.

'Please reconsider. I'd love to follow you and see how you do it.'

Dot's earlier hesitancy was completely absent. Now she seemed pushy enough to get into a revolving door behind you and still get out first.

'I work alone, Dot.'

'Please, Rebecca, it would mean so much to me. Sooo much.'

There was something in the way she elongated the vowel that irritated Rebecca. Or perhaps she was already irritated before the girl even pitched up at her table. Perhaps the source of that annoyance was really herself. Either way, she was hacked off, but she tried to keep the vexation from her voice.

'Dot, let me give you another lesson. Learn to know when no means no. Thank you for your interest, though.'

Thank you for your interest. God, that sounded so lame.

Dot's face fell. 'But . . . I came all this way.'

'And I'm sorry you did that, but I am one of those people you should have forewarned by necessity.' She drained the last of her coffee, wrapped what remained of her pastry in the paper bag. 'Now, I'm sorry, but I really have to go.'

Rebecca picked up her bag but stopped beside Dot's chair, feeling suddenly very guilty. The girl was dejected.

'Look,' she said, 'here's my advice. Find a story, any story, but one that speaks to you for whatever reason. Follow that up. It can be an unsolved case or one that's been disposed through the courts. Maybe there's something wrong with it, maybe the evidence doesn't add up, maybe there are family and friends of the accused or a victim who are demanding another look is taken. Believe me, there are plenty of them because there are holes in the system and people fall through them all the time. Innocent people do go to jail, guilty people avoid it and there are people inside who have been banged up for years for petty crime. Find one that interests you, read up on it, work out who you need to speak to – lawyers, cops, journalists, whoever – and go from there.'

She waited for a response, but Dot didn't raise her head from the point she was staring at on the table. Rebecca gave it another moment or two, then headed for the Falcon Square exit. When she looked back, the girl still hadn't moved. Rebecca felt like she'd just taken away a child's lollipop, burst her balloon and told her Santa Claus didn't exist.

Well done, Rebecca, you've upset the man you love, a perfect stranger, and disappointed your two best friends all in the space of twenty-four hours. Way to go, girl, you are on fire.

8

Rebecca knew she had locked the office door. Dot had confirmed it when she said she'd tried there first. And yet, it was lying slightly ajar. There were no obvious signs of damage, so it had not been forced, and she was the only one who had a key. The one Elspeth had would still be somewhere in the home she'd shared with her partner, Julie, in Drumnadrochit, but Rebecca seriously doubted that Julie had decided to pay her a visit.

She hesitated. Common sense told her that she should turn, gallop back down the stairs to the street and call the police. Her sense of curiosity was strong, though, and she really wanted to know who had broken in, and why. And what they had taken, because there was nothing of real value in there, even her laptop was in the bag over her shoulder. If they wanted the kettle that took an age to boil, or a fridge that no longer lit up when you opened the door, they were welcome to them. She'd often thought that if the office was ever broken into, the thieves would feel so sorry for her that they'd leave her new furniture.

She held her breath, listened. Nobody moved inside. No shadows passed the opening between jamb and door. If they were still in there, they were the quietest housebreakers in the world. She edged forward to better peer through the crack. There was someone in there, but not trashing the place. He was sitting in the chair opposite her desk, his hands clasped on one leg that was hooked over the other, his foot swinging in time to a tune only he could hear.

Okay, that was strange. Perhaps it was time to beat a hasty retreat and call the cavalry.

She turned slowly, her hand already reaching into her pocket for her mobile when she bumped into the solid muscle of a broad-shouldered man who had somehow loomed at her back. His long fair hair was tied in a ponytail, from a face that was the colour of copper and bore cheekbones that could slice bread. Large as he was, he must have been trained as a ballet dancer because she hadn't heard him climb the stairs. Nerves jitterbugged in her gut and she fought the urge to make an attempt to dodge around him. There was little room on the landing, and he would catch her easily.

He waved a hand towards the door like a concierge inviting her to enter.

The man inside, wearing a powder-blue suit, looked up as she stepped over the threshold, aided by a gentle shove from behind. He was whistling faintly under his breath but cut off whatever the song was immediately. His hair was so blond it was almost white and was impeccably cut. Not like Stephen's impeccable cut – his was neat because there was no other way he could be – this look was the result of money being spent. Rebecca surmised that the cost of the haircut would have paid Universal Credit to a family for a month. The suit, his shoes, his shirt, his entire demeanour told her that this guy didn't need to worry about mortgage rates. Nicely turned out though he was, his face seemed somehow lopsided. The jaw was twisted to one side, as though someone had jerked it, and one eye seemed much smaller than the other, its lid drooping; and his mouth was crooked, as though one side wanted to smile, but the other was far from impressed with the idea. Only his nose was straight.

'Ms Rebecca Connolly, I presume,' he said.

His accent was South African or New Zealand. Maybe Australian. She was useless when it came to accents.

When she neither confirmed nor denied her identity, he carried on unfazed. 'The door was open, so I came in.'

Something about this pair told her they were not here to read the meter. She now had a choice. She could show fear or she could brazen this out. As she had done on previous occasions, she went for the latter. She recalled a man she had once interviewed, a former soldier who had served in Iraq and Afghanistan, who had faced down three young thugs in the process of beating up a fourth boy. To her shame, one of the thugs was a young girl, who he said was the most vicious of the lot. She had asked him if he'd been frightened to step in. He had taken his time in replying.

You know what? he said finally. *Every day in Iraq and Afghanistan I was scared. Every day. Every single one. And my sergeant – a real professional soldier, he was – he said something to me that I'll always remember. He said, 'Son, there's at least two sides to everything, and fear isn't any different.' You have to push through it to reach the other side, and that's what I did. I couldn't walk away. I couldn't leave that boy to maybe be kicked to death, but I was scared shitless. So, I just pushed through to the other side of fear.*

Rebecca pushed through her own fear and put on her brave face to address the assertion that the door had been open. 'Yeah, picking a lock will do that.'

He laughed. 'Do I look like the kind of man who would know how to pick a lock?'

She didn't want to stand in the no-man's-land between him and Mr Ponytail behind her. She also believed that moving would keep her legs from giving way, even though she reasoned that if they had meant her harm, she would be bleeding all over the threadbare rug by now. She hoped it wouldn't come to that because she hadn't vacuumed for a week and the blouse she wore was new. No, she decided, they were here to talk. At first, anyway.

She dropped her handbag onto the desk before sitting down in her chair. Rather, falling into it, because her legs trembled, which she struggled to keep from vibrating in her voice. 'No, you look like the kind of man who gets other people to do your dirty work.'

When her eyes flicked to the bruiser barricading the doorway, the man shot a quick glance in his friend's direction. 'Mr Drood certainly is a man with skills. Some more direct than others.'

Rebecca forced herself to lean back in her chair. Find the other side, Becks. Don't let these men, whoever they are, for whatever reason they are here, intimidate you.

'Thank you for not doing any damage,' she said. 'But it would be nice to know who you are and why you're here.'

The man in the blue suit briefly whistled something under this breath again. She still couldn't identify the melody, but it seemed jaunty. She wondered if it was one of his own composition.

'You can call me Mr Quilp,' he said.

'Unusual name. Doesn't Charles Dickens have a copyright on it?'

He tilted his head. 'I'm impressed. You know the reference, that's encouraging in someone of your age.'

She ignored the patronising tone because she hadn't actually read *The Old Curiosity Shop*. She knew the name because her mum had been an English teacher.

'I needn't tell you that it is not my real name,' Mr Quilp continued, 'nor is Mr Drood actually called Drood. You have correctly spotted that we have taken the names from the works of Mr Dickens. We are keen readers of the classics, is that not correct, Mr Drood?'

'That's correct, Mr Quilp.'

Mr Drood's voice rumbled out of him like rocks down a hill. It was so deep she swore she could feel it vibrate the floor. His accent also was born in the southern hemisphere.

'We can lose ourselves within the pages of a book, can we not?' Mr Quilp continued. 'Some people enjoy cinema, some television, some poor deranged souls even appreciate reality TV, but books ... ah, books. They open up new worlds, correct?'

Rebecca thought Mr Drood looked like the kind of man who last touched a book when he burned it, but she kept that to herself. Never judge a book by its cover, or a person by their looks. 'So, what can I do for you, Mr Quilp?'

'You get right to the point, my dear, I do like that. What do you think, Mr Drood?'

'Very admirable.'

'Extremely admirable.'

'Thank you for all the admiration,' Rebecca said, 'but I'm a bit busy, so—'

'We're here to give you a bit of advice.'

She knew the word advice was a synonym for warning. Or threat. The trembling in her legs intensified and she clasped her hands together on the desktop to prevent the men from seeing that they had become infected. 'Really?'

'Yes.'

'What kind of advice?'

He paused again and whistled his happy tune, making her wonder if he even knew he was doing it. Then he stopped. 'I hear you're planning a trip.'

'I am?'

'Don't be coy, Ms Connolly, or may I call you Rebecca?'

'No.'

Again, he wasn't offended. 'Fair enough.'

He whistled again. She looked at Mr Drood in the doorway. He seemed bored. She had been confronted by men like him before, far too often. They were always bored until they had the chance to do something that was detrimental to someone's health. That flutter sprung up again but she forced it down, pushed through to the other side. Never let them see the fear. Thank God her legs were hidden by the desk because they were jiggling like a coked-up politician.

'Is that it, then?' she asked. '"Don't leave town"?'

Mr Quilp's whistling halted. 'More or less.'

'And if I did decide to take a wee trip, what then?'

A slight smile. 'Not a course of action we'd advise. Do we, Mr Drood?'

Even Mr Drood's lips twitched. 'Most certainly not, Mr Quilp.'

'But if I do?'

Mr Quilp's smile remained in place but his blue eyes were cold. 'If you do, you would regret it.'

And there it was. 'So, let me get this straight: you're threatening me, correct?'

He affected a wounded wince. 'I prefer to think of it as advice.'

'I prefer to call a spade bloody intimidation.'

'Call it what you wish, Ms Connolly, but we came here in peace, out of concern for your continued wellbeing. Do yourself a favour: stay here, find another story.'

'I assume we're talking about Stoirm.'

'You can assume all you wish, just don't go. There is no story.'

'There is nothing to tell,' Mr Drood added.

'The very fact that you're here tells me there is,' Rebecca said. 'There's an old saying in journalism, that the news is something that someone somewhere doesn't want printed. All else is advertising.'

'Stick to advertising,' Mr Quilp said.

'It's safer,' Mr Drood said.

Rebecca looked from one to the other. 'Why do you men have an interest in what happens in Stoirm?'

'Neither Mr Drood nor I have any interest in the place.'

'We don't even know where it is,' said Mr Drood.

'You're just messenger boys, then?'

Mr Quilp's smile flashed. Did this guy have a temper at all? 'You could say that.'

He stood up, smoothed the wrinkles in his trousers. Whistled again.

'Who sent you?' Rebecca asked.

Mr Quilp held up a finger. 'Ah, client confidentiality precludes us from revealing our employer's identity, am I right, Mr Drood?'

'You are correct, Mr Quilp.'

'So, if you told me, you'd have to kill me?'

Rebecca regretted asking that flippant question even as the words left her lips. Mr Quilp's smile froze while Mr Drood's face had reverted to its studied inscrutability.

'All you need know, my dear, is that the principals in this matter prefer to remain hidden.'

'Like, under a rock?'

Mr Quilp laughed and wagged a finger at her. 'You know, Ms Connolly, I like you, I like you a whole lot, but that mouth of yours will get you into trouble someday. Luckily Mr Drood and I were prepared for it.'

That caused her to frown. Prepared for it? So, whoever sent them had previous knowledge of her. Her mind flicked through the usual suspects, but she was none the wiser. Most of them were dead.

'But take sound advice when it's given,' he said. 'Sit this particular dance out. No good will come of it if you do, and people will get hurt.' He let that settle for a moment before he added, 'I really hope we don't have to repeat ourselves, Ms Connolly.'

He whistled as they left, clearly a man who enjoyed his work. Rebecca listened to their footfalls descend the stairs until she heard the door to the street open and close, and only then did she let her breath escape in a choppy exhalation. It was at times like this that she wished she smoked – it would give her something to do with her hands, which were shaking in concert with her legs. She didn't even have any alcohol in the office.

In the end, she did the only thing she could do.

She put the kettle on.

And by the time it had worked up the enthusiasm to boil, she knew what she had to do and picked up the phone.

9

She saw one car, but instinct told her it wouldn't be the only one.

Rebecca had thought she was being followed when she left the office. On previous occasions she'd experienced the same sensation and been proved correct, but she recognised it could still be little more than paranoia. As she walked to where she had parked her car, she sensed eyes upon her, feeling like hands gently tickling her, but though she kept turning around, nobody paid her the slightest heed. Shoppers carried bags. Schoolchildren walked in pairs or groups. Tourists took selfies or shots of husbands, wives, partners, offspring on phones.

Even when she threw some clothes into a suitcase, she continually moved to the window of her flat to scan the parking bays outside for strange cars. Not that she would know which of them was strange or not; she never paid much attention to cars, hence the reason why her own was in such a state. When she had bought it, Chaz had urged her to take good care of it. Like that was going to happen. She had tried for a while – a while being perhaps two months – but eventually it was left unwashed, unpolished and unkempt.

She turned her mind to whoever had sent Quilp and Drood to warn her off. She believed him when he said that he was merely following instructions and had no interest beyond doing what he was told. Had it been two years before, she might have seen the hand of lawyer-turned-dog-whistle-politician Finbar Dalgliesh, but he was dead, having apparently taken his own life to avoid trial and disgrace. Lord Henry Stuart would have been another suspect, but a fatal failure of his brakes while driving at speed on a country road in France took him out of the running. There was the mysterious Thomas Smith, who had headed up a bogus cult-like community on the island a few years before, but he had vanished. Mo Burke came to mind, but what interest would a drug-dealing local crook have in the sale of Stoirm? Unless there was some connection to the Glasgow boys, the McClymont crew, with whom she was in partnership, uneasy though it was. No, they weren't the type to issue warnings, and she didn't see them laundering their money by buying an island estate. They had tried-and-tested means of cleaning up their drug profits, and such an enterprise was too risky.

Whoever it was had told Quilp that she had a tendency to be smart-mouthed. She couldn't deny it, her tongue did run away with her, especially when nervous. And she had been nervous – she still was – but she had learned that action was the best way to push through to the other side of fear. Keep moving and you're less of a target.

She checked her rear-view mirror as she drove out of Inverness and headed southwest on the A82. It was almost a three-hour drive to Oban and she had lost too much time to catch the last ferry to Stoirm, so she'd messaged Fiona that she had booked into a hotel for the night and would catch the first one in the morning.

She first saw the car as she drove through Drumnadrochit, near the shores of Loch Ness. She had just passed the book-shop and tearoom in the converted barn which had once been owned by Elspeth and her partner Julie. She had considered calling in but decided against it. The memories were still raw and, anyway, the tearoom was doing a roaring trade in the late-afternoon summer sun. The tables in the courtyard being almost fully occupied, she knew Julie would have her hands full, so she kept on going.

The car was a blue Mini Cooper, about two vehicles behind. There was no reason for it to catch her eye. It wasn't driven erratically. It wasn't overtaking. It matched her own speed exactly, never closing in or widening the gap. It was just there. It was still there when she drove through Fort Augustus at the tail of the loch. Okay, she reasoned, this was the only major road heading this way, so whoever was driving might simply be going in the same direction.

She stopped at Fort William for a coffee and comfort break. When she picked up the A82 again, there it was. It was still a couple of cars behind, still matching her speed.

It didn't look like the sort of vehicle Quilp and his pal would drive. For one thing, she didn't think Drood could comfortably fold himself into it, and even Quilp might crease his suit. She also remained unsure if they would keep such close tabs on her. After all, whoever paid their wages would soon find out that she was on the island. Unless, of course, they had kept watch to ensure she took a telling and wanted to stop her even getting there. That thought made her nervous again but at least she was prepared this time.

There was nothing she could do about it now, so she settled in for the rest of the drive, Robbie Williams on the CD, and enjoyed the scenery.

She reached Oban just as the sun was setting behind the peaks of Mull across the water. She pulled into a car park near to her waterfront hotel. And so did the car. Rebecca already had formed a suspicion as to the driver's identity. The car was impeccable. It practically gleamed.

She decided to go straight on the offensive. 'Are you following me, Dot?'

Dot Blair wasn't surprised to see her glaring at her. She shrugged. 'I'm not following you.'

'You've been at my back all the way from Inverness.'

She looked away. 'I'm not following you, okay?' she insisted, her voice just a little too strident, like a child denying that they had taken a biscuit even though their hand was stuck in the tin. 'We just happen to be going in the same direction.'

Rebecca grunted. She didn't often grunt but she felt the need this time. 'So, you're just out for a nice drive, is that it?'

'Something like that. I've decided to spend a few days in the Highlands, as I'm here. I've got nothing to do back in Edinburgh and the weather's good.'

It was possible but unlikely. Rebecca jerked a thumb over her shoulder towards the hotel. 'Don't tell me, you're booked in here, too.'

'No, I'm not booked in anywhere. I thought I'd find somewhere when I arrived.' She made a show of studying the Victorian exterior. 'This looks as good as any, though.'

It was a large hotel and the chances were they would have rooms. Rebecca had already decided that this young woman wasn't short of cash. There was something about her that screamed entitlement. However much her suspicion that she was indeed following her was pissing her off, she couldn't call the girl a liar. Yet.

'I'm not going to take you along on this story, Dot, you have to understand that.'

She returned Rebecca's steady gaze with open defiance. 'Yes, you've made that quite clear. Again, I'm not following you. I've got my own reasons to be here.'

'And they are?'

Dot gave it a beat. 'My own reasons. I didn't know I had to clear everything with you before I did anything. I must have missed that bit of legislation. Tell me, is it a reserved matter, or were they able to vote on it at Holyrood?'

Rebecca was impressed by her response and almost laughed. Maybe there was something more to this girl, after all.

'Okay, have a nice break,' she said and turned away to hide the tickle of a smile. She returned to her car to heave her suitcase from the boot and didn't look in the Mini Cooper's direction as she wheeled it across the car park to the hotel entrance.

She enjoyed a late dinner in the hotel restaurant, with Dot Blair sitting alone at another table. Neither of them exchanged words or even direct glances, although Rebecca did steal a quick peek at one point to see her engrossed in something on her laptop while also scribbling on a large yellow notepad. When she ate, it was as if she was distracted, each spoonful or forkful directed at her mouth as if programmed. Rebecca would have loved to know what held her attention so intently but there was no way on God's green earth that she was going to instigate another conversation. She didn't hold anything against the girl but she had made her position clear, so to show any sign of interest ran the danger of being deemed a sign of weakness. She did make a point of passing her table as she left, but Dot closed the laptop before she could see anything on the screen. She did catch one word on the notepad, though.

Island.

She fired off a text as she rode up in a lift so ancient the buttons used Latin numerals, then considered Dot Blair and what she was up to. Though she couldn't prove it, the girl was not out for an unplanned break in the Highlands. Perhaps she was telling the truth when she said she hadn't followed her. It was entirely feasible that she was heading off for a break on any one or more of the islands reached from Oban, including Mull, but Rebecca's gut told her different. If she was a betting person, she would lay a month's income on Dot

Blair being headed to Stoirm. But why? She had no way of knowing where Rebecca was headed. The story she had told her she was following, the one on which she had refused to let the young woman tag along, could be here in Oban, not necessarily on Mull or Coll or Colonsay or Lismore. What was the girl up to?

The lift door rattled open and Rebecca stepped out onto the narrow, dimly lit corridor. Her room was at the end of the long passageway, just as it dog-legged to the left towards a fire exit. The room itself was small but comfortable, though the TV wasn't working. The receptionist had explained that they were having trouble with their satellite input so there wasn't even council telly – the basic five channels – available. It didn't matter. Rebecca wanted to do some reading on community buy-outs and general land reform, and if she still felt like watching something, there was always the BBC iPlayer on her laptop. Thankfully, the Wi-Fi signal was strong.

She was reading about the creation of the Stornoway Trust in 1923, which took up the offer of Lord Leverhulme, who deeded his estate on Lewis and Harris to the islanders as a gift and gave birth to Scotland's first extensive community-owned land scheme, when there was a knock at her door. She opened it, knowing it would be one of three parties.

'Evening, Ms Connolly,' said Mr Quilp, leaning against the doorframe in what she could only describe as an insouciant manner. Mr Drood stood behind him like a dread shadow, his face in near darkness thanks to the poor lighting in the corridor.

'What a surprise,' she said, not meaning a word of it.

'I feel certain it's really not, don't you, Mr Drood?'

'I'm convinced it's not, Mr Quilp.'

'You are, after all, not a stupid young woman, Ms Connolly. We did make ourselves very clear that if you decided to follow this line of enquiry then there would be repercussions. We did make that very clear, did we not, Mr Drood?'

'Crystal clear, Mr Quilp.'

They hadn't made any move to force their way into her room, which was a good thing. She had to keep them talking because if they did push past, then she was in trouble.

'How do you know I'm not going on a little holiday?' she asked.

'We know a lot about you, Ms Connolly,' said Mr Quilp.

'You don't take little holidays,' said Mr Drood.

'And even if you do go on a break, there's always a story to follow.'

'You're a workaholic, Ms Connolly.'

'That's not good for your health.'

'It's detrimental to your mental wellbeing.'

'And your physical wellbeing.'

'Too much work and no play . . .'

'. . . can make Rebecca a very sick girl.'

'A *very* sick girl.'

They said nothing further, Quilp doing his whistling thing again but his eyes never leaving her. Ordinarily, such deep focus would make her feel uncomfortable but this time she wanted it. She needed it.

Finally, he spoke again, his voice very soft. 'I think we should step inside, Ms Connolly.'

'And if I don't want you to step inside?'

'Then we would have to insist.'

'Forcefully,' amplified Mr Drood, as he stepped forward, the light from her room falling onto his features to reveal his hard eyes, one hand pressed against the door and pushing it open. She pushed back but he was too powerful. Rebecca couldn't stop him, couldn't stop them. She'd played for time for as long as she could, but the clock had run out. All she had left now was to scream, to attract attention. She took a deep breath, opened her mouth . . .

And then a new voice joined the conversation. 'Hello there, lads, is this a private party or can anyone join in?'

10

It was a voice she knew, a voice she welcomed. Quilp and Drood's heads jerked in unison to the corridor behind them, where Bill Sawyer stood, his right hand cupped around the cuff of his jacket, his left buried in the pocket. She had seen him stand in that way before. She knew what he had up his sleeve, both literally and figuratively.

'This is a private conversation, sir,' said Quilp.

'I'm making it public,' said Bill.

Drood made a show of waving his big hand towards the otherwise deserted corridor. 'This isn't so public.'

'We're never really alone any more, big man,' said Bill affably. 'CCTV is everywhere.'

'Not here, sir,' observed Quilp.

'True, that's why I decided to make my own arrangements.' Bill drew his hand from his pocket to reveal a mobile phone, which he held high. 'You're on the line to DCI Val Roach in Inverness. Say hello, lads.'

They didn't say hello. They were silent.

Bill manoeuvred the device in one hand, flicking the screen with his thumb, then selecting something. 'Smile, lads.' Both men instantly raised their hands to cover their faces, and the silence was further broken by a click, the corridor suddenly but only briefly brightened by the flash. 'Camera shy, are we?'

Although they maintained their silence, Quilp did exhale loudly. Drood shot him an unspoken query and, on receiving a nod in return, made a move towards Bill.

'Ah-ah, big man,' said Bill, flicking his right wrist to let the baton he had concealed up his sleeve slide into his hand. He jerked it in a well-practised motion to extend it. 'Don't be stupid now. You're big and you're fit, but your nose, your elbows, your knees can still be smashed. And I've grown quite expert with this thing over the years.'

Rebecca knew that was no idle boast. Quilp eyed the phone, obviously making up his mind as to whether Bill was bluffing. In the end, he clearly decided not to take the risk. He waved a hand towards Drood, who seemed about to protest at being held back, but Quilp put a finger to his lips, then pointed it at the phone. Drood understood and stepped back again, but he breathed deeply and tightened his jaw. He was not pleased. Without saying anything further, they both began to move in Bill's direction, but he took a step back and raised the baton to rest it on his shoulder.

'No, I'll thank you to go the other way, if you don't mind.' He paused. 'In fact, even if you do mind. My old mammy gave me two rules to live by, and one was don't let a big fella who you've recently pissed off pass you in a narrow corridor.' He waved the baton. 'So, lads, off you pop and it will be our pleasure if we never set eyes on you again.'

Quilp, with a final and extremely malevolent look in Rebecca's direction, led his friend away down the corridor. Bill moved closer to her in order to watch them vanish through the heavy fire doors and then to the stairway.

'Did your mum really give you that advice?' Rebecca asked.

Bill seemed to be surprised she had asked the question. 'Of course. Do you think I'd lie? Very forward-thinking was my old mammy.' He stepped past her into her room, looked around. 'You've got a nicer room than me.' He peered out of the window, with its view of the street. 'Mind you, I've got a sea view, which you haven't, so swings and roundabouts.'

Rebecca closed the door, locked it and put the security chain on. If she wasn't afraid of losing face, she would have dragged a chair over and shoved it under the handle, like she had seen done in the movies.

Bill watched her, a smile glinting in his eyes. 'They won't be back.'

'How can you be so sure?'

'They've been outed. Those guys will be in their car and heading for home.'

'Were you really on the phone to Val?'

He took the phone from his pocket and thumbed at the screen. 'You still there, Val?'

The detective's voice was loud and clear from the speaker. 'Yes, that was better than the telly.'

'Thank God the battery held out,' Bill said. 'It's not been holding its charge very well lately.'

'You need a new phone,' Val Roach said. 'That one's so old I'm surprised it doesn't have a dial.'

Rebecca asked, 'How much did you hear?'

'Not much until Bill took the phone from his pocket, and then they weren't so chatty once you told them I was listening.'

'So, you didn't hear any threats?'

'Afraid not.'

'I heard them,' Bill said. Rebecca had no idea whether he actually had or whether he was only saying that. Bill Sawyer had a spotty record for truth when he had been a police officer, and she knew it. She sometimes wondered if the services he had provided for her over the years were a means of making up for past sins.

'My God, Becks, you certainly have a knack of getting yourself into trouble,' Val Roach said. 'Have you ever considered a less stressful occupation? Skydiving without a parachute, for instance?'

Rebecca took a seat on the bed, her legs suddenly heavy as she realised just how tense she had been holding herself during the encounter. 'Do you think you would be able to identify them?'

'Unlikely, I'd say. I'll take a flyer and say that Quilp and Drood aren't their real names. Where the hell did they pick them up, anyway?'

Before Rebecca could reply, Bill said, 'Charles Dickens. Quilp's from *The Old Curiosity Shop*, and Drood is from *The Mystery of Edwin Drood*.'

He noticed Rebecca giving him a stunned look.

'Hey, I know stuff,' he said, adopting mock offence.

'I didn't think you'd read Dickens, Bill.'

'Well,' he said, giving her a bashful smile, 'I've got to confess I've only read *Great Expectations*, and that was at school and I was bored rigid by it, but I did see a film with Anthony Newley as Quilp, and the BBC made a series out of *Drood* a few years ago.'

'We ran the number plate of the car they're driving, provided by Bill,' Val Roach said, bringing them back to the matter at hand. 'It's a rental but not to anyone carrying those names. I'll check the name of the person on the forms, but I'll stake my pension that it will be fictional, too.'

'Don't they have to present valid ID to rent a car?'

'Yes, but I've got a sneaking suspicion that they're not ordinary rent-a-thugs. These men are professionals and would have no bother getting documents mocked up.'

'These guys *are* pros,' Bill said, having dropped himself on the two-seater couch under the window and placed the phone on the small table beside it. 'You did the right thing calling me, Becks.'

She had made the call to Bill Sawyer pretty soon after the men had left her office. She had contemplated calling Val

Roach herself but thought the detective chief inspector would require some kind of proof of threats made before she could do anything. The fact that she was on the other end of that phone call meant that this was an off-the-record act of ear-wigging, or Bill had been able to convince her that she should do something without concrete evidence. Rebecca had come to suspect there was something more than friendship between those two. Bill, who had nominated himself as her unofficial protector, had devised this plan to smoke them out. He had followed Rebecca when she left Inverness, keeping an eye out for anyone answering the descriptions of Mr Quilp and Mr Drood in pursuit. Obviously, he had.

'How did you manage to pick them up?' she asked.

'They're pretty distinctive,' Bill replied, 'that big one, in particular. It wasn't hard to spot them in the car.'

'I didn't see them.'

'They waited on a street leading from the one your flat is on to the route you'd take to hit the A82. Their car was nothing special, just a common old rental, nothing that would catch your eye. They had guessed where you were going, anyway, so they were able to hang well back.'

'They didn't spot you.'

'They weren't expecting anyone to follow them – their focus was pretty much on you.'

'So, what is it you're into, Becks?' Val asked.

'I don't really know yet. The community are trying to buy the Stoirm estate but are meeting opposition.'

'Who from?'

'I don't know that, yet.'

'What level of opposition?'

'Not sure of the full extent, but it's been bad enough for them to contact me.'

'And not the police?'

'I don't know that, either.'

'Christ,' said Bill, 'you don't know a hell of a lot, do you?'

'That's the job, Bill. You start off not knowing, then you ask some questions, dig around and then you find out.'

'Like police work,' said Val.

'Sort of,' said Rebecca, knowing that in some cases they know from the start, or think they know, and then dig around in order to make their theory work. It was such a case that introduced her to Bill Sawyer in the first place.

'But there's obviously something in it, otherwise Quilp and Drood would never have been sent to see you.'

As soon as she'd seen them, Rebecca had known for certain there was a story to tell.

Roach sighed. 'And you couldn't do anything about this story on the phone, right? You have to drop everything immediately and go to the island?'

'Yes, I have to be there,' she said, trying to ignore the bit about dropping everything immediately. 'I have to see people's faces.'

Another sigh. 'I don't suppose there's any point in me warning you against following this up, is there?'

Bill's laugh was sharp and loud. 'Val, allow me to introduce you to Rebecca Connolly, you obviously haven't met.'

Val's own laugh rippled from the device on the table. 'Okay, I'll contact the local boys on the island, see what I can find out. And you, Becks, watch your back.'

'That's my job,' said Bill, and Rebecca gave him a grateful smile.

'You watch your back too, but not for the same reason,' said Val. 'You're not getting any younger, you know. Don't you be doing anything strenuous. You be careful not to strain anything.'

Bill's smile was strange, secretive. 'I won't strain anything important.'

There was something in the way he spoke that made Rebecca think, *Eww, too much information.*

Val gave a girly giggle – she had never heard Val Roach giggle, let alone in that way – and signed off. Bill, still sporting that smile, pressed the red button to completely cut the line. She wanted to ask him about that final little exchange as she was now certain there was something going on between them, but she decided not to. They'd tell her when, or if, they wanted her to know, but she did wonder if she had to buy a new hat. That, and Val's observation that she had dropped everything to rush off to Stoirm, had made her think of Stephen's proposal. Was it the story that had drawn her, or did she need distance to think? Stephen had told her to take a few days to consider, and a twinge of shame stabbed her when she thought of the childish, selfish glee she had experienced when he made the suggestion, as if she'd had some sort of victory over him.

What the hell is wrong with you, Becks?

It wasn't the time for this. She could eat away at herself when she was alone, not with Bill Sawyer in the room.

She forced some lightness into her tone. 'What was the other bit of advice your mum gave you?'

He frowned. 'What?'

'You said there were two bits of advice. One was never let someone like Drood squeeze past you – what was the other?'

He laughed. 'Oh, yeah. It was never go into a lift with someone who has eaten a plate of baked beans.'

Rebecca thought about this, then laughed. 'Good advice.'

'Words to live by.'

11

Rebecca was unsurprised to see Dot Blair on the ferry. She was sitting at a table, the wide window at her side revealing all the splendours of a summer crossing: the ragged outline of Mull slipping by to the left, the low-lying Lismore behind them and to the right. The sky was blue, the water an even deeper shade. There might have been dolphins cavorting at the bow, though they usually made an appearance much later in the voyage, closer to Stoirm, which lay a few nautical miles to the northwest, very nearly the final part of Britain before the vast expanse of the North Atlantic.

Dot, though, was taking none of this in. She was intent on her laptop, again scribbling notes on her pad, and she didn't see Rebecca and Bill approach her until they were by her side. She hastily closed her laptop and looked at Bill closely.

'You're beginning to become a pest, Dot,' said Rebecca.

The girl's gaze was defiant when she switched it to Rebecca. 'I'm only doing what you said I should.'

'What was that?'

'I've found a case and I'm following it up.'

Even though she had already guessed the answer, Rebecca asked, 'What case?'

In the pause that followed, it was obvious to Rebecca that Dot had contemplated refusing to reply, but then there was a little flick of her brow, like a shrug. 'The murder of Mhairi Sinclair.'

Bill Sawyer didn't flinch, but he would have felt something when he heard the victim's name. It was the case that had brought them together in the first place, that first took Rebecca to Stoirm. It was the case that still cast a shadow over them, albeit it faint now that Lord Henry Stuart was dead.

'Roddie Drummond killed her,' he said.

'He was found Not Proven,' Dot replied.

'Not Proven isn't Not Guilty,' Bill countered. 'He admitted to killing her in an interview.'

Dot studied him. 'An interview that's open to question. That section wasn't recorded and there was only one police officer present to hear the supposed admission. The jury didn't accept it, so that's why they returned a Not Proven.'

Bill grunted. He was that police officer, and even though Rebecca herself was unsure that Roddie Drummond did actually confess, she had no other firm evidence that he didn't murder his ex-lover. Nobody knew what really happened on that night so many years ago. Of the three people known to be there, two were dead and the third was only a baby at the time.

'Nobody will talk to you, Dot. Not on Stoirm,' Rebecca said, speaking from experience. 'They won't tell you anything. It's an island thing.'

'Maybe, but I'll try. But there are questions that need to be asked, and that's what I'll do.'

Questions to be asked. Rebecca had once used those same words when she confronted Lord Henry Stuart, but nobody had asked the questions – and both Bill and she had vowed to remain silent about what they knew, to protect themselves and others.

'Where did you hear of it, Dot?'

The young woman rifled in her voluminous bag and produced a dog-eared copy of Elspeth's first book. 'It's mentioned here, not in any detail, but it piqued my interest. She wrote that it was the first big case you worked on, so when I looked into it, I wondered why it was still unresolved.'

'It's resolved,' Bill said dismissively. 'Roddie Drummond killed her in a fit of jealousy. End of.'

Dot's eyes narrowed. She had been researching the case so would have seen photographs of him, though younger, slimmer and with more hair. She continued to study Bill, perhaps trying to place him, but Rebecca wasn't about to help her out. Her presence was annoying, her choice of case more so, but she had to admire the girl's tenacity. She didn't just give up when Rebecca knocked her back. She had found something and was following it through. There was hope for her.

'Fine, good luck, Dot,' said Rebecca.

They walked away from her table and, once out of earshot, Bill asked who she was. Rebecca explained quickly.

When she was finished, Bill asked, 'What is she? Some bored little rich girl looking to pass the time?'

'What makes you think she's rich?'

'Look at her, those clothes didn't come from Matalan. They're all designer – I thought you women noticed that sort of thing?'

'That's a sexist generalisation, Bill,' she said, even though she had actually noticed it when she first saw her, 'and unbecoming of a gentleman.'

He laughed. 'I'm no gentleman and you know I'm about as un-PC as you can get.'

That was true; he was so far from woke he was practically catatonic.

He looked back at her again, his voice serious. 'So, are we just going to let her poke around into the death of Mhairi Sinclair?'

'What do you suggest? We throw her overboard?'

Bill seemed to favour that idea.

'I don't know, Bill.' She looked back at the girl, who had opened her laptop again and was paying them no further attention. She had found a new quest, and they weren't going to be part of it. That pleased Rebecca, for some reason. 'Maybe someone should be looking into it. You and I are too close to it.'

'And what about the men who were working with the late and entirely unlamented Lord Henry back then?'

Lord Henry Stuart, in a bid to maintain his estate, had joined forces with some shady businessmen – gangsters, really – in a people-trafficking scheme, landing illegal immigrants from the Baltic states at Thunder Bay, a remote spot on the island's west coast. They had very little proof, and the one person who knew about it would never go on the record. But they did know the name of one of the men behind the scheme, an old university friend of Lord Henry. That name had last come up the year before, during her final conversation with Finbar Dalgliesh. He had led the fringe political party Spioraid nan Gáidtheal, on the surface a nationalist party that was spurned by real nationalists in Scotland. The truth was, they were just another bunch of extreme-right nutters who used migrants and anyone who wasn't white, Christian and heterosexual as scapegoats for all that was wrong with the world. Dalgliesh wasn't a true believer, she had suspected, but instead saw the party as a way of furthering his political aims. And perhaps to make his wallet bulge a little. He had said that the SG – as his party was better known, much to his annoyance – was backed by a group of men who cared nothing for politics or ideals.

They only care about profit, he had said, *and they support – you might say, infiltrate – all parties. The groundswell of support for independence, the backlash against immigration, even pulling out of long-established unions – these things can be destabilising . . . and such instability can be taken advantage of.*

He claimed this group had been in operation for centuries but in more recent years had recruited from men who were shadows within shadows. When Rebecca pressed him for a name, Dalgliesh at first hesitated, unwilling to even say it out loud. Finally, though, he said the name both Bill and Rebecca had heard before on Stoirm, though he said it in almost a whisper.

Have you heard of the Nikoladze brothers?

12

Jarji Nikoladze's hands itched and he absently scratched his left with his right as he spoke. It had been some time since this skin complaint had flared up, years in fact, but it had returned with a vengeance in recent weeks. The mobile phone lay face up on the desk before him, the speaker facility activated.

'I am very disappointed,' he said.

The man on the other end of the phone, who had given his name as Mr Quilp, expressed further apologies.

Jarji cut him off. 'I'm not interested in apologies, my friend, only results – and even then only the results that I want.'

'She's just a girly reporter, Mr Nikoladze.'

Quilp was dismissive. Despite having been operational in the USA and in the UK for many years, his South African accent had never weakened. On the other hand, Jarji had left his Georgian roots behind many years ago, and an expensive British education had removed all but faint traces of his native accent. His brother, Ichkit, was older and had retained his accent, though he could temper it when dealing with the men in power in London and beyond. Granted, a taste of the harsh realities of his upbringing rose to the surface when Jarji was angry, but he wasn't angry right now. He was, as he had told the man, disappointed.

'She is more than a girly reporter,' he said, fishing in his drawer for some skin cream.

He knew all about Rebecca Connolly, of course. He had first become aware of her when she investigated the unfortunate death of that young woman on Stoirm. Jarji had backed his old friend Henry Stuart's attempts to turn his estate into a resort for those with the funds to appreciate it. That fell apart, not necessarily due to Connolly but she certainly didn't help. She had then crossed his path, though she didn't know it, when she poked her nose into a somewhat lucrative little scheme involving a bogus cult, again with connections to Stoirm. That had led to a female police detective visiting him in his Edinburgh office. That had been an irritant. Then she had been instrumental in seeing Finbar Dalgliesh exposed and the near collapse of his party, forcing Jarji to divest himself of any interests he had in it, just as he had the cult. Neither was any great hardship – they were spent forces, and he had no need for spent forces. Now here the reporter was again, her name popping up in connection with another scheme he had for Stoirm, one that would fulfil a long-harboured desire. It was totally legal but did require certain moves that were not so legitimate.

'I thought you to be more efficient,' he said to the South African, whose real name he neither knew nor wished to know. He had told him his name was Mr Quilp, and that was all Jarji needed to know. He checked the expiration date on the tube of cream he'd found at the back of the drawer, saw it had expired two years before. Never mind, what is life without risk?

'Sometimes things don't go according to plan, *boet*.'

Boet. Jarji understood this was a term for 'brother'. But he was not this man's brother. Nevertheless, he allowed the informality to pass.

'I was led to believe that you would get the job done. You have not done so. You can therefore understand my disappointment.'

A slight laugh made Jarji bristle. 'We underestimated her resolve,' Quilp said.

'You underestimated her resolve,' Jarji repeated.

'That's about the size of it, *boet*.'

This time he would not let it pass. 'I am not your brother, Mr Quilp, and I am deeply disturbed by the cavalier manner with which you dismiss this failure. I expect better from people in my employ.'

Another laugh. This time Jarji's jaw clamped.

'Oh, *boet*' – the man added extra emphasis to the word – 'do I need to remind you that I'm not in your employ? Mr Drood and I were contracted by the Corporation who were doing you an obligement, as I understand it, for the service you have shown and the profits you have generated. Or, more accurately, your brother. We delivered the warning to the woman, and we would have followed through with something more . . . tactile, had she not engaged someone possessing at least a basic level of competence.'

Jarji dabbed cream on the worst part of his hand. It was cool and, he thought, soothing, but given its age this was more likely along the lines of a placebo effect. 'Who was this man?'

'We weren't formally introduced but he had the whiff of law enforcement about him. He claimed to have a direct line to some police detective.'

'And you took him at his word?'

'*Boet*, he was prepared for violence and, despite what the movies may tell us, a hotel corridor is not the place for such activity.'

'Was he armed?'

'He wielded a baton with considerable dexterity.'

'But you and your colleague had firearms, yes?'

'No, unlicensed weapons are not permitted in the UK, you know that. We abide by the rules of the land.'

'You are joking.'

'No, *boet*, it's our policy. If either Mr Drood or I were caught carrying, it might reflect badly on our employers. We're not hired killers. We're negotiators.'

Jarji gritted his teeth as he rubbed more cream into his hands. He regretted calling on the Corporation for aid in the matter. He had thought by doing so he would place a buffer between him and the reporter, but now perhaps he should have despatched his own man. Tamasz, a fellow Georgian who had been at his back for many years, had suffered a heart attack two years before and had been forced to retire, with a generous settlement from he and Ichkit, but even in his debilitated state he would have done better than this pair. Not that Jarji would require him to do so. He had been a loyal servant all his life and deserved his rest now.

'Then what do you propose to do about the matter, Mr Quilp?'

'Do? We propose to do nothing.'

'That is unacceptable. I will contact my brother, and his friends in the Corporation will—'

'Your brother's friends in the Corporation have instructed us to take a step back, *boet*. As I said, we were sent as a favour, but frankly, and I'm talking a little out of school here, they don't understand your obsession with this island. They gave me a message to relay to you.'

'And what is this message?'

'If you want to play lord of the manor, then you may proceed. But don't embarrass them. That would not be recommended.'

Jarji felt his temper rise. 'You dare speak to me like—'

'We will remain in Glasgow for a few days, again on Corporation instructions. If you require our services, then you must request them through your brother. I say again, we are not in your employ. We take our instruction from New York, not Edinburgh. Perhaps in the history of the Corporation that was the case, but no longer. Take care, *boet*.'

It took Jarji Nikoladze a moment or two to realise that the man had cut the connection. He resisted the urge to throw the phone across the room. How dare he talk to him like that? Did he not realise who he was? Of what he was capable of? The man was a mere functionary, a contractor brought in to do work; he had no right to treat him like some sort of subordinate and give him advice. As for the Corporation, his brother would smooth things with them. Ichkit was, after all, on the board and, as Quilp had stated, between them they had generated considerable income for them over the years. His brother had once harboured dreams of becoming chairman, but that position was always filled by a Scot. They may have changed their name over the centuries, but they clung to the traditions of their founder.

The purchase of the estate, once through, would not embarrass the Corporation, he would make sure of that. It was, to be honest, none of their business. They were correct in their assessment that he wished to be lord of the manor. He had coveted the land since Henry Stuart had first taken him there, when they were at university. He liked the idea of a poor boy from Georgia becoming master of all he surveyed, which was part of the reason he'd eventually had Henry removed from this earth. That and the fact that he had become a danger due to his knowledge of previous illicit enterprises, including some financial irregularities that he had helped cover up.

Rebecca Connolly knew something of at least one of those enterprises. That she'd been allowed to continue walking and breathing had perhaps been a miscalculation, but Ichkit had advised no further action, and she had never made what she knew public, suggesting that she actually knew nothing. But here she was again, sticking her nose where it did not belong. He had thought a warning from Quilp and Drood would have been sufficient to keep her away from Stoirm, but he had been wrong. He didn't know who the individual was that had helped her, but it mattered little.

He glanced at his watch. If she had caught the first ferry, she would be well on her way to the island by now. Quilp and Drood had retreated, but Jarji wouldn't. Tamasz may be on a well-earned retirement, but he had others on whom he could call.

He used a tissue to wipe the greasy cream from his fingers, removed a second mobile from his desk and punched in the only number stored on it.

Mr Quilp dropped the phone on the bed and moved to the window to stare out at the city below him. The River Clyde was to his right, a large dark crane hanging over it like a gaunt sentinel guarding a past that was long gone. His grandmother had come from this city, moving to South Africa after she married his grandfather, who had studied veterinary medicine at the University of Glasgow. This was his second visit, but he felt no kinship with the place. His grandmother had told him stories of Argyle Street crowded with shoppers even on weekdays, of the bustle of Sauchiehall Street. She had talked of the camaraderie of tenement life, of families taking turns to wash the floors and walls of what she called 'the close'. She talked of being in the street with her friends, where an old, abandoned car could become a makeshift plaything, with the boys imagining they were racing cars or pretending to be Hollywood stars they had seen in the cinema. 'The pictures', she called it. She would often show him a photograph of herself as a child, standing in front of a red sandstone tenement in a tartan skirt and grey cardigan, the wall behind her streaked with lines where children had walked along with chalk in hand.

She had been born and lived in Springburn, in the north of the city, and he had visited the area on a previous trip to the city. The tall tenements that had lined the streets were gone. The buildings themselves had been replaced by more modern constructions or gap sights overgrown with bushes. He found the steps leading from her street – Adamswell Street – down to Valleyfield Street, where he found the last vestige of the tenements of which she had spoken. There were no children playing, no old cars, and the cinema in another street she had spoken of so fondly, The Princes, was gone. The area she had loved was not even a ghost of what it had once been, because what it had once been had been all but eradicated. The cavernous workshops where mighty steam engines had been built and sent across the globe, empty when she was still young, were gone, the area's fame for fine locomotive engineering now consigned to local history books. He had been sad to see it, but he knew the world turned, moved on, and the past was often sacrificed to the great god of progress. He understood these things because his employers were often in the forefront of making that progress.

He kept these observations to himself, for Mr Drood would not have understood. His own lineage went back many generations. He was a pure-blood Boer, and his people had fought the Zulus at Blood River, had been with Fran Joubert when the Kommando ambushed the British at Bronkhorstspruit and had helped besiege Ladysmith, Mafeking and Kimberley. He sprawled on the hotel room's couch, his legs propped up on the arm, one hand tucked behind his ponytailed head. It irritated Quilp slightly because this was not his room. Quilp followed the adage that wherever he hung his hat was his home, and even though he was not one to wear hats, for the time being this room was his home and Drood had no right to make himself so comfortable without permission. He didn't say anything, though. It wouldn't make any difference because Drood would do what he pleased, anyway, at least as far as making himself comfortable. Quilp had worked with the man long enough to know that professionally he was very precise, but personally he could be lax. Quilp himself was neat and liked order, but if he went into Drood's room down the hall, he would find it in complete disarray, even though they had only been in the hotel a matter of days, apart from their overnight sojourn to the Highlands. They had been in Scotland on other business for the Corporation and had been seconded by New York to perform the favour for the Nikoladzes.

Drood watched him carefully. 'I take it our Georgian friend was not pleased, Mr Quilp.'

They made a point of calling each other by their chosen soubriquets even in private, that way there would be no accidental revelations of their true identity. They tended to use names from literature relating to whatever country to which they were sent. In the UK, it was the Dickens characters; in the USA, they were Mr Grinnup and Mr Sutpen, drawn from the works of William Faulkner. In France they were Victor Hugo's Messieurs Enjolsas and Grantaire. In Germany Thomas Mann's Herr Peeperkron and Herr Castorp. He knew it was a pose, but such literary allusions amused Quilp.

'He was not, Mr Drood,' he said.

Drood considered this. There were those who believed that, because of his size, he was a stupid man, but he wasn't. He wasn't as sharp as Quilp, but he was no lumbering ox. He was well read and had suggested some of their aliases himself. Like Quilp, he found it entertaining to adopt them.

'Does New York harbour concerns over the situation?'

'They didn't say,' Quilp replied. 'But we have been ordered to await further orders.'

Drood shrugged, resumed staring at the ceiling. 'That's good, we could do with a break.'

Quilp couldn't disagree. They had been jetting around the globe for months dealing with various crises on behalf of the

Corporation, for both he and Mr Drood were gifted trouble-shooters, well able to handle issues with staff or local officials who were proving difficult. On occasion, their task even called for actions that were not in any way threatening.

'So, we simply wait here then, Mr Quilp?'

'Yes.'

Drood said nothing further, his study of the ceiling taking up his attention. Quilp didn't enquire as to what he found so fascinating, because he knew that the man was lost in his own thoughts, and a man's thoughts were private. He himself stared from the window again, whistling under his breath, and thought of his grandmother, who he had loved but who had passed two years before, never having visited the land of her birth again. Would she have approved of the changes to her beloved Glasgow? He thought she would have, in some ways, but she would have mourned the loss of the streets of her childhood. But change was inevitable.

13

On the mainland, things changed, structures came and went, but Portnaseil remained forever a collection of buildings that had seemingly been thrown at the hillside. However, as Rebecca drove down the ferry's ramp to the jetty, she noticed one thing that had not been present the first time she had visited. On the brick wall of the old harbour master's office, words had been scrawled in white paint. Just three words, but Rebecca found them disturbing, nonetheless.

COLONISTS GO HOME

She frowned. She thought that attitude had died years before, but obviously someone here still held those who came to live on islands in low regard. She shook her head as she drove up the incline towards Portnaseil.

She had only returned to the island once since her initial visit, and that was to attend Chaz and Alan's wedding. Chaz had been brought up here and had met Alan when he worked for the estate in an administrative capacity. On her first trip, to look into the Mhairi Sinclair murder, she had left her car on the mainland and manhandled a decrepit suitcase with a broken wheel because she knew Chaz would be chauffeuring her. This time her suitcase was in far better condition – it should be, it cost her £150 and Alan had described it as the Rolls Royce of suitcases as he cast covetous eyes upon it.

However, she had brought her car because she didn't know how much of the island she would have to traverse.

As she drove, she glanced at the houses spread across the waterfront and up the hill. Portnaseil wasn't a big place, the residences were scattered, but there was a focal point, known as the Square, which she now passed. The road formed one side of it, the other three being comprised of a mix of Victorian buildings made of solid grey granite, imported from the mainland back when ladies wore bustles and men had manners, and slightly more modern constructions. Among the former was the Portnaseil Hotel, which she recalled as being so old-fashioned that she felt she'd been transported back in time. Donnie had said it was being renovated, and not before time. Olde worlde charm was one thing but even the dust could have been appraised on the *Antiques Roadshow*. The hotel had been bought by a London-based chain which specialised in boutique hotels.

Another old building once housed the police station but was now an arts centre, while what had once been a bank had been empty but sported a sign for a bed and breakfast. The more modern buildings, if the 1960s and '70s could be called modern, included the Hub, comprising a small police station, health centre, library and community hall. Two low-lying buildings were taken up by a butcher and a hairdresser.

She wondered briefly where Dot Blair was staying. She experienced a little guilt over not telling her the hotel was closed, but then dismissed it, for Blair's accommodation wasn't her problem. She was obviously not short of a bob or two, so she'd find a guest house somewhere, perhaps the one in the Square. Maybe even Daddy had bought her somewhere outright, she mused, but then the guilt returned. She had no idea of Dot's personal circumstances and to profile her in that way was unforgivable.

She drove up the hill, waving to Bill Sawyer who had elected to walk, a large backpack slung over one shoulder. He was staying with an old pal who had a house on the island. He had been coming to Stoirm for years and had once contemplated buying a place himself but had decided that, though he loved the place, island life wasn't for him. Rebecca and he had their differences, but she had cause to be grateful for that decision, the previous night in Oban being only the most recent example.

She turned right on the Spine, the road that ran the length of the island. The church sat at the top of the hill, dominating the skyline and looking down on the settlement like a shepherd guarding its flock. She stopped by the cast iron gate that led to a series of steps and then to the kirkyard. To her right, Portnaseil clung to the hillside, then there was the small marina filled with yachts and motor boats. Once, that enclosed harbour would have been home to a fishing fleet, but those days were long gone. She heard the thrum of the ferry's engine as it idled while taking on passengers and vehicles for the return to the mainland, which she could just see through the summer haze across the Sound. A solitary fishing boat surged across the calm water back to port, the bow wave making the blue water bleed white. She wondered if that was the *Kelpie*, Donnie Kerr's boat. He had inherited it on his father's death and, with the fishing industry drying up and the Stoirm fleet going with it, had turned it into a pleasure craft for dolphin and whale watchers. Donnie had made it work against all the odds – well enough, anyway, that he was still in business – and had put his own chequered past behind him.

She drove on a few more yards and turned into the driveway outside the manse. It was a solid granite building, like the church, the result of Victorian architecture and construction. The Reverend Fiona McRae must have heard the crunch of the wheels on the gravel because she appeared in the doorway just as Rebecca hauled that Rolls Royce of suitcases from the boot. Her smile was broad and genuine, and she folded Rebecca in an embrace.

'It's good to see you, pet,' she said.

'It's good to be seen,' Rebecca said, wondering if her ribs would stand the strain of the hug.

Finally, she was released and Fiona took the handle of the case. Rebecca insisted that she could manage, but she was waved away.

'Come inside, I've got fresh-baked scones waiting,' said Fiona.

She always knew how to make Rebecca feel welcome. And the announcement of fresh-baked scones reminded her of her mother, who always ensured she had something ready when Rebecca visited home in Glasgow. She said that it was her scones that had finally made Rebecca's father marry her. Fiona had been her father's girlfriend when they were younger, so perhaps it was her scone-baking skills that had drawn him to her. Of course, that was before he fled the place, having learned an ugly secret about his great-grandmother, a secret that his parents had known about and yet thought nothing of.

She uncovered the secret thanks to Fiona, who showed her a diary kept by her great-great-grandmother, a record of sorts that was vaguely worded but, if you knew the truth, it was easy to decode. In his late teens, John Connolly had discovered the diary and had been shocked by the contents. Years later, Rebecca, coming to terms with the loss of her baby, had been equally as horrified. She had watched that diary burn in the grate of Fiona's study, the smoke carrying the words up and away. But their effect on Rebecca had remained, just as they had on her father. Shame. Disgust.

It was into that same study at the rear of the manse that Fiona led her. It hadn't changed much since that first time.

The same furniture, the same books still lined the shelf, some which had likely not been opened for years. New ones had been added on top of them or perched on tables and in corners.

'Sit yourself down,' said Fiona, 'and I'll fetch us the tea and those scones.'

She smiled and left, and Rebecca sat in the same chair as she had six years before, when the wind moaned beyond the windows and made the little tree she could see in the back garden sway. It had grown since then and the branches that had been bare on that dreary, dank day were now clothed in green leaves. The tiled fireplace was dark and cold, the vestiges of that leather-bound diary long gone, but the ghosts of its words remained. The old-fashioned clock on the mantle was the same one that had counted the seconds as Fiona had outlined the Connolly family history – how they travelled to the island from Ireland over a century and half before with other families, all members of a small religious group called the Blood of Christ.

Nowadays they'd be called fundamentalists, Fiona had said, *but even that doesn't cover how strict their views were . . .*

The word of God was the law . . .

And they adhered to it . . .

They settled in a clachan of their own in the hills, and the islanders accepted them as long as they kept to themselves. But apparently her great-great-grandmother offered a service that nobody else did.

If someone on the island discovered they had an inconvenient pregnancy, they would visit Roberta Connolly.

'They should have been taken up the hills at birth' was an island phrase meaning that some people should never have been allowed to live, perhaps because they were born bad or simply brought shame. It was to Roberta that they took the mothers in their confinement, and when the baby was born, it was disposed of.

She was a strong, highly motivated woman, Fiona had told her. *She was strong in her faith, strong in her views and strong in her convictions. To her, a child born outwith wedlock was an abomination, a thing of the devil.*

It was a horrible, callous, brutal practice – and learning of it, and his family shrugging it away as an island thing, made John Connolly leave and never return. He never spoke of Stoirm, apart from acknowledging that he had been born there, and Rebecca had never met her paternal relations, but she visualised Roberta as a large woman, severe of expression and view, her features perhaps twisted by the bitterness she felt at the world she saw as being riddled with sin. She had to be cold to do what she did, to take such innocence and to destroy it. She had to be heartless. And those who knew what she did, those who condoned it, those who used it, had to be cold and heartless, too.

Her father had done what he could to make up for the sins of his family. She knew he became emotionally involved as a police officer in cases involving children. One even led him to almost ruin his career when he assaulted a paedophile that he knew to be guilty but couldn't prove. Whatever unsympathetic gene there was that ran through the Connolly line had bypassed him.

But had it bypassed her? Did something of Roberta Connolly, of the family in general and of the islanders as they were then, live within her? Was that why she ran from happiness? Stephen had said that she was always afraid that something would come along and take the happiness away. Was she actually afraid that she would be the one who would do that? She knew she could be focused, but was she ruthless, like her great-great-grandmother? And would that make her cold?

No, she decided, she had been emotionally affected by the revelation contained in those long-burned pages. But she also recognised that she harboured something hard and sharp within her, but reasoned that she needed it to do her job. The problem, she now knew, was that it was possible that hard, sharp edge could cut even her.

She heard the doorbell and Fiona answering it. Voices in the hallway – Fiona's she recognised, but not the other – then they appeared, Fiona carrying a tray with a large teapot, four mugs, a plate of scones, side plates and butter, the woman behind her tall and slim, not young but not old either. A somewhat rotund black Labrador limped in behind her, its tail wagging, its muzzle upturned, eyes fixed on the scones.

'This is Emily Thorne,' Fiona said as she placed the tray carefully on the coffee table. 'She's part of the community committee trying to buy the estate. Emily, Rebecca Connolly.'

Rebecca nodded hello and then set to delivering a rough pat to the dog's head, which was already laid on her lap.

'That's Katy,' said Emily. Her accent was English, but from which part Rebecca couldn't say.

'She's lovely,' said Rebecca. 'I had a lab retriever once. Ben. I loved him.'

'She'll take all of that,' Emily said, nodding to Rebecca's hand still stroking the dog's head, 'but she also has her eyes on the scones, so be careful. You're quite fat enough, my girl.'

Rebecca smiled. 'Do you mean Katy or me?'

The woman returned her smile as she sat down in a chair by the fire. 'Katy, of course, there's hardly a pick on you.'

Rebecca knew that not to be quite true, but she accepted it with grace.

Fiona began to pour the tea. 'Donnie apologises but he has tours booked this morning.'

So, that had been his boat she'd seen.

'Emily is the most recent person to be intimidated,' Fiona said. 'It's the most direct threat so far.'

Rebecca asked what happened and Emily told her about her shed being set on fire and a man in a mask telling her to leave the island. She relayed the details in a clear, crisp manner, with no trace of nervousness.

'It must have been disturbing,' Rebecca said.

'It was,' she said, 'at the time, but I absolutely refuse to be intimidated.'

'And you're convinced it was connected to the community buy-out attempts? Couldn't it have just been some island nutter with too much whisky and not enough brains?'

'Yes, the local police officer hinted as such. Suggested it might have been Callum McMaster.'

'Who is Callum McMaster?'

'A man with a past,' Fiona said, handing Rebecca her cup and saucer. 'Help yourself to scones. Callum was born here but went to the mainland as a young man, as many did then and still do now.'

Rebecca placed her tea on a small table beside her chair and reached for a scone. 'In search of work?'

'In search of something. Apparently he was a troubled lad who found himself in hot water. Did some jail time.'

'For what?'

Fiona dodged the question. 'It doesn't matter. It's in the past. But he's not behind these threats, I'm sure of it.'

Rebecca wondered what it was Fiona wasn't telling her and made a mental note to seek out Callum McMaster.

'We've had murmurings against people coming here to stay from the mainland, but that was years ago,' Fiona continued. 'Stoirm is an island, certainly, but it isn't as insular as it once was, Rebecca. Most of those who are island-born understand that we need Emily and those like her to keep the island economy afloat.'

'This person wasn't an islander,' Emily added. 'He was from somewhere in the Central Belt – Glasgow, Edinburgh, maybe.'

'And you say this was the most direct attempt? What were the others?'

'Little acts of vandalism,' Fiona replied. 'A car damaged. A window smashed. Phone calls in the middle of the night with nobody saying anything. Break-ins with nothing taken. Nothing as overt as this, and nobody was seen.'

'And what do the police say?'

Emily wrinkled her nose. 'That they will investigate, but nobody has been arrested. A mention of Cal, or young men out for a laugh.'

'To be fair, there's no evidence,' Fiona said. 'And they're down to only six officers now to cover the whole island. That's a lot of ground to cover.'

Rebecca said, 'I've a friend at Divisional HQ in Inverness who will be in contact with them. That may change things.'

'What made your friend take an interest?'

Rebecca told them about Mr Quilp and Mr Drood. The two women listened intently.

Fiona's mouth flattened into a sharp line. 'The intimidation virus has spread to the mainland, then.'

'Did they say who had sent them?'

Rebecca shook her head. 'I had the impression these guys knew their stuff, so I feel they wouldn't be cheap.'

'They might have known their stuff,' observed Emily, 'but obviously they underestimated you.'

'People often underestimate Rebecca,' said Fiona. 'That's why we contacted her.'

Rebecca nodded her thanks. 'To be fair, if it wasn't for Bill Sawyer I may not have been here to tell you about it. I don't know what they planned to do if they got into my room last night but I'm sure it wasn't to read my Gideon Bible.' She bit into her scone before couching her next question as casually as possible. 'Can I ask when you first discussed bringing me on board?'

'Your name came up a few times – Donnie had advocated it and I supported him, but really it was after Emily's shed was firebombed that we decided to get in touch.'

'And was it just you two and Donnie?'

Fiona paused before answering, already working out where this was leading. 'No, we have a WhatsApp group for all those involved in helping raise the funds for the community buy-out. I put out a message and the majority came back immediately and agreed it was time.'

Emily hadn't quite caught up. 'Why do you ask, Rebecca?'

'Just wondering how you all kept in touch.'

Rebecca didn't want to say what was really on her mind. Fiona she trusted, but she didn't know Emily, though she seemed genuine enough. It was something she wanted to run past Donnie first.

14

Elton was from Edinburgh, like Ryan, but that was as far as the similarities went. Ryan had inherited his mother's love of books, though he didn't read anywhere near as many as she did, while Elton only picked up a book if he had to swat a fly. He was the only guy he'd ever met who was called Elton, and Ryan asked him how a boy from Wester Hailes ended up with it. Apparently his mum and dad shagged after a concert by Elton John in Ibrox Stadium in 1998, when the Rocket Man teamed up with Billy Joel, but they were Roman Catholic so there was no way they were going to call their boy Billy. So, Elton it was, which would have been fine if his second name wasn't McGeachy. Somehow Ryan didn't see Elton McGeachy as a name to top the charts, or wear platform shoes for that matter. And he couldn't work the wood, either. In Ryan's opinion, the only time the boy had used a plane was to fly to Ibiza.

They were both working in one of the rooms on the first floor when Matt stopped by and studied the new door. 'Can that door shut properly yet, big man?'

'I've just screwed in the hinges, should be fine,' Ryan said, closing it to prove his point.

Matt was satisfied. 'Keep it closed then, eh? Nobody else needs to know anything about this.'

Elton had been in the corner making an absolute arse of fitting skirting boards and he stood up, wiping his hands on his low-hung jeans like he'd been working hard. 'What's up, Matt?'

'Boss has been on the blower,' said Matt. 'Seems we have a problem.'

Ryan thought perhaps Elton's match-striking fun the other night had proved to be a step too far and the law was onto them, but Matt soon scotched that notion.

'There's a reporter called Rebecca Connolly on the island, come to poke her beak into things that aren't her business, you know what I mean, lads?'

Elton nodded. Ryan didn't respond but he knew what Matt meant. Something inside him flipped a little. The press getting involved wasn't quite as bad as the police, but it still wasn't something he welcomed. Again, he told himself he should never have taken this job, good money or not.

'The boss wants us to dissuade her from taking an interest.'

Elton's smile was eager. Too eager, if you asked Ryan, which of course nobody had. 'Dissuade her?' Elton asked.

Matt nodded, but at least he didn't smile. The impression Ryan had of Elton was that he welcomed the chance to flex the muscles he was so proud of, but Matt was more professional. He'd do it but wouldn't necessarily enjoy it.

'You know what I mean, son. Show her the error of her ways. Make sure she's on the first ferry back home.'

Elton's smile broadened. 'Not necessarily in one piece, though, right?'

Before Matt could reply, Ryan spoke up. 'Whoa, hang on, Matt, surely doing anything like that will only draw attention to what we're up to? I mean, breaking a window here and there is one thing, but threatening a reporter? That could cause even more trouble.'

Matt sighed. 'Ryan, I know what you're saying but the boss wants us to sort her out.'

'But—'

'Ryan – mate – you can question all you like but he's the guy that bungs you the readies, right? I mean, you like having cash in your pocket, don't you?'

Ryan wondered if Matt had been talking to Rina. He fell silent. He didn't like the way Matt and Elton looked at him, as if he was some sort of weak link.

'So, here's the Hampden,' Matt said. 'We find this reporter lassie and we have a word in her shell-like, right? And if she doesn't play ball, then we've been authorised to get a little rough.'

Ryan felt something catch in his chest, but Elton grew even more excited. 'A wee bit of action, at last.'

Matt raised a warning finger. 'But you cool it, Elton, okay? A slap is all that's needed, just to drive the point home.'

'Aye, no bother, Matt, just a wee warning. Got it. How we going to know her, Matt?'

Matt held up his phone. 'Got a screenshot here of her. She's been on the telly.'

Elton sniggered. 'Ooh, a celeb!'

Ryan grew even more uncomfortable.

Matt put the phone away. 'Okay, you boys get back to work now and let me get the locals onto it to see what they can find out. If she's here, they'll find her and then you can get the job done.'

Elton slapped his hands together, rubbed his palms as though they were cold, and turned back to carry on mucking up the skirting board. Ryan knew he would have to fix it later but for now he followed Matt from the room, catching up with him on the stairwell.

'Matt, can we no take a minute here, eh?'

'Ryan, mate, I know you have reservations.'

'Bloody right I've got reservations . . .' Matt's face hardened at the sharpness of his tone, so Ryan softened it. 'This isn't right, Matt, you know that.' Matt didn't respond. He just waited. 'I mean, what the fuck are we doing here? Working on this place, fine, it's good work. But the other stuff? It's not right.'

Matt stared him in the eye, took a deep breath. 'You're earning, Ryan. What more do you need to know?'

'I came here to work.'

'And you *are* working, mate. You knew when you signed on that there was other stuff to be done. You didn't question it, did you? You just took the dosh and kept your mouth shut.'

'Aye, getting Elton into people's houses and shifting some stuff about . . . I mean, I don't know what that's all about, but it seems harmless. But I didn't—'

Matt rested a hand on his shoulder. 'Ryan, mate, listen to me. Just do what you're told, pocket the scratch and keep your mouth shut. It's all hunky-dory.'

'It's no hunky-dory, Matt. We're talking about maybe hurting a lassie.'

'So? You've hurt people before.'

He wanted to scream that was then, this is now, but he knew that wouldn't play well. 'Aye, but this is different. I never hurt nobody that wouldn't have hurt me. But a reporter? And maybe a famous one? That's no on, Matt, you must see that.'

Matt gave him a reassuring smile, patted his shoulder now. 'Don't worry so much, Ryan son. It's all fine.'

It wasn't fine. It was far from fine.

'Then listen, Matt, don't put Elton onto it.'

Matt frowned. 'How no?'

'He's no right in the head, eh? I mean, last thing a couple of nights ago, the woman's shed . . .'

'What about it?'

'Was he supposed to torch it?'

'Aye, that was the plan.'

Ryan suspected it but he'd hoped it wasn't the case.

'So, what's the issue, Ryan?'

'He's unpredictable, you know? He's inexperienced, I think you know that.'

'He's got plenty of experience and you can keep him in line, Ryan.'

Matt patted him on the arm and turned away, but Ryan tried one last thing.

'That woman, the one the other night – he spoke to her, did you know that? Did you tell him to do it?'

He was taking the gamble that Elton hadn't been told to interact with her. Matt stopped and turned back, a frown beginning to gather. 'What did he say?'

Ryan felt hope for the first time. 'He told her to get off the island, that she wasn't welcome, the English people aren't welcome. Is that what this is all about, Matt? Are we scaring off English folk?'

Matt was thoughtful. 'Never mind what it's all about, son. That's not in your job description.'

'Awright, fine, but Elton was all jacked up – I think he'd been taking something before, which isn't on, you know that. And talking to the woman, that's dangerous, right? I mean, she could remember his voice and then the game could be a bogey.'

Matt played this over in his mind. 'You're right, it's no on.'

'So, maybe we shouldn't go nowhere near this reporter lassie, eh? I mean, threatening the press isn't good.'

Matt laughed. 'Son, reporters are threatened all the time, more often than not because they deserve it. But as I said, this has come down from on high and ours is not to reason, you know what I'm saying?'

'Who are we working for, Matt?'

'That's no in your job description either, son. Just trouser the cash, do what you're told and when the job's done, go home to the wee woman, okay?' Matt laid his hand on Ryan's shoulder again. 'Relax, Ryan, it's all okay. We know what we're doing, right?' He smiled. 'Don't think so much, mate. It's not good for you. Now, leave everything with me the now, okay? You get back to work and keep an eye on Elton.'

Ryan watched him head down the stairs, then turned back into the corridor. He needed him, he'd said. For what, though? To watch Elton? To do a good job with the joinery? Or something else?

Ryan had harboured doubts before. Now he was truly worried.

15

Rebecca found Donnie Kerr at the harbour. She had enjoyed dinner with Fiona, then, feeling restless, decided to go for a walk. She headed down the hill, enjoying the warmth of the evening and the comparative silence. Inverness was a busy city and there was seldom anything like the peace and quiet there that could be found on the island, unless you were one of those crazy people who got out of bed at oh-my-God o'clock to go jogging. Rebecca didn't jog. She didn't go to the gym. She attended a self-defence class and that, apart from the sex with Stephen, was the only exercise she took.

Stephen. Guilt lanced through her. She hadn't even called him to let him know she had arrived safely and she'd left her mobile back in the manse. Shit. Oh well, she'd call him later. He was used to her being inconsiderate. She tried not to be but when she was focused on something then she tended to forget the niceties of social interaction.

The niceties of social interaction.

Jesus, what a way to think of what she had with Stephen. As if it was some sort of ritual – or duty, more to the point, rather than an emotional connection. Was that why she hesitated? Was it because she wasn't as invested in the relationship as she had thought? She'd perhaps convinced herself that what she felt was love when really it was . . . What? What was it? Come on, Becks, you're not some fluttery wee girl, analyse your feelings, get to the root of them.

But maybe that was the point. Maybe she analysed too much and felt too little.

Stop overthinking, you idiot. Enjoy this walk. Breathe. Relax, for God's sake.

She walked on, forcing the guilt and mental self-flagellation into that corner of her mind marked 'To be dealt with later', which sat next to 'To be Ignored Completely', and fixed her attention on the here and now. Of course, it wasn't completely silent. Birds sang in the few trees that were dotted here and there, and insects buzzed busily from the hedges, as if gossiping about that bee nobody liked. The occasional engine purred on the Spine and a couple of cars even passed her on the road winding down towards Portnaseil, but mostly there was just the sound of her footsteps on the tarmac and the faint swish of the waves on the pebbled shoreline. No ferry idled at the quayside, so that particular throb was absent for now. The sun was beginning to sink behind her, turning the water of the Sound an even deeper blue, and across it floated a solitary yacht, its two sails – the headsail and the mainsail, Stephen had told her – billowing before the slight breeze. It was probably heading into the harbour for the night. Portnaseil Marina, as it was now called, was a haven for pleasure craft, and she could see the masts of a few yachts clustered together at anchor rising above the raised quayside. The harbour's solid walls afforded some protection from the elements, but they wouldn't be needed this night. The island could be battered by storms but, if the forecast was anything to go by, certainly not for the next few days.

She passed by the Square and spotted a knot of young men standing outside the open hotel bar, idling in the way that gatherings of young men often do, their demeanour at once casual and self-conscious. They were comfortable with one another but they were also striking a pose, not only for any passers-by but also their friends, perhaps even the solitary female in their midst. She could pick them up, drop them anywhere in Scotland and they wouldn't look out of place. There was about half a dozen of them, most with the hoods of their sweaters up, even though the evening was warm and dry. Their trousers were loose and baggy, mostly some form of jogging wear but a couple wore jeans over trainers or boots. Two were larking about with each other, pushing, laughing, dodging around, the girl egging them on. Another two leaned against the bar's wall, watching their friends' horseplay while also maintaining a watch for something that might stimulate them, an excuse to preen other than the girl or for a reason to cause trouble.

Rebecca caught herself profiling again, but it was because they reminded her of the gang Alan dubbed the Moron Squad, who had worked for the estate's gamekeeper when she first visited the island. They had the same look, the same surly and mocking expressions.

One, though, was different. He was tall, his blond hair shaven at the side while the fringe was gelled to make it rise up so high a surfer dude could hang ten under it. He had eschewed the hoodie for a white T-shirt, all the better to show off biceps that looked as if they had been pumped up in a garage. He had spotted her and studied her for too long as she headed down the hill. She looked away, kept walking, hoping they wouldn't decide to come and annoy her.

They didn't follow, but she could feel the blond boy's eyes following her all the way. When she knew she was shielded by the buildings on the far side of the Square, she risked a backward glance, just to see if he had moved away from his friends to track her movement, but he was out of sight. She took a deep breath. She was in no mood to deal with morons, thank you very much.

Donnie was sitting near to where the *Kelpie* was moored, both arms outstretched along the back of a black metal bench, his face raised, eyes closed. He wasn't in direct sunlight, so he wasn't catching the rays. She might have thought he was meditating but Donnie Kerr had never struck her as someone who would adopt the lotus position and chant. She hadn't seen him for a few years, though, so perhaps he'd changed. The island had long been a Mecca for various spiritual groups – the Connollys were part of the Blood of Christ, after all, and then there had been the Children of the Dell, who had fleeced the lost and the lonely – so it was possible he had fallen for someone's sales pitch. Unlikely, though.

She came to a halt a few feet away and hesitated, not sure if she should disturb him. She studied his face, noting lines that she didn't remember seeing six years before, and his hair, worn a little too long for her taste, was naturally frosting. She wasn't sure if she made a noise or if he simply sensed her presence, but his eyes opened suddenly, and his smile when he saw her watching him was a little sheepish.

'You caught me having a moment.'

He shifted along the bench to make room for her.

She sat down. 'I didn't want to intrude when you were communing with nature.'

He laughed. 'I suppose that's what I was doing. Good to see you, Rebecca.'

'You too, Donnie.'

He was in his forties now, she estimated. Maybe older. She'd never asked his age, which was an omission when she first met him because he had been a source for a story, and it was a rule that a reporter ascertains the age of anyone they speak to. She never fully understood the need of it, apart from when writing court stories – when it was necessary to make it clear that John Smith, 24, of Anywhere Avenue was NOT John Smith, 45, also of Anywhere Avenue. Nevertheless, obtaining someone's age was one of the things a reporter did, and she hadn't. Elspeth would have hauled her over the coals for that omission had she been her boss at the time.

'Been a hard day?' she asked.

'Not really.'

'So, why the moment?'

His grin was sheepish again. 'You were close when you said communing with nature. I try to have a few minutes to myself as often as I can, just to sit here and let the island wrap itself around me.'

'Even if the wind's coming off the Sound as though Lewis Hamilton's behind the wheel and the rain's hitting you like a needle shower?'

'No, then I just say to hell with it and go for a coffee. I'm not stupid.'

'I'm relieved. I thought you'd gone all touchy-feely on me.'

'I suppose I have, in a way. Sorry to disappoint you.'

She waved that away, letting him know she was only joking.

'But here's the thing,' he said, his voice serious. 'This moment, right now, is one of a kind, you know? It will never come again, not exactly this way. The way the light hits the water, the way the sounds surround us, this breath . . .' He puffed his fingers in front of his mouth as an example of a breath leaving his body. 'None of it will ever come again. Life is a series of moments that never repeat themselves completely, and we should take the time to enjoy them.'

That made her think of Stephen again, and how she might have missed a moment.

She let it sit before she pulled herself out of self-examination and injected some lightness into her voice. 'Shouldn't there be tinkly music playing? Gongs, nose flutes, maybe some throat singing? You've been reading those mindfulness books, haven't you?'

He laughed. 'No, it's just that as I get older I'm thinking a lot more than I used to. You know what I was like back then. And shit happens, you know? My dad's gone. My mum might be, wherever she is, I haven't seen her for a while now. Henry Stuart. Mhairi . . .'

He paused, sighed. He'd been in love with Mhairi Sinclair but his addiction to drugs and his inability to prevent her brother from dying of an overdose in Glasgow had soured the relationship. She moved on – he never did.

'Even Roddie Drummond's gone.'

Somebody shot Roddie Drummond on the beach of Thunder Bay. The murder was never solved, just as Mhairi's murder was never solved, even though many people believed Roddie did it, the Not Proven verdict notwithstanding. The truth would never be known now.

'How's Sonya?' Rebecca asked. Sonya was the child he had with Mhairi, grown up now.

Something crossed his eyes, a fleeting shadow, as if she had touched a nerve. 'At uni in Glasgow. Studying law. Doing well, too.'

'And Mhairi's folks?'

The Sinclairs owned and ran the general store and post office in the Square. They hadn't welcomed Rebecca becoming involved in their daughter's story, perhaps because that's how she saw it, at least at first – as a story. To them it was their life. Molly Sinclair had at least spoken to her but her husband never did.

'Still there,' Donnie said. 'Hector is as uncommunicative as ever. Molly's moved on, come to terms with what happened, but still misses her daughter, still blames me in a way for what happened.'

'It wasn't your fault.'

'I know that, and she does, too, but she has to blame somebody, and with Roddie gone . . .' He shrugged. 'Did you know Campbell Drummond died?'

That was a shock. She hardly knew Roddie Drummond's father, had only spoken to him once at length, but he had seemed a rock of a man.

'He went downhill after his wife died, and then what happened with Roddie. And maybe knowing there was something he could have done to save Mhairi.'

Campbell Drummond had walked to the cottage to the south of Portnaseil on the night of the murder. He'd been outside and heard her arguing with Roddie but had decided that he couldn't interfere.

If there is one rule of nature, he'd told her, *it's that couples fight.* So, he left them to it. He regretted that forever after.

'It just ate away at him until all that was left was this . . . husk,' Donnie said. 'I think when death came, he was grateful.'

He looked out across the water and then over to the grasslands by the shore, where a breeze eased its way through the blades and caused them to whisper. They knew secrets that they only told each other.

'Do you believe in an afterlife, Rebecca?'

For a long time after he died she had seen her father, even had conversations with him, but she put it down to her own sub-conscious projecting a wish into her mind. She hadn't had visions of him for some time, but sometimes she sensed his presence. She'd heard – thought she heard – Elspeth's voice as they cast her ashes onto the waters of Loch Ness, had even fancied she saw her face within them as the breeze caught them and held them for a brief moment. But it was all her imagination, she told herself.

And yet . . .

'I don't know,' she said, and that was the truth.

Donnie nodded his agreement as he stared past her at the grasslands beyond the harbour. 'Me neither, but I like to think Campbell and Mary Drummond were reunited again and they're out there somewhere, walking the machair the way they did when they were together. All the drama, all the cares, all gone. Just the two of them, together forever.' He paused, still studying the grass as if searching for their spirits. Or perhaps wishing that he would one day be similarly reunited with Mhairi.

Then, suddenly, he smiled. 'I'm getting sentimental in my old age.'

'You're not old, Donnie, for God's sake!'

'What's the line that Indiana Jones has? It's not the years, it's the mileage? That's how I feel, Rebecca. You know I didn't look after myself when I was young. Too much booze, too many drugs, too many fags, never eating properly, getting involved in shit I shouldn't have. You know what I mean. I'm clean now, but it all took its toll. My dad died too young, just dropped dead, right over there.' He nodded to a point just a few feet away. 'I told you about that, didn't I?'

He had. Lachlan Kerr had succumbed to a brain aneurysm seven years before she met Donnie for the first time.

Ticking time bomb, Donnie had said, *but I can't help but feel I contributed to it.*

'Maybe I'll go the same way, but I'd like to leave something behind, you know?'

'Is that why you're involved in the community buy-out?'

'Yeah. I'm the last of the old gang left.' He stared out at the water again, his eyes narrowed. 'I think about those kids who used to make their way across the island to Thunder Bay, run down the path, leap around the rocks and dare each other to swim to the caves. We all had high hopes, we all wanted to leave something behind in our lives, something that would last. But then life itself gets in the way, always does, and as you become an adult the dreams you had as a kid become hazy. Henry . . . well, Henry became Henry and paid the price. Roddie was a lost soul, but he might have come back thanks to Mhairi, but then whatever happened, happened, and we lost her and he was cast adrift again, and then we lost him. I was . . . a disappointment to everyone, especially to Mhairi, to my dad. So, yeah, maybe if we can pull this off, I'll make up somehow for all the shit.'

'And do you think you have a chance?'

'We have every chance. We're the preferred option, even Lady Stuart wants us to have the estate, but we need to raise the money.'

'How close are you?'

'Very close. A little push now and we can get over the line and then we can start work.'

'What will you get if you do win?'

'The land, obviously, and everything on it, the cottages, crofts. The distillery, which is doing well – one of the more positive things that Henry did while he was here. We don't get the hotel, that was sold separately a year or two ago to the chain. That's annoying but hey-ho, that's the way it goes.'

'And you really believe you can make a go of it where Henry Stuart couldn't?'

He thought about the question and took a deep breath. 'That's the unknown factor, right? The island has a lot of problems, most of the islands do. The dependability of ferries, the weather causing issues with timetables, an ageing fleet leading to breakdowns and not enough money in the kitty to get new ones. That means in the winter we can have a problem with fresh food deliveries, so we would need to increase our food production, plant more vegetables, get some poly tunnels for fruit, that sort of thing. We have cattle and sheep grazing on the land already, but they're shipped to the mainland when the time comes.' He grimaced. 'I'm a vegetarian now . . .' He burst out laughing. 'Yeah, what's the old line? How do you know someone is a vegetarian?'

'They'll tell you,' said Rebecca.

'That's it. The idea of us having a slaughterhouse on the island is something that repulses me personally, but I can't let my personal beliefs get in the way. The point is that if the ferry issue isn't, can't or won't be resolved then we have to become a little more self-sufficient. I don't mean going full-on, forming a militia and building bunkers, but just enough that we don't have to depend totally on having food shipped in on a regular basis. Henry wanted to turn the estate into a playground for his rich pals, hunting, shooting, wild parties. We need to make it accessible to all but also make it work more for the islanders than stockbrokers and hedge fund owners and billionaires.'

'And tourism?'

Donnie grinned. 'There are still a few old diehards who show disdain for visitors, see them as nothing but a pest, but they are literally dying out. Their grandchildren, those who haven't already moved away, are more realistic. They know we need the tourist pounds, so there are plans to convert some of the buildings on the estate for other uses – a place for a writers' and artists' refuge, for instance, where people can come and take classes, and stay for a week or a month, whatever. There's money in that, and employment. The old farm used by the Children of the Dell – you know about that, I know – has already been converted for multiple occupancy, so that's something.'

'You'd need more than fresh lettuce and tourists to make it pay,' she said.

'And there is. We'd need to attract business here, set up our own. There's an old building a mile or so outside Portnaseil with its own jetty, pretty rundown, but it can be converted into a manufacturing centre to convert seaweed.'

'Seaweed? Really?'

He looked surprised. 'Yeah, don't you know how useful that stuff is? It can be used in cosmetics – we hope to create a purpose-built spa specialising in seaweed-based products – animal feeds, fertiliser, packaging that's biodegradable, even drugs and food.'

'Food? As in human food?'

'Yeah, you eat sushi?'

'Good God, no,' Rebecca replied with mock horror. 'Eating something raw reminds me too much of the coming zombie apocalypse.'

'Yeah, being a vegetarian, it's not for me, either.' He gave her an exaggerated frown. 'Did I mention I was a vegetarian?'

'You might have.'

'Okay, just as long as you know. Anyway, sushi can come wrapped in seaweed. And there's a food called dulse which is rich in vitamins and minerals. Seaweed can also be used to thicken ice cream. Back in the day – I'm talking late eighteenth century into the nineteenth – right here on the island, people made a living gathering it for the landowner, who sold it to make fertiliser.'

Rebecca had never heard of this, and she leaned forward as if eager for more. She enjoyed learning, which was why she had done so well in school and at university. Her father was forever telling her stories about Scotland's history, taking her to sites of significance like Culloden and Glencoe, where she was urged to touch the stones in an attempt to communicate with the past. She still did it and sometimes she'd felt a connection with history that went beyond the tactile, beyond imagination. A crime writer she'd once interviewed had another name for such locations, the thin places, where the boundary between time and space, between now and then, between the living and the dead, was slender and the past could seep through.

'Agriculture on the mainland was beginning to explode, round about then,' Donnie explained, warming to his lecture now. 'So, you had whole families out on the rocks and beaches armed with hooks, then curing it over a peat fire until it became brittle. Believe it or not, the industry was so big that the laird had to import workers to keep up with demand. The

133

then Lord Stuart of Stoirm, Henry's ancestor, made ten grand a year out of it, which was quite a bit in those days. Some made double that and they spent it boozing and womanising in London.'

'So, why did it stop?'

'After the Napoleonic wars ended, the price of kelp fell, duties in imports were lifted and the people became surplus to requirements. Some of the landowners found themselves bankrupt, others looked to alternative ways to maintain their income, like sheep. The islands were slow to embrace the mass evictions, but the Clearances came upon them eventually and the people who had once worked the land and worked the shores were moved away from where they had been born and where their fathers and mothers, and generations of fathers and mothers before them, had been born. One woman said that they turned their gladness into bitterness, their blessings into mockery.' His face and voice had hardened. 'And all because the lairds who did this, who traditionally were supposed to look after their people, decided that their bank balances, their wellbeing, their comfort, was more important.'

They both fell silent as they considered the desolation that greed had visited upon the poor. And often still did.

'And have all these plans of yours been costed?'

'Yes, we've had money men go through it all carefully, plans have been drawn up,' he said. 'It won't be easy, believe me, but the alternative is that the estate and all the promise that it holds falls into the hands of some consortium.'

'Do you know what they intend to do with it?'

'An extension of Henry's dream to make Stoirm a playground for the rich and shameless, importing game for hunting. Build a lodge for them to hold weekend parties. Apparently there's plans for a golf course that would desolate vast parts of the machair. We want the land to be used for the good of the community; they want the community to be used for the good of those with more than a million in the bank.'

'Who is behind the consortium?'

'We've traced a few of the backers, all companies in London and abroad. We can find the names of directors and secretaries, but it really doesn't mean anything. If anyone wants to hide themselves behind paperwork and fronts, then they can.'

'And you really think they're engaged in a dirty campaign to force you and others to back away?'

'Oh yeah. There have been too many incidents for it to be coincidental. And all targeting people on the committee or who have supported us in other ways.'

'You think it likely, though?'

'Yes, I think it likely. These people only believe their bank balances are important, not people. If they see a profit, or whatever it is they see here, then they'll do whatever it takes. Business is cutthroat, Becks.'

'And you really believe there is profit to be made?'

'We believe we can make it work – we wouldn't pursue it if we didn't. If we can see the possibilities, they probably do too, although they want to use the place as a playground, maybe even some sort of tax write-off, I don't know.'

Donnie had a poor opinion of capitalism, and perhaps with good reason, but she didn't doubt his sincerity in wishing to employ it to benefit the majority and not the few.

'I can't see London businessmen coming up here to heft stones through windows,' she said. 'So, who do you think is actually carrying out the vandalism?'

He blew out his cheeks. 'It could be anyone. It's summer, there are visitors all over the island. And we're not short of headbangers, as you know, Darren Yates being chief among them. Younger brother to Andy Yates.'

Rebecca knew that name. He had been one of the Moron Squad who had forced Chaz and Alan off the road years before.

'Andy's still banged up,' Donnie said, 'but Darren's here and he's just as bad, if not worse. He punts drugs, though he's clever enough to keep it low key and shield himself from the police, not that they have the manpower or the gumption to do much about it, and he's got a bunch of absolute meatheads at his beck and call.'

Rebecca played a hunch. 'He's not tall and blond, is he?'

'Yeah, you met him?'

'I saw a bunch of young men outside the hotel earlier. He was there.'

'Aye, that'll be his lot, the bar's still open and they use it like their unofficial headquarters. They never cause any trouble there, so there's nothing anybody can do about it, especially with the cop shop just across the Square. They might not be able to pin him down for punting gear, but a rammy right under their noses would be hard to miss. Darren thinks he's a hard man and he's had a few run-ins with Rory, one of the local coppers, but he's clever enough to make sure it's nothing too serious.'

'And you think he might be behind the intimidation?'

'It's possible. He's island-born and knows a lot of people. But though he's smart, he's still dumb enough to do it if he's getting paid or just because he's bored. He'd know who was sympathetic to our cause and who wasn't; and if he didn't know, he'd be able to find out easily. It's Stoirm, after all.'

'It's an island thing,' she said, smiling. Those word had been said to her so often on Stoirm.

He grinned. 'Aye.'

'And would he know Callum McMaster?'

Donne gave her a sideways look. 'You've been digging already, haven't you? Aye, he'd know him, and I know what's being said, but Cal's not behind any of this.'

After meeting Emily Thorne, Rebecca had looked him up on the internet. Callum McMaster had led an interesting life.

'How can you be so sure?'

'He just wants a quiet life. He's made mistakes, sure, and God knows I've made more than my fair share, so I'm not one to condemn a guy for that. He's getting on now and he's come home, simple as that.'

'I'm still going to speak to him.'

Donnie smiled. 'Of course you are. But take it from me, he's not behind these threats.'

'What about you? Have you had any threats?'

Donnie looked away briefly, out to sea. The failure to reply told her that he had.

'What happened, Donnie?'

He breathed in. 'I haven't told the others about it. I don't want to spook anyone unduly.'

She waited.

He leaned over to thrust his hand into the pocket of his jeans. 'I came back to the boat to pick up my phone, found this.' He handed her a crumpled piece of paper bearing Sonya's image.

'You think this is a threat?' she asked.

'What else could it be? They're telling me that they know where she is.'

'How recent is this?'

'Recent enough.'

She studied the face on the paper. Sonya had been attractive when a teenager, but she was gorgeous now. 'What are you going to do about it?'

'What can I do?'

'You could pull out of the committee.'

'Not going to happen.' His voice was firm. 'This is a bluff. They won't touch her.'

'You can't be certain of that.'

He avoided her eyes again. He knew he couldn't be certain. 'They can't win, Rebecca. They can't be allowed to win.'

'But what about Sonya's wellbeing?'

A faint smile eased his expression. 'She's fine. I spoke to her. She's got exams right now and after that she's heading home.'

'You're taking a hell of a risk, Donnie.'

The smile evaporated. 'I can't pull away from this, it's too important. I don't think they'll do anything to Sonya. Breaking windows, silent phone calls, even a bit of fire-raising, but making a move against her would draw too much attention. And if they know me at all, they'd know I'm not backing down, so what good would it do?'

'But if they did make some sort of move against Sonya?'

'They won't.'

'But if they did . . .'

'If they did, then it would make me more determined to see this through. And if Darren is involved, he knows me and he'd tell them that.'

Rebecca remained unconvinced. 'Have you discussed this with her? After all, it's her wellbeing we're talking about here.'

'I don't want to spook her. She's got exams, remember? And I think it's all a bluff.'

'But—'

'Believe me, she'll be fine, I promise. I won't back down, I won't let them win. I've let too many people down over the years, and I won't do it now, not Sonya, not Fiona, not Emily and the rest of the committee. Not my dad, God rest him. I've got ground to make up with everyone around me and this is the way I want to do it. This is the way I need to do it.'

There was nothing she could say that would change his mind, but he had brought the conversation round to why she really needed to talk to him.

'The other members of the committee, do you know them personally?'

'Aye, more or less. Some better than others, of course. Why?'

She didn't answer that right away. 'And had you mentioned to them that you were thinking about contacting me before you actually did?'

'Yeah, we'd discussed it a few times but we decided to hold off for a while to see if it settled down. Emily getting her shed torched was the final straw.'

'Bringing me in was mentioned in your WhatsApp group, too?'

'Yes, of course. Not everyone gets to the meetings.' He frowned, having sensed something behind her question. 'Rebecca, what are you getting at?'

She took a deep breath. 'Because within hours of you contacting me yesterday morning, I was visited by two men who warned me against getting involved.'

'Who were they?'

'Never seen them before. They followed me to Oban and tried again, but I'd already made arrangements to sort them out.'

She told him about the encounter in the hotel and Bill Sawyer.

Donnie smiled. 'Bill does enjoy that sort of thing.' His smile died. 'Obviously these guys were sent by the consortium.'

'And if they'll threaten me, they can threaten Sonya.'

His head slumped a little to his chest as that thought sank in. 'Sonya's safe,' he insisted.

'You can't be sure.'

His head raised again. 'She'll be fine, I promise you.'

'Okay,' she said, finally convinced by the hardness in his eyes and the tightness of his lips. There was something he wasn't telling her, and she had to trust him. 'There is another

139

point I'm making, though. Let's just say they were sent by the consortium—'

'Of course they were, who else would it be?'

'Fine, but the point is that I hadn't even packed a bag and yet they were at my office. They knew I was coming. And they must have been on their way before you even asked me to come over.'

She let this sink in and saw understanding dawn on Donnie's face. 'Oh my God . . .'

'Yes. I think someone in your WhatsApp group is batting for the other side.' She paused to let that sink in. 'Someone's telling tales.'

16

Dot Blair didn't think she was much to look at. She thought she was too skinny, too angular, too bookish, she supposed, though she did know that her auburn hair was eye-catching. Boys don't make passes at girls who wear glasses, someone had once said, but she'd found that wasn't true. Whatever she thought of herself, others thought differently, it seemed. Her mother and father always said that she was beautiful, but she'd put that down to parents being parents. What she saw in the mirror was not what others saw, and that was proved by the attention she received through high school and university. She was genuinely popular, not in a sexually profligate way, but boys asked her out. Some were direct and arrogant, some were shy and sweet, others were downright sleazy.

All that meant she was used to men looking at her. It didn't mean she liked it – her skin crawled as their eyes stroked her, weighed her up, either enjoying what they saw and lingering, or moving on in search of another girl to creep out – but she was used to it. The boys clustered around the open doorway to the bar were what she'd expect in a place like this, interchangeable with other groups of youths in Edinburgh, Glasgow and St Andrews who gathered inside and out of low-life bars she wasn't likely to frequent – unless she had to, and she knew that before she was finished on the island that's exactly what she'd have to do. She just hoped that none of the young men watching her walk across what seemed to be

Portnaseil downtown central were not in any way connected to the Mhairi Sinclair case, meaning she might need to open some form of communication. Especially that tall blond one, who studied her more closely than the others. There was a look in his eye that made him stand out as worse than his friends. The realisation that they were too young to have had anything to do with the story made her relax a little, but their eyes still made her flesh creep.

She kept her head down and stepped onto the pavement outside the general store, which she knew would still be open, thanks to the information booklet in the Airbnb she'd found at the last minute. It was a converted cottage a little way outside the town, set back from the road, with a comfortable bed, a living room with everything she'd need and a nice well-appointed little kitchen, not that she'd cook much if she could help it because she could burn cornflakes. Although the hotel adjoining the bar was closed for renovations, and with it the town's only restaurant, the person from whom she'd rented the property told her that the bar provided food of a basic nature. There was also a seafood restaurant on the south of the island that did a decent meal, and not all fish, either.

On the way to that restaurant she had passed the cottage in which Mhairi Sinclair had died, recognising it from an online photograph. It hadn't changed much. Some new windows, a new door, the small garden to the front better tended than back then. She had contemplated knocking on the door but decided against it. Chances were, the present occupants wouldn't be able to tell her anything. She would have dearly loved to have gained access but though she parked up for quite some time at the side of the road, she eventually decided against it. The present occupants would be unlikely to allow a strange woman from the mainland access to have a look around, even if they knew that a murder had been committed in their home twenty years previously. With a last look at the cottage, she'd driven on, wondering if Rebecca Connolly would have tried to get in anyway, to get a feel for the locus.

The locus. It was a term she had picked up from her father, who was a KC.

It was Samuel Blair who had instilled in her the fascination with crime, and he would have preferred that she follow him into the law, but she had no desire to go down that route. She was idealistic enough to wish to get to the heart of a case, to the truth of it, something that didn't interest lawyers involved in either prosecution or defence. The law was only about what could be proved, not about truth. Despite protestations from her father, she instead focused on journalism, excelling in her degree and receiving offers from the so-called mainstream media, both press and broadcast. She declined them all because she wanted to make her own way. There were no money worries, as her grandfather, Lord Rodney Blair, had been a respected High Court judge, and her grandmother, the daughter of a billionaire who had built his tyre repair business from scratch and diversified into various other enterprises, had left her a considerable sum in trust.

The food was excellent – she truly believed that if the owners opened an outlet in Edinburgh they would make a fortune – and then she had returned to Portnaseil, intent on beginning work. She peered through the shop window, hesitating, knowing it would close soon and if she didn't get a move-on, she'd miss the opportunity to talk to Mhairi's parents.

Following this case was a good idea, even if it had come from Rebecca Connolly, who had turned out to be nothing like she'd expected at all. Dot had believed – had made herself believe, perhaps – that she would have been willing to take part in the podcast. So, she had been seriously dismayed when she refused. Why was she so dead-set against it? It was only an hour or so for the interview itself before letting her tag along on whatever story she was doing, to bring colour and context to the interview. Show, don't tell. Okay, Dot recognised that shadowing her on a story was a long shot, but she didn't see the problem. Her mother had always said you should never meet your heroes, and it certainly proved true in this case.

Still, maybe it was for the best. Maybe following up on this case was the better direction to travel. If she could find out anything new, perhaps even get to some sort of truth, then that could be the making of her. Maybe the podcast would be picked up by BBC Sounds. That would make her father so proud.

At first, she had chosen the case because she thought it would piss off Rebecca Connolly, but the more she read about it, the more intrigued she became. Mhairi Sinclair's murder was never officially solved. Yes, Roddie Drummond stood trial, but he was found Not Proven, Scotland's controversial third verdict which some said told the accused that even though the proof wasn't present, they knew he was guilty. Her father had been in the forefront of those who wished to retain the verdict, which often came under attack by politicians and, understandably, victims and their families. He argued that the presence of what was known as the Bastard Verdict – neither one nor the other – went to the heart of an accused being found guilty beyond the famed reasonable doubt. If it were to be removed, then the simple majority needed for a conviction – at least eight of the fifteen jurors voting guilty – would have to be changed to something that was very near unanimous.

Dot understood the anger of victims and their families that someone they believed to be guilty walked free from court when found Not Proven. But when she looked at the evidence against Roddie Drummond, even she saw that it didn't seem particularly compelling and wondered why the Crown thought it strong enough to merit an indictment in the first place. It was largely circumstantial, and the only seemingly solid piece was the alleged admission, made when the interview tape was switched off and only one police officer, Detective Sergeant Bill Sawyer, was present. 'Thunder Bay' had been the final words Mhairi said as paramedics had struggled to save her after she was found hideously beaten in her home. Roddie Drummond, her boyfriend, had been the one who had called the emergency services, claiming he had come home to find her in that condition, had tried to revive her, which was why he was covered in blood. Fifteen years after his acquittal, he had returned to Stoirm only to meet his own death, which also remained unsolved. Rebecca Connolly had written in a magazine article later that what she had learned suggested he could actually have been guilty, but there was no certainty. There were no other known suspects.

And yet Rebecca Connolly never did anything further on the story. Elspeth Taggart never wrote a book on it. Dot found that strange. No, she found it intriguing. She had read an interview with her that came out around the release of the Netflix documentary in which Rebecca claimed to have an insatiable curiosity. It was this need to know that drove her to go further in a story than some other journalists. If that was the case, why did she not pursue this one to its conclusion? There were so many unanswered questions that, to Dot's mind, she should have been unable to resist digging further, yet she gave up.

Dot wouldn't give up. She wanted to find out what she could, then present Rebecca Connolly with her findings and demand that she comment on them. It would make a great story. It would make a great podcast. As long as she could get people to talk.

She looked through the window again at the woman behind the till. She was in her sixties maybe, but looked older. Her

145

hair was grey, her face sagged, her eyes were sorrowful. Dot had seen a pic of her online at the time of the court case and though she was younger, her hair brown, her wrinkles not so pronounced, her eyes had borne that same melancholy look. Molly Sinclair was Mhairi's mother, and it was clear she still mourned her loss. There had been a son, too, Raymond, who had died before her daughter. Drugs. A lot of sadness in this family, a lot of tragedy.

Dot didn't know if the woman would talk to her, but she had to try. This was the first time she had ever done anything like this – doorstepping, they called it, cold calling, and she was daunted. She had been nervous enough approaching Rebecca Connolly, but that had somehow been different. She was about to raise a matter with a woman who would probably prefer it wasn't raised. But this was what Dot wanted to do with her life, she wanted to ask the difficult questions. This was the career she wanted, but she also needed to prove to Rebecca Connolly that she was a match for her. She had been around Dot's age when she picked up this story, and look where she was now: with her own agency and, though not necessarily a household name, she was recognised by people who had seen the documentary and read Elspeth McTaggart's books. Even Dot's father had heard of her and commented that the world needed more journalists like her.

Nerves made her stomach churn, but she took a deep breath. If Rebecca could do this, so could she. She pushed the door open and stepped inside.

17

'Your assistant came to see me last night.'

The words were more an accusation than a statement, delivered in a tight, strained tone, as if the woman speaking was trying in vain to hold them back but they were too powerful. Molly Sinclair's eyes burned at Rebecca in the manse study. Thankfully she didn't speak loudly, so none of the other community buy-out committee members present caught it, apart from Fiona whose head jerked sharply in their direction as she set some sandwiches on the table.

'I don't have an assistant, Mrs Sinclair,' Rebecca said, already guessing who she meant.

'That girl, Blair she said her name was. Very polite, well-spoken girl. Are you saying she's not connected to you?'

'No, she's working on her own.'

'You didn't send her?'

'No.'

Disbelief burned from Molly Sinclair's eyes. 'You honestly expect me to believe you?'

'It's the truth, Mrs Sinclair.'

'She asked the same questions you did the first time we met.'

'She's nothing to do with me, I promise.'

That wasn't quite true, though, was it? She had inadvertently set Dot on the trail. Granted, she hadn't meant Mhairi Sinclair's case specifically, but she had put the idea of following a cold case into her head.

'I'm telling you the truth,' she insisted.

'You don't know what the truth is, none of you do. You're intent on digging it all up again.'

'No, I'm not.'

'You people just want to rake through old ashes.'

'I'm not involved with Dot Blair, Mrs Sinclair.'

'So you say.'

'I give you my word. I've done everything I can on—'

'You people just lie all the time, as bad as politicians.'

'Honestly, I'm not looking into Mhairi's story—'

'MHAIRI IS NOT A STORY!'

This time her voice cut through the babble around them. Everyone in the room fell silent and looked in their direction. Rebecca felt her face flush, through embarrassment, through shame.

'Molly' – Fiona stepped forward to try to smooth things over – 'Rebecca is telling you the truth.'

The woman gritted her teeth and repeated, more quietly this time, 'Mhairi is not a story. She is . . . was a person. She was more than you people could ever know, more than a picture in a newspaper or a name on a gravestone. More than that. And she's dead and Roddie Drummond is dead, but you people can't let them rest in peace, always picking at their memories, pick, pick, pick, like . . . like . . .'

When she couldn't think of a simile, Fiona stepped in again. 'Molly, take it easy, okay? Rebecca is here to help us.'

'Help? Like she helped last time? And what happened then, eh? We still don't know for certain who killed my Mhairi.'

Rebecca was the first to admit that her story was inconclusive, that the doubts remained over Roddie Drummond's guilt or innocence. Someone, though, had been certain he was responsible, otherwise why was he shot on that beach? Certainly, there were other matters to which he was privy, and perhaps he had been killed to prevent him from revealing

148

what he knew of other events surrounding the young woman's death. Unfortunately, Rebecca had resigned herself to the knowledge that it was likely she would never know. Also, and Molly didn't know this, she had vowed to leave it alone.

'I'm sorry, Mrs Sinclair,' she said and meant it. Sometimes the work she did could bring about change, right a wrong, help someone – comfort the afflicted, afflict the comfortable – but sometimes it also opened old wounds and brought sorrow to people who didn't deserve it.

'Sorry doesn't bring my daughter back. Sorry doesn't bring my son back, or Roddie Drummond back. Sorry doesn't change anything. So, you can keep your sorry, thank you very much.'

She stepped back to take Rebecca in from head to toe, her eyes disparaging. No, those eyes were filled with hatred. Rebecca had experienced antagonism before, it went with the territory, but this was the first time she had been on the receiving end of this level of loathing.

'You people,' Molly Sinclair continued, 'you people . . .' She shook her head. 'You don't care who you hurt, as long as you get your story. You come to places like this and you dig up the past and cause all kinds of trouble and then you leave, without a single care as to the damage you cause. All to get a *story*.' The last word was spat out as though it was something unclean. 'You're nothing but parasites, that's what you are—'

'Molly,' Fiona interjected.

'I'll not wheesht, Fiona McRae. I don't care what collar you wear, you'll not silence me.' Molly turned back to Rebecca. 'You came into my home and you showed me sympathy, and I thought you were different, but you weren't. You didn't care about Mhairi and you didn't care about us. All you cared about was getting your story. So, you stirred everything up and people died. I wouldn't put it past you to have been the one to convince Roddie to come back.'

'He came back for his mother's funeral, Molly, you know that,' Fiona said.

'Aye, he did. But maybe he wouldn't have. Maybe this one talked him into it. He knew he wasn't welcome here, he knew there was talk. But he came back and so did she, and look what happened. Two more dead, Donnie ending up in hospital, he almost died, and for what?' She jerked a thumb towards Rebecca. 'So she could get her name under a headline and her face on the television.'

Rebecca could have denied it all. She hadn't met Roddie until he was on the ferry and even then he refused to talk to her. She had come to Stoirm because she'd been told that, after fifteen years away, he was attending his mother's funeral. She could have said that, but it wouldn't have made any difference. Molly Sinclair had made her mind up and nothing would change it.

'So, you tell that lassie to stay away from me and my husband,' Molly Sinclair continued, her voice suddenly losing much of its power. 'We've been through enough and we don't need scum like you adding more to our grief. Tell her to let it go. You let it go, Miss Rebecca Connolly. Forget it. The past is dead. Let it stay that way.'

Fiona patted Molly on the arm. 'Why don't you take a seat, Molly.'

A shake of the head, her eyes aimed at the floor, as if she couldn't bear to look at Rebecca further. 'I'll not be staying. I wasn't going to come – you know I was against calling on this girl from the start. I only came because I wanted to speak my piece.' Molly Sinclair looked back at Rebecca again. 'You Connollys were always trouble, right from when you came to the island. You weren't welcome then and you're not welcome now—'

'Molly,' Fiona began but Mrs Sinclair held up a hand.

'I'm going now. I've said what I wanted to say.'

Rebecca was about to apologise again but Molly turned away, her head down again, shoulders hunched. If she was aware of the looks of the handful of people present, some pitying, some shocked, some confused, she showed no sign. The front door slamming was the only sound to break the silence that covered the room.

'I'm sorry, Rebecca,' Fiona said eventually.

Rebecca shook her head, to say it was fine. But it wasn't fine. Everything Molly had said was at once false and true. She *had* seen Mhairi as a story when she came to the island for the first time, but it wasn't that black and white. It didn't mean she had no feelings for those affected. She'd hoped to find the truth behind her murder, but that didn't mean she didn't care. She'd met journalists who truly didn't give a damn for the people they touched; all they wanted was to beat the others into print or on the air, to have their name connected to something exciting, to use it to move on to greater glory. She liked to think she wasn't like that, liked to think she was more responsible, and yet she still grew excited at the prospect of a story. It was her job.

18

The thing about Darren Yates' mother was that she insisted he have decent meals. Breakfast was porridge followed by a fry-up, there was a lunch usually made up of the previous night's leftovers reheated, and then at teatime something fresh. He had to come home every day at midday to make sure he was eating properly, because she believed a growing lad had to eat. She served basic, plain food, nothing fancy, but it was good. The fact that he ate too much and too well, however, meant that he had to spend additional hours in the small gym in the community hub to work it off. The last thing Darren Yates wanted to be was a bloater.

He liked the way he looked, liked the muscle definition. His arms didn't bulge like he was competing with Big Arnie but they were well developed, his stomach was flat and ridged, his pectorals firm, his shoulders powerful, all progress achieved without steroids. Darren disdained the use of substances to help build body mass – he did it through hard work and sweat, though he was prone to sampling his own product. Nothing heavy, no heroin, but a puff now and then, occasionally some coke. He was proud of his body and when he was alone he'd stand naked in the bathroom, admiring himself, turning sideways, flexing and extending his muscles to see them move and expand, the veins standing out against his flesh. More often than not he ended up experiencing an erection as he stared at his own body.

So, he ate his mother's meals and he worked out and he managed to keep himself in shape.

Darren loved his mother; his father not so much. Howie Yates was too weak, whereas Morag was the real strength of their family. His dad often sat in the living room, his face in a newspaper – who reads them any more, Darren often wondered – letting his wife deal with the family. It was Morag who told her boys, Andy and Darren, that they had to stand up for themselves, that they had to do whatever needed to be done for whatever it was they believed in. It was she who told them that the world was heading to hell, that it was time for people to stand up and be counted. She had MacAllan blood in her veins, and her people had come to Stoirm over two hundred years before from the mainland to help harvest the seaweed. They had married locals and spread across the island until now there was no saying who was a distant relation and who wasn't. She loved the island, though, and she hated to see it fall into the hands of incomers.

'They buy up the property until we can't afford it any more,' she often said. 'It's an invasion, that's what it is. The island has been colonised by the English and Lowlanders who know nothing of the heritage and who care nothing for the past. All they want is their nice little house by the sea, their widescreen tellies, their Netflix and broadband. They've made their money and they don't spare a thought for those of us who have to graft here for pennies.'

Howie Yates was a plumber and he made not a bad living, not only working on the island but also taking contracts on the mainland, which meant over the years he was often away for extensive periods of time. His wife, who was a dab hand with a needle and thread and who brought in extra cash altering clothes and embroidering Stoirm tea towels for the tourist market, was furious that he hadn't been given the contract to replumb the Portnaseil Hotel, that workers had been brought in from Glasgow and Edinburgh.

'That's a travesty, that is,' she had railed. 'More colonisation. You watch, Darren, that bar you're so fond of will be transformed into a wine bar or something like that and will cater only to the colonists. And you wait and see, we'll be getting those migrants here soon and they'll take our homes away from us . . .'

Darren didn't hold anything against the men who were working on the hotel, especially as their boss, Matt, had sought him out specially for a little work. Punting a few drugs to tourists and islanders who fancied a puff or a snort kept him in beer and clothes money, but he was always happy to bring some extra into the house, especially as Andy's wages dried up when he was arrested and convicted. That was another prompt for Morag to rage against the world.

'So what did he do that was so wrong? It was an accident, in the name of God. They two gay boys were driving too fast, they skidded on the wet road and hit the rocks. But they needed a scapegoat, and Andy and his mates were there, so they must be guilty. All local lads, and that mainland court crucified them.'

Darren loved his brother and was also of the opinion that he had fallen victim to a miscarriage of justice. It wasn't Andy's fault – he'd said so and Darren believed him. He'd seen that Chaz Wymark and his boyfriend a couple of years ago in the hotel restaurant and they'd given him lip, suggested he was maybe gay too, and that had pissed him off. He would have given them both a hiding if that Rory Gibson hadn't interfered. That big cop had it in for him, but Darren was too smart for him.

He looked across at his mum as he ate his food. His dad was in the living room, watching a news channel. Darren didn't watch the news; he didn't care about the world, only about his family. He didn't read books, he didn't do social media. His pals all did but he didn't. All he wanted to do was cement his family's place in the island, to protect it from incomers, to defend his brother's name whenever someone passed comment.

'You know who's back on the island?' he said, chewing his leftover stew.

'Don't talk with your mouth full,' his mum said. 'Chew and swallow. I don't need you to spit your food all over my plate.'

His mum watched and, when satisfied he had chewed and swallowed, asked, 'So, who's back on the island?'

'That reporter.'

'What reporter?'

'Rebecca Connolly.'

Morag laid her knife and fork down. 'Why?'

'Something to do with the sale of the estate.'

Morag blamed her for Andy now being in the jail. Word was, she had convinced that murdering bastard Roddie Drummond to come back. If he hadn't, then life might have moved along as it always had. In Morag's mind, Rebecca Connolly had fractured her family.

'That one has a nerve showing her face here,' she said.

Darren said nothing. He speared another lump of beef and made sure he chewed it thoroughly.

'She's friends with those gay boys,' Morag reminded him.

He swallowed. 'I know that, Mum.'

'Are they back again?'

'Not that I've heard.'

That was something to satisfy her. 'Aye, you would have heard, right enough, son.' She watched as he ate. 'So, what are you going to do about it?'

He chewed slowly but risked a smile. She wouldn't chastise him for smiling while he chewed. 'It's all in hand, Mum, don't you worry.'

He didn't tell her that Matt had already asked him to keep an eye out for Rebecca and report back if he saw her. He'd spotted her the night before walking down the road to the harbour, had managed to keep an eye on her as she spoke to Donnie Kerr. A local that his mum had no time for. A junkie and a waster, were her words. His mum knew how her youngest son made some of his money but had decided to shield that knowledge from her mind. As long as he sold the stuff to tourists and incomers, that was fine. She was unaware that Darren had no such restrictions to his commerce. He sold to anyone with the cash to pay. He bought his gear from the Burke crew in Inverness, and they in turn got it from the McClymonts in Glasgow. His mum didn't need to know that, either. She mistrusted city folk, too.

The thing was, he'd also seen another lassie, same red hair as Connolly, going into Molly Sinclair's shop. She could be a tourist, but he didn't think so.

19

Donnie appeared in the study doorway supporting an elderly woman by the elbow. Her face was heavily lined and darkened by many summers and winters on the island, her white hair thinning to reveal a scalp punctuated by brown flecks, in one hand a carved walking stick that looked as if it had been in the family for generations. Everyone greeted her, called her Peggy, and Rebecca was grateful for the focus shifting away.

Donnie settled the woman into a comfortable chair that by some unspoken agreement had been left vacant and joined Rebecca and Fiona. He gave Rebecca a narrow-eyed look that was part frown and part query. 'We need to have a word after the meeting.'

'What about?' she asked.

'Not now, Rebecca, but we do need to talk.' He jerked his head towards the woman with whom he'd arrived. 'I want you to meet Peggy McCormick, one of the first people to come on board.'

His tone was clipped and though she wondered what caused it, Rebecca said no more and followed him while Fiona attended to her other guests. Donnie made the introductions, and the woman regarded Rebecca with sharp eyes. 'You'll be John Connolly's lass, then?'

'I am.'

A nod. 'Aye, I see him in you. He was a clever boy, though a wee bitty sensitive. You'll ken about your people, will you not?'

Rebecca didn't want to pursue that subject. 'I do.'

'And how do you feel about it?'

'I'm ashamed.'

There it was. She'd never said it out loud because, apart from Fiona, and only then by necessity, she'd spoken to nobody about her great-great-grandmother. Not Chaz, not Alan, not Stephen. Not even her mother, who she suspected already knew, though she had always denied knowledge of why her husband had left the island.

Peggy accepted Rebecca's statement. 'Aye, no doubt, but the past is not to be judged. Life was different back then. It's to your credit that you find shame in it, but you cannot change it. It is what it is. Your father knew that, in his heart, but he couldn't accept it, and no doubt it haunted him. Don't let it haunt you, lass, for no good will come of it. Roberta Connolly was as she was, and you are as you are, and that's that.'

Donnie was neither curious nor surprised by the exchange. He was also island-born and, though she had never spoken with him about it, would know of the Connolly clan and the Church of the Blood of Christ. Anyway, he still seemed angry about something. When she caught his eye, there was a distancing that had not been present before.

'Peggy's great-great-grandfather is something of a legend on the island,' he said, his voice still clipped. 'And it's very much in his memory that we pursue this buy-out. I thought you'd want to meet a living connection to the first attempt at land reform on Stoirm.'

Rebecca's curiosity rose. 'There was an attempt at a buy-out previously?'

'No, lass,' said Peggy. 'But there was a protest at the way the laird treated his tenants. My great-great-grandfather was John McCormick, a crofter on a spit of land over on the northwest of the island.'

'When was this?'

'This would be in 1887, the year of the Battle of the Machair, as it became known. The old Lord Stuart had died – he had been as kindly a man as he could be, given he was laird – and times were hard. Don't get me wrong, hard times for the Stuarts were different from hard times for the people, but the old laird at least tried to protect his tenants. His son, the new Lord Stuart, had none of his virtues.' A bitter little smile stretched the wrinkles of her lips. 'Aye, and history was to be repeated when the last Lord Stuart came into his inheritance, eh, Donnie?'

Donnie nodded and Rebecca recalled being told that Henry Stuart's father had been judged as a good laird, while he was not.

'So, the new Lord Stuart – William, he was called – he wanted the tenants off the land to make way for the Cheviot sheep, but they refused to budge. John McCormick led the protests. They withheld their rents and chased the factor away when he came with the eviction notices. A sheriff officer was sent from the mainland, and they chased him away, too.'

'So, what did the new Lord Stuart do?'

'He did what other lairds and other owners did when faced with tenants who refused to bend to their will. He brought in the authorities.'

'More than the sheriff officer?'

Peggy smirked. 'Och, that man was no more than a functionary. A petty official whose only power lay in words on paper, and they meant nothing to the islanders who couldn't read.'

'So, who then?'

'On other islands and on the mainland it was the army who moved in. Even naval vessels anchored off shores, all to cow those who protested the clearances. There was a ship here, just off Portnaseil, but it wasn't sailors who came to enforce the laird's will, it was two dozen police officers brought up from the city.'

'Glasgow? Edinburgh?'

'Glasgow. Highlanders, too, most of them, or sons of Highlanders, to their eternal shame and that of their kinfolk, here to oust their own people from land they had worked for generations. They came ashore from the navy ship and marched to the north, where they were met on the shore by around forty locals, some there to show their support from other parts of the island. The sheriff officer was back with his papers and his acts and his authority, but he fled as soon as the missiles began to fly.'

'They fought back?'

'Aye, they fought back, valiantly, too. They threw rocks and lumps of peat, and they fought with sticks like this one.' She raised the gnarled wooden stick. 'This was the one used by John McCormick himself in the battle. He laid out two police officers, by all accounts, pushed back others. The police were just doing a job, I suppose, they had no blood in this land, so they fell back. But their truncheons were sturdy and left many an islander on the machair with broken bones and broken heads.'

'What happened then?'

'What they call the full majesty of the law was brought to bear on the poor folk.' She breathed a sharp little laugh. 'Majesty. If you look it up, it says it means magnificence, but there was nothing magnificent about it. These people committed no crime but to defend their families, their livelihood, from greed. My kinsman and two others offered themselves as scapegoats to spare the others, and it was accepted. They were sentenced to two months in Inverness Castle, back when it was a prison.'

'And the people?'

Despite the fact that she had no doubt told this story many times, Peggy's eyes watered and she didn't reply at first.

Rebecca had learned that history in the Highlands is not necessarily a thing of the past. People long gone still lived in the memories of folk like Peggy – they remained part and parcel of the land, as if the blood, sweat and tears they had shed had been drawn into the fissures in the land and rocks.

Finally, Peggy said, 'They were moved on, to the mainland, some across the ocean there to America and Canada. And their crofts were allowed to fall to ruin and the land to go fallow, with only the sheep left to roam it.'

'But your family stayed?'

'Aye, my great-grandfather, John McCormick's son, had taken himself a trade, as a smithy. His shop was where Campbell Drummond had his workshop. Although that's gone, too, now.'

Campbell Drummond had been a mechanic, and Rebecca detected sadness that the property was no longer providing a service to the islanders.

'And when John McCormick was released, he came to stay with him, here in Portnaseil. He would often roam the machair, though, with this stick, as if looking for a face he knew, but all he saw was the sheep. He died before his time – broken, they say, by the sadness that weighed him down. But he's out there, walking the grasslands and the beaches, and feeling the wind upon his face.'

She fell silent then, as if picturing her great-great-grandfather walking alone on the shoreline, the wind whipping at the grasslands, the surf surging on the sand, the seabirds wailing like voices from the past mourning the loss of a lifestyle. Rebecca thought about Donnie's vision of Campbell and his wife Mary, and she had a momentary flash of all those souls from different times but joined by the common bond of being Stoirm islanders walking together on land they could no longer feel beneath their feet.

'Peggy was the first to sign up to the scheme,' Donnie said quietly.

The woman surfaced from her reverie. 'Aye, I couldn't contribute much myself, but I have relatives in America and they have done well for themselves, so they have. They have pitched into the fund. I even have a grand-nephew who works in Hollywood; in the films, he is, not an actor, though, but behind the cameras, although all that is a mystery to me. But he has spoken to Ray McAllister, whose people came from Stoirm.'

Rebecca was impressed. Ray McAllister was an action star who had hit it big in a hugely successful TV show and then transitioned to the movies. She made a mental note to find out if she could speak to him. Some quotes from him would sell this story to the nationals, maybe even TV. Her mind turned to Leo Cross. Their involvement of a Hollywood star could swing the interest of broadcasters towards commissioning a documentary – not only a 'David and Goliath' story but also a Hollywood star in the forefront. It worked for that guy who played Deadpool and the football team in Wales.

'That Ray is a lovely boy,' Peggy continued. 'I spoke to him on the telephone. He doesn't bear a trace of his roots in his voice, of course, for his kin left the island, oh, must be one hundred and fifty years ago now, to make their fortune in America. But he's eager to do what he can to help us. He's already contributed.'

'How much?' Rebecca asked.

'We can't reveal figures, Rebecca,' Donnie said, his voice finding its curt edge again, his eyes still not making contact.

'Of course,' she said, 'but we can mention he's taken an interest?'

'We'll discuss that later,' Donnie said, standing up. 'Let's get this meeting started.'

20

From a distance, the person approaching Bill Sawyer looked like Rebecca, but then he reminded himself that she was at a meeting up in the manse. She had asked him if he wished to attend but he had declined. He'd been to enough meetings when he was in the police force and it was his view that talking about things seldom achieved anything other than more talking. On two or three occasions he had even attended meetings organised to discuss other meetings, which he thought was a colossal waste of time. Well, his time, anyway. There were those above him who were of the belief that holding a meeting to discuss what steps should be taken was what the job was about, but not him. Meetings didn't bring results, only action did that. Anyway, he wasn't on Stoirm to get involved in the story, as much as he loved the island. He was there solely to protect Rebecca, who he had come to care about, even though she was a liberal.

He'd never met her father, who'd been on the Glasgow force while Sawyer had been based in the Highlands, but he had mates in the city who had worked with him and, to a man, they said he was a good cop, even if not the angel Rebecca believed him to be. He made one very big mistake from which only his solid reputation, and the high regard in which people held him, saved him from being crucified. Rebecca knew about that now, and understood that when John Connolly had beaten up a known child molester he had been acting as a human being and not a police officer. That his conscience bothered him for many years later spoke well of him, but that would not have been Bill's problem. As a police officer he'd delivered many a slap, had covered for colleagues when they had felt forced to do it, and had even lied on oath. He didn't do any of it out of spite. He didn't do any of it just because he could. He did it because he had to, that was the way he looked at it. Crooks and scrotes and pervs didn't play by the rules, so why should he? He never did it to anyone who didn't deserve it, or anyone he thought was innocent.

Instead of attending the meeting he sat on a bench on a grassy knoll above the harbour, taking in the view across the Sound. The breeze coming off the water was warm, which was something of a miracle. He'd sat on this very spot at other times when the wind from the water would have shaved a minister, as his mammy used to say. He had never fully understood what that meant and had once asked her, and even she wasn't sure, suggesting perhaps that it was because ministers were clean-shaven and the wind was so sharp it could remove what facial hair was left. Sawyer wasn't sure that worked: he'd seen men of the cloth sporting beards that would make a hipster drop their tofu burgers with envy. Still, it sounded good and he'd often used it himself. His old mammy had taught him many things. Don't run with the pack; don't take shit from anyone; if you think someone is going to go for you, get your retaliation in first. Sadie Sawyer had been a two-fisted kind of girl but was loving and nurturing. He'd been desolate when she died in his late teens. He wondered if she would be proud of him.

He saw the girl climbing the knoll and, as she came closer, he realised it was the lassie Rebecca had been speaking to on the ferry. Dot Blair. Bill Sawyer remembered names, and he remembered faces as easily as he remembered what crimes even the lowest of scrotes had committed, even if unconvicted. In his mind, there were no innocent scrotes, just those who got away with it.

She stood two or three feet away, pushing her auburn hair away as fingers of wind draped it over her face. 'Mr Sawyer, right? Bill Sawyer?'

He squinted up at her, the sun angled just to the left of her head. 'Aye.'

'Dot Blair. We met yesterday.'

'Aye.'

'On the ferry. You were with Rebecca Connolly. When we met, do you remember?'

'Aye,' he said again. 'I'm not senile yet, hen, I can remember as far back as yesterday.'

Her smile was tremulous but pleasant. 'Of course, sorry. I didn't mean to suggest anything like that. Sorry.'

'That's okay. What can I do for you?'

'I thought I recognised your face when we met but I wasn't sure, so I checked my research materials last night and confirmed it. Once I got into my Airbnb, which has decent Wi-Fi. I'd heard that broadband on the islands isn't great, but I found it was good enough for basic research. I mean, I wouldn't like to try streaming or anything like that, but it was fine for a Google search—'

He sensed she was nervous. She wasn't used to this, and that nervousness made her ramble, but he wasn't one to let someone ramble. 'Hen, if there's a point to this, I'd like to get to it before I do grow senile.'

He softened his words with a smile, and she gave him that twitchy little thing with her lips again. 'Of course, sorry.' She took a breath. 'Anyway, I did some digging online, looked at the cuttings on the Roddie Drummond case, that sort of thing.'

He sighed, made a show of looking at his watch.

She flushed a little, then rushed out her next words. 'You *are* the detective who *claimed* that Roddie Drummond confessed to you, aren't you?'

He caught the emphasis on the word claimed but let it go. He knew what had happened. 'Aye, that's me, though I'm retired now.'

'And working for Rebecca Connolly?'

'No, I work with Rebecca Connolly, not for her. I work for myself.'

He had his police pension, a little bit put by and made some cash on the side doing investigation work for Rebecca and others. He wasn't heading for tax exile, but he was comfortable, especially since he didn't need to pay his ex-wife maintenance now that she was hitched to someone else.

'You're friends, though, right?'

'Yes.'

'Why?'

That floored him. He didn't know why. They had got off to a rocky start: she suspected that he had lied when he said that Drummond had confessed. However, over the years he had come to like her and had adopted the mantle of her unofficial protector, although he had seen her in action and she didn't need too much of that. Still, everyone needed someone at their back, and he was there for her. He still couldn't explain why. Val Roach, who he had begun to see in a non-professional way, said it was because she was the daughter he'd never had.

God knows he'd wanted children, but his wife didn't. His ex-wife, rather, because she was off getting humped by a guy who owned a garden centre. He's strong and steady, she'd told him during one of their frequent arguments when they were still talking. Humphing all those potted plants must have made him like Arnold Schwarzenegger, he'd said, knowing full well that she meant the bloke was dependable and wasn't away for hours chasing some scrote. Or drinking. He didn't do that now. Gave up smoking, too, and dedicated himself to a fitness regime consisting of hill-walking, swimming and occasionally giving someone a slap when they got out of hand. He'd broken a leg during that time he was on Stoirm with Rebecca and since then his exercise routine had taken a hit, meaning he'd put on a bit of weight, so he didn't do much hill-walking these days, though he kept the swimming up. And of course the scrote-slapping, although he had found the delights of an extendable baton took the strain out of delivering the pain.

Anyway, the question as to why he and Rebecca Connolly had come to be pals puzzled him, although he realised that they had one thing in common. They both believed in justice. Hers was a purer approach, in that she approached it head-on, while his route was often somewhat more circuitous. He wasn't going to tell this lassie that, though.

'Beats the hell out of me, hen,' he said. 'Why do you ask?'

'She seemed to believe that Roddie Drummond didn't murder Mhairi Sinclair, and that means she thought your evidence was suspect.'

'Aye, she made that clear.'

'So, why would you be friends with her?'

'Why is it important for you to know?'

'Because I need to know where you stand before I ask you what I want to ask you. If you're friends, then I'd have to judge whether or not you're telling the truth. If you just work for her—'

'With her,' Sawyer corrected.

'*With* her, then you might be more amenable.'

He laughed. 'Hen, you just get right to it, don't you?'

'I believe in being upfront about things. That's the way I was brought up, and I think it's important to let people know where you stand. I mean—'

He cut her off before she could ramble again. She wasn't that upfront. 'Well, let me tell you this, I've never been amenable in my life.'

'So, you won't answer my questions?'

'I've been answering your questions since you pitched up here and harshed my mellow.'

She frowned. 'Harshed your mellow?'

He sighed. She was young. 'What do you want, hen?'

'Roddie Drummond.'

'What about him?'

'Did he confess to murdering Mhairi Sinclair?'

He saw the man's face, in that little interview room. Heard his voice. 'I testified as much.'

'People don't always tell the truth.'

'I was under oath.'

'People still don't always tell the truth. My father is a KC and tells me that I would be surprised by how often people lie under oath, including police officers.'

Bloody lawyers, as if they were all pure as the driven. 'I stand by my testimony.'

'The jury didn't believe you.'

'I can't help what the jury thought.'

'He walked from the High Court a free man.'

He knew she'd say that. 'But not without a stain on his character.'

'In your opinion.'

'Not just mine.' He checked her hands then eyed the bag slung over her shoulder. 'You recording this?'

'No.'

'You sure?'

'I'm a journalist. I have ethics. Unlike some people, I don't lie.'

That made him laugh. 'You've not met many journalists, have you?'

'I would tell you if I was recording it. I'm not out to trap you, Mr Sawyer.' She paused. 'Why did you come back here when he returned for his mother's funeral?'

'I like the place.'

'A bit coincidental, don't you think? The man you may have perjured yourself over coming back here after fifteen years, and you just happen to arrive too?'

He was tempted to say that Roddie Drummond's return was precisely why he'd come back. The fact that he'd avoided jail with that bastard verdict had annoyed him intensely and he wanted to pass on some of his annoyance. Now he felt that annoyance return.

'Coincidences happen.' He stood up. 'But we're finished here, hen. I've said all I want to say about Roddie Drummond.'

'Who do you think killed him, Mr Sawyer?'

She was insistent, he had to give her that. She had settled down a little but was still nervous – he could tell from the tremble in her voice and the way she clutched the strap of the bag.

'I don't know,' he said.

'Was he killed because he knew who really did murder Mhairi Sinclair?'

He started to walk away from her. 'I've got nothing to say, hen.'

She yelled after him, 'You know more than you're saying, Mr Sawyer. I'm not going away. I'm going to pursue this, and your friend Rebecca Connolly won't stop me.'

169

21

The meeting ended and the committee members filtered away, apart from Donnie and Fiona. Rebecca had listened to what those present had to say, heard more about acts of vandalism and the mysterious phone calls in the night where nobody seemed to be on the line. Emily Thorne repeated what happened to her shed. One man said that he'd returned home one night to find his Amazon Prime viewing history revealed films he'd never watched, adult movies. Rebecca wondered if this was true, but he seemed like a decent man, and nobody laughed when he related the story. In similar break-ins nothing was taken or damaged, but things were out of place, pictures slightly slanted on the wall, cups taken from the cupboard and laid out on the kitchen surface. All the reports seemed random, some thought at first the work of incomers because there was no way islanders would behave this way. Rebecca couldn't help but think about the Moron Squad and their attempt to kill Chaz and Alan. They were all local.

But the incidents weren't random. Each was aimed at the people in this room or those connected to them and, relatively mild though the threats were, they had worked. Folk were rattled, with two stating their intention to pull out of the bid, others nodding their agreement. Donnie and Fiona managed to convince them to reconsider but Rebecca had sensed the fear in the room.

They discussed the opposition consortium, and Rebecca took a note of everything they knew about the group, thinking this was a job for Alan's internet whizzery. He loved to dig deep into the web and uncover secrets that Rebecca would have zero chance of ever finding. She could research material for stories, but the kind of forensic key-bashing that company searches required was beyond her skill, not to mention her patience.

Donnie arranged for someone to take Peggy home and once the last person had left, he turned to Rebecca.

'I saw Molly walking back to Portnaseil when I arrived with Peggy,' he said. 'She was crying.'

How easily fury turns to tears, Rebecca thought, especially when it was motivated by grief and hatred.

'She's unhappy with Rebecca being here,' Fiona explained. 'We knew that, but I didn't expect her to be so emotional about it.'

Rebecca shrugged, unwilling to attack the woman, though she could still feel the heat of her glare. 'She's entitled,' she said.

Donnie pursed his lips and exhaled. 'Yes, she is.'

'She was out of order,' Fiona said.

Rebecca shook her head. 'No, she wasn't.'

'Yes, she was,' Fiona insisted. 'I understood when she spoke against bringing you in, and I understand her feelings over your first visit, as I'm sure you do, too, Rebecca.'

'I do, to an extent. I was doing my job, that's all. I suppose I was trying to help.'

'I warned you the first time we met about raking it all up,' Donnie pointed out, his words sharp. 'Old wounds are best left alone, I said, and Mhairi and Roddie are wounds a lot of people would prefer were never even seen, let alone touched. I loved Mhairi and I let her down, and I'd dearly like to know for certain what happened that night after she left that beach, but at the same time I don't want people hurt.'

Mhairi had discovered something she shouldn't on Thunder Bay that night. Donnie, at the time an addict, had been with her for a time but had left her to go in search of his dealer. As far as was known for certain, Roddie Drummond was the last person to see her alive. But both he and Donnie had been present on the beach, and there had been others too, men who were ruthless and dangerous. Donnie hadn't seen anyone following, but Roddie's father, who had walked to the cottage because his wife had experienced a premonition that something was wrong, told Rebecca that he had seen an upmarket four-wheel drive parked near the cottage. Neither Roddie nor Mhairi owned such an expensive car, but he'd never told the police because he'd also overheard the argument and knew that didn't look good for his son.

Rebecca had a rough idea what had happened. So did Donnie. But neither could know for certain because there was no evidence. The evidence, such as it was, pointed only at Roddie Drummond.

Donnie pulled her from her thoughts. 'Who's Dot Blair?'

And suddenly Rebecca understood his change of attitude. 'She's a podcast journalist.'

'Is she working with you?'

'Did she talk to you, too?'

'She did most of the talking, but I refused. Is she working with you?'

'No, she's on her own.'

'But she spoke to Molly, right?'

'Yes. I think that's what made her so angry. She thinks those old wounds are being reopened.'

'She's not wrong, is she?' Donnie paused, looked at Fiona, who was listening intently, her eyes fixed on Rebecca. She should have told her about Dot. She should have warned Donnie. She had failed them because she was so focused on following her own story.

Donnie asked, 'Has she got any new information?'

'I don't think she has anything apart from what's already out there.'

Fiona asked, 'So, she's just doing this for . . . what reason?'

Rebecca took a deep breath. 'I think to get at me. She wanted me to work with her, appear on her podcast. I refused.'

Donnie squinted at her. 'Why?'

'Because I . . .' She paused. 'I don't know why, to be honest. She caught me at a bad time. Also, I don't like being the story.'

'But you did the TV thing.'

'That was for Elspeth and also a business decision, because the production company use the agency now and then. I wasn't totally comfortable with it. I've still not watched all of it.'

'So, this Dot Blair is out for some kind of revenge? Journalistic rivalry, is that it?'

Rebecca thought about that. 'Yes . . . No . . . I don't know. She took my refusal badly, and I had the impression she's a girl who hasn't been told no often enough. But I felt guilty, so I suggested that she find a case and follow it up. I never for a minute thought she would choose Mhairi's case, but she did, I think to try to outdo me, to prove that she's as good as me.'

Donnie said, 'Or trying to be you.'

'I don't know, Donnie. I really don't.' She felt uncomfortable being questioned. She wasn't used to it. It was normally her doing the questioning, another reason she had body-swerved the podcast. 'Look, I just do what I do. I blunder my way through as best I can, often not knowing where the hell I'm going and trying not to have any preconceived notions, talking to people here, reading something there, pissing people off. I don't think of myself as being anything but a reporter doing a job. Yes, I think I'm better than the press release processors and social media collators that some journalists have been reduced to, and Elspeth taught me too well to believe that is what the job should be, but I'm not a role model, I tried to tell her that. I'm far from perfect and I make too many mistakes. I'm certainly nobody's mentor. But she seems to think I'm some kind of superstar.'

'That's the TV effect for you,' Fiona chimed in.

'Maybe. And, if I'm honest, Elspeth's books didn't help.'

Sorry, Elspeth, but it's true.

Donnie considered her words. 'Can you stop her from looking any further into Mhairi's death?'

'Doubtful. She's seriously pissed off with me.'

He sighed, glanced again at Fiona. 'We really don't need this right now, Rebecca. Old wounds. Old scandals. We're trying to do something here, and bringing all this up won't help. We need the islanders to trust you, and this woman asking questions about what happened twenty years ago will get in the way of that.'

'But she's nothing to do with me. I've done my stories on Mhairi. Yes, there are unanswered questions but—' She stopped. She had been about to say that she had agreed with Donnie and Bill Sawyer that they wouldn't pursue the answers to those questions. They were unlikely to find answers, but if they did, it would place them on a direct path to people best left alone. Rebecca hadn't liked having to pull back, but she had. In some ways, the work she had done since was a way of making up for that failure. For that cowardice. The thing was, Fiona McRae knew nothing of that.

Donnie seemed to sense her thoughts because he jumped in swiftly. 'The islanders don't know that, Rebecca. All they know is that a mainlander is here, asking questions of people you spoke to before. You're both in the media, and that means you not only know each other but will be working together. That could close doors and harden hearts and minds.'

'Can you have a word with her?' Fiona asked.

Every journalistic nerve in her body protested the idea. 'I don't know if I can.'

Donnie pressed, 'But you could try, right?'

No, she couldn't try. Shouldn't try. She had no right to interfere with a journalist making enquiries. She wasn't the island's PR person or the community buy-out group's PR person. She was here to do her own story.

She shook her head. 'I'm sorry, but I can't do that.'

Donnie asked, 'Why not?'

The word ethics popped into her head, but she couldn't say it because it would sound pompous and self-important. 'I . . . It's not something I can do, even if I thought she would pay any attention. When I said I do what I can do, I meant it. Dot Blair has to do what she thinks she should do. I have no right to try to stop her. I'm sorry, but that's the way it is. I didn't put her onto the story, not directly, and I've done nothing to encourage her. I can't stop her.'

Donnie stared at her for a moment, then stood up. When he spoke again, his voice was sorrowful. 'Okay, I suppose I understand, to an extent anyway. But you know that Stoirm islanders don't like people prying into their business. Fiona and I had a helluva job convincing the buy-out group that bringing you in was a good idea and most of them are incomers. The island-born might – no, they bloody well *will* – take exception to this all being dredged up again for no reason.'

'And what about you, Donnie, and you, Fiona? Do you take exception to it?'

They exchanged a look, and it was Fiona who replied. 'We're on your side, Rebecca, but, as Donnie said, others might not see it that way. My advice is to dissuade this young woman, if you can. No good will come of her digging into this. If there was any possibility that there was anything fresh to uncover that would give everyone closure, I firmly believe you would have found it when you first came here.'

Rebecca shot Donnie a quick glance, but he avoided her eyes.

22

'And how is the lovely island of Stoirm?' Alan asked.

'Lovely, and still an island,' Rebecca replied.

'That's a shame, I'd planned walking over later.'

'Alan, I thought you could walk on water.'

'I gave that up for Lent. I ruined more shoes that way.'

She smiled. Sometimes talking to him was very much a random, even surreal, experience; he talked utter nonsense but always made her smile.

'Where are you?' he asked. 'I can hear the birds a-chirping.'

'I'm walking down to Portnaseil from the manse to meet Bill.'

'Walking and talking. Multi-tasking, I like it.'

'I have many talents.'

'Decision-making not being one of them.'

He was talking about Stephen. 'Don't start, Alan.'

'I have not yet begun to start.'

She knew he would say something about Stephen because his filters were faulty. It was the price she paid for having him as a friend. 'It's complicated, Alan.'

'Only because you make it complicated.'

'I thought you always said that marriage was society's way of saying, "fun's over"?'

'You should know me well enough to know that you must never confuse what I say with what I think. I married the blond lunk, remember. Have you spoken to Stephen?'

'He said don't contact him until I made a decision.'

'Oh, that's convenient for you. And have you made a decision? Have you even thought about it?'

Not for the first time she was amazed at how little his questioning irritated her. Anyone else doing this would have been cut off by now, but Alan, Chaz and Elspeth, when she had been alive, could say what they liked and she didn't mind. 'Yes, I've thought about it.'

'And?'

'I'm still thinking about it.'

An exasperated sigh hissed down the line. 'I really wish I was there, Becks.'

'You miss the island?'

'Yes, but more so I could take you over my knee and give you a spanking.'

'Oh,' she said breathily, seeking to divert him from this line of questioning. 'I didn't know you were into that.'

Another sigh. 'Why did you call, Becks?'

Relief washed over her. 'I need to tap into your expertise, Alan.'

'Like you, I also have many talents, you need to be more specific.'

'Your facility with web searches and knowledge of the financial world.'

Alan's family was heavily involved in the financial sector. He had avoided being sucked into it but had learned a thing or two while growing up.

'Check your email,' she said. 'I've sent you everything we know about the consortium making a bid for the estate here.'

'Fine. When do you need this?'

'Guess . . .'

'Yesterday it is, then.'

A figure she recognised headed towards her. Dot Blair was striding up the road, her step purposeful and, when she saw

Rebecca, she picked up the pace. It looked like a confrontation was imminent.

'I need to go, Alan, there's someone here I must speak to.'

'Fine – but Becks?'

'Yeah?'

'Think carefully and do the right thing. Don't fuck this up.'

She knew he wasn't talking about the story. 'I'll try not to.'

'Try harder.'

And then he was gone. He could do that, hang up without saying goodbye, usually leaving her with a one-liner or, in this case, a two-word lecture. She put her phone away and pushed the thought of Stephen away (again) to concentrate on Dot Blair, who had veered to block her path.

'What are you worried about?'

Rebecca guessed what she meant but decided to play bewildered. 'What do you mean, Dot?'

'You're telling people not to speak to me.'

'That's not—'

'Oh, don't deny it. When Mhairi's mum said no, I understood, even when her ex-boyfriend refused, I thought it was understandable. But the cop? Bill Sawyer? He seemed willing but then he clammed up. He's your friend, he's travelling with you, working with you, and that told me all I needed to know. You're trying to stop me from following this story up.'

'Dot, I've told no one to—'

'You expect me to believe that? You're worried I might steal your thunder, that's it, isn't it? Worried that I might find something that you missed, so you've told all your pals here to clam up.'

'That's not the way it—'

'Even the police won't tell me anything.'

'They're not likely to.'

Dot ignored Rebecca's protestation. 'The sergeant over there, he more or less told me to eff off.'

'Dot, believe me, the police are unlikely to do anything on my say-so.'

'Yeah, sure.' A finger was suddenly pointed at Rebecca's face. 'You're nothing but a diva, Rebecca Connolly. Too big for your bloody boots and scared of competition. You see this story as yours, and yours alone, so you're doing all you can to keep anyone else out. But I'm not going to stop, you hear me? I'll get someone to speak, don't you worry—'

Rebecca had heard enough. She'd been attacked by Molly Sinclair, had seen Donnie's trust in her erode, perhaps even Fiona's, and now she was being accused by this young woman of something she didn't do. It was time to take some control, so she raised her voice. 'Dot, for God's sake, take a breath and let me speak.'

Dot stopped, clearly debating with herself whether she should do as Rebecca said, then gave her a curt nod.

'Okay,' Rebecca began, taking a breath herself and ditching the sharp tone, 'whether you believe me or not, I haven't asked anyone not to speak to you. Frankly, they wouldn't take a blind bit of notice of me, even if I did. But I do believe you've chosen the wrong story to follow. It's very difficult to get people to talk about these things at the best of times, and here it's damn near impossible. The people of Stoirm go their own way, have their own set of rules. I had a lot of problems when I came here but I was lucky – Roddie Drummond coming back for his mother's funeral made it a little easier, though not by much. The problem you face is that many of the people who knew about what happened are dead, and those who remain don't want to talk.'

'That's because you—'

Rebecca held up a hand. 'No, I have nothing to do with it. Now, I can't stop you from doing this, but I would advise you against it.' She took a breath, unsure whether she should say what had formed in her mind. 'Look, I was probably too hasty when I refused to take part in your podcast. I'm not perfect, I make mistakes, and that was one. It was very kind of you to ask me and I was a bit abrupt.'

'You were downright rude.'

Rebecca didn't think she had been, but she let that pass. 'So, here's what I propose. You wanted to follow me on a story, so why not do that now? I'm here on Stoirm for what could be something big, if I can do it correctly.'

'Don't try to mollify me with charity.'

'It's not charity and I'm not trying to mollify you. To be honest, Dot, I don't need to. It's no skin off my nose if you pursue the Mhairi Sinclair story. But I do feel guilty over blowing you off when I shouldn't have, and I don't want to see you wasting your time on something that experience tells me isn't going to lead anywhere.'

She had first considered this approach after she left Donnie and Fiona in the manse but hadn't fully decided on taking it until this conversation. The problem was, Dot wasn't buying it.

'Why should I believe you?'

'Okay, let me be totally frank, Dot. I know for a fact you will get nowhere with the Mhairi Sinclair case. It's done, it's dead, and whatever happened here will remain a mystery. I know it's tempting to think that you will crack it, but you really won't. You have to believe me on this.'

Dot's expression softened as she thought about the brick walls she had already encountered.

'You can take this offer or leave it,' Rebecca pressed, 'but it's genuine, Dot.'

She chewed the inside of her lip as she considered. 'So, what's on the table? Unlimited access?'

Rebecca smiled. 'Well, I'm not Taylor Swift or a member of the royal family, but you're welcome to help me as I follow the story. One proviso – you don't broadcast anything without my say-so and certainly not until we have the story locked down.'

Dot's face stiffened again. 'You want to censor me?'

'No, not censorship, but I do need to know what you're putting out there. This story isn't about me, it's about other people, and we have to be mindful of that, concentrate on the issue and the facts behind it. Yes, I'll be using personal stories to humanise the issue, but I can't have you broadcasting something that might hurt someone for no good reason. And there are always legal ramifications that we would have to clear first. We'd be working together on this, and that means we work as a team. Agreed?'

Dot thought about it, her teeth gnawing at her lips again, her eyes fixed on Rebecca as she tried to find any suggestion that Rebecca was attempting to fool her. Rebecca was satisfied that she wouldn't see anything, as she meant what she said. That didn't mean Dot wouldn't imagine it, though. It all depended on how angry she was.

Finally, Dot blinked a few times and her head bobbed. 'Fine. Okay. It's a deal.'

She held out her hand and Rebecca almost smiled as she took it, thinking it looked as if one of them had sold the other a used car.

'I won't let you down, Rebecca,' Dot said, her own smile finally breaking out and loosening her tongue. 'I told you I was a fan of yours and I'm sorry if I annoyed you by taking up the Mhairi Sinclair story, but I really wanted to follow in your footsteps, and it's so fascinating, a real-life murder mystery. We'll be great together, really we will, I can help in a lot of ways, interviews, research . . .'

Rebecca let her talk. Over Dot's shoulder, at the road leading into Portnaseil, she saw Darren Yates watching them. When he saw her looking in his direction, he turned back toward the Square, his phone already to his ear.

*

181

Jarji Nikoladze frowned as he listened to what his contact on Stoirm had to tell him.

'What do you mean there are two of them?' he asked.

'Two reporters. The one you know about, Rebecca Connolly, and another one, another girl. I haven't got her name yet, but I've got the local boys on it.'

The Connolly girl wasn't alone. That complicated matters. They now had two annoyances to deal with when he really only wanted one.

'Are they investigating the sale of the estate?'

'I don't know that for certain, but one of them has been asking people about some murder twenty or so years ago. A lassie was beaten to death in a cottage down the road from Portnaseil. A bloke was charged but got off with it.'

Jarji knew of the case. He knew it well. So, Rebecca Connolly was back on that? She hadn't made any moves regarding it for six years, so he wondered, why now? Did she have something new?

'There's another problem,' the voice added.

'I don't like problems, you know that.'

'I know, and I'm not even sure this is one.'

'What is it?'

'They might have a minder.'

Jarji was already aware of that. 'Who is it?'

'Some ex-cop, name of Bill Sawyer. He arrived with them on the ferry yesterday.'

Sawyer. He had heard that name before in relation to Connolly and Stoirm.

'He's a fit-looking bugger,' the contact continued, 'though running a wee bit to fat.'

'I'm not interested in his physique, man. I'm sure you can deal with him if the need arises.'

'My point is that dealing with the Connolly lassie is more complicated than we thought.'

Jarji recognised that fact, but he didn't let this man know. It was best never to let subordinates know that you were at a loss.

'It is what it is,' he said. 'You will have to deal with it.'

'What? You mean, go for all three?'

'No, that would be ridiculous and would draw attention. Keep your people watching the Connolly girl, and they can move when they get the chance.'

'How bad do you want it to be?'

Rebecca Connolly had been an irritant for too long, but he was wise enough not to be too specific. This affair should have been so simple. Show these people on the island the error of their ways, buy the estate – shielded by a complex series of shell companies – and fulfil his ambition. His instructions were that discretion was to be the watchword, but perhaps now it was time to loosen the gloves, if not take them off entirely.

'Send her some sort of message.'

'That won't be easy.'

'I don't pay you to handle the easy things. I pay you because you were supposed to be a man who brought results, and so far I have seen precious little evidence of that. These islanders are still holding together. But make sure that it doesn't trace back to you or any of your men. I would advise you not to let me down.'

'I won't let you down, don't you worry.'

Jarji put a smile into his voice. 'I never worry.'

There was a silence for a moment on the line before the man broached another matter. 'Donnie Kerr.'

'What about him?'

'He didn't take a telling.'

Jarji processed that. He had been led to believe that the tour operator was devoted to his daughter and the veiled threat of doing her harm would have been sufficient to have him think twice about his involvement.

'Then we shall have to follow through,' Jarji said. 'He will learn I don't make threats, I make promises.'

'She's in Glasgow.'

'I am aware of that.'

'I can't deal with it in Glasgow.'

'You won't need to,' said Jarji. 'I will take care of it. I have the very people in mind.'

He was unaware that, as he spoke, he was clawing the flesh of his hands.

23

She found Bill sitting at the bar, a late lunch of Scotch pie, chips and beans as well as a tall glass of lager in front of him. In the corner Darren Yates was with two of his cronies. The trio looked her up and down as she walked the short distance from the entrance to the bar.

'I can hear my arteries hardening just looking at that,' Rebecca said as she took the stool beside him, ignoring their gaze.

'The menu is pretty limited, thanks to the renovation work, apparently,' he said, tucking a crinkle-cut into his mouth and chewing. 'I think it's reduced to whatever can be cooked in an air fryer or microwave.'

She smiled. 'You'll just have to put up with it, then.'

He swallowed the chip down. 'It's a dirty job, but some-one's got to do it. Sorry, there's no tofu or avocado available.'

'Damn,' said Rebecca, catching the eye of the young man behind the bar. 'I'll have what he's having. But a gin and tonic first.'

Bill's eyebrows raised and he made a show of looking at this watch. 'Before the sun sinks over the yardarm? Slippery slope, Becks.'

'I've had a day,' she said, then told him about Molly Sinclair and Dot Blair. Bill ate as he listened, expressed no surprise.

'I kind of thought there might be some trouble when that girl tried to get me to speak. I had the feeling she'd already had some knockbacks.' A forkful of pie with beans clinging to it went the same way as the chip. Watching him, Rebecca began to feel hunger gnaw.

Once he swallowed, he asked, 'You think it's a good idea to bring her on board?'

'Not really, but I can't think what else to do.' She thanked the barman as he set the gin glass before her with a bottle of tonic. 'Letting her carry on noising up the locals could bugger my chances of getting this story. And you never know, maybe she'll be of some use.'

'You think?'

She wasn't certain but it was the best she could come up with. She would have liked a bit more time to work out the permutations of the arrangements, but sometimes events move faster than plans. She took a long sip of the drink and glanced around. 'Do you know those boys in the corner?'

Bill didn't even turn to look, meaning he'd already taken note of them. 'The surfer dude and his hangers-on?'

'Yeah.'

'Not seen any of them before but they're local, by the sound of their accent. And they're as thick as shit.'

'How do you know?'

'I've overheard some of their conversation. Their fields of knowledge seem to run the gamut from A to B.'

She laughed softly at his propensity to keep track of his surroundings and the people around him. 'Do you miss anything?'

'My youth, my dreams, my waistline.'

'Eating that won't help the latter.'

He forked the final helping of pie crust and beans into his mouth and washed it down with a mouthful of lager. 'No, but it goes down real smooth. Why do you ask about them? They given you any trouble?'

'No. The blond one is called Darren Yates. His brother was one of the gang who forced Chaz and Alan off the road that time.'

Bill shot a glance at them, this time with renewed interest. Darren Yates saw his look and returned it, his eyes mocking. 'Stupidity runs in the family, then,' Bill said.

'I've already seen him a couple of times since we got here, and each time he's shown more interest in me than is comfortable.'

'Well,' Bill said, 'you're a passable-looking lassie.'

'Thank you. Passable, that's, eh, something . . .'

'You're welcome. The point is, maybe he's admiring you. I did say they were as thick as shit.'

Rebecca was used to men looking at her in that way, but she didn't think that was it. There was curiosity in the boy's scrutiny, not lust. She risked a glance and saw him and his friends stand up. As Yates walked past them, he gave her another long look.

'No,' she said to Bill, 'that's not it. I think there's more to it than that.'

'She's in the bar right now.'

'What's she doing?'

'Going to eat, as far as I can tell.'

Darren had phoned Matt Coyle, even though he was only a few feet away, standing on the pavement outside the hotel. Matt was at a window and could see the boy with his pals.

'She alone?'

'No, she's got that bloke with her.'

'The minder?'

'Aye.'

Matt swore softly. He'd have preferred Rebecca Connolly to be alone.

Darren asked, 'What do you want me to do?'

Matt considered. The reporter needed to be pressured into keeping her nose out of the estate sale, but the presence of the minder complicated matters. He would have preferred that Ryan and Elton dealt with it, but right outside the hotel wasn't the place for that. Time was getting on, though, and the longer they left it, the more chance there was that she'd find some sort of story. She hadn't been on Stoirm long enough yet to get much, maybe a few wee tales, but nothing that could lead to them. He cast his eye across the Square. There was nobody about, but that didn't mean there weren't people who could see. And the cop shop was just across the way. He'd been told to do something, and this might be the chance to do it without sending in the heavy mob. Also, if things did have to turn more forceful, then this boy doing something now would put any blame on him. If that was necessary, Darren wouldn't grass, he knew that. Matt had already made it clear that if things went pear-shaped and he opened his mouth about anything he'd done, it would go badly for his brother in the jail.

'Have a word,' he said.

'Just a word?'

'Aye, for now.'

'If you're frightened of that bloke . . .'

'I'm no.'

'I mean, I can handle him. He's old, flabby. He must be at least fifty.'

Cheeky bugger, Matt thought, who was fifty-six. 'No, let's not have any aggro, no in daylight and no in the middle of the town square.'

'I'm not scared of him,' Darren insisted.

'Darren, son, do as I'm saying, right? Talk to her. Don't draw attention. Urge her to leave it alone, tell her she's not wanted on Stoirm – you told me people here don't really want her back.'

'Aye, but—'

'Aye, but nothing. Do what you're told, okay?'

He hung up then but kept his eye on the boy. He could tell by the way he snapped his flip phone shut and thrust it in his pocket, then spat something through his gritted teeth, that he wasn't happy. Darren and his pals had been handy up until now. Matt hoped he didn't prove to be a liability.

24

They were waiting for them outside after they had finished their lunch. Darren in the forefront, his mates at his back doing their best to look mean and moody. They were so very young, even to Rebecca, who was no Methuselah. One looked as if he hadn't even begun to shave yet.

Neither Rebecca nor Bill were surprised when they pushed themselves off the wall on which they'd been leaning and blocked their path. They had that look about them, as if their stupidity dictated that it was time they took it for a walk.

'Help you, lads?'

Yates ignored Bill and spoke directly to Rebecca. 'You're that reporter, aye?'

'I'm that reporter,' Rebecca confirmed. 'What can I do for you, Darren?'

He liked the fact that she knew his name. She regretted using it, because it gave him ideas above his station. 'You know who I am then, darling.'

'Aye, the way you maybe don't know someone's farted, but you know it's there,' said Bill.

Darren's glance towards Bill was appraising. 'I've seen you here before, old man.'

'I've visited the island once or twice.'

Darren's smile was like a sneer. 'Looking for somewhere to retire, aye?'

'Maybe one day. I'll come hear you play your banjo on the porch.'

Darren's forehead puckered as he struggled to understand Bill's allusion.

'Morons say what,' Bill added.

'What?'

Bill grinned at Rebecca. 'I hate being right all the time.'

Darren ignored him again and addressed Rebecca. 'You shouldn't be here, darling.'

She didn't have the time or the inclination for this, and an altercation in the middle of Portnaseil's Square wasn't something she relished.

'You're right, I've got an appointment to get to. And I'm not your darling.'

She made to step around him, but he moved with her. Bill wedged himself between them. Irritation flashed through her. She could handle this bawbag, and she really didn't want what was nothing more than a testosterone explosion to turn into something more serious. Bill enjoyed this kind of exchange, and with him they more often than not turned into physical encounters, but she had other things to do.

'Take my advice, son,' Bill said, 'fight your instinct to be an arse.'

'I'm talking to her, not you, old man. What are you? Her bodyguard?' He peered round Bill at Rebecca and gave her that up-and-down look again. 'Or is he your sugar daddy, aye? You like it old and wrinkly? Maybe you should try some younger meat, eh?'

'Maybe I'll do that,' she said, 'if I'm ever desperate and have thirty seconds to spare in order to be sorely disappointed.'

The words were out before she realised. The young man's forehead crinkled again.

'Morons say what,' Bill repeated.

Darren looked at him again. 'What?'

Bill laughed and shook his head. 'Seriously, son, a goldfish has better recall than you.'

Darren's jaw tightened as he realised he'd been made to look foolish again, and in front of his pals, one of whom had the temerity to snigger. He jerked his head round towards the boy and stifled the amusement with a glare, then stabbed a finger at Rebecca. 'You, reporter lassie, my advice is keep your nose out of island business, right?'

Okay, it didn't matter what she said now because her angry genie was out of its bottle. 'And if I don't, what will you do? Force my car off the road, like your big brother did to my pals? Oh, yes – I know who he is, and I know who you are. There's a family resemblance, the same stupid look. How is jail working out for Andy, by the way?'

That annoyed him even further. 'You don't talk about Andy . . .'

'Really?' Rebecca lowered her voice to a conspiratorial whisper. 'Is he someone's bitch? Don't you want to talk about it?'

Darren reached out for her, and she was prepared for it, but Bill grabbed the arm and twisted it sharply to force him away and round one hundred and eighty degrees, then placed the fingers of his other hand on either side of his windpipe. Rebecca heard Darren's breath catch as pressure was applied. He froze, instinct telling him that struggling was not the best course of action under the circumstances.

'Now, take it easy, son.' He looked at Darren's friends as they moved towards him. Rebecca steeled herself to utilise her self-defence moves, which were more advanced than ever before but still not in the action-hero class. What she had would take them by surprise, though.

'Ah, now lads, stay where you are,' Bill warned. 'Because if I get nervous, my fingers might twitch, and any more pressure than this might mean Darren here ends up sucking his meals through a straw for a few weeks. Maybe months if I get really, really scared.'

Darren held up a hand to tell his friends to keep away, his breath slightly compressed by the pressure of Bill's fingers, the air rasping in his throat.

'Now, here's my advice, Darren son. Do yourself a favour, stop acting the big man, okay? You've not got the wherewithal to pull it off. You don't want to end up like your brother.'

He released the young man and gave him a push towards his friends.

'And one other thing – get a proper haircut. You've got a head like a bleached lavvy brush.'

Darren's face was dark with fury as he rubbed at this throat.

'And a wee tip for you,' Bill added. 'See, before you start anything, know who it is you're starting it with.'

'You don't know me, old man.'

Bill's smile was thin but disdainful as he looked him up and down. 'Aye, I do, son.'

He kept himself between Rebecca and the youths as they walked round them. Darren massaged his neck as he glared after them, his face coloured by rage and perhaps even embarrassment that his cronies had seen him bested by an old man and a lassie. For boys like him, the appearance of indomitability was important, and he'd just been proved to be someone who was easily dominated.

'How to make friends and influence people,' Rebecca murmured once they were far enough away.

'I'll settle for the influencing part,' Bill replied, casting another quick look backwards to ensure that Darren hadn't decided it was time for round two.

Rebecca said, 'I could have handled him, you know that, right?'

'Yeah, I've seen you in action, but I need to get some fun out of this trip.'

193

She risked a glance back, saw them still watching as they crossed the Square towards the Hub. She shouldn't have let her own mouth run off like that. She could have handled it better and not given Bill the chance to have his fun. Something told her that they might regret it.

A movement drew her eye to the hotel windows, where she saw a stocky man with thinning hair looking down at Darren and his pals, and then at her.

The hotel's reception area was in a state of disarray. The green tartan carpet had been hauled up; the wood around the desk, so old it was burnished black, had been ripped out; paintings of animal slaughter that had adorned the hideously papered walls had been binned. The office behind the desk, though, remained intact. It was cramped, made even more so by wooden slats that had been propped up in a corner, but Matt Coyle had decided it would be useful for him when he was on the phone to the boss.

Ryan was outside the slightly open door, ostensibly rifling through a sack for the proper-sized dowels for some shelving he was erecting in what would become the guest lounge. He wasn't eavesdropping purposely, at least he didn't think he was, but even though Matt spoke softly, Ryan could still hear every word.

'The local lads had a wee set-to just outside here, but her minder was there. He's older, aye, but he's handy, you know what I mean?'

A sigh. 'Aye, sorry, I know you've been around a bit. I know you know what I mean. Sorry. But my point is, this guy has got that girl's back and he's no daisy. Darren, the local lad, did as we asked, tried to scare her, you know? Told her she wasn't wanted here, the usual, but this bloke stepped in . . .'

Darren. The boy he'd seen Elton talking to when that woman's shed was torched. Fancied himself as a hard man. He'd be laughed off the street back home. Stupid haircut, too.

'. . . He stepped in because Darren lost his rag and made a move, but this fella hit him with some sort of choke hold . . . I know, I know – he wasn't supposed to, but he did and that's that. Now that I've seen him, I know for a fact he's ex-polis. I mean, he's in his fifties easy, but he's no let himself go overmuch and he had this feel about him, you know?'

Ryan knew what he meant when he said the bloke had a feel about him. The thing about cops, even if they were retired, was that guys like Ryan and Matt could spot them across a crowded room. They had a way of looking at a fella, sizing him up, of checking out a room.

'. . . I told you, Darren lost his rag. He's a boy, and that lassie got his goat.'

That lassie had to be the reporter, Ryan decided, and her having a former cop with her obviously didn't please Matt. Good. Ryan hoped maybe that would make them think twice.

A footfall on the stairwell made Ryan step away, shoving the dowels he'd found into his jeans pocket. He looked around for a reason to be lingering in the lobby that didn't include standing by the door, saw a drill lying on the floor, picked it up and began fiddling with the bit, while also keeping an eye on the door leading to the stairs. When nobody appeared and there was no further sound of feet on the steps, he carefully placed the drill back on the floor and crept back to the doorway.

'Look, all I'm saying is, these local boys, that Darren, they're going to be hard to handle, you know? The lads I brought, they're professionals, they know what's what . . .'

He stopped, listened. Ryan wished he could hear what the other person was saying.

'Duffy's fine. He's done a good job so far.'

Another pause.

'No, he doesn't know, of course not.'

What didn't he know? Ryan leaned in closer to the open door, his body suddenly tense.

'Aye, he was pointed out to the boy. Darren knows the score. I've laid it on heavy with him, and he knows what'll happen if he doesn't play ball.'

He was pointed out. Ryan thought about Elton nodding towards the car that night and the blond boy's intense stare as he passed by, as if he was memorising his features. What the fuck was going on here?

'Aye, I'll emphasise it with him, don't you worry. My baws could be on the line if he doesn't do as he's told. But he will, otherwise it won't be good for his brother . . .'

Ryan didn't have a brother, so it had to be Darren's. What happens if the shit hits the—

Ryan kicked a wedge of wood as he eased closer. It skittered across the manky carpet and thudded against the door. Fuck!

'Hang on,' Matt said.

Ryan didn't have the time to get away, so he had to brazen it out. He rapped the door with his knuckles, pushed it fully open, and poked his head into the small office and plastered a big shit-eating smile across his face. 'Sorry, Matt, you know where Elton is, mate? I need him to hold some shelves steady while I fix them.'

Matt stared at him for too long, and Ryan knew he was trying to figure out what he'd heard. He looked at the phone in his hand, then back at Ryan, then finally said, 'He's cleaning out some shit in the kitchen, chucking it all in the skip out the back.'

That was about his level, Ryan thought. 'Grand, I'll go get him. Thanks, Matt. Sorry for interrupting.'

He walked across the hotel lobby as nonchalantly as he could, feeling Matt's eyes on him all the way.

25

PC Rory Gibson stood behind the counter in the small police station with a full view of the Square through the glass doors, so he would have seen them approach. He might also have seen the exchange with Darren and his chums, but if he did, he didn't acknowledge it. Rebecca had seen the police officer before, when she was on the island for Chaz and Alan's wedding, but she hadn't actually spoken to him. He bore a similarity to Darren, in that he was tall and filled his uniform well, but his blond hair was cut short and his features were not scarred by the need to appear tough.

'PC Gibson,' she said, laying a business card on the counter. 'Rebecca Connolly . . .'

He studied the card as if it had that week's lottery numbers printed on it. 'Aye, I remember you, Ms Connolly.'

'This is Bill Sawyer, my associate.'

Rory and Bill shared a nod, but the young officer's gaze lingered a little longer. 'How can I help you?'

'I'm looking into the spate of vandalism on the island.'

He didn't seem surprised. Word had obviously circulated. 'Oh aye?'

'And wondered what you could tell me about it?'

'I'm not at liberty to speak to the press, Ms Connolly.'

'Even off the record?'

He smiled. He had a nice smile. This was a man people could trust, she decided.

'My dad was a policeman, Ms Connolly, and his dad before him. They told me there's nothing off the record with reporters.'

'Your dad and grandad were smart,' said Bill. 'I never trusted them, either.'

Rory cocked his head, gave Bill another once-over. There was a sharpness about his scrutiny that told Rebecca he was no fool. 'You were on the Job, right?'

Bill inclined his head. 'Retired as a DS, based in Inverness.'

Understanding dawned. 'DS Bill Sawyer. The Mhairi Sinclair case.'

'You know about it? It was way before your time, son.'

'It's one of the first things I heard about when I was posted here. The only unresolved murder on the island, maybe even the whole of the Hebrides.'

Rebecca noted the use of unresolved and not unsolved. He was trustworthy, smart and careful.

He addressed Rebecca again. 'And it's back in people's minds again, thanks to you.'

'I'm not here about that, PC Gibson.'

'The other reporter is. You saying you're not working together?'

'We weren't but we are now.' She heard her words and realised how lame they were. She gave him her best smile. 'It's complicated. It's almost like an island thing.'

He returned her smile, knowing that dealing with life on Stoirm could be complex.

Rebecca thought they'd made a connection. 'It's Rory, isn't it? Is it okay to call you that?'

He glanced at a door leading somewhere, as if making sure it was tightly closed, then waved a hand to give permission. 'But if my gaffer comes back, call me PC Gibson.'

Rebecca nodded her agreement, while Bill asked, 'Who is your gaffer?'

'Pete Nisbett, you know him?'

Bill's mouth hardened, clearly unimpressed. 'Aye, our paths have crossed.'

Rebecca resolved to ask him about that particular history later. 'These acts of vandalism, Rory, do you think they're connected?'

'I can't comment on them, Ms Connolly.'

'Rebecca.'

'Unless your gaffer comes back,' Bill said. 'You wouldn't want to be seen getting too chummy with a reporter. But come on, Rory, there's only us here.'

Rebecca hadn't agreed to the bar on quoting him, but the die was cast now. The chances were, she wouldn't have quoted him directly, but she would have preferred it to be her decision.

The police officer hesitated, another glance at the door. 'It's more than my pension's worth . . .'

'One cop to another, Rebecca's not recording you or taking notes, and she won't quote you, so you can speak freely.'

PC Gibson continued to hesitate.

'Look, son,' Bill said, leaning his elbows on the counter and clasping his hands in front of him, 'following the book is very laudable, but sometimes you need to close it and make up your own mind. I give you my word as a fellow cop that you can trust her. She won't drop you in it.'

'I'm only looking for some background,' Rebecca pledged. 'Some context. You know that the locals involved in trying to buy the estate are convinced this is an organised campaign of intimidation.'

'Yes, I know that.'

'So, what do you think?' She saw in his eyes that he had thoughts of his own, but he wasn't about to voice them. 'I'm asking Rory, not PC Gibson. You have an opinion, right?'

He looked beyond them to the Square, then over his shoulder to the door. He placed both hands on the counter as if he was going to use it as a means of lifting himself off his feet, took a breath. 'I think it's possible.'

'And is it possible that Darren Yates is behind it?'

'Is that why you and him had your wee chat outside?'

So, he had seen it. Rebecca wondered why he hadn't come out when he saw it turn physical.

'He started it,' Bill explained. 'He warned Rebecca to keep her nose out of island affairs and tried to flex his muscles. I had to point out to him the error of his ways.'

A slight smile. 'He's fond of flexing his muscles. I've had to explain the very same to Darren on a few occasions.'

'Why didn't you intercede?' Rebecca asked.

The smile broadened. 'Mr Sawyer here had it under control. If it had turned nasty, I would have got into it.' He looked around him again, leaned in closer. 'Anyway, I was hoping Darren would get a wee bit of a skelp. He's got it coming. I've wanted to do it myself for a long time.'

He clearly didn't always follow the book.

'Why haven't you?' Bill asked.

'I'm savouring the anticipation. He's a cunning lad but he's not infallible. One day he'll put a foot wrong, and I'll be there to catch him.'

'So, you think young Darren is behind these threats, then?' Rebecca pressed.

A frown. 'I didn't say that. I can't say that because, a) I don't know for certain that these are threats, and b) I've no evidence to link him to any of the incidents.'

'But he could be, right?'

'Anyone could be. I think you'll know that islanders don't like outsiders poking around, and some of the older ones don't like them being here at all. There's very few but there are some who are arseholes.'

'Darren's not old,' Rebecca pointed out.

Bill added, 'No, but he is an arsehole, right, Rory?'

The police officer refused to be drawn on whether Darren Yates was an arsehole.

Rebecca asked, 'So, do you agree that there has been an increase recently in hostility towards incomers?'

He hesitated again. 'You might say that.'

'I saw the graffiti at the harbour,' Rebecca said.

'That's fairly recent. But people all over the world have grown hostile about something or other, I suppose. I've been here five years, and they still don't fully accept me. The incomers, aye, but not the island-born.'

Bill said, 'But, son, see if I was to press you – off the record, remember – would you say that if there was a connection to the reports, then Darren is the boy most likely to be behind them?'

Rory didn't want to be drawn on that, if he could help it. Rebecca pitched in to see his reaction. 'Maybe he sees himself as a defender of the purity of the island blood, something like that. Maybe it's just something him and his mates are doing for a laugh. What do you think?'

'I'll say it again, I've no evidence to suggest he is behind these incidents and nothing concrete that links them to the buy-out.'

'But it's only committee members who have been targeted.'

'That's not true. There have been other cases, all over the island, even some stock being stolen. We found the animals later, but in another grazing area.'

Donnie hadn't told her that, but then she was experienced enough to know that people only tell her what they want her to hear, or what fits their own scenario. She was never surprised. People are what they are, and it is her job to take what they say and find the other side of the story.

There are three sides to a story. Elspeth's voice. *Their version, the other version and the truth.*

She was disappointed in Donnie and Fiona, though. They should have told her.

'The thing is,' Rory continued, 'all this could be something as simple as kids carrying out pranks, a bit of mischief.'

'And Emily Thorne's shed being torched? Is that a prank?'

She almost mentioned Donnie finding Sonya's photograph on his boat but then remembered he hadn't reported it.

His face grew more sombre. 'No, that was more serious, I admit.'

'The person responsible more or less said it was because of the buy-out.'

'No, he said it was because she wasn't an islander.'

'Sometimes you have to read between the lines, son,' said Bill.

'There's nothing between the lines but empty space, Mr Sawyer, unless you write something there yourself, and that's not something I like to do.'

Rebecca glanced at Bill and saw him smile approvingly, even though in his time he had written entire books between the lines. They weren't going to get anywhere with this questioning, so Rebecca decided it was time to take another direction.

'And what about Callum McMaster?'

Bill asked, 'Who's Callum McMaster?'

'There's no evidence linking him to any of this, either,' said Rory.

'Who is Callum McMaster?' Bill asked again.

'That doesn't mean he isn't linked,' Rebecca said. 'Didn't you mention him yourself to Emily Thorne?'

That prompted a grudging shrug from the police officer and a look that suggested he was ashamed of being so open with the woman.

Bill grew insistent. 'Will someone please tell me who the hell Callum McMaster is?'

Rory was unwilling to enlighten him, so it was left to Rebecca. 'He was born on the island but left when he was in his late teens. He met a man called Morton White—'

'That name rings a bell,' Bill said softly.

'A former army demolition expert,' Rebecca nudged.

Bill's face brightened as he dragged something from the recesses of his memory. 'Back in the seventies, wasn't it? The bombing of the barracks down south and the attempt at the Post Office Tower in London, right?'

'He was nabbed when he was transporting a load of high explosives towards the Houses of Parliament. He was also involved with criminal gangs in Glasgow, Liverpool and London, using bombs to intimidate witnesses, bump off rivals, that sort of thing.'

'I remember him. The actual case was before my time on the Job, but I read he died after he got out the jail . . . what, six or seven years ago?'

'Yes.'

'So, what does this McMaster character have to do with him? He a bomb maker, too?'

'He didn't build them, but he helped plant them. Drove the van for White, who was a handy bloke with dynamite and Semtex but couldn't drive worth a bugger. If he got behind the wheel of a car, it was only a matter of time before it crashed into something, which was not advisable if you were carrying high explosives in the back.'

'You said White worked for the boys in Glasgow, but if I remember rightly from the reports when he copped his whack, the bombings were political. It wasn't an independence thing, was it?'

'No, good old-fashioned anarchy. He believed society was corrupt to the core and he wanted to blow it all up. The work with the criminal gangs was merely to pay the bills.'

'So, McMaster went down along with him?'

'Yes.'

'And he agreed with White's views on society?'

'He did. He served his time, bummed around the mainland for a while before he came back here, right, Rory?'

Rory considered his reply. 'So I understand.'

Bill asked, 'But if he was just a nutjob who thought society was going down the tubes, why would he be in the frame for the incidents here?'

Rebecca watched Rory carefully for any change of expression, but he remained stone-faced. 'His views were extreme. He was a clever man, very erudite. He left here to go to university, got a PhD in sociology, wrote for some dodgy publications, letters to newspapers, that sort of thing.'

'Don't tell me, some of what he wrote was about English people coming to the Highlands and buying property, right?'

'He called them colonists, just like the graffiti. He was quite vicious in his invective. And not just about the English – anybody with money, really. He wasn't too keen on Lowlanders using the Highlands and Islands as holiday-home heaven, either.'

Bill looked at Rory. 'And that's why you think he might be involved now?'

'I didn't say he was involved.'

'You suggested that to Emily Thorne,' Rebecca reminded him.

Another aggrieved look. 'I spoke out of turn. I shouldn't have done that.'

'Leopards and spots,' Bill said. 'First rule of policing, son.'

'No, the first rule is evidence, and there is none.'

'Have you spoken to him?'

He sighed. 'Rebecca, Callum McMaster is well liked around here. I've no reason to link the incidents to him. The person who spoke to Ms Thorne was not from the island, but Mr McMaster still has his local accent, despite being away for a long time. Even she doesn't think he has anything to do with it.'

Neither did Donnie or Fiona, Rebecca thought.

'But you did,' she insisted, 'otherwise why mention him in the first place?'

'As I said, I spoke out of turn.'

Bill said, 'I'll tell you what you did, Rory. You put two and two together, son, and that's another rule of police work.'

'Sometimes two and two don't add up to four, though.'

'So, what you're saying is, you haven't spoken to him?' Rebecca said.

'That's a police matter, but I'm satisfied he has no involvement.'

PC Rory Gibson was good. He was giving the appearance of being open without telling them anything. She didn't blame him for not opening up to her. He didn't know her, and her dad had told her that any good police officer should be wary of the press until they know the individual involved.

The media is useful but only to an extent. There are good and bad reporters, and it takes time to know which is which . . .

'Before I left the mainland, I was warned off this story,' Rebecca said.

'I know,' Rory said. 'A DCI Roach phoned from Inverness. Off the record, of course. She asked the same questions you are asking.'

'And what did you tell her?'

'The same as I'm telling you. We've logged all the reports, issued crime numbers, and they are being investigated but there is nothing to follow. No eyewitnesses. No physical evidence.'

'No CCTV? No doorbell camera footage?'

He gave her a wry look. 'This is Stoirm. We don't have a lot of that.'

'You will now,' Bill said. 'Word's out about these incidents, and I'll bet there's a run on getting them fitted.'

'Not necessarily a bad thing,' Rory said, but there was sadness in his voice, as if marking the end of an era.

'What do you know about the rival bidders for the estate?' Rebecca asked.

'Only what everyone else knows.'

'And what's that?'

'That there's a rival bidder for the estate. A consortium of businesspeople.'

'Have you had any contact with them?'

'No, why should I?'

Rebecca couldn't think of a single reason. 'Are there people here sympathetic to them?'

'A few. They think that a group with capital behind them have a better chance of making a go of it, of improving employment opportunities, than some well-meaning locals.'

'What do you think?'

'It's not my job to think either way.'

'Is there anyone who is sympathetic and might take matters into their own hands?'

'Not as far as I know.'

'What about strangers on the island?' Bill asked.

'We always have strangers on the island.' He smiled. 'They're called tourists, Mr Sawyer.'

The sound of hammering reached Rebecca. 'What about the people working on the hotel? Are they local?'

'No, they've been brought in from the mainland.'

Bill asked, 'Have you checked them out?'

'We're not a vetting agency. As long as they keep their noses clean, there's no reason for us to pay them any attention.'

'And have they? Kept their noses clean?'

'Not a peep out of them. They live in the hotel, they work in the hotel, they buy groceries at Sinclair's store, they drink in the bar. They've given us no reason to even look in their direction.'

The door behind him opened and his sergeant appeared carrying a mug of tea in one hand and a bacon roll in the other. He stopped when he saw them, his eyes flicking first from Rebecca to settle on Bill.

'Fuck me,' he said, 'the sights you see, eh? Bill Sawyer. I thought you were dead.'

'No, I was just in Dundee,' said Bill.

Rebecca had recognised that the sergeant's accent was from somewhere on the Scottish east coast but she didn't pin it down until Bill spoke. She was useless with accents. But she did identify a certain tension in the air when Rory's gaffer appeared. She'd noticed Bill's reaction when he heard his name earlier, and now she knew there was bad blood between them.

'But you'll be heading for the grave sooner than you think if you keep piling them into your gut,' Bill said, nodding first to the bacon roll then to the sergeant's ample stomach straining his uniform. The plate of pie, beans and chips he had consumed earlier popped into Rebecca's mind and she thought of pot and kettle calling each other names. Then she thought of her own plateful and unconsciously pulled her shoulders back and sucked in her gut.

Sergeant Nisbett's lips tightened as he laid the mug and roll on the counter. 'Aye, you weren't always in shape. I saw you throwing a few of these down your throat back in the day.'

'I realised the error of my ways.'

'No them all, I'll bet.' He faced Rebecca. 'What are you doing here?'

'This is Rebecca Connolly, gaffer . . .' Rory began.

'I know who she is, lad. I was asking why she's here.'

'I'm looking into the reports of increased vandalism on the island,' Rebecca replied.

'And why would that interest a famous investigative journalist like you?' The way he said investigative journalist made it sound as if she was something he'd just scraped off his shoe.

'There's a suggestion they might be linked to the community buy-out of the estate.'

'They're no.'

'You're certain?'

'Aye. You can print that in your story, too.'

Bill asked, 'You've looked into it, then, Pete?'

'Aye, I've looked into it and I'm telling you there's no connection. The increase in vandalism is just kids getting out of hand.'

'Kids like Darren Yates?'

'Darren Yates is a would-be gangster. We'll sort him, don't you worry.'

'I am worried, Pete, that's the problem. I think there's something more here.'

'And what business is it of yours, eh?'

'He works with me,' Rebecca said.

'Does he now?' He stared at Bill. 'You used to hate the press.'

'I used to eat bacon rolls, too. Sometimes you realise you're wrong.'

Sergeant Nisbett took a deep breath, then jerked his head towards Rory Gibson. 'What's this one been telling you?'

'Nothing,' said Rebecca, which was more or less true.

Nisbett weighed this up. 'Aye, well, that's because there's nothing to tell.'

'We think there is,' Bill said.

'I can't help what you think.'

'We've got a series of reports, most of them connected to the people involved in the buy-out. We've got an increase in anti-incomer hostility.'

'How do you work that out?'

'There's graffiti down at the harbour, for God's sake. And a woman was told to leave after an attack of wilful fire raising.' He jerked his thumb towards the door. 'You've got a gang of neds across the road there who just threatened Rebecca, and you have a known terrorist living here. It doesn't take Albert Einstein to put it all together.'

'I told you, it's nothing. High jinks. It'll calm down. As for Cal McMaster, I don't care what this one here has told you, but he's looking for a quiet life.'

Rory had obviously raised his own suspicions about the man. 'I told you that PC Gibson said nothing,' Rebecca insisted.

Nisbett was unconvinced. 'Aye, so you said. But Cal's done his time, you know? He's paid his debt and, as far as I'm concerned, that's it. As long as he keeps his nose clean, then we leave him alone, and I've made that clear to my officers.'

All which confirmed that Rory had wanted to talk to Callum McMaster.

'I suggest you do the same,' Nisbett continued.

'I don't think we will be, Pete,' said Bill.

The sergeant took another breath. 'You were always a fucking troublemaker, Bill Sawyer.'

'That's not the kind of language you use in front of the public, you know that, Sergeant Nisbett.'

The sergeant's thumb jerked in Rebecca's direction. 'She's no the public, and neither are you. So, why don't you both just fuck off out of here and do whatever the hell it is you want to do, stir up muck in order to sell newspapers or books or telly shows . . . Aye, I saw you on the telly, darling, speaking up for that killer, the one who murdered the undercover cop. And I read that book about the Murdo Maxwell case. You helped get that bastard out of jail on that one, eh? You like the crooks and the killers, don't you, darling? You like nothing more than embarrassing Police Scotland.' His head snapped back to face Bill. 'And you're helping her do it. You're a disgrace to the Job, Bill fucking Sawyer.'

'Now, you wait—'

'No, don't be getting all holier-than-thou with me. I know you, remember. I know you've got more skeletons in your cupboard than a careless fucking undertaker. So, off you pop, the pair of you, but I'm warning you – if I receive one complaint

209

about you bothering people, I'll have you picked up and off this island so fast you'll no need the ferry, 'cos you'll fly across the Sound. Understood?'

Bill was unimpressed by the speech. 'You were always one for the gab, Pete. While proper coppers were doing the job, you were the one giving it all the chat. I'm not surprised you've ended up here, out the way of real police work.'

Before Nisbett had the opportunity to retort, Bill turned and pushed through the glass door into the street. Rebecca was caught by surprise by the suddenness of the move and stood for a moment, feeling she should say something but unable to come up with any words, though a smile was beginning to form as Nisbett's face turned red with anger. She gave Rory a quick sideways look and followed Bill out.

She caught up with him outside. Darren and his pals were gone, and the Square was deserted. She sensed Bill's rage and so said nothing as they walked towards the Spine. She risked a look in his direction, saw the tightness of his facial muscles. Finally, she couldn't keep it in.

'I didn't know you disliked Dundee, Bill.'

He started to laugh quietly, the tension beginning to dissipate. 'I don't, it's a lovely city, and I still eat bacon rolls. It's him I don't like.'

'Why not?'

'Because he's a lazy bastard and I don't like lazy bastards. He's never done a decent piece of policing in his puff. How he ever got to be sergeant I don't know, but then I've seen tossers rise higher than that. That young cop, he thinks there's something wrong here – I saw it in his eyes, but he was playing the game, which is fine – but Nisbett? He either doesn't see it, or he sees it and he doesn't want to address it.'

'Why would he not want to address it?'

'Don't get your hopes up, it's not because he's taking backhanders.'

'I didn't think that.'

'Aye, right, there's nothing gets your blood pumping more than the prospect of a bent cop. He's just a lazy bastard, that's all. Simple as that. To address it might bring more work and he's too busy stuffing his face to want that.' They walked on a few spaces before he continued. 'I didn't know he was stationed here because I've not been for a few years. But now I do know, I'm all in. I wasn't sure about this, Becks, I was only here because I owe it to Elspeth to look after you.'

'I don't need looked after, Bill.'

'Aye, you do. We all do, in a way. And Val would have my guts for knicker elastic if I let anything happen to you.'

'Why?'

'Because if anything happened to you, it might cause her paperwork and she doesn't like paperwork. It makes her cranky and the last thing I need is Val to be cranky.'

Okay, it was time to broach this. 'Is there something going on between you and Val Roach, Bill?'

'Define "something going on",' he said, avoiding the question.

'Are you and her getting it on?'

He laughed. 'Dear God, you're a child out of your time. Getting it on? I don't even use that expression any more, if I ever did.'

'Stop stalling. Are you and her an item?'

'A gentleman never tells.'

'May I remind you that you're no gentleman?'

'True, but I'm still not telling.'

'I'll take that as a yes.'

'You're a reporter, so you'll take it whatever way that suits your story, I suppose. Anyway, from here on, I'm all in, Becks. We're going to prove there's something dodgy going on here, if only so I can rub it in Fat Pete's face.'

26

Mr Quilp found Mr Drood in his room, stretched out on the king-sized bed, a necessary expense for a man of his size. He was watching *The Quiet Man* on TV. He was very still, his ankles crossed, his hands resting on his chest, fingers threaded. Quilp had a keycard so had let himself in. Drood had a keycard for his room, too. They had been working together for many years and understood the need, if only occasionally, for access to each other's sleeping quarters, because standing outside and knocking was not for the likes of them. It was much easier if they could simply walk in. If one or other was perhaps engaged in practices of a private nature, then the 'Do Not Disturb' sign was an adequate precaution to prevent being disturbed. Drood was a calm man, often a quiet man like John Wayne on the TV screen, but he had a most energetic libido so had on many occasions taken advantage of that arrangement, but Quilp, whose ability to forego the pleasures of the flesh with ease would make a celibate monk green with envy, had never found the need.

As Quilp had expected, the room resembled the sight of a small riot. Drood's clothes were scattered hither and thither. There were empty plastic water bottles on the floor and chocolate bar wrappers surrounding the waste bin as if laying siege. Quilp resisted the urge to tidy up. If Drood was happy in such bedlam, then it was no business of his.

Drood's eyes didn't leave the screen as the Duke dragged Maureen O'Hara across half of Ireland. A woman had just offered him a stick with which to 'beat the lovely lady'.

'They wouldn't get away with that now,' Quilp observed.

Drood shrugged. In the pursuit of his employment he had assaulted a number of lovely ladies in his day. He derived no pleasure from it, it was just something he did when ordered. In all the time Quilp had known him, he had never shown any real emotion, no sympathy, no empathy. He was as close to a machine as a man could get. Even the ladies he enjoyed were sent away as soon as he had spent himself, for post-coital intimacy was not his way. The ladies, those who were not professionally orientated, often took offence to such treatment, and more than once Quilp had been required to quell not just their ire but the distaste of hotel management for the unseemly disturbance created in their normally silent hallways. Quilp himself took his pleasures with young men whose discretion was assured by the exchange of considerable sums of money. He was not ashamed of his sexuality, but he did guard his privacy most jealously.

'We have a task,' Quilp said.

Drood's eyes shifted and he waited for amplification.

'For Jarji Nikoladze,' Quilp said.

'I thought Head Office was done with him,' Drood said.

'They are allowing him to proceed, for now at least.'

'Why?'

Quilp shrugged. 'I have no idea, but it's not my job to question. His brother has contacted them, requested our services on his behalf, and they have granted them.'

'What have we to do?' Drood's eyes drifted back to the screen. He had no further interest in the why, just the what.

Quilp held up the slip of paper on which he'd written an address provided by Head Office. 'We have a young lady to visit.'

'Where?'

'Here in Glasgow.'

Drood grunted and focused on the film, where Wayne and Victor McLaglen were about to throw punches at each other. 'Good. I have an appointment later.'

Quilp left him to it, hoping that whoever was receiving his ministrations this time was a professional. He liked this hotel and didn't relish having to pacify its management.

27

Callum McMaster had been a handsome man. Actually, Rebecca decided, he was still a handsome man. His thick hair had once been jet-black but was now pure white and worn unfashionably long, his face was lined but the jawline was firm, though his neck was slightly wattled. Her research had told her that he had been in his mid twenties when he was arrested and jailed, so that made him in his seventies now. He was tall and looked fit, even if he wore double denim – shirt and jeans. She would lay odds that he had Old Spice in the bathroom cabinet.

Donnie had told her where he lived: a small, 1960s-built cottage near a little bay to the north of Portnaseil. Strangely, she had never travelled to this part of the island. She'd been to the south, and west to Thunder Bay, but never to the north. She found it quite beautiful, if lacking in trees, or any sort of vegetation apart from grass. They had picked up her car at the manse and then drove up the Spine through a flat landscape broken by lochans and rocks, while the seaward side was slashed by inlets and small carved bays ringed with sand, the still water turquoise blue and clear. They pulled up beside an old Toyota Rav 4 that badly needed a wash, though Rebecca was in no position to judge as she had to wipe her feet on the way out of her own car. A few yards further north the roof of another property peered over the top of a high hedge. A further little cottage clung to the western edge of the bay beside a short stretch of sandy beach. She stared at it for a few moments, wondering what it would be like to live in such a spot – idyllic in summer, she decided, but utter hell in winter – then turned to walk up the short garden path.

She would have preferred doing this alone, but Bill had insisted on accompanying her, citing his decision that he was 'all in' but adding that there was no way he was letting her visit an ex-convict alone. Bill took the leopard-never-changing-its-spots idea too far sometimes. It was true that she had been apprehensive about doorstepping the man, not because of his past but because she was always anxious beforehand, but she knew it had to be done.

When Callum McMaster answered the door, she had introduced herself, explained what she was doing, and – to her surprise – she was greeted with a smile.

'Why do I get the impression you were expecting us?' she asked.

'Because I was, Ms Connolly. Word gets around.'

'It's an island thing, right?'

'Exactly.'

He invited them in and his Highland hospitality extended to an immediate offer of tea, to which he would brook no refusal, and while he busied himself in the kitchen at the rear of the cottage, they settled in the small front room, enjoying the view through the wide window towards Skye, where wisps of mist clung to the jagged peaks, giving the island's profile a strangely prehistoric look. Bill remained on his feet studying the paintings on the wall, the furniture – functional if not overly expensive, and some of it obviously predating the cottage itself – and then the line of framed photographs on the high mantelpiece over a wood burner. He looked as if he was hunting for clues. She half-expected him to whip out a magnifying glass and drop to his knees to examine the spotlessly clean rug. He picked up one of the pictures, shot a brief glance at the door, and handed it to Rebecca, an eyebrow raised. She was surprised to see the man standing next to a somewhat younger Callum McMaster in the black-and-white photograph. Murdo Maxwell had been a Glasgow lawyer with political connections who was murdered in his holiday home in Appin. His young lover was convicted of his murder, and Rebecca's investigation of the case formed the basis of Elspeth's second book, *A Rattle of Bones*. Leo Cross was currently looking at making a follow-up documentary on the case. He'd had a two-picture deal with Netflix and although he already had interviews with her and Elspeth in the can, her boss's death had hampered progress. She studied the faces in the picture. Murdo Maxwell was also much younger than other images she'd seen of him, and she would estimate this photograph was taken at least fifty years ago.

Callum returned just as she was handing the photograph back to Bill and a guilty smile crept up on her. 'You knew Mr Maxwell?'

He didn't seem in the least perturbed as he set a tray down with a large pot of tea, three cups and saucers and an array of sandwiches on a coffee table. He held out his hand for the framed picture and Bill handed it over. He looked at the photograph with a sad little smile.

'Aye,' he said. 'I was younger then, as you can see.' He ran his fingers through his hair. 'Not so much snow on the roof, you know?'

'How did you meet?'

'Originally, he was speaking at a meeting of the GWP, urging us not to be so bloody stupid, that change would come but it would be brought politically and peacefully, not the way we wanted it.'

The GWP was the Glasgow Workers' Party, the members of which believed that social change would only come through civil disturbance. Through the party, Callum had also met

Morton White, who took the whole idea of civil disturbance to an extreme, and explosive, level. Other members had taken to bank robbery to finance the revolution that never came.

Callum poured the tea and indicated the sandwiches. 'I thought perhaps you'd be hungry, so I made up some sandwiches. Nothing too fancy, I'm afraid.' He smiled. 'I'm on a budget.'

The carb hit of the pie, beans and chips she'd had at the bar sat heavily in her stomach, but she took a sandwich triangle to be polite. Ham and cheese slices. He really meant it when he said it wasn't fancy. 'That's kind of you, Callum.'

'Cal, please. Callum makes me sound like that wee creature in those Tolkien films.'

Despite being away from Stoirm for many years, he still retained his island lilt. He had a nice voice and a pleasant, easy manner. It was difficult to believe that this snow-haired, elderly gent who was pouring tea into dainty little china cups was the same man who had once written that all English people who had bought properties in the Highlands should be forcibly removed and sent back home. Not to mention the man who assisted Morton White with his bombs.

She watched Bill ladle three sandwiches onto the plate, wondered where the hell he put it, then asked, 'So, Murdo Maxwell? You said you originally met him at a meeting – does that mean you met him again after that?'

He had wheeled round an armchair facing the window, where she presumed he sat regularly to take in the view, and sat down. 'I did, many times. He was a decent man, was Mr Maxwell. He was very helpful when I had my difficulties, which I'm sure you know about.'

His difficulties. That was a delicate way of being convicted of helping a terrorist bomber. She hadn't spotted the lawyer's name in the reports, but she had only scanned them to get the gist.

'He couldn't act for me, you understand, because I was arrested and charged down south, but he did offer advice. Not that it helped, of course,' Cal said, with a laugh. 'But then, I was guilty.' He handed her a cup of tea. 'In fact, it was Murdo who told me I should contact the authorities when Morton made it clear he was going to go after Parliament.'

He seemed very relaxed talking about his 'difficulties', so Rebecca pressed on.

'Do you regret what you did back then?'

He sat back in his chair as he considered the question. 'I'm asked that often, you know, and the answer is yes, of course I do. In my younger days I was' – he stopped to find the word – 'intemperate. I had my views and I wanted to inflict them on others by any means necessary.'

'Do you still hold those views?'

He breathed in deeply before he replied. 'Some of them, yes. I believe we live in an unjust society. We did then, we do now. The only difference is that back in those days they hid the injustice better than they do these days, and if they were caught, they resigned. Decades before that they would even have retired to a side room and done the decent thing with a pearl-handled revolver. Now anything goes, and when they're found out, they simply shrug their shoulders, apologise and carry on their merry way. And if they do resign, they still have some cushy job lined up somewhere.'

She liked to think that was changing, but didn't contradict him.

'Do you do anything about it now?'

That charming smile returned. 'You mean like helping someone set bombs?'

'Or write pamphlets, give talks, even write to the press?'

'Och, no. That's a young man's game. I'm happy here. I have my wee garden out the back, I have this place, I have the sun

219

in the morning and the moon at night – when the island lets me see them, of course. I'm content with that, Rebecca.'

'How did you manage to afford this place, Cal?' Bill asked, chewing on a sandwich.

'It was in my family. My parents moved here from the south of the island when I was a child. My brother lived here after our folks passed, and when he died, God rest him, it fell to me. I'd bummed around after I left prison, doing jobs here and there, never settled, so it was good to come home. The law of inheritance pays no heed to a man's criminal record, Bill, does it? Even though some people do hold it against you, eh?'

The way Cal's eyes crinkled, and the slightly bantering tone, suggested to Rebecca that he had recognised that Bill had once been a police officer.

Bill didn't care. 'You said you still hold the same views you did before?'

'Some of them.'

'Aye, some of them. So, don't you get angry with the way things are?'

'Don't you?'

'Yes.'

'So, what do you get angry about, Bill?'

'How we're ripped off constantly.'

'And who are we ripped off by?'

Rebecca was enjoying this. Cal had taken Bill's frankly adversarial approach and put him on the spot.

'Everyone. Banks. Insurance companies. Energy companies – don't get me started on the whole smart meter con. Lying politicians.'

Cal smiled. 'I agree with you, Bill. See? We're not much different in our views, really.'

'But I don't advocate forcibly moving folk from their homes.'

'Neither do I, not now, that was an example of my intemperate behaviour. Back then, I saw the way life here on the island was going – the decline in population, in living standards – and I needed someone to blame.'

'So, you chose the English,' Bill interjected.

Cal accepted that with a slight inclination of the head. 'I chose anyone with money, English, Scottish, whoever, and on all accounts I was wrong. Don't misunderstand me, I'm not in favour of houses being bought up as second homes to lie empty most of the year or to be rented out as those Airbnb things. That only pushes the price of property to such a level that they are unaffordable to the working folk here and contributes to depopulation. But I don't blame people for doing it, either. It's the way of the world, isn't it? Money talks. I fought against it when I was little more than a boy, but I'm not a boy any longer.'

'So who is to blame?'

'The people you mentioned, whether English, Scottish, American, German, French, Chinese, Russian. The people who control the money, who see humanity not as figures on a landscape but as figures on a balance sheet. They are the ones who should be targeted, not some retired schoolteacher or civil servant from Hampshire who wants to live the island life in the clean air.'

'But you didn't target financial institutions,' Rebecca said, 'even though some members of the GWP went for banks.'

'No, but perhaps we should have. We went for other targets to raise awareness of our message. It's like these protestors who spray paint over works of art or ancient monuments. They do it to draw attention, and it does, but in the end it's self-defeating. You lose any sympathy of the very people who you claim to be fighting for – the working people – and those with the money capitalise on that, twist it, sell it, and even though you have the best intentions, you become the villain.'

'You don't see yourself as a villain?' Bill asked.

Another smile from Cal. 'What I did was villainous, I suppose, but not my motive. I went about it the wrong way. I still believe what I believe but I've also come to learn that I can't change the world. I just want a quiet life.'

There was sincerity in the way he spoke, a sadness in his voice, which made Rebecca believe him.

'Are you aware of the community buy-out scheme for the Stoirm estate?'

'Of course. As I said, word does get around.'

'Are you also aware that members of the committee have been the victims of some curious incidents?'

'Aye, I'm aware.'

'What do you think?'

'I think there's some young folk with a most curious sense of fun here on Stoirm.'

'Do you think it's possible that some of these incidents are more serious than that? They do suggest a pattern.'

'PC Gibson asked me the same thing,' he said.

'He's spoken to you?'

'Oh aye, off the record, he said. He's a very diligent young man is PC Gibson. Hard-working. He knows about my past difficulties, and it would be remiss of him not to raise this matter with me, even if it was off the record. It seems his sergeant had instructed him not to pursue the matter.'

Rory hadn't mentioned that, but then, he had no reason to confide in them. It did suggest that he thought that there was indeed a connection. The slight smile curving Bill's lips showed that he approved of the young officer disobeying an order.

'So do you have any theories as to what lies behind these attacks?'

He laughed. 'Attacks, are they? I would say that's a very strong word for what I've been told has happened.'

'Someone had their shed burned down a couple of nights ago.'

His expression darkened. 'Aye, Emily Thorne. Nice lady. That was serious, I grant you.'

'A change in the wind could have made it even more serious,' observed Bill.

'Aye, you're right. That was going too far, right enough.'

'So do you have any theories?' Rebecca pressed.

'As I said, young people, bored perhaps, having what they think is fun. In Emily's case, taking it too far. I understand there have been other incidents involving people who are not connected to the buy-out.'

'They could be a smokescreen,' Rebecca offered.

'Or they could just be part of someone's idea of fun. We won't know until they are caught.' That smile again. 'Let me assure you, my dear, I've got nothing to do with what's been going on, whatever it is. I did my bit years ago, misguided though it was, and screwed it up into the bargain.'

'You made the call about Morton White, though,' Bill said. 'That wasn't screwing it up.'

'I should have done it earlier.'

'Why didn't you?'

'You know, Bill, I've asked myself that same question for nigh on fifty years and I still don't know. Was it fear? Was it my belief system? I can't say. But when he decided he was going to go after Parliament like some twentieth-century Guy Fawkes, that opened my eyes. The other bombs were not designed to injure anyone, let alone kill them. He planned to drive that van right into the gates – there wasn't the security then that they have now, even with the IRA threats of the 1970s. In doing that he would both hurt and kill, of that I was certain. I didn't get into the movement to shed blood, and that's the truth whether you believe it or not. I wanted to bring the money manipulators to account. In my naïveté I thought that our actions could help draw attention to the iniquities and inequalities of this country, which was then deeply corrupt. It's even worse now. But killing people was not part of my plan, so I contacted Mr Maxwell, asked him what he thought I should do, and he told me to inform the authorities. He warned me there would be a price to pay though, meaning jail time, but I couldn't allow Morton to go through with it. I told the police the route we'd be taking and arranged for us to be intercepted somewhere safe, in case Morton decided to fight it out. He carried two automatic weapons in that van, you know. I tried to spirit them away, but I wasn't able to and I was scared he would shoot it out with the police.'

'You helped the authorities, then. Why didn't your defence team reach an agreement that you wouldn't be prosecuted, or that you be treated leniently?'

'I could have, but I didn't want that. The scales had fallen from my eyes, Rebecca. I'm not religious but I've enough Presbyterian cant in me to know that we should be punished for our transgressions.'

He shot a glance at Bill.

'I can see I'm not convincing you. You're ex-police, aren't you?'

So he had sussed that.

'Aye, a retired DS.'

'It comes with the job, doesn't it? Such mistrust? I'm an ex-convict and therefore everything I say is suspect, right?'

Bill didn't look uncomfortable over having been accurately assessed. 'Aye, something like that.'

'Well, it's understandable. You and I have seen some of the worst humanity can offer, haven't we? You from one side, me from the other. To tell you the truth, I sometimes suspect myself. I have to damp down feelings of anger and revulsion at the injustice I see, which is why I've stopped reading newspapers and watching the news on television. But still sometimes it seeps through, you can't fully avoid it. And I feel the old rage building, at how corrupt and unfair this country is, and I need to remind myself that I'm out of it all and that's where I want to stay.'

He paused for a moment, his eyes wandering to the pictures on the mantelpiece.

'I was almost married once, did you know?'

Rebecca followed his gaze and picked out a colour shot of Cal with his arm around a woman with long dark hair and wearing a denim jacket and flared jeans.

'Flora,' Cal said, his eyes softening. 'A fitting name for what you might call a flower child. She was into peace and love, back when we thought that was remotely possible in this world. We met in the Muscular Arms in Glasgow. It's gone now, but back then it was a busy pub.' He faced Rebecca. 'You're from Glasgow, Rebecca, I can tell by your accent. Have you heard of the Muscular Arms? On the corner of West George Street and Buchanan Street, opposite what's now called Nelson Mandela Place, though we used to call it St George's Place? No, of course not, it was long before your time.' He looked back at the photograph. 'Flora was a student at the drama college, which was on the other side of the road. The Athenaeum, they called the building. It's a restaurant and a hotel now, I understand. Anyway, Flora and I met in the pub and fell in love over a few joints – the air of the Muscular Arms was ripe with marijuana smoke. All you needed to do was breathe in deeply and you were high.'

Bill studied the photographs. 'She was a bonnie lass.'

'Aye, Bill, she was that.'

There was a new sadness in Cal's voice, different from his earlier tone, and it was one that Rebecca recognised. This was born out of loss. 'What happened?'

'I let her slip through my fingers. As I became more embroiled with the GWP, and more and more intense in my beliefs, she pulled away from me. I felt it happen, knew in my heart that I was losing her, but did nothing to prevent it. She tried to pull me back from the excesses, tried to cool the heat of my rage, but I ignored her. Eventually she told me she was moving on, and I let her go.' He blinked. 'Biggest mistake of my life, because if I'd seen sense, then perhaps I wouldn't have made my next mistake, which was joining up with Morton White.' He inhaled as his mind travelled back in time, perhaps reliving that final conversation with Flora. 'What's the film? The one about life going two ways, with that Scottish actor and the American lassie?'

'*Sliding Doors*,' said Bill, and Rebecca shot him a surprised glance. He shrugged. 'I've got Sky.'

'Aye, that's the one,' Cal said. 'I suppose that was my *Sliding Doors* moment. If I'd listened to her, maybe my life would have been very different. No Morton White, no bombs, no prison and all that came after.'

'What happened to Flora?'

'I never saw her again. She graduated, got a job as a drama teacher in Perth. When I got out of prison, I contacted mutual friends and they told me she died of cancer.' He stared at the mantelpiece again. 'So very young to be taken. She'd never married, it seemed. Such a waste.' He fell silent for a moment, then repeated, 'Such a waste.'

Rebecca couldn't be certain whether he meant Flora's life, or his own.

'I'll tell you something, Rebecca,' he said. 'One thing I've learned over the years and through all the mistakes I've made is that you should never miss the opportunity for happiness. It's like sand – the trick is to scoop it up and hold it tight because it can easily slip through your fingers. That's what happened to me. I didn't hold onto it tightly enough. I let my own issues blind me to the path I should have taken, and that path led me to places I really wish I hadn't been.' He paused. 'But now it is what it is. I screwed up and I have to live with it. I wish I didn't, but I do.'

He was staring directly at her, as if he was trying to get something through to her, as if he knew about Stephen.

28

Sonya Kerr was packing so she could leave early in the morning for Stoirm when she heard her letterbox rattle. The security lock on the exterior door of the tenement had been out of order for weeks now – it had been reported to the landlord, but nothing had been done, which she had learned was par for the course in this building. The same man rented out every flat in the four-storey block and he only performed the bare minimum of servicing, the security buzzer not being deemed vital.

Angelique had gone out with her boyfriend, so she was alone to get on with throwing clothes into a bag. She had been due to go home in a few days anyway, so her dad's suggestion that she come back soon wasn't a hardship. Exams were done, the pub in which she worked at nights was closing down . . . Good God, a pub in Glasgow closing down. Time was, she'd been told by one of the regulars, that would have been seen as science fiction, but these days it was becoming, if not common, then certainly nothing to raise an eyebrow.

It wouldn't be Albie at the door, as she had finished with him the week before and he'd gone off in a strop. She'd caught the bastard shagging someone else, and he wouldn't come back to try to make up for things – he was too arrogant, too full of macho bullshit. Her dad had always told her to steer clear of boys who thought themselves manly because they went to a gym and/or played sport competitively. Playing for fun was fine, Donnie had said, but watch out for those who only liked to win. Because when some of them lose, they lose badly, and it's always everybody else's fault. Albie had taken the break-up very badly indeed and was no doubt spreading lies about her with his pals. It didn't matter, his friends were never really her friends – she'd never much liked the posh twats anyway. To be honest, that was one of the reasons she was glad to be going back to Stoirm, just in case she bumped into any of them. They would all take his side and that would irritate her intensely, so much that she probably wouldn't be able to keep her mouth shut.

The letterbox rattled again.

She finished zipping up the bag and walked from her bedroom to the front door. Through the spyhole she saw nothing. She frowned. Was it that bloody kid upstairs playing games? She swore softly, using words that would have her Gran reaching for the soap, and returned to the bedroom.

The letterbox rattled a third time.

She stormed back quickly, peeped through the hole again, still nobody. Little brat needed a lesson.

She rested one hand on the keys in the mortice lock, the other on the snib of the Yale, and waited. Within a minute she heard movement beyond the door and squinted through the peephole but saw nobody.

The letterbox rattled.

She twisted the key and the snib, loosened the security chain and jerked the door open.

Almost immediately a man stepped into view from where he'd been flattened against the wall and pushed her back with one hand on her chest. He was big and wide, his skin tanned, his broad handsome face impassive, his fair hair tied back in a ponytail. He was followed by another man, smaller, very blond hair, looked like an accountant in a smart blue suit, white shirt and blue tie, but he had a face that didn't quite add up. He closed the door behind him carefully, as though it might break if he wasn't gentle. She didn't like the look of them one bit, but she forced her voice to be calm.

'Who the fuck are you?'

'That is language unbecoming to a lady,' said the small one, his accent South African, his eyes flicking around him. 'But who we are doesn't matter. We're here with a message for your father.'

'My father? He's—'

'Yes, we know, he's not here, he's on Stoirm.'

Fear really took hold now. They obviously knew who Donnie was.

'But we have a message for him, anyway,' he added.

She swallowed hard, glanced at the large man whose hand still rested lightly on her chest. His eyes were languid, as if he found terrorising a young woman boring.

'Okay, tell me what it is and I'll pass it along.'

His mouth twisted into a smile. 'Aw, my dear, it's not the sort of message that you *tell* someone. It's the sort of message that you *show* someone. Isn't that right, Mr Drood?'

'That is correct, Mr Quilp,' said the large man. His South African accent was thicker, his voice deeper, as if someone had turned his bass level up to maximum.

The names registered belatedly. Quilp? Drood? What the hell sort of names were they?

Quilp reached into his pocket, pulled out his phone and raised it in their direction. 'I'd say smile for the camera, dear, but you're not going to be able to.' He then nodded to his friend. 'Get it done, Mr Drood.'

Drood's fingers tightened on the front of her T-shirt as he raised his right fist. She knew what was going to happen but couldn't stop it. She wasn't Wonder Woman, she wasn't some action hero, she couldn't stop that fist from landing. She felt

230

her legs weaken, then wilt, and she began to slump, forcing him to hold her up and press her against the wall. His facial expression still hadn't changed; even now when he was about to inflict pain, he remained deadpan. To him what he was about to do was routine, something he had done many times before.

Quilp was whistling through his teeth.

Drood's fist pulled back.

Sonya braced herself.

The letterbox rattled again.

Drood looked to the smaller man for guidance, who stopped whistling and raised his hand to tell him to hold back. The fist was lowered. Sonya almost wept with relief. The small man stared at the door, as if he was trying to see through it, but he wasn't a superhero either.

The letterbox clattered once more.

Sonya tried to call out for help, but Drood clamped his hand over her mouth to stifle any noise. It was a firm grip, not painful at least, but she managed a little squeal which she doubted would be heard in the hallway. The doors to these old tenements were solid.

Another flap of the letterbox.

She wasn't particularly religious but she prayed now. Please God, don't let it be that kid upstairs playing silly buggers. Don't let him just do this and run away.

Quilp gritted his teeth in irritation and thrust his phone back into the inside pocket of his jacket as he stepped closer to the door and asked, 'Who is it?'

'Pizza delivery,' said a voice.

Quilp gave Sonya a querying glance, and she had the presence of mind to nod. Whoever it was – whether the delivery man had the wrong door, whatever – this was her only chance.

'Just leave it out there,' Quilp said through the door. 'I'll pick it up.'

'Sorry, mate, it's cash on delivery. Need £10.50 from you. There's chips and all.'

Quilp breathed heavily as he tried to decide what to do.

'I'll tell you something, mate,' added the voice outside, 'this food's no getting any warmer and time's getting on, you know what I'm saying?'

'We've changed our mind. We don't want it.'

'That's your choice, pal, but it'll still be £10.50. See, if I go back without the wherewithal, they take it out of my wages, you know? So I'm no moving from here till I get it.'

Quilp motioned that Sonya was to be hauled out of the line of sight, and she was propelled towards the bathroom door. When he was satisfied that they couldn't be seen from the open door, Quilp took a couple of deep breaths, stretched that off-kilter mouth into some semblance of a friendly grin, then opened the door, his hand reaching into his pocket for money.

As soon as the lock turned, the door was thrown wide, the edge catching him full on the face. He hissed something that might have been in Afrikaans and reeled back, blood bursting from his nose. A man stepped over the threshold, what looked like a pickaxe handle in his hands, and threw Sonya a cheeky wink. She didn't know who he was, but she was glad to see him. Drood bellowed, released her and threw himself across the narrow hallway, but the man was already swinging, the solid wooden club catching the big man on the side of the face. Sonya was fairly certain she heard something crunch. Drood's forward momentum came to a halt, and he spun and slammed into the wall behind the door, but he didn't fall. He pushed himself away with both hands and actually growled as he lunged again, but a thrust to his gut with the flat end of the pickaxe handle doubled him over. A crack across his shoulders brought him down with a groan.

Quilp took the opportunity to make an attack, but the man whirled and jabbed his weapon straight into his face, sending more blood spraying, and this time Sonya knew she heard something crack. Quilp backed away, both hands covering his nose, blood streaming through his fingers and dripping down the blue suit. The man swung the club at his knees, and the impact made Sonya wince, even though he deserved it. Quilp cried out as his legs folded and he hit the floor hard. He wasn't whistling now.

All of this had played out in a matter of seconds, maybe even micro-seconds, and the silence that followed was intense. Sonya felt she should say something but couldn't find the words.

The man gave her a reassuring smile. 'Sonya, right?'

She nodded. In the aftershock of her terror, even that took an effort.

'I'm an old pal of your dad's.'

So many questions filled her mind and she didn't know which one to ask first. 'My dad? How do you . . .? I mean . . .' She aimed a trembling finger at Drood first, then Quilp, who was blubbering in the corner. 'How did you know . . .?'

'You dad and I met years ago – it doesn't matter how or why. He asked me to keep an eye on you, and I saw these two charmers arrive and followed them up.'

'But who are they?'

The man studied their face. 'Not a clue, though this one' – he swung the handle at Quilp, catching him on the shoulder, making him flinch and wail – 'certainly isn't from around here.'

'I think he's South African.'

'That right? I went out with a South African lassie once. She was tougher than these two put together. Anyway, let's get you away from here. You got a bag?'

She nodded and collected her bag from the bedroom while the man knelt beside Quilp.

'What's your name, pal?'

233

Quilp gritted his teeth. 'Fuck you.'

'Is that Mr You, or can I call you Fuck?'

'He's Quilp,' Sonya called from the bedroom. 'The other one's Drood.'

'What the hell kinda names are they?' He didn't wait for an answer, instead leaning in closer. 'Here's the deal. I'm taking the lassie here away and you better not try to follow, okay? I've already broken your face, and I'll break more if I catch you again. Your pal over there is still out of it, anyway. Tell who- ever sent you that the lassie is out of bounds, right? We don't involve family. I don't care who sent you but whoever they were, if they have an issue with Donnie Kerr, they take it up with him, not her. Now, I'm going to stay with her for a while, till I know she's safe, and if I see you again, I might not be so lenient, understand?'

A mumble that might have suggested some form of com- prehension seemed to satisfy him, so he leaned over Quilp and cupped his chin with his left hand and raised his head. 'Jeez, mate, you were no Brad Pitt before, but now you'd make Quasimodo swing back up to his belfry in fright. That nose needs some attention, mate. But first it's time for a wee nap. Night-night.'

He slammed Quilp's head against the wall and his eyes fluttered as he slid sideways.

Sonya followed the man as he slipped the keys from the door, stepped from the flat then closed the door behind him. At the top of the stairs she realised she was leaving with a strange man. 'I don't even know who you are.'

'I told you, I'm a friend of your dad's.'

'I mean your name.'

'Oh, aye.' He glanced at the door to the flat, as if checking it was still closed. 'The name's Malky Reid.'

Another thought struck her. 'Are we just going to leave them?'

'What do you want to do? Take them to hospital?'

'I mean, there in my flat?'

She was thinking about Angelique returning to find them till there.

'You're right.' He reached into the pocket of his leather jacket and handed her a car key fob. 'It's a blue Vauxhall, parked just outside the door. Get in, lock it, and don't unlock it until I come back, okay?'

'What are you going to do?'

He smiled as he selected the Yale from the key ring. 'I'm going to take out the rubbish.'

29

The problem with having an older brother like Ichkit was that he always acted like an older brother. Jarji had left his childhood long behind him and he no longer needed his big brother to look after him, but still Ichkit did. Jarji had heard them referred to as the Russian brothers, but they certainly didn't see themselves as Russian. They barely saw themselves as Georgian now, having found their respective places in the United Kingdom – Ichkit now living in London, where he oversaw their various enterprises, both legitimate and otherwise; Jarji remaining in Scotland, where he could pretend to others, and even himself, that he was his own man.

But he wasn't, not really, and deep down he always knew that.

His hands itched.

In the language of his childhood Jarji meant 'herald', and for many years he saw himself as just that, an advance man for his brother, looking after his interests, relaying his messages, following his orders. He longed to break free of that, to have something of his own, something he had built without Ichkit's help. That was why he was so focused on obtaining the Stoirm estate.

Yet, he hadn't been able to get this far without Ichkit's help. When word had reached him that the islanders were about to contact Rebecca Connolly, it was his brother who had smoothed the way for the assistance from the Corporation, because Jarji hadn't wished to use his usual people. After all, should the girl not heed the warning, then matters might turn unpleasant, and he hadn't wished to risk anything being traced back to them. The Corporation had agreed, as a favour, to send Quilp and Drood.

Now Jarji wished he had used his usual people. Asking Ichkit for assistance, and by extension that of the Corporation, had been an error of judgement, not simply because the men they sent had failed to dissuade her from taking an interest, but because it gave his brother the leverage to believe he could influence proceedings.

'I have the feeling that matters are getting out of control, Jarji.'

His brother had called him on the direct line they shared. Jarji had a number of cell phones, each with a different purpose, none of them registered to him. This one was reserved solely for conversations with Ichkit.

He took a breath to control his anger, looking at the flesh of his free hand. It had been scratched raw in the past few days and he'd forgotten to replace the cream. 'Everything is under control.'

'Nonetheless, my feeling remains. And I'm not alone.'

Jarji closed his eyes tightly, willing himself not to claw at the damned itch. 'I've told you, brother, I am in complete control.'

'The reporter has not been convinced to leave well enough alone.'

'That was because the men the Corporation sent were incompetent.'

'They are very competent, brother. I have used them myself.'

'Then they must have had an off day. I have tasked them with something new, so let's see if they can carry that out with any sort of proficiency.'

Ichkit's sigh was long and laboured. 'I don't understand your obsession with this enterprise, Jarji.'

Obsession. Quilp had used that word, saying it had come from the Corporation. Ichkit was part of the Corporation, so it had perhaps stemmed originally from him.

'It's not an obsession, it's a business arrangement,' he insisted.

'It's a plaything, brother, nothing more. You have had your eyes on this place since you were first taken there by Lord Henry Stuart all those years ago. You came home to me full of talk about it and you have never stopped since. I've allowed it because it gratified me to see you so full of enthusiasm. You were always a sullen child, Jarji, never showing any spirit about anything.'

'That's not true.'

'Oh, you were efficient, of course. You were committed. But you were never passionate about anything, not truly ardent. Except for this island and its land. So I encouraged it and have assisted when you requested it.'

Jarji wanted him to stop talking. To just stop. He gave in and began rubbing the hand on the top of the desk. 'And I thank you, Ichkit. I appreciate all you have done.'

Ichkit was silent for a moment, as if he didn't believe him. Then he continued. 'But your obsession is not restricted to the land, is it?'

'I don't know what you mean.'

'The reporter, Jarji. I mean the reporter.'

'She is a danger to us.'

'She is no danger to us.'

'She knows about the importing of labour, using the island.'

'That was many years ago, and there has been nothing to connect us with it since. And she has not reported on it. If she does know, then she cannot back up her information and, at this late remove, there is little fear of her finding anything of note.'

'She interfered with our Children of the Dell project.'

238

'Ah yes, but that had outlived its usefulness anyway, you said that yourself. We are insulated from both endeavours, Jarji, you know that, just as we are insulated from our current projects. She has neither the talent nor the resources to trace us, just as I'm sure you have placed many roadblocks and blind alleys between you and this current purchase.'

'She brought down our political outlet.'

'Mr Dalgliesh and his party were of little use to us in the long run. There was a chance at one time, but the political landscape changed, at least in the UK. And, if you remember, Mr Dalgliesh betrayed us.'

'He paid the price.'

'Nevertheless, it was his choice.'

'He betrayed us to her!'

'If it hadn't been her, it would have been someone else. But that does raise another point. Thanks to Dalgliesh, we became persons of interest to the police.'

'We are well insulated. They looked, they found nothing, they left us alone again.'

'Alone, for now. Jarji, this must end. The woman is not a threat. She never has been. The most she can do is nibble at the edges of our enterprises, but she will never get to the heart of them. She works alone.'

'She's not alone.'

'She has helpers, yes I know, but they are not experts. They don't have the resources or the funding to truly make a difference. And though we are well hidden in all our enterprises, there is always the possibility that someone with real ability traces us down.'

Jarji recalled a meeting with a police officer after the Children of the Dell incident and again with another after Dalgliesh had stupidly dropped his name within their hearing. Ichkit was correct, they were well insulated, but the police were aware of them.

'New York is unhappy,' Ichkit said.

'They have no reason to be.'

'They have every reason to be, brother, and if you would put aside your fixation on this enterprise, you would understand.'

'This is a business deal.'

'As I've already said, it's more than that. I know that and New York knows that. They have entertained you so far, but their patience wears thin. My patience wears thin.'

'Is that a threat?'

A sigh. Another long one. 'No. You are my brother, and I would never threaten you. It's because you are my little brother, my little Jarji, that I implore you to cease this obsession. Let it go. We have other work.'

Jarji could barely keep the rage from his voice. 'And if I don't, *brother*?'

'Then all it will take is another mis-step and New York's patience will evaporate.'

'And then?'

'And then we have a situation I would rather avoid. Think on this, Jarji, see sense. There is no profit in this for us.'

Ichkit hung up then. Jarji was angry but he had also recognised the rage building in his brother's voice. They both kept a rein on their temper, for a man who loses his temper loses everything, but like a geyser the pressure grew, and it had to blow. Jarji's had now blown. He wanted that estate. He deserved that estate. New York wouldn't stop him, his brother wouldn't stop him, Rebecca Connolly wouldn't stop him.

His hands itched.

Someone was snoring.

Mr Quilp thought it was himself, but when he awoke, he found Mr Drood propped up against him. At first he didn't know where he was but then pain sliced through his head,

240

front and back, and he remembered a man's face and the pick-axe handle and felt it slam into his face again. He touched his nose, causing fresh agony, looked at his fingertips, but he couldn't tell if the blood that coated them was fresh or the memory of what had happened in the flat.

Another snore.

He nudged the large man with his elbow, the movement sending a fresh stab of agony through his body. Drood protested in a desultory way, then gave a further snorting inhalation. Quilp steeled himself for further aches and nudged him harder.

'Wake up, for God's sake.'

Drood began to surface, grunting and groaning as he felt his own discomfort. Quilp gave him a moment and looked around. They were sitting on the ground, their backs against a wheelie bin, the lights of the tenement's rear windows looking down at them as if in judgement. The sky was dark. He had no idea how long they had been lying there and he didn't want to risk moving and generating a new wave of pain.

He gently probed his nose again. The man had said it would require attention and he agreed. The bastard had broken it. Mr Quilp had been very proud of his nose. It was straight and perfect, or had been. Aquiline, his mother used to tell him. Noses ran in the family, his father would joke. It was aquiline no longer.

He made tentative moves to rise, noting the blood that had spread down his suit, wondering if it would come out. Perhaps not completely. Once on his feet he paused to let the world stop spinning, his hand on the bin lid, which was filthy, but that was the least of his worries at that moment. His nose hurt, his suit was ruined, his head waltzed, but worst of all he would have to report this failure back to Head Office. It wasn't something he looked forward to, especially coming off the back of their failure to convince the reporter that following the story would be detrimental to her health.

Drood had roused himself and was standing unsteadily in front of him, slowly arching his back and then rubbing his gut. 'Who was that goddamned *bliksem*?'

His words were slurred, his jaw swollen and discoloured, perhaps not fractured given he was speaking.

'I don't know.'

'If I get my hands on him . . .'

'I don't think that's likely.'

They were professionals, he and Drood. *Bliksem*, Drood had called the man who had overcome them with apparent ease. Bastard. But he was more than that. He was also a professional, that much was clear. He came in fast, dealt with them without hesitation. He had handled men such as them before. A primary rule in their profession was never to underestimate the opposition, and that was exactly what they had done: first the reporter, now this. Quilp's mind turned to how he would present this failure, for failure it was. New York had little enthusiasm for this business and they would pull them out, of that he was certain. There was nothing to gain.

He began to walk across what his old gran had told him was called a back court. The shed which housed the wheelie bins was the midden. He was beginning to hate Glasgow.

30

'You sure that's the right thing to do? I mean, if that's what you want, fine, but . . .'

Matt Coyle had known it was heading this way all along, but he still felt the prickle at the back of his neck that told him it was the wrong way to go.

The voice on the other end of the mobile was firm. 'Let them off the leash.'

'Fine . . . fine,' Matt said, knowing there was nothing he could do to dissuade this guy. 'But my guys didn't sign on for that, not the really heavy stuff. There's already been rumblings . . .'

'Who?'

'Believe it or not, it was Duffy.'

'With his record?'

'Aye, I know, who'd've thought it, eh? But he's no chuffed with what we've been doing. I mean, he's been fine with the wee stuff, getting Elton into places to shift stuff around and that. The boy Darren and his pals handled the phone calls. But Rory wasn't happy with the torching of the shed.'

'I don't care what he's happy with. He's not here to be happy.'

'Aye, I know why he's here and it may come to that, but you know I'm no comfortable with it.'

'I also don't care what you're comfortable with, you understand me? You've got a job to do, so just do it.'

'Aye, right, you're the boss, but I've been thinking, why not use the local lads?'

There was silence on the line.

'Here's the deal. Darren's already had one run-in with the Connolly girl, right? And he's "known to the police", as they say, right? So let him and his crew handle it, give her a slap, maybe put her out the game for a while. He's canny enough to make sure that he has an alibi for whenever it happens, but if things do lead back to him then we always have Plan B, right?'

The silence was long and worrying. Matt didn't fully trust Ryan, but he didn't want to say that out loud. He'd chosen him, after all, abetted by Pat Murphy, who didn't like him and felt his daughter would be better off without him. And if Plan B wasn't needed, then the extra money Ryan put into the house would be handy, was Pat's way of thinking. He was only looking out for his lassie.

'Have you made it clear to Darren Yates what will happen if he grasses?'

'Aye,' Matt said, 'he knows the score.'

He heard breathing down the line. 'Fine, use the local boys. Just get it done, and get it done soon.'

Dot Blair had asked her father about Terence Williams, the solicitor who acted for the consortium intent on buying the estate. Rebecca had performed a quick check online and had learned that Anthony Blair KC (no relation to another Anthony Blair who once had the keys to the executive toilet at Number 10 Downing Street) had been toiling in the trenches of the legal profession for over forty years and had worn the silk for half of that time. Given Dot was only in her early twenties, she was presumably a late-in-life baby, for him at least.

'He always tells me that the legal world is both vast and small,' Dot said. 'There are lots of lawyers, yes, but it's never difficult to find someone who knows someone else who might know someone else.'

'And did he find someone who knew Terence Williams?' Rebecca asked.

Outside, darkness had dropped like a curtain and somewhere they could hear an owl hooting. Fiona McRae was in the church, attending a meeting of the WRVS in the vestry, so they had the study of the manse to themselves. She had kindly left them some coffee and scones, though. Rebecca's laptop was open to Zoom and on the screen Alan watched and listened. Chaz was out working, he'd explained. Bill was buttering a scone before laying some jam on it with a spoon. She had never seen him eat so much and she wondered if he had a tape worm. Either that or he was keeping his strength up for energetic bedroom activity with Val Roach. She closed her eyes momentarily against the image of wrinkly sex.

'He did,' Dot replied. 'In fact, he'd already heard of him but hadn't actually worked with him, so he spoke to a friend in the Society of Advocates—'

Alan butted in. 'This Terence Williams is a solicitor advocate, then?'

The legal profession was one of hierarchies. Solicitors were the bedrock in civil matters while, if accused of a criminal offence, they are the first line of defence. A solicitor can speak – argue a case – in the lower courts, but if the charge is more serious, a solemn procedure, then they are rendered mute in the higher courts and must retain the services of an advocate or a KC. That is, unless they trained to be a solicitor advocate, a hybrid granted special rights of audience in the High Court of Justiciary in criminal cases, or the Court of Session and Supreme Court in civil matters. In court they would wear a gown but not one that was silk-lined. That distinction was reserved for KCs.

'No,' said Dot, 'but the members of the society obviously deal with solicitors all over the country, as does my father. Mr Williams specialises in civil and company law but does do a little criminal work for one specific client: the McClymont family in Glasgow. Have you heard of them?'

Rebecca had heard of them. Joseph McClymont had inherited an empire based on drugs and intimidation from his ageing father, Big Rab, who she had heard was debilitated after a massive stroke. Joseph's name had come up during the investigation into the Murdo Maxwell case, though she had never had cause to meet him.

'So he's a bent lawyer,' Bill said, with a snort.

To Bill Sawyer, any lawyer who represents known criminals was bent. He had never said as much, but she suspected he thought the same of Stephen, who had acted for many a miscreant in Inverness.

'No, my father says he's honest, in the broad sense of the word,' said Dot.

Another snort from Bill. 'An honest lawyer. Now there's a contradiction in terms.'

'What does he mean, "in the broad sense of the word"?' Rebecca asked.

'Well, he suspects Mr Williams might not break any laws, and he emphasised the word "might", but he will advise clients how to circumvent them. He's as old as the hills, my father says, and over the years he's built up a list of contacts that would fill a library. He's reputed to be very experienced at hiding money and the identities of those clients who might not want their name attached to ownership of a particular company, which is why he is retained by the McClymonts. Legend has it that he knows, literally, where the bodies are buried.'

'These boys need to wash their dirty money,' said Bill. 'Bastards like this Williams character know where it comes from, but they don't care as long as they get their cut. They use dodgy accountants to funnel it to legitimate businesses, hedge funds and shell companies and the like, clean it up, send it out of the country to off-shore accounts.'

Bill also thought all accountants were dodgy. Bent lawyers, dodgy accountants, crooks who never changed. Bill's world was filled with larceny and mistrust.

'He knows about dark money?' asked Rebecca.

'Almost certainly,' Dot said.

Alan cleared his throat, and all eyes turned to the screen. 'And looking at what I could find on this consortium, if I was a betting man, I'd say that there was dark money here most definitely.'

'Can you prove that?'

'Nope. It's just a feeling. I searched online through Companies House, online registers, deep searches, et cetera, and ran what I had past my father and one of my brothers, and they agreed that yes, on the face of it, given the brick walls I hit, that there were investment sources involved here that the consortium didn't want traced, and so it follows that a clever man like Mr Williams had gone to great lengths to keep them hidden. If that was the case, it would take a team of forensic accountants years to unravel the complex web.' He paused, then added, 'Or, in the interests of balance, it's all legitimate and the people behind it just don't want their identities known in case it inflates the price. If a seller knows that, let's say, some software giant is interested in buying a company, then the share price can go through the roof. If it's an estate, then perhaps they don't want the seller getting greedy, thinking there's a bottomless money pit.'

Rebecca hadn't been given the go-ahead to contact the Hollywood star Ray McAllister, but would Lady Struan play hardball if she found out he was involved, she wondered.

'So this Williams guy could be acting for legitimate companies who just don't want their presence known?'

'Exactly.'

'But you don't think so?'

Alan shrugged. 'Let's call it intuition.'

Rebecca had learned to trust Alan's intuition.

'Let me recap what we have so far,' Bill said, polishing off his scone and carefully brushing his fingers free of crumbs over the plate. 'We have two bids for the estate, one a community buy-out that gets first dibs if they can raise the scratch, the other a consortium that may or may not be made up of dodgy finance being hidden by a clever lawyer with links to the underworld and who knows what else.'

'Sounds about right,' said Alan.

'In the meantime, we have intimidation attempts on members of the community group.'

'Allegedly,' Rebecca said.

Bill waved that away. 'I've no time for allegedly. We either work from the premise that it's true or it's not and, frankly, I think it's true.'

'What about the reports of people not involved also being tormented?' Alan asked, no doubt playing devil's advocate. Rebecca knew him well and he wouldn't be able to resist a conspiracy theory.

'Smokescreen,' Bill said, repeating Rebeca's earlier response to Rory Gibson. 'Hide the real targets among people they don't really care about. Now, some houses have been broken into – nothing taken, but things moved around. There's been nothing too serious yet.'

'Apart from Emily Thorne's shed,' Rebecca pointed out.

Bill conceded that. 'Aye, apart from Emily Thorne's shed, but everything else is fairly minor, right?' Something must have shown on Rebecca's face because he stared at her. 'Everything else *is* fairly minor, right Becks?'

The Kelpie wheelhouse being broken into and the photograph of Sonya Kerr had flashed in her mind. That had been a veiled threat, Rebecca was certain, but Donnie hadn't told anyone but her. Dot was leaning forward, her face eager, her earlier anger dispelled by being part of the team. Had she not been there, Rebecca might have told Bill and Alan, but she still didn't know if she could fully trust the young woman.

'Yes, all fairly minor,' she said, catching Alan watching her with an expression she knew well. He knew she was hiding something. Damn his intuition. She needed to throw something in the mix and, luckily, she had the ideal thing. 'Apart from Mr Quilp and Mr Drood.'

Dot was puzzled. 'Who are they?'

Rebecca told her about their visit to the office and the subsequent encounter in the Oban hotel.

Dot was silent after she had finished, no doubt considering her own position. Then she asked, 'Does this sort of thing happen often?'

'More than you'd believe,' said Bill. 'Rebecca attracts trouble like a shite does flies.'

'Thank you for that analogy, Bill, it's most flattering,' said Rebecca.

'Anytime,' said Bill.

Concern flitted across Dot's face. Not a bad thing. Perhaps she should learn that doing this kind of work could have consequences.

'That does tend to lend weight to the argument that there is a campaign of intimidation,' said Alan.

'Okay,' said Bill, 'so we're agreed and we have some heavy money at the back of it. Then we have Darren Yates—'

Alan's eyebrows shot up. 'Oh my God, is he not in jail yet?'

'You know him?'

'Chaz and I had a little set-to with him when we were on the island for our wedding.'

'Who is Darren Yates?' Dot asked.

'Local drug dealer,' Bill said, 'and would-be hard man. I'd say him and his compadres are behind the vandalism and maybe the phantom phone calls.'

'Can you back that up?' Alan asked.

'You're not the only one with intuition, son.'

Dot asked, 'But you don't think they're behind the break-ins?'

'We think they're professional jobs,' said Rebecca. 'There was no sign of forced entry, no damage at all, just things left out of place. Whoever did that, knew what they were doing, and I don't think Darren Yates knows much.'

'What about the arson attack?' Alan asked.

'Wilful fire raising in Scotland,' Dot corrected, as if by rote. She realised what she'd done and flushed. 'Sorry, force of habit, my father is a stickler for getting these things right. I didn't mean to correct you, so sorry, Alan.'

Alan gave her a mock glare.

'We don't think it's Darren's handiwork,' Rebecca said.

Bill disagreed. 'Him and his buddies are just the type who would get a kick out of arsing around with matches.'

Alan smiled. 'Or wilful fire raising around with matches.'

'The man who spoke to Emily wasn't from the island,' Rebecca said, 'even though Darren gave me some of the same kind of chat today.'

'What kind of chat?' Alan asked.

'Incomers poking their nose into island affairs, that sort of thing.'

'That does sound like him. Like his older brother, Darren is not the welcoming sort.'

'Which brings us to Callum McMaster,' Bill said, then waved a hand towards Rebecca so she could explain who he was.

When she was finished, she added, 'But nobody on the island believes he has anything to do with it and, I've got to say, having spoken to him, I agree with them. He might still hold his views but he's old enough to let them lie.'

'Rory Gibson might disagree with you,' Bill pointed out.

'Rory Gibson's a police officer and, like you, tends to believe that leopards don't change their spots.'

'Rory's a good man,' said Alan. 'But he's a police officer first and foremost.'

'Doesn't make him wrong,' Bill insisted.

'And it doesn't make him right, either,' Rebecca said. 'You met Cal today as well – do you still think he's carrying on some sort of campaign?'

'I don't know,' Bill admitted.

'Why would he do it? If he still holds enmity for southerners buying property up here, then why would he target the locals who are part of the buy-out bid? Would he really work for some shadowy consortium? It doesn't make any sense.'

'People don't make sense, Becks, you know that. They can seemingly act out of character, do things they wouldn't normally do for reasons only they know. But most of all, they don't change. They might say they do, they might look as if they have, but they don't. Not deep down.'

Rebecca shook her head. 'No, he's clean, I know it. He just wants a quiet life.'

Dot asked, 'So what do we do now?'

'I need to take tonight to get my head straight, maybe jot down a few ideas. There's a story here but we've not got it yet, not fully. Give me till morning then I'll have a clearer picture. But we need to know more about this consortium, Alan, which means I may need to speak to this Mr Williams. Dot, can you find me a number?'

'Yes, I can get that for you,' Dot said, beaming.

Rebecca knew she could do it herself easily, but she wanted to make her feel part of the team.

31

Dot enjoyed being part of the team. If she was being honest, she could understand why Rebecca had reacted the way she had in Inverness. By simply turning up, Dot had made an error, she saw that now. She thought it would show initiative, show her that she was serious, but now, with hindsight, she understood that such tactics should only be employed with those who are not likely to speak. Had she contacted Rebecca first, then Dot really believed she would have been more amenable. Suggesting that she find a case had been her way of holding out an olive branch, she supposed. Yes, she was aware that her being invited on board this buy-out story might be a means of diverting her from the Mhairi Sinclair case, but she didn't care. She wasn't anywhere near as experienced as Rebecca, who was only a few years older but had done so much in her career, which was why Dot had modelled herself on her. She would learn a lot in the next few days, or however long this took. And Rebecca was still engaged in this despite the fact that she had been threatened by those two men. What were their names . . . Quilp and Drood? What kind of names were they?

Rebecca had said she'd left a notebook in the car, a big one in which she noted background details. Dot, eager to please, happy to please, said she'd fetch it, bring it back. Rebecca gave her the key fob.

It was cooler in the dark. The day had been warm, not unpleasant, but now that night had fallen, it was fresher, a lazy breeze drifting up the hill from the water. She paused on her way out of the manse doorway, waited until the security light clicked off and stared up at the sky, wondering at how many stars appeared the more she looked. They didn't have skies like this in Edinburgh, even if she walked out in The Meadows at midnight. There was too much light pollution. There was no moon tonight, so it made the stars even brighter. Thousands, maybe millions, clustered in a strip making them appear like a band of mist stretching across the heavens. And the air was so sweet and, well, clean. She had never before enjoyed simply breathing.

She thought about home. Her mother and father would have finished dinner by now; he would be preparing work for the following day, she would be painting in her studio. Her mother loved art and had tried to instil that love in Dot, but while she could appreciate a beautiful landscape or portrait, any appreciation of technique, texture, even brush strokes, passed her by. Dot smiled as she recalled her taking her as a teenager to the National Galleries, dragging her round the various halls, with Dot being appreciative but unmoved by the artistry and beauty surrounding her, and then returning home and telling her father, with a laugh, that their daughter might as well go into law because she had no soul.

She hoped they were taking care of her cat, Woodstein, giving him the correct food, giving him love when he wanted it. She loved that little guy with all her heart. When she had that heart broken by a boy who turned out not to be the person she thought he was, it had been Woodstein who had helped her through. Her father was angry at the boy, of course, and her mother sympathetic, but even though the words 'You're young, you'll get over it' were never actually said, they hung in the air like a sign. Woodstein understood that she was sad, she was certain of it. He had been unusually clingy for the few days it had taken for her to bounce back. And it was only a few days. Dot was resilient and realistic.

She knew she was young, that she'd get over it, she just needed a little time to process it, file it under experience. The cat's purr as he nestled close to her in bed helped.

She pushed the button and Rebecca's car clicked, the lights flashing. When she moved again, the security light above the small open porch clicked on again. Rebecca had said the notebook was in the back seat, so Dot pulled the rear door open, the interior light activating, and she spied the book, a big one with a bright floral cover, on the other side of the seat. She half-climbed in, stretching for it. The manse security light clicked off. Then clicked on again.

She heard the slight movement, just a scrape on the gravel, then almost immediately felt the hands on her. Her cry of surprise was cut off when the back of her head slammed against the top of the car door as she was hauled out. She was thrown face down onto the gravel driveway and immediately the agony of a boot to her ribs coursed through her. She tried to get up, but another kick between her shoulder blades forced her down again. She tried to speak but a third blow to the side of her head splintered her vision into tiny bright lights, like the stars she had been admiring, but there was pain, too, a ringing, singing pain. She was being pummelled now, whoever it was moving around her, his breathing heavy, as he swung his feet at her shoulders, her sides, her legs, kicking, stamping, pain flooding, overtaking her. And she couldn't speak or breathe because the kicks kept coming, kept coming until another powerful blow to the side of her head jerked her body over and over again and she couldn't stop it, couldn't move her arms, and her legs were numb, and she knew this one was bad because something happened, something different, not just pain – it was as if she disconnected but she saw the stars again, the real stars, not the ones inside her head, and she had time to think how beautiful they were, and to think of her mother at her easel and her father at his desk and her cat curled on her and hoped he would be continue to be cared for and wouldn't miss her too much, before another blow to her head extinguished the stars and blew the thoughts from her mind and she felt nothing more.

32

When Jarji's phone rang at just before eight in the morning, he knew it was trouble. Ichkit was not an early riser and never called him before ten.

His hands began their damnable itching as soon as he heard his brother's voice.

'Are you alone?' Ichkit asked, knowing that Jarji often had women staying over.

Jarji could hear the anger in his brother's voice. Ichkit believed that to show anger was a sign of weakness, that it should be channelled, used, wielded like a weapon. He was always controlled, his tone always even, and he had urged Jarji to follow suit, but this time it was a struggle.

'Yes, I'm alone,' Jarji said.

'Have you heard the news from that island of yours?'

Alarm bells rang in Jarji's mind. A call at this hour from Ichkit was disturbing. To hear something had happened on Stoirm that he knew about first was even more so.

He began to scratch his hand unconsciously.

'No, what?'

'Tell me this, Jarji, did you order the death of that reporter?'

'No,' Jarji said truthfully. 'I only wanted her urged to leave. Why?'

'There's been a death. A young woman. Murdered.'

Scratch

That had to sink in. 'How do you—'

'I have a news alert for anything relating to this precious island of yours.'

'Why?'

'Why? Why, he asks. Because you are inserting yourself into that island's affairs, and I need to know what is going on.'

'When did it—'

'Just a few hours ago.'

Scratch

Jarji's mind raced. He had told them to let the local help off the leash, but he hadn't ordered a killing. If that had been necessary, he would have arranged professional assistance and Rebecca Connolly would have vanished, simple as that. He had toyed with the idea, but in the end decided against it. Even Quilp and Drood, who had proved incompetent but who he had been informed were not averse to taking lives, had been warned to intimidate only.

'This is a mess,' Inchkit said, his voice strained. 'And it needs to be contained.'

Jarji had keyed the words 'Stoirm' and 'murder' into Google, and scanned a brief report on the BBC News app. 'It doesn't say it is her. It could be any young woman.'

'It could be, but I find it something of a coincidence that there is a sudden death, declared murder, on the island, don't you? A young woman, not local, it says. A visitor, it says.'

'*Believed* to be a visitor,' Jarji corrected, angering his brother even further.

'Do not interrupt, Jarji. You are not in a position to correct me.' He paused, his breathing harsh as he controlled himself. 'I have heard from New York regarding the men they sent.'

Jarji frowned. That was more than he had.

Scratch

'It seems their latest attempts on your behalf have failed. There was another player in the game who injured them and took the girl away.'

They had allowed themselves to be bested again, by some cheap Glasgow thug by the sounds of it. First it was that man with Connolly, now this. If they truly were the best the Corporation had to offer, then he would hate to see their worst.

He almost said that to his brother, but now was not the time.

'What do you wish me to do about it, Ichkit?'

A long pause down the line. He could almost hear his brother reining in his temper. 'You know what I'm going to say, Jarji.'

He did but wanted to hear Ichkit say it. 'I really don't.'

'End this ridiculous quest of yours.'

'No.'

'Don't defy me on this.'

'This is my money, my enterprise, not yours, not any of our companies, not the Corporation—'

'And yet, you requested assistance.'

'I requested a referral to some professionals as I didn't wish to involve my usual contractors. Always maintain buffers between us and the work, Ichkit, remember? They are your own words.'

Even without seeing his older brother's face, he knew that would hit home. He could visualise him gripping the handset tightly, his mouth set in a thin line, as he concentrated on maintaining his composure.

Scratch

'I've spoiled you, Jarji,' he said. 'I ensured you had the best education, that you were trained in this business of ours, that you understood the need for discretion, the need to remain hidden—'

'And I have.'

'Let me finish!'

Jarji was startled at the rage and frustration in those few words. His brother seldom raised his voice but when he did, it was effective. He almost apologised but instead waited for him to speak again.

Finally, he did. 'I've indulged you in the past because you have also shown acumen and distinction in our other endeavours, but this particular indulgence must stop. End this and end it now.'

'Ichkit—'

'Do not defy me on this!' His voice was not raised but there was a tension present that gave Jarji pause. 'Those men have already reported back to New York and they take a dim view of proceedings on the island and in Glasgow. There is a danger that too much attention will be brought to bear, that the returns will be too nebulous.'

'It is not their enterprise.'

'In the name of God, Jarji, everything we do is their enterprise, don't you understand? Our fortunes are inextricably linked with theirs. Our successes are their successes, our failures are their failures and, let me assure you, Jarji, as you have obviously forgotten this, they don't respond well to failure.'

'I'm not failing.'

'Yes, you are. In their eyes.'

'And in yours?'

Another pause, then Ichkit's voice softened. 'Yes. I'm sorry, but I've never understood this need of yours to possess this island. But it must end, and it must end now.'

'And if I refuse?'

'Don't refuse, brother. Just do as I ask.'

'You're not asking, Ichkit, you are ordering.'

'Then do as I order. Pull back from this scheme. Sever all ties before it's too late.'

'And if I don't?'

Another pause. Another deep exhalation. Then a voice filled not with threat, or anger, but with sadness. 'Don't test me on this, brother. Do what you know has to be done. Or I will. And do it now, Jarji.'

Scratch

And then he was gone. There was no goodbye. No protestation of brotherly love. One second he spoke, the next the line was dead.

Jarji was unwilling to abandon his dream, but he knew he had to. He knew his brother, knew his moods, knew the cadences of his voice. He meant what he said when he said he wasn't to be tested. Jarji knew that he had made a mess of things, that was always the risk when he was forced to use buffers – but that was what Ichkit had taught him. Until now the system had worked. In this case, the buffers he'd put in place were insufficient, inept, incompetent.

Ichkit had been a good brother, but Jarji was uncertain how far filial love went. If New York ordered direct action, he might not take an active role but he wouldn't do anything to stop them. Couldn't do anything to stop them.

He checked the time again, made a mental calculation. Ichkit had said to draw a line under this, and he would do it. He didn't have time to contract the work out, and he didn't trust those fools sent by New York to do it. He would catch the first ferry he could to Stoirm and take care of business personally.

Despite his disappointment at his dream collapsing, Jarji felt a thrill he hadn't felt for a long time. He had been behind a desk for too long, but now he would take decisive action. Perhaps that would help stop this damned itching, he thought, as he reached out for the new tube of cream.

33

Sonya Kerr stood on the bow of the ferry and watched the dolphins cavort in the waves below. They leaped and swam, leaped and swam, as if they were herding the ship towards shore, which loomed ahead in the early morning haze. She always loved to stand here when she returned to Stoirm, watching the dolphins welcoming her home, and enjoy the sight of the island ahead. She loved the place and was always glad to be back, even though this time her thoughts were dark and confused.

Malky Reid had driven Sonya all the way to Oban and found her a hotel to stay the night. He even paid. Along the route, despite her persistent questions, he didn't tell her who those men were, what they had against her dad, or even how he knew her dad – or much about himself, come to that. All he said was ask Donnie, ask Donnie. His reluctance to explain anything only added to her unease.

That unease deepened when she hopped on the first ferry, which was often fairly quiet, but found it bustling with a number of uniformed police mixed with plainclothes cops. At least she assumed they were plainclothes cops, because they all clustered together, sipping coffee, having a breakfast roll bought from the ferry's café, talking quietly.

Something had happened on the island.

She had phoned her dad as soon as she saw them, but the call jumped straight to voicemail. So she phoned her gran, but

261

it went to voicemail, too. She looked at her watch, not even eight yet, but she would be at the shop, serving early customers. Her grandad didn't have a mobile phone, he hated them, but he'd be heading to the harbour to pick up the morning papers. He liked to get there very early, the only quiet moment of the day he'd say, and look at the water and the sky and the seabirds, perhaps throw some fish they hadn't sold the day before to any seals who showed their face.

She climbed to the deck, walked as far forward as she could and waited for the dolphins to find her.

Darren Yates lay in bed, the panic rising. He hadn't slept much and when he had, it was filled with visions of the girl lying on the gravel, the security light at the manse clicking on and off as it picked up his movements.

He hadn't meant to do it. He just wanted to teach her a lesson. And when he got the word from that bloke in the hotel, he thought it was fate giving him a sign, like it was meant to be or something.

Too much booze, that was the problem. And snorting the cocaine was a mistake, too. He only had one rule, one fucking rule, and he'd broken it, and now look at the shit he was in.

He'd only wanted to teach her a lesson. Rebecca Connolly. It wasn't until the girl had rolled over onto her back that he realised it wasn't her, but by that time it was too late.

His hands shook as he covered his face, trying to blot out the image of the girl's body flopping on the gravel. It had only taken a few minutes, maybe less. That last kick, the one to the side of her head, that was the one that did it. He'd really put his back into that one.

He took his hands away, looked down at the foot of the bed, at the clothes he'd had on. Get a hold of yourself, Darren, cover your arse. He sat up, scrambled down the bed to examine them. He couldn't see anything but there might be blood on the jeans. They would have to go, the boots he'd worn, too. In fact, everything had to go, there'd be forensic shit all over them. He'd seen it on the telly. *CSI*, *Silent Witness*. They could find tiny traces of blood and snot and saliva and hairs. DN-fucking-A.

Wait . . . Did he leave any on her?

He'd hardly been with her, was that enough to leave anything? He'd grabbed her shoulders to pull her out the back of the motor, but that was all. Apart from that, he hadn't touched her with his hands, just his feet.

Fuckfuckfuckfuck.

Cool it, Darren, he told himself. Calm down. One thing at a time. Get rid of those clothes and boots, have a shower, a right good scrub, just in case she left anything on you. Stay calm. Think. He needed to think. He needed an alibi. He couldn't trust any of the lads – they would burst under pressure.

Kayleigh. She would cover for him. She fancied him rotten, would do anything for him. And if she didn't, he'd make sure her boyfriend knew that they'd been shagging for weeks.

Felling more relaxed now that he had a plan, Darren rooted around under his bed, found an empty plastic bag and gathered his clothes in a bundle.

He'd fucked up but he could still get out of this.

34

'They fucked up, but it was nothing to do with me.'

Ryan had heard about what had happened to the girl reporter and had challenged Matt Coyle as soon as he saw him that morning. Elton stood by, listening.

'You should've sent me, Matt,' said Elton.

Fuck, Ryan thought, this was exactly what he'd been trying to avoid, but it had happened anyway. He wanted to say that things should never have reached the stage where they were giving someone a doing, but he didn't. He kept his mouth shut. He knew there was something more going on here that he couldn't put his finger on.

'I told you, it was nothing to do with me,' Matt insisted. 'That boy, Darren? He'd got himself into an argument with her – I saw it, right outside there – and he came off worse. He obviously got himself worked up over it, all doped up or boozed up or whatever, and went after her.'

'And got the wrong lassie.'

'Aye, tosser.'

Ryan didn't believe a word of it. He knew Matt had sent the boy after the reporter.

'So what do we do?' he asked.

'We keep our heads down, that's what we do. This island will be crawling with polis from now on.'

'I told you, you should've let me do it,' Elton said.

'Fuck's sake, for the last time, I never had nothing to do with it.' Matt was losing it now and he gave Ryan a stare that told him that he was blaming him for this fuck-up.

'We should leg it, surely,' Ryan said. 'Get away from this island on the next ferry.'

Elton giggled. 'Don't call him Shirley.'

Matt's sharp look cut the giggle off. 'Why should we worry?'

Because I heard you talking about me on the blower, pal, Ryan thought. And you're up to something.

'I mean, how would that look?' Matt continued. 'Naw, we stay cool, get on with the work in this shithole.'

'Christ, Matt, can you no see that the shit has hit the fan big style? They boys might drop you in it.'

'There's nothing to drop me into.'

'Okay, maybe no this,' Ryan conceded, but didn't mean it. 'But they were with Elton when he torched that shed.'

'Relax, Ryan, for God's sake, you'll give yourself a hernia or something. Elton wore a mask, right? At the fire?'

'Aye, I put it on before they arrived.'

But I didn't, Ryan thought, *and Elton pointed me out to them. There was something specific about the way he did it.* He didn't say that, though, because something prickled at the back of his neck, reminding him that this set-up was well iffy.

'They boys are smarter than people think,' Matt said. 'They'll have got themselves covered, I'm sure of that. The only one I had contact with was Darren, and even then never face to face, and he knows that dropping me in it is not recommended.' He paused, thinking. 'But maybe you're right. If he's no been hoovered up, maybe he needs to be reminded what side his bread's buttered.'

'Are you nuts, Matt?' Ryan said, that prickling growing. 'We need to stay well clear of him and his pals.'

265

'A wee word, maybe. A message. What you think, Elton?'

Elton shrugged. 'I'm up for it. The boy needs a slap for his haircut, anyway.'

'I'd rather Ryan did it,' Matt said.

Ryan held up his hands. 'I'm no hurting anybody, Matt,' he declared. 'I've got us into a few houses but I'm no hurting nobody.'

'You'll do whatever you're told, Ryan, because see the guys that hired us? They don't like being let down, and when they feel let down they take steps, you follow?'

Ryan had wondered who it was that had hired them, who it was that Matt spoke to in those secret phone chats in the office, but he had never asked about them. In their life, you didn't ask questions. But he did now. 'Who are they guys, anyway?'

'All you need to know about them, son, is that they're no the kind of blokes you want to piss off, right? Unless you want someone to hold a hot iron to your wife's face.'

That kindled Ryan's anger. 'You don't involve family, Matt.'

'Fuck that!' Matt laughed dismissively. 'See these notions you have of honour among thieves, they don't exist. They'll involve family, they'll even dig up your dead boy and mess with his corpse if that's what they feel like. They pay well, don't they?' He didn't wait for an answer. 'And anyway, we have to make sure we're no dropped in it.'

Ryan's anger broke free. 'Don't threaten my family, Matt.'

'I'm no threatening anybody, I'm telling you the way it is. You signed on for this job.'

'I didn't know—'

'Aye, you did, so don't come it. You knew you weren't being brought up here and paid a Klondike just to hammer a few nails. It was your other skills we needed. You can get into any house you fancy and you have the muscle to handle anyone that comes at you. We've used the first part, and now the time has come to use the second.'

266

'I told you, I'm no going to hurt anyone.'

'Don't test them on this, mate. They will fuck you up and anyone whoever said hello to you.'

Ryan looked from Matt to Elton, mind filling with all that he had heard or been told or had witnessed. In that moment, Ryan realised that he had walked into a trap with his eyes closed.

Rebecca was numb.

They had found Dot lying in the driveway, and Rebecca immediately knew. She saw the blood streaming from her ears, her nose, from a gash on her cheek, and she knew. She saw the way her limbs were splayed, as if they were detached from the hips and the shoulders and being held in place only by her clothing, and she knew. Bill had knelt by Dot's side to gently brush his fingers first across her cheek before placing them on her neck to feel for a pulse, and his shoulders slumped and his head drooped, and she knew.

'No,' she'd said.

Bill had looked up then. 'Phone the police, Becks.'

'No,' was all she could say.

He stood up, gripped her by the shoulders. 'Becks, go inside, call the police.'

Rebecca hadn't moved. She'd stared at Dot's lifeless body. 'I can't leave her.'

Bill understood. 'It's not your fault, Becks.'

She didn't reply but she knew it was. It really was.

'Don't touch her,' he said. 'Don't go near her, okay? Keep the locus clean. Do you understand, Becks?'

She'd stared.

'Becks?' He gripped her by the chin, forced her to look at him. 'Do you understand? Don't contaminate the locus.'

She'd managed to nod. She understood. Evidence. Forensics. So she went back to staring.

Bill sprinted back into the house himself. When his crunching footsteps ended, she was left alone in the dark. No, not alone, Dot was there. But she wasn't, not really. The air around her was warm but she was cold. Somewhere an owl screeched. The sound of the sea kissing the land drifted up the hill.

She didn't move when Fiona returned from the meeting, Bill already back out and heading her off at the gate, taking her to the other side of the garden. Don't contaminate the locus. Don't disturb evidence.

She didn't move when Fiona approached her, put her arm around her, held her.

She didn't move when the police car pulled up and two officers, male and female, climbed out. Bill spoke to them, the flash of the lights on top of the vehicle casting an intermittent blue glow over everything, and then they set about securing the scene.

She moved then, awkwardly, unwillingly, but she moved. Fiona gently dragged her back into the manse. Later, Dr Charles Wymark appeared. He was never called Chaz, that was for his son. Of course, she thought, he would have to be there. Not to treat Dot's injuries, because she was beyond that. But the rules of death had to be observed, so he would have to pronounce life extinct. She heard him talking quietly outside, then he came in and crouched in front of her, holding her hand.

'Rebecca,' he said. 'How are you?'

She stared again, not at Dot's lifeless body this time but at his face, and she saw the beginning of Chaz's features there. The same strength, the same kindliness. She told him she was fine, but he held her hand and told her to drink the hot sweet tea that Fiona had made. Rebecca repeated that she was fine, and he said to drink it all the same, so she drank it, and it tasted good, and the heat was welcome and the sugar was welcome, and she was even finer than she'd been before, but Dot wasn't fine and she wanted to scream that was the problem, because Dot would never be fine again and it was her fault.

So she sat there in the manse study while outside the business of death followed the rules. She heard more engines and more voices. One of the uniformed officers, the female, asked her a few questions.

What happened?

She was murdered.

Where were you when it happened?

I was here.

(I shouldn't have been, she thought. I should have been out there.)

Did you hear anything?

No.

Did you see anything?

No.

(That wasn't true. I saw Dot's body lying out there on the gravel, her body limp, her blood flowing, her life . . . extinct.)

What can you tell me about her?

Her name was Dot Blair, short for Dorothea – who's called that nowadays? And she wanted to be . . . no, she was a journalist. And she was young and irritating and keen and smart, and her father's a KC in Edinburgh, and I don't know anything else about her. I don't know her age, I don't know if she has a boyfriend or a girlfriend or a pet or her favourite colour. All I know is, she's dead and it's my fault.

The police officer left her. Rebecca hadn't caught her name and she doubted that she could pick her out in a line-up even though she had sat only two feet away during the interview. Was it an interview? Or just a chat? Rebecca didn't know. Didn't care.

She was numb.

Rory Gibson appeared briefly, then went away. That sergeant poked his head in, said nothing, left. Bill moved back and forward, making sure she was all right. Fiona, too. They knew she needed to be alone but also needed to know they were around.

The birds had heralded the rising of the sun, and the island had awakened. She heard a man's laugh, and she wondered what he had found to laugh at. Life goes on, she supposed. But not for Dot Blair.

It was her fault. She should have agreed to do the interview with her back in Inverness, should never have suggested she find a case, then Dot wouldn't have decided to take up the Mhairi Sinclair story, wouldn't have come to Stoirm, wouldn't have been noticed.

Wouldn't have been mistaken for her.

Rebecca was convinced of that. The attack was meant for her. It was her car she'd been at, and Dot had the same colour hair, was the same rough height and build. In the dark she would have been easily mistaken for her.

Rebecca closed her eyes against another image, of Elspeth in a Glasgow hospital, wires, machines, the beeps.

Then there were other images, flashing against her eyelids.

Her father, emaciated, old before his time, sitting up in bed, his eyes wide in terror as he faced something that Rebecca couldn't see.

A shot in a rain-filled darkness and a young man lying dead at her feet.

And the faces of others, people she had met, people she had interviewed, people who might not be dead if she hadn't interfered, if she hadn't been so intent on telling a story.

Grab hold of happiness, Cal McMaster had said, but how could she when she walked with death all the bloody time? And that was true. Death followed her like a shadow. How could she open Stephen up to that? He could have died while they were on holiday, for God's sake, gunned down by an idiot on steroids. She almost died herself because she had been too intent on finding the story to care about her own safety.

Too many stories, too much death, not enough life.

The sun climbed over the windowsill, slanted into the room, awaking motes of dust; at least that's how it seemed. Bits of dead matter, of dead skin, dancing in the warmth, showing more life than Dot Blair would again. The shaft of sunlight angled towards her, hit her feet, its energy melting the numbness. One of the police officer's questions came back to her.

Who do you think might have done this?

I don't know.

But she did know. She couldn't prove it, but she knew.

She stood up suddenly, aware of what she had to do.

35

Donnie met Sonya at the harbour. He took her bag without a word, scanning the other foot passengers as they alighted.

'Do you want to tell me what this is all about, Dad?'

He watched the marked police vehicles drive up the ramp, following the Police Scotland Incident Unit bus. He saw Ryan Gibson and Pete Nisbett meet a slim woman with short dark hair, shake hands, then lead her up the jetty.

'It's all connected to that,' he said.

'And what is that? I've been worried sick all the way over.'

'Not here, Sonya.'

He spoke in a distracted manner as an expensive 4x4 caught his attention. The driver's window was down and he glimpsed a profile he thought he recognised. He wasn't sure but it seemed familiar. Then the vehicle was gone, skirting past the police officers as they continued their way towards Portnaseil.

He led Sonya along the quayside to where the *Kelpie* was berthed. He didn't need to help her down the ladder, as she had been climbing on board and off since she was a child. Once they were settled on the deck benches usually used by tourists, he leaned forward, his elbows on his knees. He didn't say anything for a long time.

'Why don't you start with who those men were who attacked me last night, and who Malkie Reid is,' she suggested.

'Okay,' he said. 'First, I don't know who those men were, but I know they were sent by the people who want to stop the buy-out.'

'And who is that?'

'We don't really know. They've hidden themselves behind a screen of paperwork.'

'And Malkie?'

He took a breath. 'An old friend.'

'Yes, he said that too, but you've never mentioned him before, and he's never visited here as far as I know.'

'He was here, oh, a couple of years ago, maybe three. He was in Inverness on, eh, business and came over for a flying visit. You didn't meet him.'

'What sort of business?'

Donnie didn't know how to explain what Malkie Reid did for a living. She searched his face then nodded as if she'd found the answer.

'He was pretty handy with a pickaxe handle. Don't get me wrong, I'm glad he was, but I don't think he digs roads.'

He smiled. 'No, he doesn't. The main thing is you're okay.'

'No, Dad, the main thing right now is that you tell me what the hell is going on. Begin with Malkie. Where did you meet him? Why have you never mentioned him?'

He gathered his thoughts. 'You know I was . . . lost for a time, back when I was your age, right?'

'Yes.'

'You know I drank and did drugs. Went to Glasgow with your mum's brother.'

'Is that when you met him? When you were in Glasgow?'

'Yes. Malkie was . . . is . . .'

He stopped, looking for the words again.

'A criminal?' she offered. 'A hard man?'

'Not then. He was like me. Lost. Kind of angry at the world. He was younger, hadn't proved himself, and he wasn't going to as long as he was hitting the brown.'

'The brown?'

'Heroin. He realised before I did that it wasn't doing him any favours, so he weaned himself off it. Cold turkey. I think you know he's pretty tough.'

'Oh yes, I know that.'

'He's also one of the most honest people I know.'

'For a criminal, you mean.'

'Aye, but also honest people can be pretty dishonest. Malkie's a crook, there's no doubt about it, but he's an honest one, if that makes sense. When he was a boy, there was a guy who kicked around his streets, name of McCall. He was a hard man, too, but Malkie looked up to him, heard all sorts of stories about him. I suppose he wanted to be him, and in a way that's what he's done.'

'And you stayed in touch all these years?'

'Yeah, on and off. I didn't get clean as quickly as him, I had a wee bit to fall before that happened. He helped as much as he could. I caused a lot of trouble back then, Sonya, for my dad, your mum.'

Sonya didn't want him to go there. She had known for years there was something eating at him concerning her mother's death, but she wasn't ready to hear it. She sensed that him taking so much interest in island affairs was in some way a means of atoning for past sins.

'Did you know those men were coming after me?'

'Someone broke into the wheelhouse, left a picture of you taken recently outside your flat. It was a message. That was why I phoned you the other night, to get you to come home.'

'Why didn't you tell me the reason?'

He rubbed his chin, looked away. Rebecca had asked him something similar and he couldn't articulate it properly then. He was still having trouble. 'I don't know, Sonya. I should have, I suppose, but I didn't want to scare you, especially with

274

your exam coming up. Anyway, it could have all been just a bluff on their part.'

'But it wasn't.'

'No, it wasn't.'

'You asked your old friend Malkie to keep an eye on me?'

'Yes.'

'I'm glad you did.'

'So am I.'

She stood, craned up to peer over the quayside wall. Time was she would have had to stand on something to do that, but she had grown into a tall young woman. Like her mother. So like her mother. Donnie felt an old familiar pain stab at him.

'And why are the police over here in force?'

He rose and joined her, seeing the incident unit turning towards the Square. They'd park it in there, he thought, for the duration of the investigation.

'There's been a serious incident,' he said. 'A young woman was attacked up at the manse.'

'Dead?'

He nodded. Sonya blinked. She didn't know the girl but felt a kinship with her. His daughter was a lovely young woman, Donnie thought. She'd been wilful as a teenager, but who wasn't? He had been a wreck as a teenager and as a younger man.

'Who was she?'

'A reporter, helping Rebecca Connolly with a story about the buy-out.'

'Rebecca Connolly is back?'

She had first met Rebecca when she was at school, when the journalist was looking into her mother's death.

'Yes, I invited her over.'

A faint, grim smile. 'I'll bet that pleased Gran and Grandad.'

'No, it didn't, but we need the publicity and she's the only person I trust.'

Sonya sat back down. 'So who killed this young woman?'

'We don't know.'

'Nobody's been arrested?'

'No.'

'Do you think this is connected to the buy-out?'

'I really don't know. Maybe. Maybe not.'

But he knew it was. Somehow. And he felt grateful that it wasn't Sonya.

The bar had just opened and was busy. Rebecca wondered if it was always so packed, or if it was because word of Dot's death had swept across the island like a virus and people had flocked to Portnaseil to listen to the gossip. Stoirm islanders might be different, but they were still people, and murder always brought out the curious.

Eyes turned in her direction as she pushed open the door, some querying who she was, others knowing. She heard, thought she heard, her name being whispered, passed back and forward, but she didn't care. She was here for only one person, and she found him sitting at the same table as the day before, two of his friends at his side. They might have been the same two, but they were so interchangeable she couldn't be sure. She wondered if they were part of the crew who had jumped Dot.

Customers moved from her path as she walked straight towards him. He saw her coming, of course, and for a brief moment she saw surprise splash across his face.

'Surprised to see me, Darren?'

The shock had gone and he managed a small, but slightly mocking smile. He didn't reply, though, and his flesh was pale; there were smudges below his red-rimmed eyes. He did it, she knew he did it.

'Did you think I was dead?' she asked.

His eyes flicked slightly behind her, at the faces watching them. 'I heard someone had died up at the manse.'

'And you hoped it was me, didn't you?'

He shrugged. 'Don't care either way.'

She leaned on the tabletop, bent closer. 'I think you do, Darren. I think you came after me last night, but you made a mistake, didn't you? You got the wrong woman.'

He made a dismissive noise, his eyes darting away from her. 'You're talking rubbish. I don't know anything about what happened.'

'You're a liar.'

His eyes finally focused on her and flared a little, but he didn't rise to her. She wanted him to rise to her. She had to try harder.

'You're also a coward.'

His body stiffened. It was only a slight change in his position, but she saw it. Time to press harder.

'Just like your brother. Andy was a gutless piece of shit, too. It obviously runs in the family.'

That got to him. He stood up, his chair flying back and toppling over. 'You don't talk about my brother, you bitch.'

She didn't flinch, but she was ready if he did make a move towards her. 'You want to hit me, Darren? Eh? You want to punch me to the ground and then you and your pals can stomp all over me? Just like you did last night?'

She looked to his two friends, who were studying something very interesting on the tabletop. Yeah, they knew, too. She couldn't say that he'd boasted about it, but they knew. Darren's fists clenched and unclenched, but she knew now that he wouldn't try anything, not with so many witnesses. He was a liar and a coward, but he wasn't completely stupid.

'Her name was Dot Blair,' she said. 'I thought you'd want to know that.'

'I had nothing to do with what happened to her.'

'She was bright and hard-working, everything you're not. She had a future, but you took it away from her.'

'I didn't have—'

'She would have contributed something. You won't—'

'I told you!' he yelled. 'It wasn't me!'

'Yes, it was, you piece of shit. You, maybe others, maybe not. But you jumped her and kicked her to death. And all because you thought she was me. You were so stupid that you didn't even realise, did you?'

'That's libel, I'll have you—'

'We don't have libel in Scotland – it's defamation, dickwad. And it's only defamation if it's not true. And it is true; you know it, I know it, Tweedledum and Tweedlethickasshit here know it's true. So I will see you in court, but you'll be in the dock, and I'll be cheering the jury on when they find you guilty and you join your brother in jail.'

'I had fuck all to do with that lassie's death, can you no hear?'

'All I hear is a coward lying through his teeth.'

'That's enough, Rebecca.'

The voice came from behind her. She turned to see Val Roach in the doorway, flanked by Bill and Rory Gibson.

Darren pointed a shaking finger towards Rebecca. 'I want to make a complaint, she slandered me.'

Rebecca sneered. 'Defamed, Darren, don't you listen?'

Val Roach moved closer. 'Are you Darren Yates?'

'Aye, but she accused me of—'

'We'd like a word with you, if you don't mind.'

Darren swallowed, took half a step back, his face blanching even further, then he realised he was being watched and forced himself to save face. He adopted a defiant sneer. 'Am I under arrest?'

'No, just helping us with our inquiries.'

'I don't know anything.'

Rebecca's laugh was sharp, but Val's glare was even sharper. 'We'll see what you know and don't know. We won't keep you long, just a chat in the police station.'

Darren's cocky attitude was well in place. 'And if I don't want to go?'

Val looked around at the audience, her face severe enough to have most of them turn away lest she turn them into stone. 'Then you would hurt my feelings. And I don't like my feelings being hurt.'

'Darren, son, you're busted,' Rebecca said.

'Rebecca, be quiet, let us handle it from here,' Val snapped, then half-turned. 'Bill, take her away, will you?'

Bill took Rebecca by the elbow, murmuring, 'You need some food and some sleep.'

As he guided her towards the door, she twisted around and gave Darren an exaggerated wink. 'Maybe they'll let you and Andy share a cell,' she shouted. 'Won't that be cosy?'

Val Roach gave her another glare as Bill dragged her into the sunlight of the Square.

'Now tell me, Becks, what good did that do?' he asked as he steered her towards the road out of Portnaseil.

She felt a little drained. The adrenalin the anger had generated was beginning to dissipate. 'None at all, probably, but it gave me satisfaction. That bastard killed her, Bill. He might not have meant to, but he killed her.'

'Aye, I know. But it has to be proved, so let Val do her job, okay?'

'You would have done the same.'

'I would but I would have been wrong.'

'He killed that girl, Bill. She went out to fetch my notebook from my car and he killed her. Because he thought she was me. Can you understand how that makes me feel? She's dead because I pissed him off.'

He didn't say anything as they climbed the hill towards the Spine. Then: 'Val will get him.'

'Are you sure?'

He gave her a sideways look. 'What do you think? Right now you've got Darren Yates, boy blunder, one side of a table, and on the other is Val Roach. Who would you put your money on?'

She didn't want to say. Val was good but there were no witnesses and, as far as she knew, no physical evidence linked him or his pals to the murder. All he had to do was keep his mouth shut and he'd be home free.

36

Darren Yates wasn't under caution. He wasn't under arrest. He didn't request a solicitor. He was too cocky for that. He sat in the small interview room, one arm over the back of the uncomfortable plastic chair, a little grin playing. Or perhaps it was a sneer. If he'd had gum, he would have chewed it.

Val Roach thanked him for agreeing to the interview. Rory Gibson sat by her side.

'I didn't think I had a choice,' Darren said.

'You could have declined,' Val said.

A slight exhalation showed what he thought of that. 'Aye, and then what would have happened?'

'Nothing.'

He gave her a little squint, the smile dropping. 'Nothing? You wouldn't have lifted me?'

'Have you done anything that I should lift you for?'

What is a mix of a smile and a sneer called, she wondered. A snile? A smear? Whatever it was, it returned. 'No.'

'Well then, you have nothing to worry about.'

He looked at Rory Gibson. 'He's always trying to get me on something.'

'Never mind PC Gibson, concentrate on me, Mr Yates.'

Darren's eyes moved back to her and flicked up and down what he could see above the table. 'What do you want to know?'

'Dot Blair.'

He feigned innocence. 'Never met her.'

'But you know who she is?'

'Aye. She was the wee lassie that died last night.'

'Murdered, Mr Yates. Dot Blair was murdered.'

He shrugged. 'Nothing to do with me.'

'Did I say it was?'

'That bitch Connolly did. You heard her.'

'Has she any reason to say that?'

'No, she just doesn't like me.'

'Why is that, Mr Yates?'

'You'd need to ask her.'

'I'm asking you.'

He didn't answer.

'Have you had any sort of argument with Ms Connolly?'

Darren gave a little laugh. 'You know I did, otherwise you wouldn't have asked.' His chin jutted a little towards Rory Gibson. 'He probably saw it the other day.'

'What happened?'

'Ask him.'

'Why don't you tell me?'

One hand raised to rest on the table and then he began to slowly rotate it, as if he was washing the top. 'She insulted me. Her and that old guy, her minder.'

'In what way did they insult you?'

'He called me a moron. She said something about my brother.'

Val lowered her head to glance at the notebook in front of her, partly to hide the smile tickling her lips. 'Your brother would be Andrew Yates, correct?'

'Aye.'

'Who is currently serving time for attempted murder.'

'Aye, it was a fit-up.'

'You're saying that he didn't' – she made a show of reading the note again, even though she was already aware of the circumstances – 'drive his vehicle with reckless disregard, causing the one containing Charles Wymark and Alan Shields to leave the road and crash into the rocks known as the . . .' She searched for the name of the rocks.

'Seven Sisters,' Rory Gibson provided.

'Thank you, the Seven Sisters?'

'No.'

'The driver of a car travelling behind them said differently.'

Darren shrugged. 'It was an accident.'

'So which was it? A fit-up or an accident?'

'That Chaz Wymark bumped Andy's motor first. Then he lost control on the wet road and went flying off.'

'That's not what the witness said. That's not what Mr Shields or Mr Wymark said.'

'The witness was wrong and they two were lying. But what does it matter? Andy got the blame and was jailed. End of story.'

Val paused for a moment. 'You hold your brother's conviction against Mr Shields and Mr Wymark, don't you?'

'Of course I do. Those two lied through their teeth in court.'

'And you had an argument with them three years ago, in the hotel restaurant, I understand.'

Darren gave Rory another look. 'Aye, he told you about that, eh?'

'You delivered homophobic slurs—'

'I didn't slur anybody.'

'You threatened violence.'

'I'd had a couple of drinks, and they got my goat.'

'People get your goat very easily, don't they, Mr Yates?'

'What does that mean?'

'Did Dot Blair get your goat?'

'No, I told you, I've never met her.'

'But you'd seen her in Portnaseil, right?'

'Maybe. How would I know?'

'Come on, Mr Yates, it's not exactly Metropolis, is it? She'd been here for a couple of days. She was an attractive young woman, so I'm sure a big strapping lad like yourself would notice her.'

'Maybe I saw her once or twice.'

'And in one of those once or twice sightings, did you see her with Ms Connolly?'

'No.'

'Are you sure?'

'Aye, I'm sure. Why? Are they together? Are they lezzers or something?'

Val ignored that. 'Where were you last night, Mr Yates?'

'I knew it – I knew you were going to accuse me.'

'I haven't accused you.'

'Near as.'

'It's a routine question, Mr Yates. Where were you?'

'I was with someone.'

'Who?'

'Kayleigh Connors.'

Rory Gibson wrote the name down. Val glanced at him, and he nodded to let her know he knew who she was. 'What were you doing?'

'What do you think we were doing?'

'Where were you doing it?'

'In her place. She lives in a wee flat above the butcher shop next door.'

Another glance to Rory, another nod.

'And she'll corroborate this, I take it?'

'Well, she might need some persuading. She's seeing another guy, and she wouldn't want him to know that we were shagging, you know?'

'I can be very persuasive, Mr Yates.'

'You'll need to be.'

'I got you here, didn't I? Her reputation will be safe with me. Was there anyone else with you?'

'No, I'm no into threesomes.'

'So you weren't anywhere near the manse?'

'No, I told you, and I told that cow Connelly, I had nothing to do with what happened to that lassie.'

'Do you think there's anybody that would know?'

'Naw, no on the island. We're law-abiding here, right PC Gibson?'

PC Gibson remained silent but his face betrayed his scepticism. Val Roach stared at Darren for what seemed like a long time. It was a piercing stare, as if she could see through to his soul.

Darren's confident demeanour withered a little under the gaze and he squirmed slightly. 'Is there anything else, or can I go?'

'You can go, Mr Yates. I know where to reach you if I have to.'

He rose, flexed his broad shoulders and rotated his head back and to the side. 'Feel free. But next time I'll probably bring a lawyer.'

Rory stood and opened the door for him. A female constable waited outside, and he told her to escort Mr Yates from the police station. The formality sounded grudging, and Val couldn't blame him. She'd found it difficult herself to remain polite.

'What do you think, boss?' Rory asked after he'd closed the door.

'He did it.'

'Aye,' he said, folding his arms and leaning against the wall. 'So what do we do now?'

'Get a warrant to search his house, his clothes, go through them carefully. The victim bled profusely during the attack and there would be transference. It'll take time for the forensic and DNA tests to come back, given the body has to be taken to the mainland.'

'I didn't see any blood or skin under the deceased's fingernails, boss. It doesn't look like she managed to defend herself at all.'

Val Roach nodded. She knew that. The only hope she had was that Darren Yates would have been stupid enough not to destroy the clothes he'd worn, or that someone would fire him in.

'Let's go talk to this Kayleigh Connors,' she said.

37

Ryan hung around outside the manse. There were other people there – not many, all drawn by news of the murder – and they watched the investigation team go about their business, two of the island's constables making sure they didn't get too close. A tent had been erected over part of the driveway and Ryan assumed that was where the girl had been killed. He'd seen Rebecca Connolly being guided through a side gate back to the house by the guy he presumed was the man they said was her minder. He had the look of police about him, more likely ex-police. Ryan had wanted to speak to her, but his presence put him off. He didn't much like cops, whether serving or not. So he lingered, watching the comings and goings in the big tent.

He should be getting back to the hotel, as they would wonder where he was. But maybe he shouldn't go back. Maybe he should just get on the next ferry and get back home, leave everything behind, this whole mess. But that prickling in his neck told him he should stay, try somehow to get himself clear of the mess he had walked right into.

He was being set up. He'd worked it out now, put it all together. The conversation he'd overheard between Matt and whoever the hell was on the other end of the phone. The way Elton had nodded in his direction outside that cottage. The way that Darren had stared at him, as if he was clocking him specially. Matt saying that he'd never met the boy face to face.

Matt wanting him to threaten Darren, not Elton. It all added up. He was being set up as a fall guy if anything went pear-sharped, and it had.

He must've stood out there for an hour or so, trying to decide what to do next. He couldn't go to the law, as they wouldn't believe him. He was a known offender, and for violence, too, so they'd bang him up just for being there. He could maybe find a solicitor but he didn't know if there was one on the island. He couldn't phone his own guy in Edinburgh because it was Saturday. He couldn't talk about this with Rina because it was her dad who had put him in with Matt Coyle in the first place. That old bastard must have known what it was all about. If he got out of this with his liberty intact, he'd have a wee chat with Pat Murphy. He might be a hard man but so was Ryan. It was a chat that was long overdue, anyway.

The ex-copper came round the side of the manse and headed straight for him, making eye contact, too. Shit, that wasn't what he wanted. Ryan turned away and began walking back towards the village. He looked behind him, saw that the guy was following. Ryan picked up the pace, so did he. He didn't want to run, that would be an admission of something. But admitting what? He hadn't done anything. What the fuck was he worried about?

Ryan stopped and turned. 'Can I help you, mate?'

The guy stopped a couple of feet away, studied him with a practised eye. 'I wanted to ask you the same thing.'

'What do you mean?'

'You've been standing outside the house for over an hour.'

'Aye, so? I was watching what was going on.'

The bloke shook his head. 'No, son, you hardly looked at the actual locus.'

Locus. Ryan had been right: this guy was police.

'You were watching the house.'

'No, I wasn't.'

The guy studied him again. 'My name's Bill Sawyer. What's yours?'

Ryan knew when a cop was trying to worm his way into his good graces. He hadn't come up the Forth on a water biscuit. 'What's it to you?'

Bill Sawyer's jaw tightened. He was doing his best to be pleasant here. Ryan would have laid money on him being a hard bastard when he was with the police. 'Son, I've watched you for an hour. You're nervous about something. You've been hopping from one foot to the other, and it wasn't to keep warm. You never took your eyes off the house for little more than a second or two. I saw you looking at Rebecca when we arrived.'

The bastard had missed nothing. Ryan realised he should never have come here. He was out of his depth. Get back, grab his stuff, get the fuck off this island, that's what he should do.

'The minister – you know that's her manse, right?' Sawyer didn't wait for an answer. 'She says you're one of the guys working on the hotel. Up from Glasgow, she thought, but I hear Edinburgh in your voice, am I right?'

'What of it?'

'Nothing. But I think you've got something on your mind. Maybe you should tell me what it is.'

Another mistake, Ryan, what the fuck have you been thinking? You've not made a right move since you got out the jail. You listened to Pat Murphy, the bastard. You came up here, you agreed to do the break-ins, you should have legged it as soon as it turned nasty with the fire. And now this, hanging around in broad daylight and getting clocked by this guy, an ex-cop no less.

The guy edged a little closer. 'Son, do you know something about what happened to that lassie?'

'How the hell would I know anything? I'm just a joiner.'

'There's something on your mind. I was a police officer for thirty years, son, and I was good at it. We learn to read people and I'm reading you right now. You should've walked away from this conversation ages ago but you're still here. What's on your mind?'

Ryan looked over his shoulder, as if he expected Elton or Matt or anyone to be there watching him. This guy had sussed him perfectly. He did have something on his mind.

'I need to speak to that reporter.'

'Rebecca?'

'Aye.'

'What about?'

Ryan didn't answer.

'You're not going to tell me, are you?'

Ryan shook his head.

The guy sized him up again. 'You've been inside, right?'

'Does that make a difference?'

'It might. I'm sure she'll speak to you, but I'll be there, too. Does that change things?'

Ryan thought about that. He seemed okay, for a cop. 'I suppose not.'

Bill Sawyer gave him a stare, a hard stare, a cop's stare. Finally . . .

'Okay, let's go talk to her then.'

Matt Coyle had positioned himself at the window overlooking the Square. He'd spotted the police leading Darren Yates across to the community hub and wanted to see if they let him go. As he waited, he grew even more concerned. Things were going pear-shaped, and he didn't like it. This was supposed to be a simple job. Fix up the hotel, he had proper guys for that, but also convince some locals that they might be better off not being so keen to buy the estate. Matt didn't know who it was that had employed him, not for certain. He didn't care whether the land went to the community or to the rival bid. All he cared about was the money he was getting, which was good. He'd been told to have boys like Ryan and Elton on hand – Ryan to get them into the houses, Elton to mess the stuff around, maybe some rough stuff if needed. Matt had handled the Yates lad, but only by phone, so he was insulated there, he was certain. Elton had gone a bit far with the woman whose shed they burned. Him and the locals were only supposed to scare her a little. He'd exceeded his brief. Of course, there was another reason why Ryan was on board.

Now this lassie had got herself killed. That wasn't in the game plan, not as far as Matt was concerned. Scaring people, aye, maybe giving them a kick up the arse if necessary, but murder? No way. The local law was easily handled, but murder had brought the heavy mob over.

He stepped back a little into the shadows when he saw Darren emerge from the door to the community hub and stand in the sun for a minute, as if soaking up the warmth. He seemed relaxed. He saw him look up at the window, but Matt knew he couldn't see him. The boy then walked towards the bar, his cocky walk in full swing. Matt thought that the boy could swagger even when he was sitting down. Okay, he seemed confident, but too confident maybe? Matt had wanted him to be given a wee reminder of what was at stake if he opened his mouth, but the police had moved too quick. Or too quick for Ryan Duffy, who had dragged his feet.

He found Elton on his tod in the room Ryan was supposed to be working on.

'Where's Ryan?'

Elton was staring at a hammer in his hand. 'Beats the hell out of me. He said he had something to do.'

'Like what?'

'Didn't say. Saw him going out.'

'Out where?'

'No idea. He was heading towards the road up the hill.'

Something about that didn't appeal. Elton was still studying the hammer.

'You use the heavy end to hit things, by the way.'

'I know that,' Elton said. 'I was just getting the feel for it, you know?'

Matt didn't say anything further. Elton getting the feel for a hammer might prove useful. He left the hotel to go in search of Ryan.

38

Rebecca was cold so she sat in the study wrapped in a blanket sipping a cup of homemade soup Fiona had provided. Soup was the answer to all of life's ills, she'd said, along with the word of the Lord. It was Scotch broth and Rebecca felt it warm her, though there were some parts it would never reach.

The man sitting on the chair opposite was powerfully built. His hair was dark and a bit too long, his face pale. The mug of tea Fiona had provided was like a demi-tasse cup in his hand, and he hung onto it like it was the last lifebelt on the *Titanic*. He was nervous and hesitant and he kept glancing at Bill, who was positioned behind her wing-backed chair like a sentry.

'Mr Duffy, why are you here?' she asked.

'The truth? Because I'm shit scared. I'm getting put in the frame for things I've not been involved in.'

'But you did participate in the intimidation, right?' Bill said.

'Aye, but I don't want nothing to do with folk getting hurt. That lassie—'

'Dot Blair,' Rebecca said. 'She had a name.'

Vestiges of her anger remained, she realised. But who was she angry at? This man, who had nothing directly to do with it, at least according to him? Perhaps not. Darren Yates? Definitely. Herself? Without a doubt.

'Aye,' he said, 'Dot Blair. Sorry, I never met her. What happened to her was . . .'

His voice trailed, he shook his head, waved both hands in front of him as if trying to pull the words out of the air and not reaching them. Rebecca felt he was sincere.

'What do you want me to do?'

He took a breath, stood up and stepped to the window, from where he could see the tent outside. 'Help me.'

'How?'

'Speak up for me.'

'I don't know you – how can I speak up for you? What would I say?'

'That I had nothing to do with all this.'

'But you did,' Bill insisted.

Duffy didn't reply, and his shoulders drooped.

'If you have information, you should go see the police,' Bill said.

Duffy turned back. 'No way. I talk to them and I'm banged up right away, with my record. That's what this was all about, that's why I'm scared. I've been put in the frame for all this right from the beginning.'

'Maybe you are responsible,' Bill said.

'Think about it, would I be here talking to you if I wasn't telling you the truth?'

'Could be you're trying to be clever,' Bill said.

'I'm no that clever, believe me. If I was clever at all, I'd not be on this island in the first place. Look, I'm a joiner, right? But that's no why I was hired, not really. The bloke that hired us, Matt Coyle, he's never been inside, neither has Elton McGeachy, but they're not straight arrows. I kinda knew that straight off when I met them.'

'How did you know?' Rebecca asked.

'You get a feel for these things.' He jerked his head in Bill's direction. 'Same way as you spotted I was an ex-con. You had a feel for it, right?'

'That's right.'

'Okay,' said Rebecca, exhaustion building despite the soup.

Duffy moved back to the chair he'd been sitting in, but remained on his feet, desperation clear in his expression and voice. 'Miss Connolly, I just need to . . . I just want to . . . Look, I need you to help me make it clear that I've had nothing to do with what's going on.'

'But you *have* had something to do with it,' Bill insisted again.

'Aye, I know but . . .' He walked back to the window, stared at the activity. 'I've been stupid, I know that, but I needed the money, you know? I had the chance here to make some real cash, maybe put some aside for once, so I ignored the other stuff that was going on, thinking it was chicken feed, you know what I mean? I mean, it wasn't anything serious, not really, apart from that fire. But now it's turned heavy, the lassie—'

'Dot Blair,' Rebecca repeated.

His shoulders slumped again. 'Aye. That shouldn't have happened.'

'But it did,' Rebecca said.

Bill asked, 'Did this guy Matt Coyle order it?'

Ryan turned to face them again. 'It was talked about, but not her . . .' He gave Rebecca a sorrowful look. 'You know . . .'

'Me,' she said.

'Aye. But just a warning, maybe . . . you know . . .'

A beating, she thought. Maybe a beating. But beatings can go too far.

Bill asked, 'Who wanted it done?'

'Whoever it is that Matt talks to on the phone. The guy who told him about the local lads.'

'And you don't know who that is.'

A shrug. 'He just calls him the boss.'

'Any ideas who it could be?'

A shake of the head. 'He said they're heavy, dangerous, that I wouldn't want to cross them, that they'd come after my family if I did.'

He fell silent, his look from Rebecca to Bill imploring. He needed them to believe him, Rebecca understood that even through her exhaustion. But she found it difficult to care.

'Bill's right,' she said, 'you should go to the police.'

He was emphatic. 'No way.'

'The DCI in charge is a friend of mine,' Bill said. 'She'll treat you fairly.'

'No, you can tell her if you want, tell her I had nothing to do with it.'

'You need to tell her yourself.'

Duffy set the mug on a table. 'No, I can't.'

'You have to,' Bill insisted. 'If you're in the clear, like you say, then you've got nothing to worry about.'

Duffy's laugh was sharp and bitter. 'Aye, right. Matt said the folk behind all this were bad news, and I'm not putting my wife in any sort of bother by doing that.'

He was genuinely fearful. He was a large man, and Rebecca had the impression that he was no stranger to violence, but he was scared. She had seen such fear before. She had felt it herself, but she always managed to push through to the other side. She wasn't sure she could do it this time. There had been too much death around her. She needed stability. She needed security. She needed Stephen.

Then something else whispered in her mind. Something the man had said.

'This guy, the one on the phone to your boss, you've no clue, no inkling at all who he was?'

'No.'

She reached for her point, which was just out of reach, her mind sluggish. 'And he only spoke to him on the phone, right? You never saw him?'

'Yeah. And Matt only spoke to Darren Yates on the phone as well.'

'And you said . . .' She saw it then, recalled his words. 'You said this man knew about Darren Yates in the first place?'

'Yeah.'

Rebecca looked at Bill, who had realised what she was driving at. 'Only someone who was on the island could know about a ned like Yates,' he said.

Rebecca nodded. 'Whoever is behind this is local . . .'

Matt Coyle had walked up the hill to the road they called the Spine, where he found himself with a choice of left or right. He remembered an old uncle of his telling him that when you have two ways to go, always go right. He'd asked him why, but he never explained, probably because the old bugger didn't know himself. Still, he turned right and followed the road above Portnaseil. He hadn't seen that much of the island since he'd been here and, truth was, even though he was concerned about Duffy and where he was, he was enjoying this moment of peace and quiet. He'd been told Stoirm could be pretty tough in the winter, but today it was bloody gorgeous.

Up ahead on a rise to the left, he saw the church and a graveyard that looked ancient. Maybe Ryan had found religion and was up there praying. He'd certainly not been what Matt had anticipated. Yes, he'd got Elton into the houses, but his squeamish attitude to anything heavy was a surprise given his background. Matt had been unwilling to use someone he didn't know, but when it was explained to him why they needed someone like Ryan Duffy, he understood. Even so, Duffy's reluctance was unexpected.

He slowed when he saw the police car ahead, sitting outside an old house set back from the road. He saw the top of a white tent that experience told him was something they put up to protect a crime scene. That must be the manse where the lassie got herself killed. He didn't fancy walking past it. He might never have been banged up but that didn't mean he hadn't had brushes with the law, so he did his best to keep below their radar as much as possible. He looked back the way he'd come, then back at the manse, trying to decide whether to brazen it out. After all, it wasn't a roadblock, they weren't likely to stop him and ask any questions, and for all they knew he was just a tourist out for a walk on a nice day.

And then he spotted Ryan coming out of a gate at the far end of the manse garden. And with him was that bloke Matt had seen the day before with that Connolly woman. They stopped and exchanged a few words, then Ryan moved in his direction. Matt swore out loud and glanced around for somewhere to hide. He edged along the hedge, the leaves and twigs scraping his face, until he found a gate opening on the steps that led to the church. He pushed it, hoping that it didn't creak, then dodged through and crouched behind the hedge. He heard footsteps approach then saw Ryan's big frame walking past. He let him go, anger and suspicion growing in equal measure.

39

Rebecca wasn't sure she had the energy to do what she must do next in order to confirm her suspicions. She also had to do it alone. To take Bill with her would smack of intimidation, and there had been enough of that on the island. She knew he would argue that she needed some rest – and my God, that was true – but she had to see this through now. Dot's murder had knocked the breath from her, but now that she believed – no, she *knew* – that whoever was behind this was local, she had to follow it up. She owed it to Dot.

She made a show of going to bed, of being so tired that she couldn't think straight – there was a considerable measure of truth in that, after all – and waited until the house quietened down. Bill had said he was going to speak to Val Roach about Ryan Duffy, which was fine. Fiona had parish business to conduct, spending some time with a very sick member of her congregation. Once she was certain the house was empty, Rebecca dressed quickly, grabbed her bag and notebook, and crept downstairs, just in case she was wrong. The only sound she heard was the activity in the driveway as the forensic teams continued to conduct their searches.

Her legs were reluctant to move and she didn't think she had the strength to walk down the hill, so she decided to drive. Her car had been released by the forensic teams and moved into the church's small car park because the driveway remained sealed, so she took the side gate and walked sluggishly the few yards.

You can do this, Rebecca. You have to do this.

She parked outside the general store on the Square, gathering her thoughts and strength. Through the window she could see Molly Sinclair at the checkout, two customers waiting. Hector was at the post office counter, tapping at a keyboard, his glasses perched on the end of his nose, occasionally dipping his head so he could see over them at paperwork on the counter. He should get varifocals, she thought.

The last customer left and Rebecca shot a quick look towards the police station, in case Bill appeared, before climbing from the car. Molly saw her as soon as she pushed through the store's door.

'You're not welcome here,' she said, her voice making Hector look up from the monitor. He took off his glasses, dropped them on the counter and unlocked the counter door.

'Get out,' he said.

'Mr Sinclair—'

'Get out,' he repeated, advancing on her, his face tight with anger. 'My wife said you're not welcome.'

'I've got questions.'

'You always have questions,' said Molly. 'And your questions always lead to tragedy for somebody. That poor wee girl would be alive if it wasn't for you.'

That hit home because Rebecca had already shouldered that blame. But she had to focus. She had to get straight to the point.

'Who did you tell I was coming to the island, Mrs Sinclair?'

Her directness took the woman aback. 'What do you mean?'

'You're on the committee, you were present when Donnie suggested I be contacted to do a story on the buy-out. You were against it.'

'Yes, I was against it, of course I was. You bring nothing but heartache.'

Rebecca couldn't argue with that, but she had to press on. 'Who did you tell?'

Hector cut in. 'Don't you come in here and interrogate my wife.'

'I'm sorry, but I need to know, Mr Sinclair. I was threatened on the mainland, warned not to come.' She paused before she said her next words. She hadn't cleared it with Donnie, but she had to know. 'And Sonya was terrorised by the same people.'

That made him fall silent.

'But I saw her today,' Molly said, much of her aggression diluted. 'She didn't say—'

'But it happened. It was only because Donnie had arranged to have her protected that she's not injured. Or worse.'

Donnie had called her earlier that morning when he heard about Dot's death and had told her that Sonya was on her way home, filling her in on what had happened in Glasgow. The fact that their granddaughter had been threatened seemed to defuse much of their rage. Rebecca felt guilty about using it, but this was too important.

'Someone was told that I had been contacted and I think that person is here on Stoirm. I was threatened, Sonya was threatened and now someone is dead.'

'Because of you,' Hector accused.

Rebecca let that go. She couldn't wallow in introspection, not now. 'Some very nasty people want the community buy-out halted, Mr Sinclair, and they don't want anybody shining a light on what they're doing.' She returned her eyes to Molly Sinclair. 'I need to know who you told.'

Tears began to form in her eyes. 'I didn't tell anyone.'

'You did, Mrs Sinclair. It could only have been you. Nobody else on the committee was as dead set against me becoming involved.'

'I didn't.'

'She told me,' said Hector quietly.

Rebecca wasn't surprised. 'And who did you tell?'

'Cal McMaster.'

Ryan had packed up his gear and was about to leave when he was confronted by Matt and Elton in the hallway outside his room. Matt had a grim look. Elton had a hammer. This wasn't a good sign.

'Who were you talking to, Ryan?'

Matt spoke. Elton smiled. This really wasn't a good sign.

His first instinct was to bluff it out, but Matt got in first. 'I saw you, son, getting all chummy with that reporter's minder.'

Shit. He knew he shouldn't have come back to the hotel, but he wanted – needed – his tools. He'd hoped to get in and get out without being seen, or at least without anyone knowing where he'd been. He wasn't sure what he'd do after that, right enough.

'What were you talking about, Ryan?'

'Nothing.'

'There seemed to be a lot of words saying nothing. And he smells like ex-polis to me. You weren't talking out of turn, were you?'

'No.'

Elton looked at the tool bag in his hand. 'Where you taking your tools, Ryan?'

'Just packing them away properly.'

'Your clothes too?'

Ryan looked at the rucksack in his other hand. 'Thought I'd give them a wee wash. The washing machine in the kitchen's working, right?'

Elton began to walk around him. 'You're telling porkies, Ryan.'

302

Ryan turned with him. 'No, I'm not.' He glanced over his shoulder at Matt. 'Honest, I'm not, Matt.'

He shouldn't have taken his eyes from Elton. He knew it as soon as he did it, but by that time it was too late. Seconds was all it took . . .

Elton swung the hammer but at least Ryan was quick enough to dodge out of the way. It still caught him a glancing blow on the shoulder, which was painful enough, but it didn't lay him out, which was a good thing.

Seconds . . .

Ryan dropped his bags, launched himself at Elton, throwing a right which connected sweetly on Elton's jaw, sending his head rocking back, giving Ryan the opportunity to snatch the hammer with his left hand and throw it down the hall then follow it with another right to the same sweet spot to make Elton stagger.

. . . was all . . .

He grabbed handfuls of Elton's shirt and thrust him back against the wall, slamming him against the plasterwork, cracking it – that'll piss Jim, the plasterer, right off, Ryan thought – then buried his fist into the boy's gut, making him double over with a grunt.

. . . it took . . .

Ryan drove his knee into his face, straightening him again, then he finished it by gripping his face with both hands and slamming his head hard against the wall, sending flakes of new plaster cascading. Elton's eyes rolled and he tipped over.

Ryan let him go and spun towards Matt, who hadn't moved.

'That's what you wanted from me, right?' Ryan said, feeling the thrill of the action coursing through him. He hoped Matt would go for him, he really did, because he would pound that fucker into dust. But he was no threat. Matt was older and fatter, he was a talker and a leader, and Ryan didn't reckon he was up for the rough stuff.

Elton groaned behind him, began to move, so Ryan picked up his bags and stared at Matt until he had the sense to step from his path. He was at the head of the stairs when Matt finally found the balls to speak. 'You're fucked, son, you know that? They'll come after you for grassing.'

Ryan stopped, dropped the bags, turned, considering going back and delivering punishment, but decided Matt wasn't worth it.

'I've no grassed, no really,' he said, believing that talking to the reporter didn't amount to it. 'But you know what? Maybe it's time I did.'

He picked up his bags. Matt's voice raised. 'You're a dead man, Ryan Duffy. You hear me? You're a dead man.'

Ryan smiled. 'Speak up, Matt, maybe there's one of the other guys working around here who didn't hear you. Anything happens to me, you'll maybe need to go on one of they killing sprees.'

And then he skipped down the stairs and out into the Square, almost colliding with a slim woman with short, dark hair. She had a blue suit, a white shirt, flat sensible shoes and a look that could only be perfected after years with Police Scotland. Behind her was the young cop Ryan had seen around the place.

She looked at the bag in his hand. 'Mr Duffy?'

He didn't see any point in denying it. She'd have found his mugshot somewhere. Stoirm was an island, but the internet was everywhere.

'I'm Detective Chief Inspector Val Roach,' she said. 'This is Police Constable Rory Gibson.'

Nobody offered to shake hands. This wasn't a social occasion.

Roach nodded to the bag. 'Going somewhere?'

He almost laughed. 'I'm guessing across the road to the cop shop.'

She smiled. It wasn't filled with humour. 'That would be very kind of you.'

The reporter hadn't wasted any time telling the law about him, which was fair enough: he'd told her to do it.

40

Rebecca didn't want to waste any time. She was uncertain if Hector Sinclair would try to warn his friend that she was coming. She didn't think so, but it was possible that his hatred for her would outweigh his feeling of remorse for having perhaps placed his granddaughter in jeopardy. She had to get to Cal McMaster to ensure he didn't leave the island, which he might do now that events had turned lethal.

But then, he might be innocent. Just because Hector had told him about Rebecca coming didn't mean he was the person that Ryan Duffy's boss had been speaking to. Again, she thought about contacting Bill, getting him to come along, but there had been an edge between the two men at their first meeting. No, best leave him out of it. She could handle it.

Where have I heard that before?

Stephen's voice. Always cautious.

Stop and think, Becks.

She parked in a passing place far enough away from the cottage that he might not recognise her car if he chanced to look that way. Cal's car sat at his gate beside a powerful 4x4, suggesting he had a visitor. Or perhaps he was planning on fleeing the island and had called in a friend to help.

The sun was waning and a lamp was already turned on in a window of the small cottage on the bay, the light reflecting on the still water. She couldn't see the property behind the high hedge nearer to Cal's because it was obscured as the road curved to the left.

It was isolated here, and she began to wonder if she had been too impetuous. Maybe she needed someone with her. Cal McMaster was an old man, but he obviously kept himself pretty fit. And he was no choir boy.

She thumbed Bill's number on her phone, but it went straight to voicemail. He'd either switched it off or he was in a dead spot. If they were successful with the buy-out, Donnie and the committee would have to really work hard to improve mobile reception on the island. Or perhaps his phone had finally packed in. Damn it, get a new one, Bill. She left a message and settled in to wait.

DCI Val Roach was hard to read. They were seated in the small interview room in the police station, which to be honest wasn't much of a place. Just the public area at the front, an office at the back with two desks and two computers, a wee kitchen area, a toilet, this room. But then, it didn't need to be much of a place on the island, given there probably wasn't a lot of crime to speak of. At least until Matt had arrived with his crew.

'Tell me why I should believe you, Mr Duffy,' she said, her eyes boring into him. They didn't move away from him. He wasn't even sure she had blinked since he'd met her. That was freaky.

'Because it's the truth,' he said. 'I mean, why would I tell you all this if it wasn't?'

'To divert suspicion from you.'

'Aye, that's right, I'm a criminal genius and I thought all that out. If I'd been guilty, you know what I'd've done – I'd've legged it right away.'

'I don't know how your mind works, Mr Duffy. You could be Lex Luthor for all I know.'

Despite his nervousness, the image of this cop sitting up in bed reading a Superman comic made him smile. 'But I'm no.'

'No, you have too much hair.' She looked at the sheet of paper in front of her. 'You've got a bit of a record, haven't you, Mr Duffy?'

'I told you I did. Right upfront, I told you that.'

'That you did.' She read it again. 'So, knowing the full extent of your violent tendencies, and the fact that you have been involved in criminality for most of your life, I'll ask you again, why should I believe you?'

He couldn't reply straightaway. He stared at her, one hand rubbing his jeans as if it was wet. Which it was. He hadn't done anything wrong, not really. Well, not much. But he was still nervous. 'I don't know, I really don't. You've got my record right there in front of you. You'll know that I've never grassed anyone up in my life, even when it would have been in my best interests.'

'But you are now.'

'Aye, that's right.'

'Because?'

He rubbed his hands on his jeans again. 'Because . . . Fuck, I don't know that either, not really. They're going to try and put any blame on me, and I'm no having that. And I'm telling you, it was that boy Darren Yates who jumped that lassie.'

'We know that.'

'You know that?'

'Yes.'

'How do you know?'

She paused, a glint of a smile but only in her eyes. 'Let's say his alibi didn't stand up.'

'You've arrested him?'

'Not yet, but we will. How did you know he did it?'

'Matt Coyle, my boss, told me it was him.'

'But he didn't order him to do it?'

'No. Well, not to kill her. Just to scare her, maybe damage her. But not her – the other reporter, Rebecca Connolly.'

Those eyes hardened again. 'And somebody else ordered him to do that, you say?'

'Aye.'

'But you don't know who?'

'No. But he's local, I think.'

'What makes you think that?'

'Well, it was that Miss Connolly who thought that.'

She moved her head ever so slightly to give him a sideways look. 'Yes, you went to her instead of us. Why?'

'Because I don't—'

'Grass,' she said. 'Yes, very noble.'

'It was her and that bloke with her, the ex-cop.'

'Bill Sawyer.'

'Aye, that's his name. Suspicious bastard.' Like you, he thought.

'And what made them think that the person was local?'

'Because he was the one who told Matt Coyle about Darren and his mates in the first place.'

'Did they say who they thought it was?'

'No.'

DCI Roach exchanged a look with the young, uniformed guy, then back at him. 'And did you get the impression that she intended to follow this information up?'

Ryan frowned. 'She was pretty well out of it when I saw her up at the manse. I mean, really knackered.'

Her lips thinned in what was the first expression he'd seen. 'Believe me, Rebecca has a knack for getting herself into trouble. And she's never too knackered to do it.'

Everything around Rebecca was still. She had slid the car window open in order to get some air and the only sound she heard was the faint, rhythmic hiss of the waves on the beach.

She would have given anything to be able to walk to the bay, take off her shoes, roll up her jeans and wade into the water. But she couldn't. She had to keep her attention on the cottage in case Cal McMaster left before Bill arrived.

Maybe she should knock on the door. She didn't really need a minder, did she? She'd knocked on many doors over the years not knowing what awaited on the other side.

Don't do it . . .

Stephen's cautious voice again. It came with being a lawyer, she supposed. But what was life without risk? Faint heart never won front-page splashes. This had the potential to be a huge story, one she could punt to print and broadcast.

Don't do it . . .

After all, Cal might be totally innocent. He could have mentioned it to someone else and the longer she sat there the more chance there was of that person taking fright and fleeing the island.

Don't do it . . .

A rapping on the passenger side window snapped her out of her deliberations. She jumped in surprise, saw Cal McMaster bent over to peer at her. For a minute she was puzzled as to why she hadn't seen him leave the cottage and walk in her direction – if she'd looked away, it was only for a matter of seconds. Then she realised he must have crossed the moorland behind his cottage in the gathering dusk.

He rolled his finger to ask her to crank the window open. 'Perhaps you should come into the house, Rebecca,' he said. 'There's somebody there who wants to meet you.'

41

Bill watched the ferry ease towards the jetty. The ramp came down, the foot passengers filed off first and right in front were Chaz and Alan. He had called them earlier that morning to let them know what had happened. He was far from amazed, though slightly annoyed, to see Stephen Jordan behind them.

'Where is she?' Stephen asked immediately after the customary nods and handshakes.

Bill pulled him to the side to allow the vehicles to disembark, and they began to walk up the slope. 'I left her sleeping.'

'She's staying at the manse, right?'

'Yes, but—'

'Okay,' Stephen said, striding ahead of them, knowing where he was headed. He had visited the island before, when Chaz and Alan were married.

'How is she?' Alan said as he drew level with Bill.

'Exhausted. Gutted about Dot Blair.'

Chaz said, 'But I'll bet she's not going to give up on the story, right?'

'That's what makes her what she is,' Bill said, loud enough for Stephen to hear. 'We need to accept that.'

Stephen stopped, faced him again. 'Was that for my benefit?'

'Does it need to be for your benefit?'

'I know Rebecca quite well, thank you. I don't need lectures from you.'

Bill had never liked Stephen, and the feeling was mutual. Each believed the other to be corrupt in some way and clashed too often in court, or by proxy in the High Court, to change their minds.

Chaz stepped between them. 'Guys, this isn't the time.'

'Sorry, Chaz, but maybe it is,' Bill said. 'Here's the thing about Becks, mate: she's got a mind of her own. Now, to me, she can be an interfering, do-gooding busybody, but she's our interfering, do-gooding busybody, and if we're to be her friends' – he waved a finger towards Stephen – 'or whatever, then we have to accept what she is and help her when it's needed, support her, you know?'

'And when she's just wrong-headed?' Alan asked.

'Then we make her see sense but still support her. My God, she can be maddening, stubborn, wilful, crazy, mixed up, complex, but that's what makes her Rebecca Connolly. And anyone who can't accept that should just jog on.'

Stephen stepped closer, his face set hard. Chaz held out a hand, but then Stephen nodded. 'You're right.'

He turned again and continued walking to the Square.

The man sitting in the same chair Rebecca had been in on her previous visit had dark hair which was slicked back like he'd been swimming the wake of the Exxon Valdez, but it was at least carefully groomed. He wore a black suit, and his blue shirt was open at the neck. She had the impression that for him that was casual. His shoes were black. His features were even, perfect. His eyes were dead.

'Rebecca,' he said, and she detected a faint accent. Even though she couldn't identify it, something told her who he was. 'It's time we actually met, given you have been nosing around the edges of my business for so long. Too long.' He held out his hand. He was wearing latex gloves. 'Forgive the gloves. I have a skin infection that requires I keep them covered. My name is Jarji Nikoladze.'

Of course it is, she thought, not making a move to shake the hand. This wasn't a meet-and-greet.

Her phone rang but she didn't make any move to answer it. When it stopped ringing, Nikoladze gestured to Cal, who found the device, hauled out the SIM card and broke it in two before slipping the phone back in her pocket.

'People know I'm here,' she said. 'They'll be here soon, don't worry.'

'I never worry.' He smiled. 'And we won't be here long.'

Cal McMaster stood behind her, and she could feel his tension reach towards her. 'We should move, Jarji.'

She had to keep them here. Bill would pick up the message. He'd get here soon.

'So how do you two know each other?'

'We're old associates,' Jarji said. He was smooth and affable. Too smooth and affable. And his eyes were still dead. 'Callum's past intersected with mine when he left prison.'

He said he'd bummed around for a while before returning to Stoirm. During that period he'd obviously come into the orbit of the Nikoladze brothers.

Her eyes fixed on Nikoladze, she said, 'You didn't learn any lessons being in prison, did you, Cal?'

'There weren't many opportunities open to a man like me,' he said.

'Callum was introduced to us by a mutual friend,' Nikoladze said.

Rebecca was about to ask if that mutual friend was Murdo Maxwell but then her mind clicked. Maxwell had a partner for a time, a man who she had learned was connected to the Nikoladzes. 'Finbar Dalgliesh, right?'

The lawyer-turned-politician had mentioned the brothers to her in the shadow of a Highland castle. He had told her that his ultra-right-wing party was funded by powerful men who sought to profit from any unrest and chaos they could cause, and he had even provided a list. Nikoladze's name was on it, but nothing had come of it. Anyone can put names on a list, she'd been told.

Nikoladze appeared impressed. 'Very good, Ms Connolly. Mr Dalgliesh caused us some inconvenience with his indiscretion. He should never have mentioned our name.'

'The police were listening.'

'I know, and my brother and I were visited by your organised crime and terrorist officers, but they only had his word for any connection we might have had to Dalgliesh and his political party. Naturally, we were well insulated and they found nothing to link us. Ultimately, of course, his unfortunate demise meant there was no case.'

'You had him killed, right?'

'People die, Ms Connolly. It's part of living.'

Rebecca felt her flesh chill. 'And have I reached that part of living?'

Nikoladze smiled but didn't reply. She searched her freezing brain for another way to keep him talking.

'What's this, then? Damage control? Did Dot Blair's murder screw everything up for you here? Maybe you should have been more careful.'

'Ms Blair's death was most unfortunate, but nothing to do with me.'

'No, you were after me, right?'

'Not everything is about you.'

'This was. Darren Yates came after me, didn't he?'

Nikoladze was momentarily puzzled by the name. 'Ah, was that his name? I had no contact with him. That was all Callum's doing.'

Rebecca detected an accusatory note in his voice. So did Cal.

'You told me to let them off the leash,' he said. 'I argued against it, but you were insistent.'

The dead eyes flashed, just briefly, and a slight gritting of the teeth were enough to tell Rebecca that Jarji Nikoladze had a temper which he had to control.

'Let's not wash our dirty linen in front of Ms Connolly,' he said, his gaze fixed on Cal behind her.

'You have a lot to wash, I'll bet,' she said.

Those slow dead eyes slid back to her.

'It's the police I told.'

'I doubt that, but no matter.' He glanced to the window then stood. 'I think it's dark enough now. We'll take my vehicle, Cal.'

'Where are we going?'

'To where it all began for us, Ms Connolly.'

Val Roach despatched two DCs from her team to hoover up Matt Coyle and Elton McGeachy. She'd also sent Peter Nisbett and another officer to pick up Darren Yates again, this time to be interviewed under caution. She'd never met the sergeant but sized him up as a lazy officer. However, he knew where Yates lived. Rory had wanted to go along but she recognised that he was both competent and efficient and wanted him with her.

He drove them up the hill to the manse, where they found Bill Sawyer, Stephen Jordan, Chaz Wymark and Alan Shields lingering outside. Val gave the forensic tent little more than a cursory glance as she'd already visited the scene of Dot Blair's murder and there was little more to be found. Instead, she homed in on Bill.

'Where's Rebecca?'

He looked worried as he stared at his phone. 'Not here. I left her in her bed, I thought she was worn out, but she must have waited till I was gone and then left.'

'To go where?'

'She left a message on my phone. She went to speak to the owners of the general store then to see a guy called Cal McMaster.'

'Why?'

'Hector had told him that she was coming to the island, and maybe that's what set those two guys in motion.'

'Quilp and Drood?'

'Yes.' He nodded to a woman with short-brown hair wearing a dog collar and climbing into the driver's seat of an ageing Land Rover. 'She's not answering her phone. We're heading up to his cottage now.'

'No, you're not,' Val said.

'Yes, we are DCI Roach,' insisted Stephen.

'This is a police investigation, Mr Jordan, and I'd appreciate it if you didn't interfere.'

Stephen was already settling himself in the rear of the Land Rover. 'You can arrest us later. Right now, we're going to see this guy McMaster.' He paused before he closed the door. 'You're welcome to come along.'

Roach gave Bill a reproving glare, but he merely shrugged. 'It's Rebecca, Val. This is what we do.'

He, Chaz and Alan climbed into the vehicle and Val stepped back to let the minister reverse from the driveway.

'Do we go after them?' Rory Gibson asked.

'No, I thought we'd nip down to the village for a cappuccino and a biscotti. Of course we're going after them.' She hauled at the passenger door of the police vehicle. 'I told you this woman has a knack for getting herself into trouble.'

42

Rebecca knew she was in trouble.

Cal had grabbed her by the arm – bloody hell, that old guy was strong – picked up an old duffle bag from beside the front door and dragged her outside. She'd tried to resist, had even tried to land one of the blows she'd learned in self-defence but failed. Nikoladze reached behind him and produced a small but stocky pistol.

'That's cute,' she said, struggling to push through to the other side of the fear. 'Is it the extension of anything?'

'In pistols, size doesn't matter,' he said. 'This is what they call a micro nine, small but deadly, I assure you.' He jerked the barrel towards the open door of the 4x4. 'Please get in, Rebecca.'

'And if I don't, what will you do? Shoot me?'

He considered this. 'I'm going to do it, anyway, and I had planned somewhere more secluded, but if you insist.'

He raised the pistol, and she decided to get in the car. Perhaps she'd think of something on the way to wherever they were going. Nikoladze handed the weapon to Cal, taking his bag in return. 'You keep her under control. I know the way.'

He threw the bag into the passenger seat and walked around the front. Cal climbed into the rear seat alongside her, the gun pointing at her side. His hand was shaking, and she hoped that gun didn't have a hair trigger. Was there such a thing as a hair trigger? She didn't know. She wasn't used to guns. She'd had them pointed at her before but had never grown used to it.

Becks, how the hell do you get yourself into these scrapes?

Stephen would tell her, she knew that. But he wasn't here. Bill would tell her, so would Chaz and Alan, but they weren't here, either. There was only her, this old man with a gun beside her and a Russian gangster behind the wheel, driving through the growing darkness.

She could feel something harsh rising in her throat and she thought she was going to lose it. She was absolutely terrified. She didn't know what to do. She wondered how Nikoladze would react if she threw up all over his nice suit. He wouldn't be happy, she thought. Maybe she'd do it, just for the pleasure of pissing him off. After all, he could only kill her once.

Shit, he was going to kill her. The thought made her tremble and she very nearly did throw up. Focus, Becks, push through. Find the other side. Don't give them the satisfaction. Think, for God's sake . . .

'Duck her head down. You too, Cal.'

Nikoladze's voice cut through her panic, and she saw the beams of two sets of car headlights speeding towards them, but then Cal grabbed her by the back of the neck and forced her head between her knees, and he crouched down, too. She struggled, hoping to get free and alert Bill and whoever was in those cars, maybe Val, but he was too strong. Damn it, why couldn't he be feeble as well as old? The pistol jammed into her ribs, made her still.

She heard the cars zip by, and he let her up. He even allowed her to look through the rear window to see their lights vanish around a curve.

'Say goodbye to your friends,' Nikoladze said, adjusting the mirror slightly so he could see her properly behind him. His eyes told her that some of his confidence had vanished now that he realised she hadn't been bluffing.

'They'll get you, don't worry,' she said, hoping her own voice was more confident than she felt.

'I never worry,' he said.

But he was worried. One hand left the wheel to scratch at the other.

'Bastard,' she said, even though she was also worried.

He forced a laugh and concentrated on the road.

Okay, the cavalry has passed you by. You need to force yourself to relax. There has to be a way out of this. Somehow. She could struggle, perhaps force him off the road. They did that in the movies, didn't they? But this wasn't a movie, and she wasn't some actress with a stunt person at her beck and call. She was a reporter from Glasgow with rudimentary fighting skills, and Cal had a gun – and guns go off.

Somewhere secluded, he'd said. They were taking her somewhere secluded.

Okay.

Maybe there'll be a chance to break away then, dodge into the dark – it was dropping fairly quickly now, as it did on the island. Yes, they'd shoot at her, but there was a greater chance of them missing if she was running in the night than fighting with this bloody weightlifting octogenarian in the back of a 4x4. Right?

Right.

Take deep breaths, Becks. Force the vomit away. Force the nerves to settle. Push your way through. You can do this.

Can't you?

'That's Rebecca's car,' Stephen said as they passed it.

'And that's Cal McMaster's up ahead.' Bill nodded to the Toyota as they drew nearer to the cottage. Lights burned at windows where no curtains were drawn.

'He's at home, then,' said Alan.

Bill wasn't so sure. Something wasn't quite right. They pulled in and piled out, the police car coming to a halt behind them.

'Leave this to us,' Val Roach said, her tone letting them know that any argument might result in heads being banged together. She was slim but she was strong. Bill knew that.

She surveyed the cottage for a moment, then looked around her. Somewhere in the darkness they could hear waves breaking on the shore. She looked at the windows, the interior light blazing, and frowned. Bill knew what was troubling her. If someone was in there, they would have heard the cars approach and the doors slamming. They would have come to the window to see who it was. They had seen nobody. Bill looked back the way they had come, instinct telling him that she wasn't here but knowing that they had to be certain. Val Roach would have come to the same conclusion but nevertheless she flicked a finger to Rory Gibson to go around the back of the cottage while she strode to the front door and gave it the old policeman's knock. Firm. Authoritative. If the door wasn't opened quickly, there would be trouble. The door wasn't opened, but Bill hadn't expected it to. He looked back down the road again, thinking the trouble had already begun.

Stephen swore softly, marched to Roach's side and reached for the handle, but the door was locked. He stepped back.

'Move aside, DCI Roach,' he said.

Roach noted his body language. 'We shouldn't do that.'

'No, we shouldn't,' he said, raising his foot. 'But we will.'

It took him three kicks, as close to the lock as he could manage, before the wood splintered and the door gave. He was first through, calling out Rebecca's name, followed by Bill, Chaz and Alan. Bill gave Roach a little shrug as he passed, but he saw her smile and knew this was what she had wanted. He loved it when she bent the rules.

The house was empty, as they'd expected.

Rory Gibson joined them. 'There's nobody at the rear.'

Roach and Bill looked at each other, both reaching the same conclusion. 'That 4x4,' he said. She nodded.

'Rory, get on the radio, get vehicles out, find that 4x4. Meanwhile, check with the people in that cottage over there if they saw or heard anything.'

It was all they could do, but Bill felt it wasn't enough. There was a lot of land to cover on the island, lots of little trails that snaked away from the Spine to remote areas. And if someone meant Rebecca harm, they could be too late.

Nikoladze sped down the Spine at speeds Rebecca would have found alarming if she wasn't more concerned with what her immediate future held. Spinning off the road might have been welcome, because at least then she might have a chance. As it was, she couldn't think of a way out of this. They had passed the manse and the kirk and the road leading to Portnaseil long ago. They passed the Seven Sisters, the fingers of rock on the foreshore where Chaz very nearly died. They passed the small cottage where Mhairi Sinclair was murdered. They all slid by in a blur.

She had already guessed where he was going and when he suddenly veered off to the right onto a bumpy side road, that guess proved correct. He'd said they were going somewhere secluded, to where it all began for them.

He was taking her to Thunder Bay.

The powerful beams of the 4x4 briefly revealed the trees on either side of the narrow single-track road, then the vehicle lurched and pitched as the surface became more uneven. She had come this way the first time with Chaz, and there had obviously been no work done on the road since. Donnie and the committee would see to that, she supposed, when they won the bid. They would now, of course. She had worked it out while she forced her brain to focus on her situation. Nikoladze was pulling out, and he was here to clean house. Dot's death, whether accidental or intentional, had ruined everything for them. She glanced at Cal McMaster, his face dimly lit by the lights from the dashboard. He stared ahead at the road, the gun still jammed into her ribs. She wondered if she could somehow take it away from him, then fire through the seat into Nikoladze. She'd never pulled a trigger before – would she be able to do it? Hell, would she be able to wrest it from McMaster in the first place?

Maybe.

If the car slammed into one of the large potholes, then the impact might jar the gun away from her and she could grab his wrist, jab her elbow into his face. Yes, that would do it. Keep the muzzle away from her, maybe he'd jerk the trigger and even if the bullet didn't hit Nikoladze, it might create enough confusion to force him off the road and she could escape. It was worth a try, surely. They could only kill her once.

She shifted her position slightly in preparation. Cal's eyes turned towards her, watching her, but she tried to be as casual in her movements as possible. She settled again and he seemed satisfied she was only making herself more comfortable. Her right arm was in a better position now. All she needed was for Nikoladze to hit a serious bump in the road.

She waited.

She waited.

The trees whipped by, the track stretched beyond the reach of the headlights, hit small holes, but not big enough, barely causing the gun to move.

Come on.

Come on.

And then the car suddenly bucked to the right, and she felt the muzzle shift from her ribs as Cal reached up with his free hand to the roof to steady himself. She shot her elbow up and into his face, catching him on the eye, and he cried out, jerked back, while she reached with both hands for the gun, wrapped her fingers around it and forced it away from her. She heard

Nikoladze demand to know what was happening and she thought, *You'll see, fucker*, as she twisted her body one way and the gun the other, and she thought, *Yes, yes, yes . . .*

And then Cal slammed a fist into her jaw, and her fingers slipped from the barrel as her head jolted to the left, cracking against the window.

'Don't do that again,' Cal said, ramming the gun back into her ribs.

Nikoladze watched her in the mirror, his eyes smiling. 'Nice try, Ms Connolly. I'm impressed.'

'Why don't you go fuck yourself,' she said, her jaw aching.

His laugh this time was more relaxed than before. He had regained his confidence.

'Not far to go now,' he said.

43

Morag Dewar had been seeing Connor Prentice on and off for a year. It had to be on and off because she was married to the master distiller at the Stoirm distillery, and Connor not only worked for him but also was himself married, in his case to the island's librarian. The affair had begun as many of these things do, with some flirting, casual touching, a few looks that were longer than needed, until they ultimately found themselves alone one night in a small room at the rear of the community hall where they'd both been helping with preparations for a Christmas ceilidh. It was there that the looks and the touching and the flirting became a whole lot of kissing and groping and, surprisingly for them both, frenzied coupling up against the door. Afterwards, both affronted by their wanton behaviour and amazed that they hadn't been caught, they decided that there could be no repeat performance. And there wasn't, not in that small back room anyway, but there had been further kissing, groping and frenzied coupling in other locations.

She had never taken to it in the car, though. It seemed so cramped, even in her roomy Suzuki Jimny, and nigh on impossible in his Ford Puma. Perhaps some people managed, but she certainly couldn't.

They were giving it another try, having parked up near to Thunder Bay. Nobody would come out to the bay after dark, so they were confident that they wouldn't be disturbed. Or, rather, caught. However, they had taken the precaution of parking on a flat piece of land in the shadow of some trees that were bent permanently back by the force of the winds from the Atlantic. Any visitors who had braved the bumpy track from the Spine to the bay would have moved on as darkness fell, and so they felt secure to have at it.

She straddled him in the back seat, and it had been awkward but she'd managed it – maybe if they were both younger, it might have gone better. They deserved full marks for effort, she had said to him, and he'd erupted in laughter, which is perhaps not the best thing to do when they were in the throes of passion, but they really didn't want to be defeated by this, even though the situation was pretty funny.

The sound of a car engine growing closer caused them both to stop laughing and instinctively throw themselves flat on the seat, her legs still wrapped around him. Her first thought was that they had been caught, that one or both of their respective partners had followed them. She risked peeping out of the window and was relieved to see that it was another 4x4, a big one, that had pulled into the makeshift car park beside the fence above the bay. Neither her husband nor Connor's wife drove a car that expensive.

The full moon provided a fairly clear view as the doors opened and a tall man climbed out of the back, hauling a young woman behind him. Another man, dressed – she thought incongruously given the location – in a dark suit had emerged from the driver's side and waited for them to join him. Then they both took one of her arms each and propelled her towards the path leading down the cliff.

'Who is it?' Connor was still underneath her and couldn't see.

'I don't know, I can't make them out,' she said. 'But I don't like the look of it.'

She eased off him so he could prop himself up to see. The trio were just disappearing over the lip of the cliff. 'Why not?'

'There was a girl being manhandled by two men.'

'Manhandled in what way?'

'Pushed, dragged, forced down the path. I don't like it, Connor.'

He was tucking in and zipping up. 'I'll go take a look.'

She rearranged her clothes as he eased the door open and slipped into the night. She saw him run in a half-crouch to peer over the edge of the cliff. She waited for a few seconds then crept to his side.

'Can you see them?' she whispered.

He gestured to a point a few yards down the path which snaked to the shoreline, and she made out the three figures, the young woman obviously struggling against them.

'We should call the police,' she said.

He hesitated, obviously thinking of the possible effects on them personally, then nodded. 'There's no signal here. We'll need to drive back to the Spine to make the call.'

Morag gave the scene below another glance. She didn't know what this was about but hoped the delay wasn't bad news for that girl.

Nikoladze stopped suddenly, his hand raised, his head cocked.

'What is it?' Cal asked.

'I thought I heard a car engine.'

They listened – even Rebecca, who hoped it was true, that there was help coming – but heard only the surf crashing on the rocks of the bay and the boom of the water in the caves that had been hollowed out of the rocks on the far side.

'Where's the boat?' Cal asked, scanning the moonlit water.

'It will be here. It will take you away somewhere safe.'

So that was why Cal had a bag. He was doing a runner. They either didn't want to wait for the first ferry in the morning or feared being nabbed by the police if they delayed too long.

Cal was concerned. 'I still don't like this. The bay's a difficult place to land.'

'I told you, the man I hired is an experienced hand,' Nikoladze reassured him. 'He'll moor just beyond the bay, where the surface is smoother, and send a RIB to fetch you. It's all arranged. Trust me.'

Never trust a man who calls you by your first name as soon as you meet him, Rebecca's father was fond of saying. *And never trust a man who says trust me*. Nikoladze had failed on both counts.

That coming to Thunder Bay had been in their mind even before she had turned up was obvious, but Rebecca sensed something about this that wasn't quite right. She wasn't sure what it was, but she turned it over as they continued their descent. It was a long way down and their pace was slow in the dim light of the moon. She made sure she delayed it further by stumbling a few times. Think, Rebecca, think . . .

'What's the plan?' she asked, feeling the need to keep them talking. 'Cal hops on the slow boat to China and you drive back to Portnaseil and catch the first ferry off the island. Nobody knows you were here, right?'

'Something like that,' Nikoladze replied.

'And I'm left here.'

'It's fitting, is it not? After all, it was events here that began the process that made our orbits intersect and gave you the licence to interfere in my business affairs, not just once but many times.'

'That wasn't my intention.'

'I should have removed you from my path earlier, but my brother prevented me. You knew little, he argued, you had limited impact on our profit. He can be ruthless, but he grows old and weak. He doesn't like to deal with the necessities of our work.'

'But you do.'

'Yes, and they are often left to me.'

'I wouldn't think a man like you would trouble himself with the wet work.'

He laughed. 'Wet work? You have been reading too many spy novels, my dear. We simply call it killing.'

His matter-of-fact tone chilled her even further.

'And yes, I have killed, many times. I will do so again tonight.'

That drove all other thoughts from her mind. This wasn't happening. This couldn't happen. She fell silent for the remainder of the descent, her stumbles this time were real because her legs were sluggish. At the bottom of the cliffs Nikoladze led them across the sand towards the water. He stopped just as they reached the high-tide line, the aroma of seaweed hanging heavily in the salty air. A few feet further away the waves that hadn't thrown themselves at the jagged rocks that peppered the bay slid onto the sand with a fizzing noise.

'You don't need to do this,' she said, annoyed at the pleading tone.

'Yes, I do.'

'Why? What will it profit you?'

He wheeled on her. 'Because I want to! Because you have denied me that thing I desired most. That estate should be mine. I have worked for it. I have killed for it. But your meddling has snatched it from me.'

In that moment she saw that Jarji Nikoladze was a spoiled brat who didn't like being denied anything.

'It was nothing to do with me,' she said. Keep them talking, Becks. It's your only chance. 'You had to spoil your chances by resorting to dirty tricks and intimidation. Not to mention murder.'

'That was not my doing.'

'No? Let me see if I understand everything . . .'

'Must we?'

'Indulge me. Call it a last request.' She was delighted that she sounded calm again, even though she was ready to collapse through fear. She had to keep the faith. She'd think of something. Someone would come. Something would happen. She wasn't going to die on this beach. 'You have Cal here find some guys in Glasgow and Edinburgh, arrange to ostensibly have them work on renovating the hotel . . . I take it you have an interest in the chain that bought it, right?'

'Through intermediaries, yes.'

'Intermediaries,' she repeated. 'That's your thing, isn't it? No straight line between you and what you own, or want. Your bid for the estate has so many intermediaries that it would never lead directly to you. Cal here was an intermediary with Matt Coyle . . .' She saw McMaster stiffen. 'Yes, we know about him. He, in turn, pulls together a team of guys, a mix of real tradesmen and a couple who have other skills. You also get him to deal with Darren Yates, who you know as being the boy most likely on Stoirm to do what you needed, right? But Matt Coyle didn't meet him face to face, did he? The only face Darren has seen is Ryan Duffy's. Another intermediary. Another buffer.' That shocked Cal; even Nikoladze seemed surprised. 'Oh yes, we know it all. So do the police.' She looked at Cal again. 'And by the same reasoning, Matt Coyle knows nothing about your boss here, does he?'

Nikoladze sighed. 'I've heard enough. Give me the weapon, Callum.'

Rebecca watched the gun being passed over into Nikoladze's hand. His latex-gloved hand. Realisation struck then.

'Yeah, you're the only one, apart from me now, who knows about him,' she said to Cal. 'And he's going to kill me.' She let that sink in before continuing. 'There's no boat, Cal. Isn't that right, Jarji?'

Nikoladze smiled, stepped closer to Cal, placed the gun to his temple and pulled the trigger. It happened so swiftly that it took a moment for it to sink into Rebecca's consciousness.

'When you're right, you're right,' Jarji said, looking down at Cal's body.

Rebecca backed away a couple of paces. 'You're going to put my death on him.'

'I am.'

'That's why you're wearing gloves, that's why you drove here and not him, why you gave him the gun, so that only his fingerprints would be found. There is no infection, is there?'

'Oh, there is,' he said, peeling off one of the gloves and holding his hand up so she could see the raw, red skin. 'It's quite unsightly and itches terribly. It's stress-related, apparently. I expect that it will ease shortly.'

'The idea is that Cal killed me and then himself, I take it?'

'You take it correctly.'

Her thoughts were gelling now. 'You couldn't do it at his cottage – the neighbours might hear, or someone might happen by and see you. This bay is ideal. Remote. He wouldn't have been found till the morning, maybe even later, but by then you'd be off the island.'

He didn't say anything, simply smiled, the gun dangling idly by his side. Keep talking, Rebecca, something will happen. It has to.

'I mean, nobody knows you're here, do they? You came across on the ferry, nobody knows you anyway, nobody knows your connection to all that's happened. Only Cal, and you've silenced him.'

She waited for him to say something, but he didn't. The waves rolled in, the tide thundered in the caves.

'And I'm what, collateral damage?'

'No, you're an itch that I couldn't scratch until now, one as irritating as my hands but more easily eliminated.'

Keep talking, Rebecca. Someone has to come. 'What about the estate? You're giving that up, I take it?'

He didn't reply, but she knew he was right. His earlier outburst proved that.

'Did your brother order it?'

That guess brought a reaction, a sharp exhalation. She didn't want to annoy him, so she pulled away.

'I don't suppose my promising not to tell anyone would do any good, would it?'

His smile was like a rictus grin. 'What do you think?'

She began to take side-steps. She didn't know why, but she couldn't just stand there. And she couldn't run, she'd never make the shelter of the rocks before he got her. So, she moved, unconsciously, slowly, to her right. He spun slowly, watching her, as if he was enjoying seeing her fear.

He raised the gun as they circled.

'Goodbye, Rebecca. I can't say it was good to make your acquaintance.'

She stiffened, waited for the bullet, but then realised his eyes were fixed on something over her shoulder. She followed his gaze, saw little pinpoints of light on the clifftop and down the path.

Then someone was running across the sand towards him. Tall, fit, a good runner.

Stephen . . .

He hadn't run like this since his rugby days, but he was glad he could still do it. They had seen the figures below and used their mobile phones to light the way down the treacherous path. When the gunshot reached them, it sounded incredibly loud and his first thought was for Rebecca, but as he careered down the final part of the path he saw she was still standing, so he sprinted across the beach, hoping to reach them before that bastard knew what hit him . . .

*

Nikoladze spat something in Georgian, leaped towards her, grabbed her and pulled her in front of him like a shield. Stephen didn't falter, he kept running straight at them, legs and arms pumping. Nikoladze swore in his native tongue again, one arm round her neck, the hand holding the gun aimed first at her head, then it moved towards Stephen, then back at her head, then returned it towards Stephen.

Stephen kept coming.

Nikoladze was panicked, she heard it in his breathing, felt the tension in his body. Rebecca forced her body to relax, to wilt, dragging Nikoladze's arm with it. The gun lowered a little. She turned her head to make sure her airway was clear, then gripped the portion of his arm near her chin, wiggled her fingers into the crook of his elbow, tucked her right leg behind his, then jabbed her elbow into her stomach and jerked her shoulder into his chest, throwing him backwards. As he stumbled, she twisted herself free and ran towards Stephen, who was calling her name. She waved him away, but he kept coming. She glanced over her shoulder, saw Nikoladze had righted himself, was swinging his gun hand up again. She shouted to Stephen to get down, but he didn't hear her, just kept running. She needed to get to him, pull him down.

And then Nikoladze fired.

Stephen swerved a little, his eyes wide with horror.

Something punched her on the back. She carried on moving for a few steps, wondering why she was slowing, why pain seared through her body. Her legs folded and Stephen caught her, lowered her to the sand. The agony was intense, glowing, burning. His expression twisted from shock, to concern and then to anger, and he looked up, said something she didn't catch, couldn't catch, because the sound of the waves was too loud. And then he was gone and Chaz, Alan hove into view, Fiona kneeling by her side, hands on her, their lips moving.

But she couldn't hear what they were saying because of those damn waves . . . Stephen, where was Stephen?

Stephen had taken off after the man with the gun, who was running off down the beach towards the cliffs at the far end.

There's nowhere to go, pal. Unless you have some climbing gear in your pockets.

He didn't know who he was, didn't care, all he knew was that he'd shot Rebecca and for that he'd pay. He heard Val Roach call after him, then ordering the man to drop the gun. She'd recognised him, had mentioned his name but he hadn't caught it, as he was so intent on getting to Rebecca.

The man looked behind him, saw Stephen coming after him, turned and loosed off a hurried shot as he backed away. Stephen didn't care, didn't know where the bullet went, was only interested in getting to him, and he threw himself the final couple of feet in a tackle he'd not done for years – but once you knew how, you never lost it. He caught him firmly in the midriff, sent him tumbling backwards, the gun flying from his hand. They both landed in the sand, rolled together, with Stephen making sure he finished on top, one hand grabbing the collar of his white shirt, the other crashing into his face. The blow hurt his fist like hell, but he didn't care. He hit him again. There was a danger he'd break his hand, but he didn't care about that, either. This man shot Rebecca. He hit him again. Blood spurted from his lips, his nose. He hit him again. The man groaned, cried out to stop. Stephen hit him again and kept hitting him until he was being dragged off by Bill Sawyer and the young, uniformed cop.

Stephen ran back to where Rebecca lay in the sand. Fiona McRae gave him a tearful look, Chaz was holding her hand, Alan stood by, cursing over no signal on his phone.

44

Stephen's face filled Rebecca's vision. He brushed her hair from her face. Said something she didn't catch. The waves were too loud. The booming was too loud. Had she fallen in the water? Her back was wet.

Everything faded.

Faded back in.

In and out.

In and out.

Like the waves.

More faces, police officers.

Then gone. Val Roach gesturing to a female police officer, sending her back up the cliff.

Gone.

Rory Gibson muttering something to Nikoladze as he pushed him before him. Nikoladze's face was bloody. Did he fall? Good.

Gone.

The pain surged. Oh my God, it was intense, like someone holding a hot iron to her flesh.

Gone.

Stephen's voice coming through.

'Help coming . . . Stay with us . . .'

Gone.

The world tilted, but she hadn't moved. Everything faded again, the faces, the waves, the thundering caves.

All was silent.

All was black.

Gone . . .

Suddenly it was daylight and Elspeth was with her. The waves still headed for shore, but she couldn't hear them smacking the rocks. Even the booming had stopped. She wasn't surprised to see Elspeth there, it seemed natural. She looked to her other side and there was her father. She'd expected that, too.

They faced the sea, where the sun bleached the white breakers. Seabirds darted and hovered but made no sound. That was freaky. There was a breeze but, unusually for Thunder Bay, it was warm.

Thunder Bay. This was where it all began, even though she hadn't been here for that. Mhairi Sinclair had mentioned it in her dying breath. She knew why, knew what she'd seen here. Roddie Drummond had died here, too.

It was fitting. This was where the spirits came to go into the west. That was the island legend. She searched the horizon for a sail. Of course it had to be a sail.

Are we going somewhere?

She hadn't been aware of speaking, but both Elspeth and her father looked at her as if she had.

We are. Elspeth's lips didn't move but Rebecca heard her voice all the same. Suddenly she understood.

Okay.

And it was. She was ready.

But you're not.

Her father, this time. She wasn't aware she had turned but she was facing him.

What do you mean?

We're here to say goodbye, she heard him say. *We needed you to bring us here before we could leave you forever.*

335

She didn't understand.

It's not your time, Becks. She was facing Elspeth again. *Not for a long time yet.*

John Connolly again. *But one last piece of advice, from both of us. Put the past behind you. Look to the future.*

She saw Elspeth's face again. Stern now. *Time for you to get your act together, Rebecca Connolly.*

Her father. *Stop being such a little diva.*

Okay, she thought, she didn't expect the afterlife to be so judgmental.

It's not the afterlife, numpty, Elspeth said. *It's Thunder Bay.*

Then both voices together.

Life is loss but it's also wonderful.

Don't waste it.

Be happy.

She felt her father's lips on her forehead, just the way he used to do it. And Elspeth hugged her. She never did that before.

And then they were gone. There hadn't been any sails. She was alone, staring out at sea. Into the west.

And then someone touched her hand.

Stephen was sitting beside her bed, her hand in his, when she opened her eyes. There were wires leading from her arms and from contact pads on her chest. She heard something whirring and beeping. She felt sore.

He smiled. 'Hi there, sleepy.'

She had a flashback to waking once before with him at her side. He'd looked worried and relieved then, too.

She tried to swallow, and he reached up to a cabinet beside her bed and brought the straw of a plastic bottle of ice water to her lips. She drew some in, swallowed, found her voice.

'I'd've preferred a gin,' she said.

He put the bottle back. 'Yeah, maybe later.'

She heard the sound of waves from outside. She was still on the island, in the community hospital.

'I had dreams,' she said. 'I thought I was dead.'

'Nah, was never going to happen.'

'I was shot.'

'You were.'

'It might have killed me.'

'Unlikely. The bullet didn't hit any vital organs. The shock was what really knocked you out.'

She felt an ache running along her back. It wasn't as hot as it had been on the beach, but it was there.

'I was shot in the back,' she said.

He looked a little uncomfortable. 'Well . . . yes . . .'

She realised then. 'I was shot in the backside?'

'Yes.'

'It really hurt.'

'It would. That bullet was travelling at about twenty-seven hundred feet per second. It's bound to smart. But if you want to take a bullet, then that's maybe the place you want it. Big muscles there, lots of padding to soak up the force.'

'Are you saying I have a big arse?'

He smiled, a lot of relief in his eyes. 'It's a very nice arse, but it was still dangerous. It might have hit an artery, but it didn't, though you bled quite a bit. That and the shock were more dangerous than the actual bullet. We were able to at least halt the flow a little until the paramedics arrived. They gave you some blood and brought you here.'

'Who's we?'

'Well, Val and Rory Gibson. They applied some pressure.'

'They had their hands on my bum?'

He laughed. 'It's all right, they're professionals.'

She moved her eyes to the water again and he duly provided it. When she'd had another long drink, he put it back.

'How did you find me?'

'Police officers picking up a boy called Yates reported seeing the 4x4. It had passed them before the call went out to keep a watch for it, but it was heading south. We were already on our way south. It was the only direction they could take you. Then an anonymous tip told us you were on that beach.' He waved a hand. 'Are you up to moving over?'

She edged to the side a bit, but carefully. It didn't hurt too much. He climbed up on the bed beside her, his back on the pillow, and put his arm around her head.

'I don't think you're allowed to do that,' she said.

'I laugh in the face of petty regulation,' he said. 'I'm a shit-hot lawyer. They can sue me.'

She laughed, then winced at the pain.

'Take it easy, it'll hurt when you laugh,' he said, holding her tight. They were silent for a moment, her head resting on his chest.

'Stephen?'

'That's my name.'

'That thing you said . . .'

'What thing that I said?'

'About the ring.'

'Oh yeah. What about it?'

'I think my answer is yes.'

He didn't say anything for a very long time.

'Yeah, about that,' he said.

'What?'

'The thing is . . .'

She waited.

'The thing is . . .' he said again.

'What is the thing?'

'Well, I'm not sure I want to any more . . .'

She hadn't expected that and felt something catch in her throat. 'Why not?'

He took a deep breath. 'The fact is, life's just too dull around you, Rebecca Connolly.'

She laughed. Winced again. Settled against his chest and fell asleep again, this time with his arm around her, and dreamed.

Author's Note

The rebellion by islanders against evictions described here is based loosely on the 1882 Battle of the Braes on Skye, although I've put my own spin on it. The island of Stoirm is, of course, entirely fictional but the issues facing it described by Donnie are based on very real concerns today.

There are many people to thank. Professor James Grieve for his always on-point advice regarding forensics and, in this case, gunshot wounds. John Corrigan, former ACC Strathclyde Police, also provided a comment or two on policing. If I've got anything wrong, it is solely down to me. Thanks to the booksellers who stocked the books, the readers who have enjoyed them, the reviewers and bloggers who have praised them.

Also, to all at Polygon for taking Rebecca out to the public – thanks to copy-editor Craig Hillsley and proofreader Debs Warner – and to my agent, Jo Bell, for keeping me right.

And to Sarah Frame, for being there, for supporting me – often forcing me to write when I'd rather do something else – and proofreading when I can't face the words again.

It's been quite a journey for Rebecca. She's come through a lot and, on reflection, that journey has in many ways mirrored my own. She began as unhappy, but has now found her happiness, as I have. She believes in the power of journalism, but sees how it has been eroded by commercial and political influences, as I do. She has lost a good friend, as I have. She's had a near-death experience, and I once had a bad cold.

If you have followed her tale through the seven books, thank you. And what was the truth of Thunder Bay all those years ago? If you don't know, but want to, then you'll have to buy the book. The selling never ends!